WILDFIRE

MYSTICAL ELEMENTS 2

MEG LYNN

GLOSSARY

People/Things

Elemental: A witch with the ability to control one of the five elements: water, fire, earth, air or spirit. Elemental power is regenerated to each Generation.

Generation: A group of five Elementals, each representing one element, born within five years of one another. A Generation is connected through their powers and are able to feel the other's powers when used.

Magister: The oldest of a living set of Elemental generations.

Seer: An Elemental who has visions of the future and is able to see into the past through memories of other Generations.

Feeler: An empathic Elemental, one who can sense other's feelings and cannot be lied to.

Talisman: An object thought to have magic abilities and bring good luck or protection to the wearer.

Archivist: A title passed down to witches that care for old texts and spellbooks, keeping them safe and the stories of the past alive.

Erebus: The legendary leader of the Renati. A powerful witch who lived centuries ago that was banished to the Shadow Realm by the last known Generation of Elementals.

The Renati: A group of witches who believe Elementals are too powerful and therefore corruptible.

Shadows: Carnivorous creatures from the Shadow Realm.

Allurement: A concentration of magic that attracts witches, bringing them to one another and strengthens their powers.

<u>Places</u>

The Dark Star Forest: A massive forest that covers the majority of Western Oregon into the Cascade Mountain Range.

   Falcon Bay, Oregon: A coastal city an hour and a half from Rifton.

   Rifton, Oregon: A small town on the edge of the Dark Star Forest.

   Pines Row: A neighborhood outside Rifton city limits where the Dansley siblings live.

   Diamond Gate: A gated community by the lake outside of Rifton where the wealthier families live.

   Eagle Loop Trail: Hiking trail in the Dark Star Forest that leads around the local lake.

   The Corner Cup: A local coffee shop in Rifton where Whitney works.

   The Cottage: Whitney's boss, Amilia Burnet's, home.

   The Hallow: A compound of witches hidden in the Dark Star Forest.

   The Shadow Realm: A dimension of darkness and danger that shares a veil with the modern world.

CONTENT

This book contains elements of

death of a loved one (on and off page),

mention of suicide and addiction,

mention of self-harm,

alcohol and marijuana consumption,

cursing,

blood,

hospitalization,

explicit sexual scenes (MF).

Listen to the playlist for Wildfire here on Spotify!

For Dave,
my everything.

Chapter One

Needle in a Haystack

Whitney

Thick raindrops fell against the windows of the Corner Cup. They hit the glass in a musical pattern before they trickled down, leaving a trail of water behind them. As if the window cried, tears streaming down its face.

The window tried to get past the fear it felt as it turned every corner, not knowing who or what would be there to greet it. It attempted to get up in the morning and live life as if nothing had happened, but all it could think about were shadows and blood magic. Everywhere it looked, a pale, decrepit hand reached out to strangle the life from its throat.

I never thought I would be comparing myself to a window but there I stood, gripping the handle of the espresso machine with white knuckles.

"Ouch." I gasped, pulling my hand back as burning hot espresso overflowed from the shot glass I held underneath the spout. I put the knuckle of my thumb in my mouth, using my powers to soothe the burning sensation. The cool metal of my mother's moonstone ring rested against my lips. Analyzing the machine, I realized I had pushed the wrong button causing the espresso to overflow.

You okay, Whit? Rayn's voice asked mentally.

Yes, just spacing out. I replied silently, quickly cleaning up my mess and finishing the cappuccino.

My siblings, Rayn and Dmitri, sat at a table against the wall with Rose McClintock and Brooke Evans. Coffee cups, open binders and stacks of papers covered their table. To the average eye they were studying, but I knew better than that.

They were witches. My brother sat with the sisters of my Elemental generation. For the past two weeks we worked to understand our new reality. We'd gone through spellbooks we'd already read, and learned more magic than we had in our entire lifetimes. On top of honing our Elemental skills, we had learned all sorts of tricks that made our complicated lives a bit easier. We'd learned to manifest our powers in the form of energy waves to knock someone on their backs like a rogue wave. We'd learned to levitate things, clean up messes and fix broken objects. All useful spells, but nothing that would close the portal we'd opened or eliminate the ancient sorcerer we had accidentally resurrected.

After making sure we had enough coverage behind the bar, I went to check on their progress. "How's it going?" I asked, reading over Brooke's shoulder at the notes they had been taking.

"Well, apparently closing portals wasn't a priority for any of the past generations." Rose slumped down in her chair. "Could I get some decaf tea? I've had so much caffeine my hands are shaking."

"Yeah, of course," I answered. "There has to be something in here. We've gone through every other book in Amilia's living room. The book you found at Dragonfly can't be the only one with info about the Shadow Realm."

My boss, Amilia Burnett, had taken us under her wing. Not only had she been my mother's best friend, but she was an Archivist. An Archivist was a keeper of old spellbooks and texts, protecting the history of the Elementals. She had countless books we had been reading through, yet none of them provided the information we needed.

"Yet here we are knowing nothing more than we did a few weeks ago." Dmitri sighed, resting his cheek on his open palm. "Even that page on opening portals Abe gave me didn't help. He swore it was important." Saying Abe's name brought a pained wince to Dmitri's face.

"The info Abe gave you wasn't even a spell," Rayn muttered, flipping the page in the book before her. "It was just a bunch of jumbled theories about different types of portals and *why* they should be opened, not *how* to open them."

Dmitri sighed. "You'd think Mia being an Archivist would mean she'd have more than old gardening books."

"They aren't all gardening books," Rayn replied, glaring at him from across the table.

Dmitri barely glanced up. "They might as well be."

"Unfortunately, these books don't like us as much as our book used to," Rayn answered, lifting her green coffee mug to her lips the moment I filled it up. "This would be a lot simpler if it would just open up to the spell we need."

Our spellbook hadn't done that since Halloween night either.

"Let's say we find the right spell. Who knows if we can even pull it off being an incomplete generation. We aren't as strong as we used to be." Brooke rubbed her eyes, taking a break from the constant reading.

Rose shook her head. "Lauren held us back."

"Lauren completed us. It's like we have a gaping wound now," Brooke snapped back.

As much as Lauren Thaner wanted to move on, we could never go back and forget about Halloween. The night Tom Campbell and Serenity Drake attacked us and resurrected Erebus. Rayn, Rose and I could never erase those memories. Lauren didn't want to accept how serious this had become. She already had one foot out the door since we met her. Brooke stayed, but she would never abandon us.

I put my hand on Brooke's shoulder in comfort. She reached up and squeezed my fingers.

"I'm tired," she answered, defeated.

"It's okay, B," Rose said to her before turning the page of the massive spellbook sitting in the middle of the table.

We cast a cloaking spell on the book before we all arrived at the Corner Cup that evening. To someone without powers, the books were disguised as old encyclopedias. We couldn't risk it. Any person in this building could have been an average person or a Renati member in hiding. Those without powers needed to stay unaware and the Renati all knew who we were anyway.

We had been driving ourselves into the ground searching for a way to close the portal at the lot that used to be Dragonfly Mystic before it burned down. The portal that slowly let Shadows into the land of the living. It was hard enough dealing with the Shadows that already followed us around Rifton, but there seemed to be more crawling around every day that passed. They were weak, but they wouldn't stay weak for long.

I already felt a shift in the energy around Rifton. The air felt heavier, and the sun setting earlier in the day didn't help the feeling that something always lurked behind me. To add to the ambiance, a missing person's flier hung up on the Corner Cup's bulletin board. But the face didn't belong to Abe Roberts. A woman in her mid-twenties smiled at me from the photo. She had gone missing on a hiking trail outside of Falcon Bay last weekend, yet to be found.

I glanced up at the clock, six in the evening. I groaned in relief.

"Let me grab Rose's tea and clock out for lunch," I told them and made my way back behind the counter.

I already untied my apron as I walked the warm water and a packet of orange spice tea with some cinnamon back to the girl's table.

"Do you guys need anything before I clock out?" I asked my coworkers after I dropped off Rose's tea.

"Nope, I'm good, boss," Robby answered from the cash register.

Boss. It came as a surprise when Amilia promoted me to a supervisor. I got a few confused looks from my fellow baristas when Amilia chose to promote me even though I'd been there less time than the rest of them, but no one said anything to my face. The promotion could not have come at a better time, I desperately needed the pay raise with Rayn's recent unemployment. Plus, being a shift supervisor meant Ashley and I worked opposite schedules, which had been a wash of relief since she'd been giving me a cordial cold shoulder since her best friend and I had stopped seeing each other.

I rushed into the employee break room down the hallway off of the main dining area. Amilia stayed back at the cottage attempting to find something to give us an edge over the Renati. One of the many pros and cons of Amilia's large collection of magical texts back at her home; so many to go through. My main focus had to be closing the Shadow Realm portal. No one in Rifton would be safe until the shadows were dealt with.

After tossing my black apron into my small locker, I checked my cell phone. Nothing from Mia. I grabbed the half dozen cupcakes I'd hidden in the breakroom and headed back to the dining area.

We have company. Rayn's voice filled my head as I opened the door. I walked out to see a tall man in a police uniform standing at the counter.

Officer Joseph Grady.

Act natural, I replied to my sister and casually strolled over to their table like his presence didn't completely strike me with nerves.

Officer Grady had been following us for weeks, watching our every move. He knew we were connected to the disappearance of Abraham Roberts, a former member of the Renati. At the end of the summer, my brother, Dmitri, saved Abe from drowning and pissed off an entire coven of dark witches.

Grady hadn't been entirely wrong. I knew Abe. I was one of the last people to see him, but none of us had anything to do with his disappearance. As frustrating as I found Abe, I would never hurt him, not when my brother cared for him so deeply. It felt like a lifetime ago that I'd seen him and Dmitri in the backyard together, their hands clasped as Abe handed Dmitri that paper about the portals.

I couldn't exactly walk up to Grady and tell him the truth. "Hey, Officer. The reason the girls and I were in the forest when Abe disappeared? Well you see...We're all witches and he had been stalking us but he was only trying to help. Yes, we were the last ones to see him but I swear, I don't know where he is." I could only imagine the shock on his face if I dropped that bomb.

"Happy–" Brooke began to sing but Dmitri cut her off as I set the cupcakes down on the table.

"Please don't sing," he begged, covering his face with an open hand.

"Fair enough." I opened back the plastic casing. "Happy birthday, Dmitri."

Seventeen years old. I remembered when he turned seven. It didn't feel like ten years but at the same time, it felt like more than a decade had passed. If someone had asked me ten years ago where I pictured us today, it certainly wouldn't be in Rifton with a generation of Elemental witches and a dead mother, but life can be unexpected that way.

"Okay, where were we?" I sat down in the empty chair next to my sister. I took a drink from her coffee cup and flipped the book around to face me.

"Whit, Grady is getting settled in," Rose whispered from across the table, watching the police officer as inconspicuous as she could.

Officer Grady had taken his cup of black coffee and moved to a table across the dining area. He sat comfortably in a chair with his shiny black boot resting on his knee. Grady took relaxed sips, watching every twitch the girls and I made. He didn't try to hide that he watched us. He wanted us to know of his suspicions. Whatever went through his head about us, I had no clue. All I knew is that this man made our search for a needle in a haystack even more complicated.

"Just ignore him." Brooke went back to her notes from previous spellbooks we had read as if hoping she'd missed something.

Rose sighed. "This is borderline harassment. Can't we file a complaint?"

"Officers in uniform get a discount here," I replied, using every bit of self-control I had to not death glare Grady into the ground. "It's not illegal for him to happen to be wherever we are. He doesn't say anything to us."

"Stalking is still illegal, Whitney." Rose played with the string of her tea bag, pulling it up and down.

I let out an irritated sigh and closed Amilia's book. Nothing in there would help us anyway. Reaching into Rayn's backpack, I pulled out our spellbook. The one we had discovered in the graveyard the night we all decided to put our trust in one another.

"I don't think the book is going to help us out of the blue," Dmitri said, watching me lay the aging text down on the table atop their piles of loose papers.

"I don't think it will, either," I answered, opening the cover to the assortment of maps that took up a big chunk of the first pages.

"You know, we've been so focused on finding something in Mia's books," Rayn paused. "Maybe we're wasting our time. We haven't even tried going straight to the source."

"Because the source is too dangerous," I replied.

Brooke crossed her arms. "Do we actually think the Renati are leaving the portal unprotected?"

"I don't know but there's only one way to find out if we are even on the right track," Rayn said.

Rose shrugged. "We don't exactly have the luxury of time."

"What about Lauren?" I asked. We were missing an integral part of our generation.

"What about her?" Rose scoffed. "We've done successful spells without her before."

I pondered. "True, but this isn't as simple as a protection potion. They used her blood too."

"I'm down to try. We have to at least try, Whit," Rayn begged.

I didn't give in. "It's in the middle of town, we can't fight the Renati in the middle of town."

"If Shadows keep leaking through, a magic fight on Main Street will be the least of this town's concerns," Rose replied. "Maybe we can find a potion in here that'll help us. Turn us invisible or something."

"Have you found anything about closing portals in the Shadow Realm book?" I asked Rose.

Rose shook her head. "No, but I have a vague idea of what's on the other side. The Shadow Realm shares a veil with our world, which is how they were able to open the portal in the first place. It doesn't seem like people exist there naturally, just raw magic and creatures like the Shadows, according to the author."

"I wonder how the author knows so much about it," Brooke pondered aloud.

"I did find a potion intended for calling energy back to you, kind of like the opposite of the one Amilia gave us. We could use it and try to call our energy back to the portal? Since they used our blood to open it," Rose suggested.

"I will try anything at this point." I went back to the map in front of me.

Rose and Rayn may have been obsessed with the potions and spells within this book. Brooke may have been consumed with Gabriel and his spirit healing. I, on the other hand, felt inexplicably drawn to these maps. Only half of them weren't labeled, as if those reading the book should have known what the maps were and why they were important. But one map in particular stood out above the others.

The fifth map had been ripped in half. The top half was missing, and by the looks of the aged, jagged edging that remained, the page had been defiled long before we found the spellbook in the crypt. The bottom of the map marked a clear coast line of a bay. What I assumed to be peaks of mountains might have been on the missing half.

"Whit, that map isn't going to magically put itself back together," my sister said, watching me analyze the page.

"I know, but there's something about it."

"Is it going to tell us how to close the portal?" Rose asked with a smirk.

"We need to go to the portal and focus all our energy on closing it. What harm could it do? Maybe it could actually work." Rayn rubbed her face with open hands.

"We could get attacked by a swarm of Shadows. Who knows what else is on the other side in the Shadow Realm," Dmitri answered, finishing off his cupcake. "Rose's book doesn't have anything useful and it's all we have on that place."

"It's not like the author had ever been to the Shadow Realm," Rose pointed out.

Rayn sighed. "Well, plan C, down the middle with guns blazing. What do we have to lose?"

"A limb," Dmitri muttered. "Can we at least practice on the meadow portal one more time before we go to the portal with all the Shadows? If we can figure out how to open the meadow portal, we could figure out how to close the Shadow Realm portal."

"I think that's a good idea," I agreed with Dmitri.

"Perfect. Loving the enthusiasm." Brooke closed her binder and began packing up her notes. "I need to go home and get some dinner. I don't want my parents to think I'm sneaking around again."

"We should wrap this up anyway." Rose's eyes wandered back over to Officer Grady, who still sipped his coffee across the room. Although he watched the front door, I knew his attention would wander back soon enough.

"Okay, meet up the day after tomorrow at the meadow?" I asked.

"I'll be there," Brooke answered.

"Be safe getting home." Rose smiled as Brooke left the Corner Cup.

Rayn grabbed our book and put it back in her backpack. "Do you guys want to grab some dinner tonight?"

Rose took one last drink from her tea. "I would love to another night, Ray, but I already have plans."

"A date?" Rayn sang, resting her cheek on her fist.

Rose shifted awkwardly between her feet. "No, I'm going to Giani's."

Rose did her best not to look at me and I avoided her, too. We didn't need to speak to know what went through the other's head when her brother's place of employment came up in conversation.

"Ah, well, enjoy your pasta."

"Let me know when you get home. Happy birthday, Mit," Rose said, leaving the Corner Cup. She gave Officer Grady a death glare as she walked past his table.

Rayn quickly changed the subject as she turned to Dmitri and I. "What do you guys want to eat?"

"I'll have a bagel or something," I answered in a flat tone.

"I don't mind bringing you something to eat, Whit. You skipped lunch, don't think I didn't notice," Rayn coaxed.

"I wouldn't be opposed if you brought me a cheeseburger." I mustered a smile.

Dmitri hummed. "That sounds incredible."

"Coming right up." Rayn sprung up with the keys to my Eclipse in hand. Dmitri followed behind her.

I ignored Grady as I cleaned up the table and went back through the employee only doors to the break room. He couldn't do anything to us anyway, and I refused to be intimidated by a local police officer who had nothing better to do with his time than scare a group of young women. He wasn't getting any kind of confession out of us.

I sighed and collapsed into one of the folding chairs. Another problem we were heading into unprepared, but I felt I had little to lose. We had to get the portal closed before Erebus and the Renati grew more powerful than we could handle. At this moment in time, the girls and I still had the upper hand and we needed to take advantage of that.

Since I already felt defeated, I decided to add insult to injury and opened up Spotify on my phone. I had searched for Bryan McClintock's account weeks ago and found his playlists easily. I picked my usual assortment and plugged headphones into my ears. This was as close as I could allow myself to get to him.

As a cover of "The Boys of Summer" began to play, tears welled in my eyes. It was the first song that came on my own shuffled playlist when I got home from breaking his heart after Halloween night. Coincidentally, I found it on Bryan's liked songs. I couldn't tell what felt worse, reopening these old wounds or knowing he had been doing the same.

As I leaned back in my chair and got comfortable, a strong headache rushed over me. I squeezed my eyes shut, hoping it would pass, but it pierced through my brain. My vision began to darken and my knees went weak. I knew this feeling. I had gone through this before. I leaned up against the table and braced myself.

The air around me chilled and I no longer sat at the Corner Cup. I stood in a dark forest, surrounded by trees. It took my eyes a moment to adjust to the sudden change of light. Once I could see more clearly, a single-story white house with a red brick chimney stood in front of me.

I spun around the forest to see if I was anywhere familiar but I didn't recognize my surroundings.

"Abbie!" a voice echoed in the night, sending a chill up my spine. I wasn't alone in these woods.

A teenage boy crawled out of a window next to the chimney and ran across the lawn. He turned back as if he expected someone to be behind him but he was alone. The teenager stumbled to the ground and struggled to get back up. His gray t-shirt had dark red blood stains across it from unseen injuries. He lifted his head and looked to the tree line where I stood. Strands of dark brown hair fell into his eyes as he frantically searched for anyone.

I stood still as a statue, staring into those broken hazel eyes. It was an odd time to notice it, but the boy was painfully handsome. Nice cheekbones and a strong chin.

"Help!" he screamed, his voice cracked into the empty forest. "Somebody help me!"

I tried to run to him, but I couldn't move. An invisible wall kept me behind the tree line.

A blood curdling scream erupted from the house, the sound of someone being tortured. The teenager turned back towards the house. He stared at it until the scream came again. He lifted both hands towards the house with tears streaming down his face. In a matter of seconds the small house engulfed in flames. Fire broke through the glass windows like a bomb had gone off and flames quickly reached the roof. He willed the flames to burn until the house was completely torched.

More screaming followed from others trapped inside. It wasn't until the screaming stopped that the teenager finally lowered his hands and passed out on the lawn. Whoever had been inside the small house surely died. For all I knew, the teenager died too.

My vision blurred again as I came back to the break room at the Corner Cup. My headphones were still snug in my ears, playing the same song as before; everything exactly how I left it. I leaned under the table and examined the ground. Thankfully my stomach didn't empty onto the floor this time.

Half of a laugh caught in my throat as I placed my hand over my pounding heart. The teenage boy had lit that house on fire with his hands. Another pyro. Before the realization that I had seen a vision of another Elemental sunk in, the screams of the people still inside the house echoed in my head. I ripped the headphones from my ears but I still heard the cries for help. Whoever that pyro was, he had killed everyone inside without a second thought.

CHAPTER TWO

DELICATE BALANCE

WHITNEY

I awoke a few mornings later with a gasp, throwing the blanket off of me. I held up my hands prepared to see blood dripping from my fingertips but everything appeared to be normal. Tom Campbell wasn't lying dead at the foot of my bed, staring up at me with vacant eyes. I wasn't covered with his blood. The screams of the teenage boy from my vision didn't fill the room and the smoke of his fire no longer suffocated me. I took in a deep breath, thankful it was only the recurring dream that visited me every night since my vision.

Since sleeping hadn't brought any rest, I decided to get up and shower. Maybe the warm water would help wash the dream from my mind. The water poured over my skin, cleansing my body but not my memories. I stayed under the showerhead until the water ran cold. After I got dressed and braided my hair, I found Dmitri on the living room floor, sketching with a piece of charcoal. His fingers were stained with a black smear across his forehead from where he had moved his dark brown hair from his eyes.

"Hey, Mit." I plopped down on the couch from pure exhaustion.

"You okay?" he asked, glancing up from his artwork.

"I didn't sleep. Weird dreams," I answered.

"Well, if it's any consultation, there's coffee made for you whenever you feel like crawling in there."

"Will you get me some?"

"I don't want to wash my hands."

"Ugh, Dmitri please," I begged, but he ignored me. "Where's Rayn?"

"She stayed at Rose's last night. Sent a text around midnight that she would be home sometime today."

"Checks out," I muttered, finally getting a decent look at Dmitri's drawing.

It must have been the charcoal giving the effects I saw because Dmitri certainly wasn't sitting in the living room drawing pictures of Shadows, right? The drawing stood on its back feet, long front limbs hanging at its sides, nearly dragging on the ground. Soulless eyes glared up from the page, its large mouth gaping open as if it would swallow me whole.

Dmitri caught me peeking and quickly picked up the paper, taking it back to his bed in the corner of the room.

"What are you drawing?" I asked, watching him walk away.

"Nothing," he answered quickly.

"Is that a Shadow? It looked weird."

"No, it's not a Shadow."

"Okay, then–"

"Whit, it's nothing. I'm just drawing. Not everything has a deep meaning or hidden message."

I sat up, leaning my weight on the armrest of the couch. "Mit, hey." I waited until he turned to me so I had his undivided attention. "Are you okay?"

"I'm fine," he muttered, turning back to his drawing.

"I wouldn't be asking if I thought everything was fine." I let out a soft sigh. "I know I've been too focused on the girls and the portal. I know I haven't been giving you as much attention, and I'm sorry for that. I'm here now though, and I want to be better. After everything with losing Mom and Abe going missing, you've been keeping it all inside. Talk to me."

Dmitri's eyes became void of any emotion. "It works for you."

"What?"

"You turn yourself into stone and say you're fine. I don't know what else to do besides do that as well."

I blinked away tears as they blurred my vision. "I don't want you to be like me. It's okay to not be okay. Maybe you need to talk to someone."

"I'm talking to you right now."

"No, I mean a professional." I chewed on my lip before I continued. "Would you be open to a therapist?"

Dmitri chortled. "What am I supposed to tell a therapist, Whitney? Hello, I'm Dmitri, a witch. My mother was a witch and she died, leaving me in the care of my two older sisters who are witches. Then everyone found out we were witches so we moved here. Then I fell in love with a witch and he's probably dead, too." He rolled his eyes. "I'm fucking cursed, a therapist isn't going to fix that."

"You aren't cursed, Mit. We all die, eventually."

"Then what's the fucking point?"

I squeezed my eyes shut, knowing I said the wrong thing. I constantly said the wrong things to him when I tried to make things better.

"The point is that emotion is human, Mit, all of it. The good and the bad. The very fact that we get to feel means we're alive and we care. Even though we lost Mom, we still got to love her and be loved by her, even if it was only for a short time. We still got to learn and laugh with her. She loved us. And Abe cared...he *cares* about you, too."

Dmitri turned his head, hiding the tears beginning to well in his eyes. "It doesn't feel worth it." He paused, letting out a deep breath. "I'm worried Abe will never come home. Being at school without him is miserable."

"Brooke has been trying to make it easier."

Brooke had been an angel the last few weeks, befriending my brother and keeping him close during school hours. It had been an absolute struggle getting Dmitri to go to class after Abe's disappearance. Brooke promptly stepped in, taking him to lunch and being a genuine shoulder. Since Brooke and Dmitri were the only two in our little family who were still in high school, I was relieved and forever grateful that they had clung to one another.

"Brooke has been great but it's..." His voice cracked. "It's not enough, Whit."

"What can I do?"

He let out a puff of air, collecting himself. "I want to transfer to the charter school."

I paused. "How would that work?"

"I've already done all the research. I'd go in every Friday and turn in a homework packet. As long as I keep up with my work, I'll still graduate on time, maybe sooner, and...and I won't have to be in physical class. I won't have to be at the school without Abe anymore. I just need your signature."

I nodded slowly. "Okay."

Dmitri shot up, his back straight and shoulders squared. "Seriously?"

"I'm not going to make you go to school if you're miserable, Mit. Especially with Abe still missing. I want you to be happy, and if this will help, then yes you can go to charter school."

I made a promise to myself when Mom died that I would make sure Rayn and Dmitri stayed in school. I wanted Mit to at least graduate high school, but he didn't have to sit in a classroom to do that.

"I'll make an appointment with the charter school." Dmitri took a deep breath. "Thank you, Whit."

"I love you," I told him simply. "I'd do anything for you."

The sound of keys in the door handle jingled before it swung open. "Hey," Rayn greeted.

"How'd it go?" Dmitri rubbed his eyes with the balls of his palms, probably attempting to hide his earlier tears.

"I got a job." Rayn hung her jacket on a hook next to the front door and kicked off her boots. "I start tomorrow."

"That's amazing, Ray!" I exclaimed.

"I haven't heard back from my other applications, so it's a huge relief. Money has been tight since my previous employer burned down and all."

"That's great timing since the Roberts are closing the mini-mart for good, so I'm officially unemployed. Where's the job at?" Dmitri asked.

"Huh?"

"What's the new job?" he repeated.

"Oh, um, a restaurant."

"Okay, which one?" I asked, taken back by her vagueness.

Rayn shifted awkwardly. "Um...Giani's."

"I'm sorry, where?" I must have misheard her. Giani's Italian Kitchen couldn't be Rayn's new job since that's where Bryan worked.

Rayn picked at her fingernails. "I stayed at Rose's last night and Bryan came over this morning to do laundry. His power went out or something. Anyway, I was talking about going out to find a job and he said Giani's is looking for a new hostess. One of them quit last night. I guess she got in a fight with one of the supervisors and quit on the spot after causing this huge scene." Rayn bit at her thumbnail, avoiding eye contact. "He took me down there this morning and I met his boss. I had no idea he had so much sway there.

He literally told the manager to hire me and she did on the spot. I need to buy some black dress shirts though."

I didn't know what to say. What did she expect me to say to all that? I wasn't mad that Bryan had found Rayn a job. Hell, the fact that he had given my sister a job when he knew we all had to work to get by. It broke me to think that after everything I had said to him the night after Halloween, he still watched out for us, for me. No, I was probably thinking too much into it. Maybe this had nothing to do with me. Somehow that hurt even worse.

"Whitney?" Rayn asked.

"What?"

"I asked if you're okay with all this."

"It's not up to me, honestly. It's your job, not mine."

"Yeah, but he's your ex."

"Technically not an ex. We never actually dated. It's fine." I huffed and retreated into the kitchen to finally get some coffee.

After a moment, Rayn followed behind me. "Hey."

"I'm fine."

"Rule number two."

Don't lie or keep secrets.

I let out a deep sigh and turned to face her. "How was he?"

"He said he's okay."

"Is he really?"

"I think so? I don't have much to gauge off of. He seemed surprised to see me but he was nice."

"He's always nice." I took a sip of coffee, expecting it to warm my soul or pick up my spirits. But I felt nothing except the hole in my heart growing a size bigger. "We have to meet Rose and B in the meadow in an hour."

"I'm ready to go. Are you coming with us, Mit?"

"If that's okay," he answered, speaking for the first time since Rayn explained the details of her new employment.

"Wait, really? You want to come?"

"If you're trying to open the portal, yeah. I don't know, I might be able to help. I may not be an Elemental but I still have magic powers." Dmitri shrugged, coming into the kitchen to wash the black residue off his fingertips.

Chapter Three

THICKER THAN WATER

RAYN

The wind rustled through the trees, blowing cold air through my hair as my siblings and I arrived at the meadow. I shivered in the breeze, wrapping my arms tighter across my chest. The crisp fall air filled my lungs and seeped deep into my bones. I let out an aggravated sigh, wishing for the heat of summer. The bright reds and golden yellows of the surrounding trees echoed against the evergreen needles of the pines. While I admired the beauty, I knew it would be a long winter.

Whitney had been quiet on the drive, but that didn't surprise me. I had dropped a bomb on my sister and stressed the entire way home over how it would land. When I mentioned that I had been looking for employment that morning, Bryan hadn't hesitated to help find me a job.

But I kept a tiny detail from my sister.

It would have only hurt Whitney to know how Bryan had tapped the steering wheel when he gave me a ride home, mustering up the courage to ask how we were doing. I knew what he really asked.

How was Whitney doing?

If she…if any of you ever need anything, just let me know. Bryan's words echoed in my memory.

I decided to keep that interaction to myself. Of course I didn't want to make my sister feel worse, but the interaction with Bryan had been accompanied by a sting of jealousy

I had been embarrassed to admit, even to myself. How easy it had been for Whit. How she had strolled right into the arms of someone willing to do anything for her, who knew exactly what she was and still wanted her. She didn't even have to try.

I always had to try. I had to try harder in school. Had to try harder to keep my temper under wraps. The last few times I had tried to put my heart out there, to give the love I longed to receive...

Both times ended with not only my life turned upside down, but my sibling's lives, too.

I brought my attention back to the trees, wishing I had brought a thicker hoodie and pretending I didn't see Tom Campbell's face whenever I closed my eyes.

Rose and Brooke seemed surprised to see Dmitri trailing behind us.

"All three Dansleys? What a treat!" Brooke smiled at him.

"How was everything after we left the CC? Did Grady stick around?" Rose asked.

"I had another vision," Whitney answered as casually as she would have commented on the weather.

"Just now?" Rose asked, alarmed.

Everyone's eyes shot to Whitney, hanging in anticipation for her to explain herself. I blinked in disbelief. There had been plenty of opportunities for Whitney to confide in me, but instead I heard the news for the first time with the rest of the group.

"After you guys left I had a vision in the break room," Whitney explained. "I saw this guy and he–"

"After I went home?" I cut her off, not possessing the patience to let my sister finish.

"No, before. Right after you all left."

Anger bubbled under my skin, threatening to take over my nervous system. "Wait, this happened while Mit and I were out getting food? Why didn't you say anything when we came back?"

Whitney ran her fingers through her hair. "I'm still processing it. I'm not really sure what I saw. I wanted to tell everyone at once."

"Okay so tell us what you saw." Brooke waved her hand impatiently for Whitney to continue.

With a deep breath, Whit described a boy she had seen in the forest. How he called for help but nobody came for him. How he cried while he burned a house down. How the people inside its walls screamed for their lives. How he passed out afterwards, likely from using too much magic at once.

How he burned the house down with magic.

"He…he burned down the house? Like with…like me?" I stammered, my vision blurring over with betrayal. "You saw someone like me and didn't tell me."

"Ray, I wasn't deliberately keeping this from you." Whitney defended herself. "I'm trying to understand what I saw."

"You don't tell us anything until you have to," I mumbled, hurt feelings seeping out onto display.

"That is not true!" Whitney's voice cracked. "You're not listening."

"Oh, I heard you!" My voice echoed off the trees. "I hear you crystal fucking clear."

"Rayn–"

"What did he look like?" Brooke asked, stepping in between us.

"He was young, probably around Mit's age," Whitney answered. "Kind of short. Dark hair."

"Doesn't ring any bells," Rose muttered, watching me pace in the grass.

"It looked like he was in the forest somewhere around Rifton, like this." Whitney motioned around to their surroundings. "And his clothes were modern, so whatever I saw, it was recent."

How were they all being so calm about this? Maybe if they had been told another Elemental exactly like them existed out in the world, they would react differently. Someone who could manipulate their elements, but Whitney had seen another pyro. Someone like me. This was life changing information and Whitney had kept this from us. From *me*. She had the opportunity to tell Dmitri and I a few nights ago, but kept it a secret.

She'd broken rule number two.

Again.

"If there's someone else in the forest like us we would know by now." Brooke crossed her arms. "One of us would have run into him at some point."

"Then he's not in the forest anymore," Whitney answered.

"Didn't Amilia say your visions were metaphoric?" Rose asked. "Like when you had that vision about Dragonfly, you were the one in the basement when it was actually Ray. So, who knows what you saw and what it actually means. Or if it's even happened yet. I know you saw a guy but maybe he was a stand in for Rayn. Maybe Ray burns something down. Maybe she's protecting us again."

Again.

"I told you already, I didn't burn down Dragonfly." My voice cut sharp as a knife. I had only told them a million times before.

"Not that you remember." Dmitri's voice was no surprise. He always stepped in to defend Whitney when she was wrong, even when we were children.

"I remember all of it. Every fucking second," I hissed through my teeth.

It had haunted my dreams and every waking moment. Sometimes I wondered if I would ever leave that damn basement. If I'd ever be clean from the marks Tom Campbell left on my soul, on my body.

Rose put her hands up. "Guys, this is counterproductive."

"What's counterproductive is keeping secrets. It's a fucking rule," I argued, turning to Rose. "You of all people should know how shitty this feels."

Before Whitney could rebuttal, Rose continued. "Whitney wasn't keeping secrets from us. Have you ever stopped to think how scary getting these visions are? There's no warning, no pattern. Suddenly you're gone and you have no control over where you go. I would need to take time to process it all, too. And we have no idea what it even meant so until we figure it out, can we focus on the portal, please? That's something we actually have control over right now."

My crossed arms softened and so did my brow as I looked at Whitney. The anger broke through enough for my hurt to show, tears stinging my eyes. "I would have told you right away," I admitted.

"I know," Whitney answered. "Ray, I...I'm sorry. I wasn't being deceitful. I'm still getting the hang of this shit."

"There are other Elementals." Brooke laughed, the reality of Whit's vision finally sinking in. "We aren't alone."

Whitney nodded, letting a smile break out across her face. "There were Elementals before us, after the Shepherds died."

Rose put a comforting hand on my shoulder, startling me. "This is the exact motivation we need to figure this portal stuff out." Rose motioned to the other side of the meadow. "Lead the way to the portal, Mit."

I wasn't ready to move past it, but I knew I'd have plenty of time to stew later. We had come up to the meadow for a reason and I didn't want to hinder the mission. As betrayed as I felt, I accepted Whitney's apology and pretended it didn't still sting.

Dmitri led us to the spot in the meadow he had fallen through. How had it only been a few months since the first time we'd been here? It felt like years. I may have looked the same since then, but my very being had been altered.

Dmitri stopped at the rock he tripped on. I wondered what life would be like if Dmitri had been running two feet to the left? If he had gone right past this patch of dirt and back to the car. Abe would have died in the lake. Dmitri would have never gotten to know him, but he wouldn't have the protection from the ritual Abe performed either.

"Are we sure this is it?" Brooke asked, glancing around as if there would be a big arrow pointing to the right spot.

"It is." Rose knelt down on one knee and held her hands towards the portal as if she warmed them by a fire. "I can feel it. The ground is...it's different here."

"Okay, let's do this."

Rose opened up the vial she had brewed and poured it over the ground. The liquid soaked into the earth and I pleaded that this would work. We needed this to work if we had any chance of closing the portal at Dragonfly Mystic. Tom and Serenity may have been the ones who opened it, but they couldn't have succeeded without our blood.

I held out my hand to Rose and met Whitney's gaze before I offered my other hand to my sister. Whitney grabbed my hand, giving a gentle squeeze. Another silent apology. I squeezed back.

"Should we say anything?" I asked, turning to Rose for guidance.

"The magic is in us, not our words. Stare at the portal and concentrate all your energy into the magic in the ground," Rose explained like she had done this a million times. It amazed me everyday what a natural Rose was at potions and spells, as if she had been the one raised by my mother.

I nodded and stared at the blades of grass and the tall weeds that grew up from the earth. At the rocks and flowers that camouflaged the once open portal and made it impossible to know it was there until someone fell through it.

My heart raced as I pulled from the energy flowing all around us and poured every ounce of it back into the earth. I pictured the passage between the meadow and the lake opening once more, strong and alive like the trees that surrounded them.

The ground began to tremble and then, nothing.

"That's it?" I asked, spinning around. "Did anything happen?"

"I don't know, honestly," Rose admitted. She let go of our hands and reached for a rock near her feet. Rose tossed the rock into the portal but it landed on the dirt.

I sighed, defeated. "What are we doing wrong?"

"I think you're right about the other night, Ray. We can't open this portal because we aren't the ones who closed it." Whitney let out a deep sigh.

"We won't know for sure until we try the Dragonfly portal." Rose tapped her lips with her index finger. "Between the Shadows and the Renati, I'm still not sure how we'll get close enough, even for a second. Who knows how long it'll take to actually close it."

"Lauren's blood was used to open the Dragonfly portal too though. Even if the four of us go there and bleed all over it, it may not close. We're not a complete generation." I ran my fingers through my red curls.

Rose shook her head. "I'm beginning to think that weakened generation stuff is a bunch of bull. I think Amilia is only saying that so we don't do anything she doesn't want us to."

"I know, I'm irritated with it too," Whitney agreed. "But it does make sense."

"Annoying or not, we can't do this without Lauren." Brooke echoed my concerns. "And she's out wherever, not returning our calls."

"We'll figure it out," Rose reassured the group.

Would we though? Together we could pull this off, only we weren't together. We needed Lauren, the missing piece of the puzzle. I huffed, realizing we wouldn't be in this situation if I hadn't put all my trust in Tom Campbell. But I couldn't change the past, all I could do was keep moving forward. I couldn't give into the darkness. I couldn't let Tom win.

The next afternoon, I filled my lungs with courage as I stepped off the sidewalk towards the Thaner's home. A clean, paved walkway led up to the front porch of the two-story white house. Trimmed rose bushes lined the perfectly manicured lawn. I pictured Lauren playing in the yard as a little girl, kicking around a ball or lying in the grass as the clouds passed by above her.

Shaking my head, I released the daydream and knocked on the door. We had given Lauren her space. We had left her alone for long enough, maybe too long; a couple weeks to pull herself back together. But we needed her if we had any chance of closing this portal and preventing the Shadows from overwhelming Rifton.

The door swung open. The older woman before me had dark brown hair and hazel eyes with a slender build. She stared at me for a moment, puzzled, probably trying to place my face.

"Hi," I broke the silence. "Is Lauren home?"

"She isn't," Lauren's mother answered. "Could I give her a message?"

"Um, I need to speak to her in person. Do you know when she will be home?"

Her eyes fluttered away from mine as she let out a sigh. "I'm not sure, to be honest. She's out of state visiting family. She hasn't booked a return trip."

"Oh."

She ran away. Lauren literally packed her bags and ditched town, leaving her generation to deal with the Renati alone. The girls and I should have known better.

"I could tell her you stopped by? I'm sorry I don't know your name."

"My name is Rayn Dansley. If you don't mind, I'd appreciate it. Please let her know it's important." I reached into my pocket and retrieved the citrine bracelet, running my thumb over the yellow gem before offering it to her. "She forgot this the last time I saw her. I know it's a family heirloom. You should have it back."

"My grandmother's bracelet." She blinked at it, a faint smile curved the edges of her lips. "Thank you for bringing this back."

"You're welcome." I nodded, stepping back from the door. "Sorry for bothering you."

Lauren's mother gave a small, polite wave before closing the door. The lock clicked the moment the door shut. I stared at the handle and sighed before I retreated to the car. What were we going to do now? Luckily, the Shadows had yet to fully form but it was only a matter of time before the people of Rifton found the witchy charm of the town unattractive.

My phone began to vibrate in my back pocket. Whitney's name lit up the screen.

"Hey," I answered, plopping down into the driver's seat of the car.

"So, I just got a weird call from Mia." Whit sounded unsettled. "She wants us to come to the cottage."

"I'm close by. I stopped by Lauren's and found out she fled the fucking country. Want me to come get you?"

"I'm not surprised. And yeah, I just got off work. Amilia sounded so off, not herself at all."

"I'm on my way." I ended the phone call and started the car. Hopefully Whitney was reading too much into Amilia's voice and they were being gathered for something mundane.

CHAPTER FOUR

A GOOD MAN

WHITNEY

Rayn, Rose, Brooke, and I all squeezed ourselves onto Amilia's couch. I glanced around her living room at all the plants and paintings as if one of them would give me some clue as to what was going on. Nothing seemed out of place; everything in its proper spot except for the heaviness that hung in the air. Amilia finally emerged from the kitchen, wringing her hands together.

"I have something to tell you." Amilia sat down on the sky-blue recliner. She looked around the room nervously, avoiding eye contact.

"What happened?" Rose asked, surprisingly calm. I wished I had her empathic abilities to get a better read on Mia, but seeing Rose relaxed helped ease my anxiety.

"There's something I've kept from you. Please understand it wasn't because you aren't old enough or that I don't trust you. I haven't told anyone. For their protection and your own," Amilia explained. "But I am sorry that I kept this from you until now. I hope you understand."

"Whose protection?" I asked. My heart pounded in my throat as every worst possible scenario crawled around in my thoughts, making my skin tingle. She had already shown us her potion ingredients, her books, and theories. Why would she keep anything from us in the first place?

To answer my questions, a man came around the corner that led down the hall to the bedrooms. He was older than us by at least a decade and only a few inches taller than Amilia with a slim, athletic build. His short, dark brown hair stuck up like he had been running his tattooed hands through it. His hazel eyes scanned the four of us on the couch, lingering on me. I studied him up and down. He wasn't as devastatingly attractive as Bryan, but he was easy on the eyes. From the way he held himself, he knew it, too. The swagger in his walk, the slight tilt of his head, lifting his chin so he looked down at everyone.

This man may not have been a teenager anymore, but his screams had been haunting my dreams.

"No way," I whispered with my hand over my heart, afraid that if I didn't feel the beat somehow my blood would run cold.

"Who's that?" Rayn asked Amilia, shifting uneasily at my reaction.

"This is Dominic Grant," Amilia said. "Nic is like you, Rayn. He's a Flame Elemental."

That's for sure. He lit a house on fire with people still in it. Now he stood in the living room of the cottage, one of the few safe places I had left in this world.

"Really?" Brooke leaned forward to take a closer look at Nic, examining him without ever leaving the safety of the couch.

He watched me. He watched my eyes on his calloused fingers and the rips in his jeans. On the traditional rose tattoo covering the back of his hand that ended the artwork inked up to his short sleeves. Nic snapped his fingers in response to our questioning gazes and that familiar flame appeared in his palm. The flame danced around in his hand, but I felt nothing when he lit it.

He may have been like us, but he wasn't one of us.

Whitney, Rayn's scared voice asked inside my head. *Is that him?*

"That is the man from my vision. Only he was a teenager when I saw him," I answered aloud, not breaking eye contact with him. I wanted Amilia to know what he did. "He killed a house full of people without a second thought, burned them to the ground as they screamed for mercy."

Nic raised his eyebrows, not as surprised as I expected him to be. Amilia seemed too calm by my words. Hadn't she heard me? He killed a house full of people.

"You must be the Seer," Nic replied, not skipping a beat.

"Whitney's visions have never been wrong before. You killed innocent people," Rose said. At least the girls listened to me, even if Mia wouldn't.

"Like there isn't blood on your hands," Nic said, his eyes locked with mine. "Like that kid at the Dragonfly Mystic drowned on his own."

"How do you know about that?" Rayn snapped, jumping up from the couch in defense.

Nic smirked, waiting for us to put two and two together. And then it clicked.

"Because you really aren't the one who started the fire at Dragonfly, Ray," I whispered. A single tear fell down my face as I turned back to Nic. "Looks like you have a hard-on for burning down buildings while people are still inside."

"Surprisingly, that still makes me one of the less murderous Elementals."

"Dominic," Amilia snapped. "Stop it."

"Mia, I saw what he did!" I shouted in frustration that she wasn't listening to me. "I saw him as a teenager and he killed people!"

"Whitney, I know what you saw and what he did. I have known Nicky since he was a little boy. I practically raised him myself. He is many things, and trust me when I say that a good man is one of them. There are bigger issues to face than the past."

"He hasn't given us any reason to trust him," I said through my teeth.

"I saved your lives," Nic argued.

"No one asked you to." Rayn threw back at him.

"What a couple of ungrateful little shits." Nic crossed his arms across his chest.

"Those two are Audriana's girls," Amilia murmured, rubbing her temple.

Nic spun around to her in disbelief. "What?"

"Whitney and Rayn are Audri's girls. She adopted them after she left Rifton," Amilia explained vaguely.

Finding out Dominic knew my mother somehow made me want to punch him even more.

Nic gaze shifted, a small crack of humanity came through his exterior before it hardened again. "Sounds like Audri is getting soft in her old age."

"She's dead," I snapped.

Nic froze in place, huffing out a deep breath but didn't speak a word.

Amilia turned to Nic. "I meant to tell you last night, but–"

"I'm fine." He cut her off. "I'm so sorry, Mia."

Amilia placed her hand on his shoulder.

"Amilia, I don't like this," Rose admitted, standing with me as a unified front.

"We just found out we aren't the only living Elementals left and you want to fight about it?" Brooke asked, turning to face me. "You guys pick the weirdest hills to die on."

"It doesn't bother you that he's a murderer?" I turned to Brooke. I loved her, but she insisted on seeing the good in everyone, no matter what their flaws.

"It bothers me that you're ready to cast him out without at least hearing his side of the story."

"There isn't time for that," Nic spoke again, casually sitting down in the second armchair. He rested his ankle on his knee and leaned back, getting comfortable like he owned the place. "We need to find the Renati hideout yesterday and stop them before it's too late. You four haven't done shit, so it's a good thing I showed up when I did. You're welcome for saving your asses at Dragonfly Mystic, by the way."

What a cocky asshole.

Nic planted both feet on the floor and leaned forward, his elbows on his knees. "Tell me everything."

"And why the hell should we trust you?" Rayn asked, scoffing at him.

"Because the Renati will never stop now that Erebus has returned. They're going to kill your friends, your parents, and everyone you've ever loved until they finally slit your throats and use your blood to bring over nightmares from the Shadow Realm. So unless you're planning to roll over and end centuries of Elemental dynasties, quick fucking around and tell me what you know before you get someone else killed."

Dominic Grant appeared to be many things, but a good man? That was the biggest lie Amilia had told us yet.

Amilia hunched forward and held her forehead in her open hand, taking in an unsteady breath.

"Mom?" Nic asked, reaching out for her.

"I'm fine." She sat back up.

I decided not to comment on her heavy, exhausted eyes.

Nic turned back to us. "Are you going to talk to me or what?"

"I'm not telling you a damn thing," I responded coldly, matching his energy.

"Then you'll take us all down with you," Nic answered, our eyes burning into each other.

"Why are you by yourself?" Rose asked him, sitting on the edge of the couch. "Where is your generation?"

"Why are there only four of you?" Nic asked. He raised an eyebrow and curled the side of his mouth into a small smile. "Where is your windbreaker?"

"She needed space," Brooke replied. "We've been through a lot."

A knock at Amilia's front door made the four of us jump. Amilia got up from her chair and began to walk to the door, but paused and faced us.

"I hoped the others would all be here before the four of you showed up, and I'm sorry for that. Be patient, please?" Amilia asked. "They haven't seen each other in a very long time."

"Others?" Brooke asked.

"Yes. Harmony and Warren, along with Nic, are the last three of their generation," Amilia explained.

"We're fine," I lied.

Nerves and anticipation rattled my core at the arrival of Amilia's guests. There were even more Elemental witches than we could have imagined. Three more besides us? An almost complete generation. Almost.

Amilia reached for the handle and opened the door, but my attention wasn't on the people she let in. My eyes were on Dominic Grant. He froze in his chair with a hardened face as emotion flurried in his eyes. He looked like he did when I first saw him in my vision, like a human being capable of empathy. As if he was in disbelief that the two people Amilia had let into the house were real, like they had been a figment of his dreams until now.

The African-American man who came through the door first stood much taller than the rest of us. His hair was buzzed short and his eyes lit up like diamonds when he smiled at Amilia.

"Hello, Mia. It's been too long." He pulled her into a warm hug and kissed her on the cheek before he finally glanced up. His arms and jaw both fell in shock when his gaze settled on who sat in the recliner closest to the fireplace. "Nicky?"

"Hey, Warren," Nic said, slowly standing up from his chair.

The tall man, Warren, practically ran across the room and pulled Nic into a bear hug. They held each other close like long-lost brothers who thought they would never see each other again.

Warren held Nic at arm's length with his big hands on Nic's shoulders. "I can't believe it's really you. Look at you! Little Nicky, all grown up." Warren laughed and gave Nic another hug. I wondered how long it had been since they'd seen each other.

"Hi, Harmony," Nic said, looking past Warren at the woman still standing by the door. He had clear difficulty saying her name.

The woman wore large sunglasses with brown hair spilling over her shoulders in wispy curls. She bit the side of her mouth and crossed her arms, jutting out one wide hip to the side. Everything about her body language said she couldn't be more annoyed with everyone present.

Harmony dramatically ripped her sunglasses off and sped across the room as quickly as Warren had. Once she reached Nic, she threw her arm back and slapped him across the face so hard I felt it in my bones. Rayn and Rose startled on either side of me.

"Fuck you, Dominic," Harmony hissed through her teeth.

"Come on, Honey. It's been thirteen years," Warren begged.

"Exactly. It's been thirteen years. Where the hell have you been? Did you think it was funny letting everyone believe you were dead? Another flamboyant, dramatic episode of the Dominic Show." Harmony shook her head in disgust. "You should have seen your mother at your funeral."

Nic scoffed, unbothered. "Did she cry? Did she put on a big show for everyone?"

"Dominic, watch your mouth." Amilia snapped like a mother disciplining her toddler in the grocery store.

What was wrong with these people?

Harmony turned to observe us. She pointed a well-manicured finger at us. "Amilia, these are children."

"Who, us?" Rose asked, pointing a finger at her own chest. "I don't know who you think you are, lady, but we aren't children."

Harmony disregarded Rose's comment. "These can't be the daughters we've heard so much about. They're so young! That one is barely twelve."

"I'm seventeen," Brooke muttered through clenched teeth.

"Honey, don't talk about people like they aren't in the same room as you. It's rude," Nic said, shaking his head. "Besides, they're about the same ages we were when everything fell apart."

"Don't you *dare* call me that," Harmony snapped in a low tone. "You lost all right to speak to me like that thirteen years ago when you faked your death. In fact, don't speak to me at all."

"Is it true, Amilia?" Warren asked, diverting away from the tension in the room.

"Yes," Amilia replied. "Whitney, show them your necklace."

Harmony turned her head and glared at me with piercing brown eyes. She looked at me like I was completely incapable of anything compared to her. I didn't want to show her my necklace. I didn't know who these people were. One of them was a murderer and another had been nothing but condescending since she walked in the room. Only one of them seemed trustworthy at all and even then, I still didn't trust Warren.

"It's okay, Whitney. You can trust them. I promise," Amilia said, reading my mind like Mom had done all the time.

I pulled up on the silver chain, exposing my aquamarine. All three of the new faces in front of me froze the second the gem hit the front of my sweater. Nic sat back down in the recliner with a loud thud and began to rub his face. Warren took a deep breath and a step towards Harmony, who stared at the gem around my neck with her ruby red lips parted in a gasp.

"This can't really be it." Harmony took a step towards me, shaking her head. I quickly took up the gem in my hand and hid it as she came closer.

"They all have one," Amilia replied. "The complete set has been reunited."

"So you're saying the Shepherd's talismans...they really do exist? The stories are true?" Warren asked, finally getting air back into his lungs. "And they went to these girls?"

"Of course they exist," Nic replied. "Why else would it be in the books?"

"What books?" Rose asked. "What else are you keeping from us, Mia?"

"It's not something you would have access to," Harmony replied matter-of-factly.

"If it was, I would have already read it. That isn't what I asked though, what book did you read about the jewelry in?" Rose asked again, hardening her expression.

"We don't have them anymore." Harmony crossed her arms. "All of those books were lost years ago."

"There used to be more books about past Elemental generations," Nic explained. "When a generation does something great, something life-changing, there is a book written about them. But they weren't story books necessarily, more like a collection of documents. But years ago, there was an attack and some were lost."

"And one of those books talked about the talismans?" I asked, meeting Nic's hazel eyes.

"There was an entire book written about the generation who those talismans belonged to," he answered. "Your jewelry are the only ones in existence and they haven't been seen for centuries."

Rayn stood up. "This changes everything."

"The books are nothing more than ashes now," Harmony informed us.

"We can't change the past," Warren said, taking a seat in the chair Amilia had been sitting in earlier. "I'd like to talk about your magic."

"What are your powers?" Brooke asked him.

Amilia answered for them. "Warren is air, like Lauren, and Harmony is water, like you, Whitney."

Ice seemed more appropriate.

"We'd like to know what exactly happened at Dragonfly Mystic, as much as you can tell us," Warren replied.

"Why should we trust you?" Rose asked.

"Because we are you," Nic answered.

I looked at Rayn and mentally asked her, *What do you think?*

Rayn stared at the four people in front of us, but her gaze paused when she reached Nic. "There was this boy in one of my classes, named Tom Campbell. He pretended to care about me, but he was Renati. He attacked me. I didn't expect it and he had me knocked out before I could fight back. They took me to Dragonfly Mystic and chained me in the basement. I was barely awake when Whitney and Rose got there."

I could see Rayn getting choked up so I stepped in. "Then Tom exposed himself as what he really was, a monster. Rose and I tried to fight but he and Serenity were too strong. They were able to finish their ritual."

"What happened next?" Warren asked.

"The floor opened and we saw Erebus, but he seemed weak. It's the last thing I remember."

"And you didn't defeat him," Harmony stated.

"Erebus? No," Rose said coldly. "Obviously not?"

"Well, I guess lesson one will be self-defense," Harmony muttered.

"Whitney didn't need your lessons to kill Tom," Rayn spoke up again, her voice stronger than when she started the story. For a moment, Harmony actually seemed impressed and I felt like the only person truly ashamed of taking a life.

"It used a lot of magic," I admitted. "Before I passed out, there were Shadows all around. They erupted in flames."

Warren, Harmony and Amilia all turned to Nic. Nic didn't try to hide a smug smile.

"How did you know when we didn't?" Warren asked Nic the question dwelling in my own mind. "Where have you been, Nicky?"

Nic shrugged. "When I got back into town, I knew something felt off. There was blood on the moon. I figured that old hag still owned Dragonfly Mystic so I went there first. It appears I got there right in time and stepped in. That is part of the job description, isn't it?"

"How convenient," Harmony mumbled.

Blood on the moon? Halloween night had been too much of a panicked blur to remember what the moon had looked like that night.

"What job description?" Brooke asked.

"We are the elder of the generations. That makes us the Magisters," Warren explained. "Although for many years we thought we were the only ones left."

"The Magi-what?" I lifted an eyebrow.

"Magisters. Your teachers," Amilia offered.

"Oh goodie, the powers do come with instructions after all." Rose rolled her eyes. "Better late than never, I guess."

"She is so much like Abbie," Warren chuckled to Amilia, nodding towards Rose.

I leaned forward in my seat. "Abbie. Nic called out that name in my vision."

Harmony spun around to me. "What vision? What did you see?"

My gaze wandered to Nic and Amilia, wondering if my vision was information to be shared with Harmony and Warren.

"She saw Abbie and I the night of the fire," Nic answered for me.

"Who is Abbie?" Brooke asked.

Amilia opened a cabinet I had dug through a million times. This time, Amilia waved her hand over it and a dim light lit up behind the wood. The same light as the brick in the graveyard. Amilia broke the protection spell and opened the cabinet, revealing books and picture frames I had never seen before. She handed us a photo in a thick, wooden frame with a small crack in the corner of the glass.

Smiling up at me were three young boys and two girls, all around the same ages that the girls and I were now. Harmony's short dark brown hair fell around her chin in a bob. Warren stood tall in the background with his arm around Harmony's shoulder. Nic was obviously the youngest of the bunch, with his round face full of freckles, giving the camera a mischievous smile. The other two were mysteries. One boy with shaggy blonde hair and a fair complexion, eyebrows and lashes so blonde they looked invisible. The girl was shorter with wavy auburn hair, her arms around Nic's waist and a mouth full of braces smiling at the camera.

The only thing I knew for sure, their complete generation seemed happy. They looked like genuine friends and not just five people who were thrown into the same forest with no explanation as to why. They truly loved one another.

"Her." Brooke nearly jumped out of her seat as she pointed to the short girl with her arms around Nic. "I've seen her. She's the spirit I saw in the cemetery, the one who led us to the crypt where we found our spellbook."

"Mia, is this Abbie?" I asked, looking up at the saddest blue eyes I had ever seen.

"Yes, that is Abigail," Amilia said, her eyes welling with tears of sadness and pride. "My daughter."

CHAPTER FIVE

FIRST IMPRESSIONS

WHITNEY

"You guys can head out if you want," I told Robby and Olivia a few days later as we closed the Corner Cup. "I'll lock up."

Olivia didn't hesitate, already halfway out the door as she told us goodnight.

I took cash from the register to the safe in Amilia's office and recorded in her books how much I put away from the night. "You can go ahead, Robby, I'm right behind you."

"I can wait so you don't have to walk to your car alone at night," Robby offered but I'd been longing for some alone time since Amilia bombarded us with ancient family drama.

"I appreciate it, but I'll be okay." I faked a smile.

"Night, Whitney."

Robby reluctantly left Amilia's office, glancing over his shoulder as I gave him a reassuring wave. Sitting in Mia's chair, I glanced over at the large oak cabinet in her office that held her apothecary away from home. I wondered if any of the other supervisors ever got curious and peeked inside. Even if they did, Amilia probably had a cloaking spell on it. Resting my face in my hands, I leaned against her desk. My elbows thudded against the hardwood; her papers and large monthly calendar crinkled under me.

How could she keep the other Elementals from us? When Amilia first revealed herself as a witch, especially one that had been so close to my mother, I thought all our problems had been solved. She had saved Rose's life from the spirit that attempted to possess her. She had given us books to read and answered questions but she still kept so much from us. I struggled to continue trusting someone that only showed us half of the picture, especially when I considered what we were up against. I wondered if Erebus kept secrets from his followers. Maybe they didn't ask questions. I had no idea what went on behind closed doors with the Renati.

The bell attached to the front door jingled in the distance, pulling me out of my pity party. I jumped up from Amilia's desk as my powers prickled over my skin like pins and needles. Whoever decided to break and enter didn't know this place was the current hideout of a witch with pent-up aggression, but they were about to find out.

I tiptoed towards the dining room, careful not to make any noise and alert the intruder. The main overhead lights were turned off, only the string of decorative ones twisted around the metal rafters illuminating the scene. My heart pounded in my ears as I slowly pushed back the door that separated me from the dining room. A man stood with his hands casually held behind his back, fingers wrapped gently around his wrist as he examined the art hanging on the wall. I recognized the flash art sparrows tattooed on his forearm.

"We're closed," I snapped at him, building up my powers in preparation for defense. The tingle across my skin slowly simmered down as he turned to face me. "What are you doing here?"

Nic Grant smiled genuinely. Something I had yet to see him do. "I think you and I need to start over."

"Start over?"

"Yeah, Monday was a rough day. Mia should have known better than to have us air out our dirty laundry in front of an audience." Nic crossed the room and sat down on the barstool at the counter where Bryan had sat during his visits. It felt sacrilegious to see someone else sitting in that seat.

"Surprisingly, that's not what has been bothering me since Monday." I moved onto cleaning the other side of the counter as if I wasn't curious to hear his explanation or excuses.

"Well, I can answer whatever questions you have. I bet you have a few." Nic folded his hands calmly on the counter, demonstrating patience I didn't think he possessed. A ring on his thumb clanked against the glass counter. *Ugh. A skull ring? How fucking tacky.*

"Why do you care about first impressions? You made your feelings about the situation quite clear." I raised an eyebrow at him.

"I don't have any friends left in this town."

I scoffed. "I am not your friend."

"You could be." Nic ran his fingers through his hair. "Look, if this is going to work we need to trust one another, and right now you don't trust me."

"Wow, audacious and insightful."

Nic chuckled, leaning further onto the counter. "I know Mia. She isn't giving you the answers you want. So I'll tell you what I know in exchange for your trust."

"Trust has to be earned."

"Isn't that what I'm doing?" Nic side-eyed me, as if he assumed I would take the bait.

"Why did you come back to Rifton?" The words fell out of my mouth as I gave in. "Amilia couldn't have called you, not if everyone thought you were dead. So why? Why now?"

Nic pursed his lips and ran his tongue over his teeth. "I had a dream."

"A dream," I repeated, lifting one eyebrow. "Like a vision?"

Nic shook his head. "No. Abbie was the Seer. This was a dream. I was asleep. I dreamt of the meadow off the Eagle Falls Loop. I'm sure you're familiar with it."

"You know about the meadow?" Of course he did, I should have expected he would.

Nic chuckled again. "I lived in Rifton for seventeen years, Whitney. I know all the hiding places."

"Not the Renati's, unfortunately."

"No, I'm not up to date on where the Renati slither back to when the sun goes down."

"So...the dream."

"I knew the meadow instantly when I saw it. Honestly, I thought I was reliving a memory until I saw two girls sitting in the tall grass. One of them held a fireball in her hands and dropped it. So the other girl created a rainstorm and cleaned up her mess."

My face fell and my heart stopped beating. I had no words, no expressions.

Nic continued. "I realized there was another generation in Dark Star Forest. I didn't know if you two had found others but I did know it was only a matter of time before the Renati found you, so I decided I had been on vacation long enough."

"Vacation," I muttered.

"Death is a vacation, of sorts." Nic shrugged.

"But...Rayn and I in the meadow... that was months ago, back in August," I muttered, pleasantly surprised I could still form comprehensive sentences.

"I had it the night before Halloween. I woke up and drove straight here."

"So that's all it took for you to come back from the dead?"

"Life isn't always complicated."

"Yes, it is... Does Amilia know about this dream?"

"She does."

"Hmm." I rested my back against the counter and glanced at Nic from across the bar. "Another thing Amilia kept from us."

I let out a deep sigh and looked into Nic's hazel eyes. He stared back at me with a soft smile, as if he patiently waited for me to come around and trust him. Part of me wondered how long he'd sit there and humor my questions. Though he remained a stranger, something about him felt familiar and safe.

"The woman has always spoken in riddles. She's worse now than she used to be."

"It's infuriating!" I shouted, letting out my anger. Only Nic and I stood in the Corner Cup. What did I have to lose? "She knows so much and keeps everything to herself, expecting us to figure it all out on our own like we have lived our whole lives knowing the truth and not spent weeks confused out of our fucking minds. We have to do it all ourselves and on a time limit, and if we don't hurry then everyone is dead. And when we didn't get everything done when she thought we should have, she called in the Magister Calvary. I'm done with it."

Nic laughed like he watched an old episode of a TV show he hadn't seen in a while. "You have Harmony's temper. Amilia didn't call us because you were on a time limit. I showed up in the middle of the night. Mia called Harmony and Warren because I came back from the dead. What do you want to know that Amilia hasn't told you yet?"

"That easily?" I felt like there should have been some kind of catch, a hoop I had to jump through.

"I mean, I could make you dance before every question but I think you've dealt with enough bullshit this week."

"Wow, you're so kind." I echoed his laughter. "Okay, tell me about the jewelry."

"Ah, the infamous talismans of the Shepherds." Nic crossed his ankle over his knee and got comfortable. "Once upon a time, there was a generation that we call the Shepherds. Legend says in order to protect their magic from being taken by Erebus, they sacrificed themselves and locked their powers inside precious gems. The generation before them is called the Martyrs because Erebus killed them and absorbed their energy."

I leaned my back against the counter. "We have the Martyr's spellbook. Abbie's spirit showed it to us in a graveyard here in town. Mia told us a bit about them a while back."

"Good." Nic continued on with a nod. "So the Shepherd's created the talismans in an attempt to protect their magic. The gems were eventually taken by Archivists and turned into jewelry to keep them hidden, but from what I read the talismans got separated from one another, lost in the world for who knows how long." Nic shrugged. "In a book Abbie read, someone said that one of the Archivists believed the Shepherds sacrificed themselves so that the generation that ended up reuniting the talismans could unlock the magic and finally put that old bag of bones in his place. The Shepherds couldn't kill him, but they were able to detain him long enough to complete their spell. I think maybe if they knew how long Erebus would sit in the Shadow Realm, they would have thought twice about killing themselves, but hey, who knows."

"How long ago?"

"Oh shit, I don't know, Whitney." Nic chuckled, running his fingers through his hair. "Long enough to make it a legend. I didn't believe the talismans even existed until I saw one hanging around your neck."

"Holy shit." I released a deep breath. "How many generations are there?"

"There's been several."

"No, I mean, how many are there at a time? I know elemental magic reincarnates or recycles or whatever."

"Three," Nic answered. "Elemental magic can manifest in three different generations at once and cannot be reincarnated until an entire generation is dead. I guess older generations used to perform this ceremony where all five of their members would die at once to make room for the new generation to be born."

"They'd kill themselves?" My stomach churned at the thought.

Nic nodded. "They seemed to live long lives. It was considered an honor to allow the youngest generation to manifest. The magic wouldn't reincarnate until all five members of the generation were gone."

"Why three generations?"

"Personally I think it's to keep the magic from being spread too thin, but I don't know for sure. There's never been more than three generations at a time. But who knows, it's just a story." Nic shrugged like he hadn't unveiled the truth behind our powers that Rayn and I had been chasing for over a decade. "That's what I remember of it. I'm sorry so many of those books were burned, but it was a messy time and we lost a lot more than a library."

"And why couldn't Amilia tell us all this? I don't understand how knowing the truth would have put us in more danger than we are already in."

"She lost her entire family, her husband and Abbie both." Nic's shoulders fell as his expression softened. "I think she's trying to keep history from repeating itself. She'd never willingly put Audriana's daughters in danger. Those women were platonic soulmates."

"Is that what the floating ink inside of the gems is? The powers of a past generation?" I picked up my aquamarine and watched the black ink float around.

"Maybe? I think so." The casualness of Nic's responses and demeanor given the topics he explained were truly mind-blowing. "Nothing I've read has ever specified."

I put my hands on my hips and huffed. "Why is this all so 'whatever' to you? Things that have kept me awake for days on end roll right off your shoulders."

"I guess after you come face to face with death so many times, molehills don't seem like mountains anymore. Knowing what the talismans are and how to actually get that magic out to use it? Two completely different things, one much more dangerous and complex than the other."

I frowned. "Why are you telling me all of this? Why leave my generation out of it?"

"Because we don't have enough time for you to sit around and hate me, Whitney. You may not see it yet but you're the leader of your generation. Once the others see that you trust me, they'll follow suit and we can get shit done." He glanced across the room. "Plus, you remind me of someone."

"Harmony?"

Nic nodded, a hint of sadness on his face. "Her too. So, do you trust me?"

"You killed a house full of people in the forest."

"And you drowned a boy in a basement." Nic shrugged like the two things were even remotely comparable.

"That boy tried to kill me and my sisters." I glared at him.

"And the people inside that house were going to kill me and *my* sister." Nic snapped. He slid off the bar stool, his shoes hitting the tile floor hard and echoing through the empty coffee shop. "I think that's enough school for one night."

"Nic, wait...I'm sorry."

He slowly turned back around. "People are not black and white, Whitney. We're all gray, some darker shades than the others but none of us are innocent in this war. I want to help you. If we don't get a handle on Erebus and the Renati before they get too powerful, everyone in this town is fucked. Everyone that they decide to set their gaze upon is fucked. We're Elementals, it's our job to protect these witches. It's our duty."

"Who decided that?" I asked curiously.

Nic chuckled. "The Elementals. We put ourselves in this position of power, it's time we start behaving like we deserve it. We have a lot to make up for, this is a good start."

"You talk about previous generations like they were villains."

"Because we were." His eyes went cold. "But we can be better. I want to do better and I believe you do, too."

I chewed on my lip for a moment before my gaze met his. Nic may have been feeding me what I wanted to hear, but I felt a pull in my heart. The one where the universe tells shows which path to take.

"Okay, Dominic." I gave in and trusted my gut. "You have my trust. For now."

Nic grinned. "Glad to hear it. Amilia wants everyone to get together tomorrow."

"Tomorrow is Thanksgiving."

"Big plans?"

"No, we don't really celebrate it."

"Good, then you'll be able to come to the cottage."

"Hey, I never said that."

"It'll mean a lot to Mia, and she may be frustrating at times but we owe her a lot. None of us would be here without her."

I sighed. "I'll talk to Rayn."

"Bring your brother. Mia has been dying to see that kid again."

"You're bossy. You came in here to coax us into dinner at the cottage."

"I'm a multitasker." Nic smirked as he turned to leave the Corner Cup.

Chapter Six

FERAL BRUTES

Whitney

Rayn pushed through the door first, strolling into the cottage like her own home. She kicked her brown boots off and hung up her jacket like second nature. Dmitri dragged his feet behind me hesitantly before he stepped over the threshold into the entryway. If I hadn't been carrying a pumpkin pie and a bottle of wine in my arms, I would have reached for his hand and pulled him the rest of the way.

Flames danced around in the fireplace, warming the living room and setting a calming atmosphere as the fire glowed across the floor. Harmony and Warren sat on the couch, talking quietly amongst themselves. Harmony barely looked up as we walked through the door, her eyes darting up to see my face then quickly turning back to Warren. Warren turned and gave us a wide smile that warmed the room as easily as the roaring fire.

"Happy Thanksgiving," he greeted us.

Amilia bustled around the kitchen; dishes clinked together and cupboard doors swung shut as she seasoned pans and stirred pots. Rayn beelined toward her, taking a wooden spoon from Amilia's hand along with a deep whiff from the pot. Ray chewed the inside of her cheek in thought before she reached for the salt shaker next to the stove. Amilia appeared in the doorway of the kitchen, wiping her hands off on an apron around her waist. She smiled at me as I set the pie and wine down on the dining room table.

"Wait, is this Dmitri?" Warren stood up from the couch, taking a few steps towards my brother. "Oh, wow. We haven't seen you since you were a little guy! You look so much like your mom."

Dmitri glanced around in sheer terror as every pair of eyes in the room were on him. Literally one of his biggest nightmares. I took my spot at his side and rested my hand on his shoulder. "He's not a huge fan of being the center of attention," I explained.

"I'm fine." Dmitri waved me off, turning his attention to Warren. "You knew my mom?"

"Oh yeah, we all loved Audri. One of the best people I've ever known." Warren smiled warmly. "One time, she and Mia were cooking Solstice dinner together and she burnt every single pie crust they had made."

Dmitri chuckled, the tension in his shoulder easing. "Sounds like her."

"Audri was a wonderful woman," Harmony said. "I remember the day she told us she was pregnant with you. It seems like another lifetime."

"Technically it was." Nic's voice filled the room as he appeared from the hallway.

"I found some old photos. There's pictures of her, if you'd like to come see." Harmony held up a thick black photo album, offering the seat beside her to my brother.

Dmitri wandered over to Warren and Harmony on the couch. I felt like an idiot standing there alone, not sure what to do with myself. I glanced across the room and caught Nic watching me. When our eyes met, he gave me a crooked smile and nodded down the hall, signaling for me to follow. I took a quick glance at my siblings before I indulged in my own curiosity.

"What?" I asked, following behind him into the bedroom at the end of the hallway. The same room I'd woken up in after Halloween. The last place I'd seen Bryan in person.

"I found something that might interest you." Nic went to a stack of books sitting on the bedside table.

"What are those?"

"Mia's books that she hid in her bedroom. She needs to put stronger cloaking spells on her stash if she wants to keep me out of them."

"Why would she want to keep books hidden from you?"

"Not just me, all of us."

"Why would–"

"Whitney, do you want to see what I found or ask a million questions?"

"Show me."

Nic took the first book from the stack and opened it back to a page he had saved with a lime green sticky note. He set the large book down on the bed and pointed to the second paragraph on the page. I stepped closer, reading over his shoulder.

The last free council seat has officially been seized by the Renati. Now all five members of city council, as well as the mayor, are Renati, members of the founding families. Drake and his minions. There is no way they are using these meetings to discuss Renati business, the minutes for those are public record. The places of business they own would also be too obvious. They have to be hiding somewhere in the shadows. Audri refuses to believe that Kyle is attending these meetings but his father sits on the council. Now that we know the true purpose of the ledger, maybe we can destroy it for good.

"Who is Kyle?" I asked, looking up from the pages to Nic's hazel eyes.

He furrowed his brow. "Seriously?" I shrugged, and he let out a sigh. "I'm not sure I'm the one to tell you about him."

"I'm confused."

"Kyle was your mom's boyfriend. He, uh, he's Dmitri's father."

"Oh..."

Mom never spoke of Dmitri's father, not directly. She told Rayn and I of a previous heartache and how women with powers like ours would always struggle with love, but I had never heard his name before. I had accepted that whoever my brother's biological father was, he belonged in the rearview mirror.

"Dmitri doesn't know anything about him," I finally spoke.

"That's probably for the best."

"Dmitri's father is Renati?"

"Amilia will be able to tell you more. I don't know exactly how things ended between them." Nic cleared his throat. "This passage explains when the Renati took full control over Rifton about twenty years ago. Though the founding families have obviously been here much longer."

"I'm vaguely familiar with the story," I replied. "The witches who founded Rifton were Renati, yeah?"

"The first group that settled here, yes. See, the Dark Star Forest is a powerhouse of energy. It's like a giant magnet, attracting witches towards it. The magic in the forest is stronger because it's more concentrated here. We get pulled here involuntarily."

Like there's these magnetic pulls that lead us on the route we're meant to take. Bryan's words echoed in my head.

"An allurement. I'm familiar with the concept," I answered quietly.

"Good," Nic continued. "It seems Mia and her coven were silently tracking the Renati. The Renati track the rest of us, trying to weed out those who remain loyal to the Elementals so I guess the coven used their own tactics against them."

"Mia's mentioned the coven before. My mom was part of it but were there a lot of them?"

Nic paused as if counting in his head. "About six of them. They were just some of the Elemental supporters in Rifton before the Renati took over. Abbie being an Elemental and her daughter made Mia the leader of their little group, but there used to be more witches in Rifton that still believed the Elementals were special because of our enhanced powers."

"None of them are left?"

"None that are out in the open. The Renati drove a lot of people out of town who refused to convert and any who remain are well hidden." Nic tapped his finger on the book. "There's a list here of where her coven believed their secret hideouts were. It's an old list but it's the best lead we have so far. If we can find out where the Renati are keeping Erebus while he gets his sea legs, we may be able to strike before he's strong enough to fight back."

"What did Warren and Harmony say about it?"

"I haven't told them," Nic admitted. "I don't want Mia to know I've been snooping and Harmony will tell her before I finish my sentence."

"Amilia told us that we had access to all of her books." I shouldn't have been surprised that Amilia hadn't been completely honest with us. This was far from the first thing she'd lied to us about, but each lie revealed still stung as bad as the first one.

"Maybe she thinks if she can figure it all out herself, none of us will have to put ourselves in harm's way. That's a pipe dream," Nic answered. "Whether we get hurt or not is obsolete. We have to do what needs to be done before Erebus takes over the town."

"What happens if he succeeds?"

"I don't want to find out." Nic turned a page in the book, revealing the list of potential Renati hideouts. "They would want to be hidden in plain sight, I'd imagine. Somewhere we wouldn't think to look."

"Like Dragonfly Mystic?"

"That place was too obvious, literally a store about witchcraft. Sure, most people thought it was cutesy and would shop there for incense but who knew it sat on top of a future portal to hell."

"Nic, I have to ask you something."

"Shoot."

"Do you know about a portal in the meadow off the Eagle Loop trail?"

"Yeah, it leads to the lake."

Of course he knew.

"We need to figure out how to open it. If we can open it and reverse engineer the spell, we could close the portal at Dragonfly."

"It won't work," Nic answered, returning to the list in the book.

"Why not?"

"The portal in the meadow is a little baby shortcut when you want to go swimming. The portal at Dragonfly leads to another dimension. It's not the same."

"But if we can figure out how to open and close the smaller portals, why can't we use the same logic at Dragonfly?" I held out my hands in confusion. "My brother fell through it when we first moved here and when the girls and I went back, it had closed."

"That's weird. Portals don't close on their own and they certainly don't close by being used. From my understanding, witches cannot close portals they didn't open. I've gone through that portal a million times." Nic scratched at the stubble on his cheek. "Did anyone go through it with him?"

"No, but when he landed in the lake...Well, he kinda fell into a mess."

"What do you mean?"

I told Nic what I had seen when Dmitri unknowingly showed me his experience saving Abe Roberts from Serenity Drake.

"Drake?" Nic snapped before I could finish the story. "As in Henry Drake?"

"His daughter."

"He had twin girls, right? They were little at the time."

"Yeah, Serenity and Emma. How do you know him?"

"He tried to kill me thirteen years ago," Nic answered.

Before I could ask any of the million questions buzzing through my head, Rayn opened the door and stepped into the bedroom. She glared back and forth between Nic and I like she had walked in on something indecent.

"Amilia is looking for you. What are you doing in here?" Rayn's eyes wandered down to the books on the bed.

Nic thinks he may have found some info on the Renati but we have to keep it between us right now. Don't tell Amilia. I said between Rayn and I.

Nic cocked an eyebrow before he closed the book. With a quick wave of his hand, the books disappeared.

"Where did they go?" I asked aloud, looking around the room.

"Back where they belong." Nic walked past Rayn in the doorframe.

"Hey, what about the portals?" I went to stop Nic before he left the room but he had already headed down the hallway.

"I'll look into it," he answered over his shoulder.

"Does he know how to close the portal?" Rayn asked as Nic disappeared into the kitchen.

"I hope so," I answered, but before I could follow after him, Rayn caught my wrist in her warm hand.

Be careful with him, she warned.

What do you mean?

I don't know. I get a weird vibe from the way he acts around you.

I don't get a weird vibe. I crossed my arms.

I didn't get a vibe from Tom either and look how that turned out.

Ray, Dominic is not going to try and kill us.

Maybe not but something is there between you guys. I don't like it. You literally just broke up with Bryan and–

I cut her off. *Don't you dare. Don't you fucking dare, Rayn. This isn't me trying to get with someone else to get over Bryan. Bryan is all I think about. Nic is an Elemental. He is the only Magister who is doing any work to try and reverse this portal we opened. I trust Nic. I'm in love with Bryan. There's a difference.*

Rayn softened like she actually believed me. *Okay, I'm making sure you're keeping your head on straight. I mean, Nic is hot but in like, an older brooding, tortured past way. Not usually what you go for.*

Yeah, he's hot, but I have a feeling he is the only one who isn't keeping things from us.

Amilia too?

Nic said she's been hiding books, that he had to break her cloaking spell on the ones he showed me. Good intentions or not, Amilia isn't telling us everything.

And how do we know Nic is telling the truth?

I just do.

"Hmm." Rayn sighed aloud. "That simple, huh?"

"That simple."

"I hope you're right."

"You don't trust him?"

"I don't trust anyone anymore," Rayn said.

I didn't blame her, not after everything we had been through. I opened my mouth to say more but Amilia called for us. My sister shrugged a shoulder at me and headed towards the dining room table.

Amilia took off her apron and hung it on a small hook in the kitchen. Moving to the head of the table, she snapped her fingers. Orange, red, and yellow flowers filled the two small vases on either end. A beautiful hay-colored cloth table runner appeared under perfectly arranged place settings. Steamy, buttery rolls filled the wicker basket and the scent of rosemary and olive oil filled the room.

"Please, sit." Amilia waved her hand around, motioning for us to take our places.

I sat in between Rayn and Dmitri, the three of us taking up an entire side of the table. The Magisters sat across from us, Warren in between Nic and Harmony. Amilia waved her hands once more as trays of food levitated into the dining room, each platter and dish taking their place on the walnut table. Amilia had poured her heart and soul into this meal. A perfectly browned turkey sat in the middle surrounded by fluffy potatoes, a slice of butter sitting in the center. The gravy was smooth and rich in color. Without a doubt, she used her magic when she cooked because only holiday-themed magazines had this perfect spread.

"Does everyone have something to drink?" Amilia peered around the table at the empty wine glasses that sat next to full water goblets.

"I'm fine with water," Dmitri answered, taking a sip from his glass.

Harmony held up her hand, calling for a bottle of white wine she left on the kitchen countertop. With the slightest wave of her fingers, the bottle floated into her hand. The moment her fingertips touched the bottle, it chilled instantly. Small fragments of frost coated the olive-toned glass as if it had been sitting in the fridge for hours.

"Chardonnay, anyone?" Harmony asked, twisting the cork off with a loud pop.

"Yes, please." Warren tilted his glass towards Harmony as she filled it up. Wisps of cold rose from the liquid as it left the bottle.

Nic grabbed the bottle of merlot I'd brought that still sat on the table where I'd left it. Without a word, he twisted off the cap and leaned across the table, filling up my wine glass before he poured some of the red wine into his.

"We're going to need it," he answered with a soft smile.

"Thank you," I said.

Nic held the bottle out in front of him towards my sister. "Rayn?"

"I'm fine," she answered, picking up her water glass.

Amilia held her wine glass and smiled, looking each of us in the eyes before she spoke. "I cannot express how thankful I am to have all of you here today. I never could have imagined in my wildest dreams that I would have the six of you here for this meal, but it means the world to me. Cheers to our next chapter together."

Harmony and Warren clinked their glasses together before toasting with Amilia. Warren held his glass across the table and clinked it with Dmitri's water glass before raising it towards Rayn and I with a gentle nod. Nic took a drink from his glass without toasting anyone. He picked up a roll and ripped off a small piece.

I ate in silence, listening to Amilia, Warren and Harmony go back and forth about their good old days. Every now and then they would bring Dmitri into the conversation, about when he was a baby or when Mom was young. Amilia made an effort to always glance down at Rayn and I when she talked about my mother but everyone else at the table seemed to have forgotten that Audrianna Dansley raised more than one child.

"Oh man, that reminds me of when Abbie convinced us to ditch school and we took a day trip to the coast. I barely had my license and I was terrified we were going to get caught." Warren laughed. "Remember that, Nicky?"

"I do," Dominic whispered.

I glanced across the table at Nic, who merely moved a small portion of mashed potatoes around the plate with his fork. He drank the last of the wine from his glass and set it down gently, his eyes never leaving the half-finished roll on the corner of the ceramic.

When I looked at the man sitting across from me, I saw the scared teenager from my vision, alone in the woods screaming for help. I saw the tears streaming down his face in my memory. No one else at the table paid much attention to him, but he shattered all over again right before my eyes.

I grabbed the bottle of merlot and refilled his wine glass to the brim before I topped off my own drink. Nic's eyes wandered off his plate and met mine across the table. He gave a silent acknowledgment that I was the only one at the table that had seen his darkest moment. He flinched every time Abbie's name was spoken. I wondered how Amilia felt, or if she even knew the entirety of the events that took place. I didn't fully understand what I had seen in my vision, but that night seemed to be the last time anyone in Rifton saw Nic until a few days ago. Thirteen years.

"So, Whitney." Harmony's attention turned to me, holding her wine glass close to her face. "I hear you can conjure a mean rain cloud. How are you with ice?"

"A mean rain cloud? That's a bit condescending, don't you think?" Nic muttered, picking up the full wine glass I'd poured him, careful not to spill any on the tablecloth.

Harmony dismissed him with a wave of her hand. "Ice?"

I met her gaze. "What about it?"

"How is your second skin ability?" she asked.

She might as well be speaking a foreign language. "I don't understand what you're asking."

"You don't know how to freeze your skin?"

I might as well have told the table that I couldn't read or do basic math equations.

"I've never tried," I admitted.

"That'll be our first lesson, then. It's a handy trick to have up your sleeve." Harmony took another sip of her wine. "So, what can you do?"

"Um," I tripped over my thoughts. "I've learned a lot the past few weeks, actually. Amilia taught us how to create energy waves to defend ourselves. We've learned how to levitate and use magic to put things back together if they break."

"Wow," Harmony replied monotone, glancing over at Amilia. "So, beginner stuff."

"They may not have received the same training at the same age you did, Honey, but the kids are powerful and capable witches," Amilia defended us.

"So Audri didn't teach you anything?" Harmony turned her furrowed brow back to me.

"She did," I answered. "But it was mostly trial and error. After I flooded the living room, I became a bit timid with my powers. I didn't start using them much again until recently."

"That sort of defeats the whole purpose, don't you think? Goodness, flooding the house. I haven't done that since I was a child."

"Looking for a medal?" Nic muttered under his breath before he took another drink.

"That's enough from you two." Amilia disciplined Nic and Harmony like a mother who grew sick of her children's shit. "Harmony, you're able to ask about the girl's abilities without belittling them."

"I'm not belittling. I'm trying to gauge where she's at and how much work she's going to be," Harmony rebutted.

"I'm not a project," I shot back. "I don't need you to teach me anything."

"That's where you're wrong. You have a lot to learn. If you were smart, you'd take advantage of the lessons we have to teach." Harmony's cold eyes met mine. "Maybe next time you face the Renati, you won't get knocked on your ass so easily."

"Ease up, Honey." Warren turned to Harmony. "We were their age once, too. Even you weren't born as powerful as you are now."

"I don't want to train with you," I announced, glaring at Harmony. "You can keep your ice-cold attitude and your bitch ass comments to yourself."

Nic snorted into his wine glass, nearly choking on his drink.

Harmony's brown eyes narrowed. "Oh, I'm sure you think that's real fucking cute. You need us whether you want to admit it or not."

"Do we need you or are you just desperate for relevance?"

"I said that is enough. You two are so thick-headed. If you want to fight, go outside and settle it there but don't bring it into my house." Amilia raised her voice at us. "I swear, Whitney, I know Audri raised you with more manners than this."

"Mia, I'm not taking the girl outside to settle it. I'm not being rude, I'm being honest. Erebus has returned and they are so far from ready it's frightening. What are we supposed to do if they get themselves killed? Even one of them, and it's game over for all of us. I'm going to assume there isn't another complete generation out there since the girls have the talismans," Harmony continued on her soapbox.

My eyes wandered over to Nic, who held his wine glass to his lips. His eyes met mine and then gazed down to my wine, silently telling me to drink up.

"You're right." The words falling from my sister's mouth hit me like a freight train. "She's right. We aren't ready. We have absolutely no idea what we are up against, we learned that on Halloween. We can't do this on our own. I want to train. I want to learn."

"Finally someone with common sense," Harmony rejoiced.

Rayn turned to me. "Whit, you'd be stupid not to take advantage of spending time with someone like you. You wanted to meet other people like us, well here they are."

"Thank you, Rayn, I'd tell you to train with your fellow Flame Elemental but generations know what he would teach you. I'll do what I can." Harmony side eyed Nic.

"Excuse you." Nic set his wine glass down on the table a little harder than the last time. "What do you know about fires other than burning down bridges?"

Harmony's ice-cold gaze slithered around Warren and met Nic's for the first time that afternoon. "We don't know where you've been. We don't know what you've been doing or who you've been doing it with. Your timing to come back is awfully convenient, if you ask me. I don't want you mentoring these girls one on one. You haven't earned anyone's trust."

"I trust him," I announced to the table.

"Then you're even more naive than I assumed." Harmony waved me off and turned back to Rayn. "Please talk some sense into your sister."

"That's enough shop talk for one evening," Warren announced, looking around the table at everyone. "This is no way to thank Mia for this beautiful meal and all the work she put into today. You're acting like a bunch of feral brutes."

"I'm sorry, Mia. You know I love you." Harmony turned to face the matriarch at the head of the table.

"I love you too, sweet girl, but remember who you are speaking to when you converse with these girls. They are the holders of the talismans and that means something," Amilia said.

"You're right." Harmony nodded.

The fact that only Amilia received an apology from Harmony was not lost on me, or Nic, who rolled his eyes as he went back to playing with his food.

Chapter Seven

FELLOW PYRO

Rayn

That weekend, I wasn't sure what to expect when training with the Magisters, but I definitely wasn't surprised to hear them arguing. I stood in the doorway listening to Harmony and Dominic's voices bounce off the cottage walls.

"You could be working with the Renati for all we know!" Harmony shouted.

"The Renati? Are you serious?" Nic yelled back. "You know me better than that, Harmony."

"I *used* to," she shot back. "All I know is Abbie died and we thought you did too. I know the Renati had something to do with the events of that night, but your involvement is murky. The Nic I knew would have never hurt Abbie."

"If you think losing her hasn't haunted every moment of my life, then you never knew me at all."

Warren's calm voice clashed with the flash of emotions in his fellow generation's shouts. "Guys, we have a lot of work to do if we are going to get back to where we were, but we will never get there if we don't try."

"Things will never go back to how they were," Harmony snapped.

I slammed the front door behind me, alerting the Magisters to my presence. Silence fell over the cottage as the Magisters seemed to realize they had company. Warren emerged first, walking through the entryway from the kitchen into the living space.

"Hello, Rayn." He smiled.

"Bad timing?" I asked, deciding not to pretend I didn't hear them.

Warren sighed. "You are always welcome. Your timing is actually perfect. Those two need an excuse to be apart for a while."

"They really don't get along, do they?"

"It wasn't always like this," Warren said.

Harmony rounded the corner, putting on a smile like she intended to pretend everything was fine. "Rayn, are you ready for some training?"

I nodded. "Yeah, I'm interested to see what you guys have to teach me." I paused. "I'm not sure you'd be much help though."

"Oh," Harmony hesitated. "I understand why you'd feel that way, but Rayn, I am not comfortable with you being alone with him."

"He's not a monster, Harmony." Warren glared at her sideways.

"I don't know who he is anymore, that's the problem."

Nic's voice startled both of them. "I didn't come back for you."

I looked at the three of them and sighed. "I've waited my entire life to meet someone like me, someone who could do what I could. It's all Whitney and I ever dreamed about since we were kids. I'll find out for myself. I'd like to train with Dominic today."

He smiled. "Glad to hear it. Let's head into the backyard."

I followed my fellow pyro through the kitchen and out onto the porch. I stopped on the bottom step and hardened my gaze. I had things to say and intended to take this opportunity to make sure Nic knew his place. I understood why Rose felt the way she did about Whitney and Bryan's relationship. Rose wasn't the only protective sibling in their group. But at the end of the day, I was Team Bryan.

"Dominic." He turned at the sound of his name, waiting for me to continue. "I love my sister more than anything in this life," I started. "She is my best friend and I will end anyone who ever tried to hurt her."

"I understand," he answered.

"No, I don't think you do." I stepped into the grass. "Whitney is in a delicate state right now. Her head is all over the place and so is her heart. I see the way you've been looking at her and I'm telling you right now, the answer is no. If you even try it, I'll put you six feet under."

"Rayn, the only intention I have is making sure she can take on the Renati. And I have the same interest in protecting you." Nic stepped towards me, filling the gap between us. "That is all I care about."

"It better stay that way," I warned.

The corner of Nic's lips curved into a half-smile. "Do you want to light shit on fire or not?"

"Always."

Nic pulled a pack of cigarettes out of his pocket and lifted one to his lips. He snapped his fingers and a flame appeared in the palm of his hand. He used it to light the cigarette before he closed his hand around the flame, extinguishing it.

I waited for something to bubble in my stomach, for some sort of indication that I'd feel him use his powers like I could feel the girls, but nothing. "I didn't feel you use. Not now or the other day." I watched Nic puff on the cigarette as I spoke.

"Because we're in different generations," Nic answered. "I can only feel my own generation when they use."

"So that's common, then? Being able to feel one another's magic?"

"Yeah, as far as I know. That's part of the bond a generation shares. We may be the same, you and I, but we belong to our generations," Nic explained.

I liked the way he described that. We *belonged* to our generations. I felt that in my bones, that I belonged to the girls. Though I wondered how much the Magister's generation truly belonged to one another.

"So, where do we start?" I asked.

"There's something I've been wondering." Nic chewed on his lip. "You and I technically use the same magic, right? Like, our powers are the same, we use the same energy."

"What's your point?" I tilted my head.

"Do you think we might be able to combine our powers? Make one hell of a big fire."

I pondered the thought for a moment. "That could be kind of cool."

"Right?" Nic smiled. "Let's try it."

I held up my hand to stop him. "Wait, how exactly do we do that? I don't want to catch anything on fire."

"So control the spread of the flames."

"How do I do that?"

"Oh, okay, let's practice that first." Nic put his cigarette between his lips and snapped both of his middle fingers against his thumbs. Flames sparked in his hands. The heat intensified and the fire grew, concentrated between his hands. He stared intently at the flames, creating a fireball similar to the one I had the first time I'd gone to the meadow.

I watched in awe as the fireball levitated into the air. Nic kept his hands steady as it floated higher up. He moved his hands apart, willing the ball of flames to increase in size. The heat licked my face but I didn't back up. The fire wasn't too hot for me, so I stepped closer.

Nic brought his hands closer together and the fireball got smaller. When his palms met, the fireball disappeared into a puff of smoke.

"Shit that was cool," I breathed. "I made a fireball like that once."

"Oh yeah?" Nic's eyes lifted to mine. "How'd it go?"

"I dropped it. Whit had to put it out before it spread to the forest." I hated admitting that. Hated making myself seem like I wasn't as experienced or as strong as the other Flame Elemental standing before me. Even though he had years on me, I was the holder of the talisman and that was supposed to mean something, wasn't it?

Nic shook his head like what I'd said was no big deal. "You just have to practice. Do you remember how you made the fireball?"

I nodded. "Yeah, I could probably do it again."

"Okay good. Instead of making it float, try to make it grow and shrink in your hands. Keep a hold of it."

"Okay," I whispered, bringing my hands together like I had in the meadow. I closed my eyes, taking in a deep breath. The weight on my shoulders melted away and I felt the fire burning inside of me; the flame that was always there in my chest. It felt like the heat bearing down from the sun. I pulled from the heat in the sky and felt it travel down my arms and into my hands.

I opened my eyes to a marble-sized fireball sitting in my palm. I flinched as the fireball sparkled but at least I didn't drop it this time.

"Don't be afraid of it," Nic told me. "The fire won't burn you. It won't hurt you, it's part of you. You are the flames."

I nodded, putting all my attention on the ball of flames in the palm of my hand. I held the fireball in one hand and slowly pulled my other hand away. I imagined the fire growing as my hand moved further away, expanding the flames. The burning in my chest intensified, filling my entire body with warmth. A tiny bead of sweat trickled down my forehead.

The fireball seemed to twitch in my hand and I swore it got the tiniest bit bigger. Barely noticeable but I saw it expand. I moved my hand back closer to the ball of flames and it twitched again before it began to shrink.

"I did it!" I yelled, pulling my focus from the fireball. The moment I took my eyes off of it, the flames slipped through my fingers.

"Careful." Nic stepped forward. With a wave of his hand, the fireball stopped midair only a foot above the grass. He brought his palms together once more and the fireball extinguished.

"Shit. Sorry," I apologized, my face heated with embarrassment.

Nic scoffed. "Sorry? That was incredible, Rayn. You did exactly what you intended to do."

"I almost dropped it."

"Eh, that's why I'm here. Think you can do it again?"

I narrowed my eyes. "You're going to make me perfect this before you try to combine our fire, aren't you?"

He smiled. "Yeah, I think that would be the smartest course of action. Don't worry, soon you'll be almost as good as me."

"Don't you mean better than you?"

"I said what I said." Nic finished his cigarette.

I rolled my eyes and brought my hands together again, ready to create another fireball when I felt eyes on me. It wasn't the same chill climbing up my spine when I felt a shadow watching my every step, but eyes were on me all the same. I glanced over my shoulder to see Harmony and Warren standing on the back porch, watching the training session intently. They didn't trust Dominic to be alone with me.

I furrowed my brow, wondering if I *should* worry about being alone with him. Nic didn't seem threatening. Annoying? Yes. I didn't like how he acted around my sister, but that didn't come as a big shock. Whitney didn't usually see it, but boys had always taken notice of her.

Dominic didn't seem dangerous, not like Harmony made him out to be. But I didn't know him, and after everything I'd been through recently, I couldn't risk it. So, I let the chaperones remain without a second thought and returned to the fireball.

When I got home that evening, Whitney and Dmitri were waiting on the couch. They both slid to the edges of their seats, eyes wide with curiosity.

"How did it go?" Whit asked before I could even close the door behind me.

I kicked off my boots and set my bag on the table. "Fine."

"Fine? That's it?" Dmitri crossed his arms.

"I made another fireball. Nic taught me how to make it grow and shrink, but I dropped it again. He's so in tune with himself and his powers. It's only a matter of time before I'm that confident. Well..." I paused. "I don't think my head will ever be quite as big as his, but still."

"So, these *Magisters* might actually be able to teach you guys something." Dmitri used air quotes around the older generation's title.

"I think so, yeah." I turned to my sister. "You should train with Harmony."

"I don't want to," Whit argued. "She's a dick. Rule number three."

Don't be a dick.

"Dominic isn't a peach either, but he still taught me something. Who cares if they're annoying? They're all we've got."

Whitney chewed on her bottom lip, letting out a sigh before looking up at me. "You really think I should?"

"Yes, I absolutely think you should. They were fighting when I got there. Dominic and Harmony were yelling at each other. She and Warren stood on the porch and watched our entire session. They don't trust him. And I don't know if we should either."

"Rayn–" Whitney began but I didn't let her finish.

"We don't know anything about these people. We should just be careful, that's all."

Whitney smirked at her. "I thought you were over being careful?"

"I changed my mind, just like you're going to change your mind about training with Harmony."

Whitney groaned. "Okay, fine. I'll do it."

CHAPTER EIGHT

NEVER ENDING

WHITNEY

"I'm glad you've come to your senses," Harmony said, watching me walk down the steps of the cottage's back deck the next afternoon.

"This is a trial run. Push your luck and it'll be our last," I warned, still unsure if Harmony could be trusted. Rayn seemed to think I could learn a lot from spending time with this woman, so for her sake, I'd give it an hour of my time.

As that hour passed, I regretted showing up more and more.

"Your feet need to be planted firmly on the ground, otherwise you'll lose your balance," Harmony instructed for what felt like the hundredth time.

We stood alone at the side of the cottage. The only patch of Amilia's property that had a lawn and not a sprawling garden. Harmony called this session my "defensive training". Apparently, my ability to keep Rayn and Rose alive in the Dragonfly Mystic basement didn't impress her. I guess having Audriana as a mother didn't mean shit to Harmony Vasquez.

"Again," Harmony ordered.

I pushed my shoes into the wet dirt, allowing them to sink into the mud.

"Feel the water in the soil, in the air. Use it, embrace it. When you channel your power, don't focus so much on the water itself but the way your energy flows through it. You aren't an Elemental simply using the water, you are the water. Pull it in and freeze it, freeze yourself."

"I know how to use my powers, I've been a witch my entire life," I said through my teeth.

Harmony sucked in a deep breath of moist air and held out her hand in demonstration. A thin coating of ice covered her skin, forming perfectly around the curves of her hand like a cast made just for her. I hated to admit it, but it was impressive.

"Gives you an added layer of protection in case you get attacked and need to punch a Shadow."

"When would I ever have to punch a Shadow?" I eased my form and crossed my arms, allowing my feet to leave their battle stance.

"When you get caught off guard and find one in your face," Harmony explained like I was a five-year-old.

"At Dragonfly, one got close and it wisped away like smoke when I kicked it," I argued back. "I didn't even feel it."

Harmony rolled her eyes. "Those Shadows were not fully formed, they were still adjusting to living in our world. The longer they are here, the stronger they will be. Next time you try to kick a fully formed Shadow in this realm, you'll break your damn leg."

"How do you know?"

"For once can you listen to my instruction and not question how I obtained the information? It doesn't matter."

"It matters to me."

Harmony huffed, her breath turning to smoke in the cold air as it left her lips. "I've done this before."

"Punched a fully formed Shadow in the face?"

"Yes."

"When?"

She rolled her eyes. "When I was in college. Now, put your feet back in the proper place and focus on the ice."

"It's not cold enough for ice."

"Then turn the fucking water to ice, Whitney. You're too powerful to be this self-destructive," Harmony snapped. "You stubborn girl."

"Reminds me of someone I know." Warren chuckled behind me as he made his way across the lawn, his shoes sticking to the mud.

"I don't think we're ready for an audience yet," Harmony said to him, no doubt embarrassed by my lack of progress.

"Pretend I'm not here. I'm just moral support." Warren put his hands into his pockets and took a step back.

"Okay," Harmony answered reluctantly. "Try again, Whitney."

I sighed, attempting to center myself despite my aggravation. Harmony behaved worse than Mom and Mia combined. One of those pestering parents who wants everything done a certain way. Someone who believed the only right way was their way and felt the need to remind you the moment you strayed from their chosen path. One thing I found helpful about having Harmony conduct this lesson, her presence alone turned the moisture in the air ice cold.

I did my best to follow her instructions, but nothing happened. My magic barely tingled under my skin.

"Have patience, Whitney." Warren encouraged from the sidelines. "It took Harmony a long time to master this one."

"Yes, but I learned it on my own. It's much easier with an instructor."

"You act like we didn't have instructors. Mia and the coven taught us a lot." Warren chuckled.

"They were not Elementals," Harmony retorted.

"Amilia mentioned having a coven before," I spoke up, and both Harmony and Warren turned their attention towards me. "Did you spend a lot of time around my mom?"

"We did," Warren answered warmly.

"Who were the others?" I asked.

Harmony spoke before Warren could. "This isn't part of the lesson. We're supposed to be learning self-defense. Protecting yourself is more important than Mia's past."

"It's not Mia's past I'm interested in, it's my mother's," I snapped back. "Stop talking to me like I'm a child. I've lived an entire life before you decided to become relevant in Rifton again. I've had an entire life of defending myself and keeping my siblings safe. I was paying my bills and putting this puzzle together before any of you Magisters or whatever you call yourselves showed up so treat me like an equal or–"

"Or what?" Harmony's voice boomed, bouncing off the side of the house. "You'll what? Please enlighten me on how you think you could possibly hurt me."

"I never said I'd hurt you, but I also don't have to entertain this. I don't have to include either of you or Nic in my life. This is *my* battle so if you aren't going to help, get out of the way."

Harmony smirked, looking me up and down, but she wasn't sizing me up. A gleam of pride reflected in her eyes as she held her hands out for me to see for myself.

My warm breath crystalized before my eyes and bits of snow danced around in front of me. I pulled back, unsure of what had happened. I slowly lifted my hand to catch a tiny snowflake in the air. One fell gently onto my palm, right in the middle of the thin sheet of ice that formed over my skin. My skin shimmered as the sunlight reflected off the ice that covered every inch of my body, almost too bright to look at. I didn't feel the cold. It wasn't until I slowly closed my hand into a fist that I felt the ice at all, like wearing a plastic glove.

"Who knew getting you so heated was the key to manifesting your second skin of ice." Harmony smiled with her teeth, the first genuine grin I'd seen on her face. "Not so hard, is it? Now drop the spell and do it again."

"I don't know how I did it in the first place," I admitted, opening my hand back up again.

Harmony huffed. "What were you thinking about?"

"What an ice queen you are."

She chuckled. "Well, that makes two of us. Like it or not, you and I are the same. The same magic flows through both of our veins. We are two different versions of the same person. You're more powerful than you give yourself credit for. You're an Elemental, Whitney. There's a reason we are the most powerful witches in our world. Now get back into your stance and do it again."

Two versions of the same person. I didn't like that.

"What does my stance have to do with my ability to create ice?"

"It's all about centering yourself and opening up your connection to energy. Besides, if you're already planted into the ground like that, you have better luck fighting back if it comes to that."

I dug my feet into the mud and repeated the same emotions in my mind with the same intentions. Once more, my skin covered with beautiful, shimmering ice.

"There's one last thing I want to teach you." Harmony threw her hand out across the yard, shooting sharp icicles from her bare hands.

"Woah!" I stepped back as the icicles stabbed into the grass like knives.

Warren didn't seem the least bit surprised by Harmony's display.

Harmony smiled over her shoulder. "The more you practice, the more these spells will become second nature. Conjuring is as simple as picturing what you want in your head, just like you do with the rain. Give it a go."

I moved next to her and imagined the big icicles that used to form on the gutters of our old house in Kansas. When the big snow storms would come through in the winter, Mom would knock them all down. She would say they were dangerous and didn't want to risk one of them falling on us, even though I begged her not to. I thought they were the most beautiful things in the world.

With a wave of my hand, a thick icicle shot across the yard. It went right through one of the icicles Harmony had conjured, shattering it to pieces.

Harmony smiled at me, true pride in her eyes. "Make sure you practice while we're gone."

"Gone where?" I asked.

"We're going to check on a few things but we won't be gone for long," Warren explained like I would be satisfied with that vague explanation.

"Care to elaborate?"

"No," Harmony answered, picking a piece of lint off her sweater. "When we get back, I expect to see improvements."

Harmony walked past Warren and up the steps onto the back porch without another word.

"When will you and Harmony be back?" I asked Warren.

"It won't take more than a few days. Nic's coming with us."

"Oh. A Magister team building retreat?"

Warren chuckled, resting a hand on my shoulder. "Something like that. Hold down the fort while we're gone."

The collection of candles and missing person flyers at the park for Abe Roberts wasn't exactly where I planned on spending the rest of my day off, but after the long holiday weekend, I wanted to be alone. A lot happened that I hadn't anticipated. The fate of my world and everyone in it depended on our success. No pressure.

I knew the path through the park well, like the drive to work in the mornings. It had become routine since the candle lighting ceremony before Halloween. At first, I would come here with Mit, but the park had turned into one of the few places where the buzzing in my brain stopped. So I started coming alone.

The list of problems was really adding up. A never-ending collection of shambles.

Erebus and the Renati.

The portal.

Officer fucking Grady.

Dmitri and helping him process.

The Magisters and their weird dynamic.

Amilia and her dead daughter.

Pretending I didn't see lily pads whenever I closed my eyes.

It's not like talking to a poster would fix any of my problems, but at least here I could get stuff off my chest without having to listen to anyone else's opinions. Here no one told me what to do or how to do it, because no one was here to listen.

I got comfortable on the frozen ground, not caring if my jeans got dirty or if there would be a giant wet mark on my butt when I stood up. No one was around to see it anyway.

"I know what you're thinking," I muttered to the photo in front of me. "I'm still a stupid girl with a magician's book. Once I feel like I'm getting a grip on something, another problem jumps into my lap. I don't know what to do with these other Elementals Amilia has brought into the picture. She expects us to trust them without a second thought because she tells us to. But the more I get to know Amilia, the more I realize she's only given us cliff notes on everything we've ever asked her. So what do I do? Do I trust their intention because they knew my mom or do I keep going at this alone, just the girls and I? Because as much as I hate to admit it, we haven't had much luck with any aspect of this."

I stopped to catch my breath, grateful for the silence. With a sigh, I reached out and ran my fingers around the rim of one of the unlit candles that sat before me.

A light breeze picked up, rustling the tree branches before the chill hit me, running up my spine. The cold reached every molecule, comforting me as if I wasn't sitting there talking to myself like a crazy person.

"It's funny," I chuckled. "The Magisters don't seem trustworthy, but then again neither did you at first. I don't know how to comfort Dmitri. He's distressed and I can't do anything about it. I feel responsible because the only reason you were in the forest that night was to follow us and now...where in the hell are you now?"

My face fell into my hands as I confronted one thing on the list that had truly been bothering me the most. I could eventually sort out and tackle everything else, but seeing Dmitri broken had been something I could never prepare myself for.

"I should have gone about things differently knowing how he felt about you." I hated admitting I had made a mistake. "I'll figure it out. I always do."

Lying all the way back, I stared up at the gray skies. The sun hid behind a blanket of overcast clouds that lingered over the city. I tried to believe that the universe would provide. I knew that we would get the answers and the help that we needed, whether that be the Magisters or something else yet to show itself. I knew that my efforts wouldn't be in vain. I couldn't place what gave me such confidence, but the warm sensation in my stomach was a good start.

An unexpected buzzing in my pocket made my blood run ice cold. I had completely forgotten I had a phone or any responsibility outside of this park.

"Hey," I answered, covering my eyes with my arm.

"Whitney," Brooke's voice shook on the other end. "My dad got called into the station. He didn't tell me anything, but I overheard his conversation. 187 on Cherry Blossom. 7329 Cherry Blossom."

"Okay," I drug out the syllables, not connecting the dots. "What does that mean, B?"

"7329 Cherry Blossom is Lauren's house. 187 is the code for a homicide."

"Oh, shit." I sprung to my feet as quickly as I could and sprinted back to my car. "I'm on my way over there now."

"So is Rose," Brooke sounded overwhelmed with panic. "Please tell me what is going on when you get there. My dad told me not to leave the house."

"I'll find out what I can."

"What if Lauren–"

"She's not in town," I snapped, attempting to convince both of us. "She's probably not even in Oregon. She's safe. She has to be."

By the time I got to Cherry Blossom, the sidewalk in front of Lauren's house had been sectioned off with bright yellow caution tape. Four cop cars with their red and blue lights on were parked out front. Police officers stood with a hand on their holstered side arms, reminding neighbors to stay behind the yellow line and telling passing cars to keep moving.

I parked down the street and braced myself as I joined the crowd that formed around the barriers. My knees shook so badly that walking took more effort than usual. No matter how many times I swallowed, my heart remained in my throat, gagging me.

"Rose!" I shouted when I finally spotted a familiar face. "What happened?"

"I just got here," she replied, her white knuckles wrapped tightly around the strap of her bag. She was out of breath with flushed cheeks and I realized she had run from her house a few streets over.

"Excuse me?" I approached one of the bystanders. "What's going on? One of our friends used to live here."

"Oh, it's awful!" the middle-aged woman cried, grabbing my arm. "Karen across the street stopped by this morning to borrow TJ's ladder, he's always so kind about letting everyone borrow his tools." Tears welled in her light blue eyes as she continued. "That's when she found them, TJ and Deb both. Poor things, such wonderful and kind people."

"The Thaners are dead?" Rose clarified, making sure there were no misunderstandings.

To answer our question, the medics came out of the house with a gurney covered with a black bag zipped closed. My entire body went ice cold and my stomach churned. I clenched my teeth to prevent myself from throwing up all over the poor woman who still clung to my arm. I didn't need my imagination to picture the contents of that bag.

"Oh," I whispered, watching the paramedics load the gurney into a coroner van. "There's only one."

"They took TJ off in an ambulance a few minutes ago. They were doing chest compressions. I'm not sure if he'll make it to the hospital," the woman replied.

Lauren's mother was the one in the black bag.

"Thank you." I gave the woman a kind smile and stepped off to the side, Rose following close behind. "Where the hell is Lauren?"

"I don't know." Rose shook her head, looking back at the police and medics. "She has to come back to town now."

I covered my mouth and sighed through my fingers. "I don't understand what is going on here. Why would someone attack her parents?"

Rose cursed under her breath and spun around, taking in a quick inventory of everyone else there. "Someone might have been looking for Lauren?"

"I guess, but she's been gone for weeks. Why now?"

"I wish I knew. There's that bastard. I knew he'd be close by." Rose nodded towards the cop car closest to us.

Officer Grady stood tall, conversing with one of the other cops. Almost like clockwork, he glanced over at Rose and I casually. He nodded slightly, almost unnoticeable, like he had been waiting for us to show up. Waiting to try and pin this one on us too.

"You think the Renati did this?" I inquired quietly.

"Has to be, but they've been watching all of us. They must know Lauren isn't here."

Nic's words echoed through my head. *They'll kill everyone you love before they finally slit your throats.*

Rose's phone began to ring from her back pocket. Frantic, she answered it quickly. "Are you okay? Have you talked to Mom recently? You're sure? Okay. No, I'll see you tonight. I love you too."

The timing to be self-indulgent was horrid, but I would have given up coffee for the rest of my life to hear the voice on the other end of that phone call.

"Come on, let's get to the cottage before Grady decides to show up at my door tomorrow morning," I replied, leading Rose back to my car.

"I can't believe they killed Lauren's mom. Who knows what state her dad is in." Rose's voice cracked once we were in the safety of my car. She wiped a tear from her cheek. "Nic was right. They won't stop until they've taken out everyone. That could have been my mom. Whitney, that could have been Byn."

I reached out and took her hand in mine. "We have magic protecting all of our houses, we are trying to stay on top of this. One step ahead of them, we didn't think–"

"No, we haven't been thinking, not clearly enough. It never even crossed my mind that Lauren's parents could be in danger. Especially after she skipped town. I've been so worried about keeping my family safe that I didn't think about anyone else..."

"We didn't kill Lauren's parents, Rose." I shook my head. I couldn't have any more blood on my hands or I would never sleep again.

Rose scoffed, as if she knew I only said that to make myself feel better. "We might as well have."

CHAPTER NINE

ASHES AND DUST

WHITNEY

I called the hospital every morning for the next few days to ask about TJ Thaner's condition, knowing they wouldn't tell me anything since I was not immediate family. They did, however, tell me his daughter had arrived at the hospital. That was all I needed.

Rifton Memorial Hospital felt eerily silent. Fluorescent lights flickered overhead as we walked into the cold and sterile main lobby. My chest constricted as I looked around the waiting area, at the fern and the magazines. As I blinked slowly and took it all in, I was no longer in Rifton. I was in Hemston, Kansas. My lungs squeezed tightly inside my rib cage, making each breath more difficult. Little black spots took over my vision before I squeezed my eyes shut, forcing myself to breathe.

Rayn grabbed my hand. "Whit, you okay?"

"I hate hospitals," I muttered, rubbing my eyes in an attempt to snap myself out of it.

"Me too." Rayn nodded, squeezing my fingers.

"Thaner is in room 198," Rose said, catching my attention. I didn't realize she had gone to the reception desk for directions.

I took a deep breath and attempted to swallow my anxiety, reminding myself over and over again that we were not in Hemston. We were not there waiting for word that our mother had died while Rayn was still being examined. We were there for Lauren.

The girls and I took an elevator to the intensive care unit on the next floor up.

Lauren sat on the floor outside of room 198, hugging her long legs to her chest. I almost didn't recognize her at first. Lauren's long blonde hair had been chopped into a bob that fell into her buried face and her nail polish was chipped.

We froze in the hall at the sight of her, unsure if we should approach her or not.

Brooke glanced over at me and widened her eyes, silently asking what we should do. I didn't know the right answer. When Dmitri and I were in the hospital after losing Mom, I didn't want to talk to anyone. I didn't want to be touched. I didn't want to answer questions from the hospital staff about coroners or insurance. I didn't have time to let everything sink in, to process what I lived through.

Lauren deserved to have that time.

When I turned back to Lauren, her gaze was on us. Her head lifted enough for our eyes to meet. I held my breath, unable to tell if she felt angry that we had shown up. Maybe this had been a bad idea. I had convinced myself we'd done the right thing; to come here and show solidarity with her. Lauren was part of our generation and she had gone through something unimaginable. I never stopped to consider that she had run away from us. I never stopped to think that maybe Lauren didn't want us there.

Her hands slowly left her knees as she used the floor to push herself to her feet. Lauren wiped her nose on her sleeve as she glided over to us as elegant as always. Her pace picked up the closer she got until she stood in front of us. I braced myself for whatever emotions she prepared to unleash as she was entitled to all that she felt in that moment. I waited for her to tell us to leave, how inappropriate it was for us to be there. Instead, she let out a heavy sigh and wet her bottom lip with her tongue. Then she began to cry.

Her chest bobbed with a heavy sob that echoed against the silent hospital walls. I stepped forward and caught her in my arms, pulling her close to my chest. Lauren bent down to my height and rested her head on my shoulder, tears quickly soaking my sweatshirt. Her painful cries attracted the attention of the nursing station down the hall, all eyes on us as Lauren released the built-up anguish she had been holding in all morning. As if everything had finally sunk in and she realized what had happened. I held onto her as tight as I could; two girls who had lost their mothers too soon.

"I got you," I whispered, gently rubbing Lauren's back. "We're here."

Rayn and Brooke both stepped forward. Brooke wrapped her arms around Lauren's waist and hugged her, nestling in under my arm. Rayn hugged Lauren from behind, resting her head on Lauren's shoulder as her hand ran up and down Lauren's arm. Rose stood still for a moment, looking at the four of us huddled together. I met her eyes, wondering if Lauren would even accept comfort from Rose. Part of me wondered if Rose even felt comfortable giving this kind of affection with all their bad blood. But Rose leaned in anyway, resting a hand on Lauren's open shoulder and gently rubbing her thumb across the fabric of her sweater.

"We're here for you, Lauren," Rose said quietly, squeezing Lauren's shoulder. "Whatever you need, we're here."

Lauren straightened her posture and the rest of us took a step back, giving her space. She wiped the tears from her cheeks with an open hand and took in a deep, unsteady breath.

"Do you still have my bracelet?" she asked, her voice nothing more than a whisper.

Rayn shook her head. "No, I gave it back to your mom after you left."

Lauren nodded in acknowledgment, as if she already knew. "They took it then," she whispered, her voice cracking. "I think whoever did this was looking for it."

"Oh fuck, I'm so sorry, Lauren. I had no idea. I went there to talk to you and when your mom said you had left, I figured she'd want it back." Rayn explained in a panic, tears welling in her eyes. "Fuck, I led them straight there...Lauren, I–"

Lauren cut her off. "They would have come for it either way. I thought leaving would keep them off of my back after what had happened to you guys on Halloween but it only put a bigger target on my parents. I left my family unprotected, that isn't on you."

"Lauren, you had no way of knowing." Brooke attempted to comfort her but Lauren shook her head.

"I was naive. Weak." Her gaze met mine with dark circles under her eyes. "Never again."

"How's your dad?" I asked.

Lauren's voice cracked again. "In a coma. He has bleeding in his brain. They aren't sure if he's going to wake up."

"Shit. I'm so sorry." I rubbed her shoulder. "We should have been looking out for them. We should have done better. I'm sorry."

"I don't blame any of you," Lauren whispered. "It's the Renati who will pay for this."

"Are you staying?" Rayn asked the question that lingered on all of our minds.

"I'm staying. I'm getting my bracelet back and then I'm going to burn every last member of that cult to the ground," Lauren said through her teeth.

"We've been searching for their hideout. We're going to get them back for this, Lauren. This won't go unanswered," I promised her.

Lauren nodded. There was a burning in her that I had never seen before. A hatred that brewed under the surface, rising up into her pupils. A wind picked up, strong enough to knock over a filing tray, sending paperwork scattering across the floor. The two nurses sitting at the computers looked up at the vents, trying to figure out where the sudden gust of chilling air came from.

"They fucked with the wrong witch. We're going to hunt Erebus down and end this before he can take anyone else from us," Lauren whispered, glancing over at the nurse bending down to gather the scattered paperwork. "Get me out of here?"

"Come on." I linked my arm in hers and led her towards the elevator.

"What do we know about the Renati?" Lauren asked from the backseat where she leaned against the window. "Who are they? Where are they hiding?"

"That's what we've been working on," I answered. "There's another generation, by the way."

Lauren's head shot up. "What?"

"Amilia hid another generation from us. The three living members came back into town a few weeks ago."

"Living members," she said under her breath, not a question. "What are they like?"

"Obnoxious."

"They aren't all that bad," Rayn spoke up. "They're older, in their thirties, but they want to help. Warren is like you, an Air Elemental."

"I'd like to meet them."

I huffed. "Harmony is a lot. She's like me, but also nothing like me at all."

Rayn laughed. "You and Harmony have more in common than your powers, that's why you don't get along. Nic, on the other hand, is obnoxious for no reason."

"He's the only one that doesn't treat us like children."

"No, *you're* the only one he doesn't treat like a child because he has some weird infatuation with you."

"Who's Nic?" Lauren asked.

"Dominic. He's a Flame Elemental," I answered.

"And the other two are dead?" Lauren asked. "Their earth and spirit?"

"That's what they said. The Earth Elemental was Amilia's daughter, but she died thirteen years ago."

"Wow, no wonder she didn't tell us. I can't imagine losing Rose and Brooke both." Lauren fidgeted with her hands. "Can we go there now?"

"They went out of town for something, but they should be back in a few days. We can still go to the cottage, if you want."

Lauren nodded. Rayn and I glanced at each other as I turned down the next street toward Amilia's neighborhood.

I was relieved the Magisters weren't at the cottage. The air seemed lighter as we walked into an empty house. We had just picked Lauren up from her father's intensive care room at the hospital. I didn't want to bombard her with the Magisters' hot mess that the other girls and I had witnessed.

"Mia?" I asked, my voice echoed against the walls.

"Up here!" Amilia called from the upstairs loft. The sound of rustling papers and shifting furniture came down into the living room. It sounded like Amilia rearranged her bedroom.

"We brought someone to see you," Rayn called up to Amilia, glancing over at Lauren with a kind smile, but Lauren didn't look at her.

Lauren gazed around the cottage, taking it in. I realized the last time she stood in this living room was the day she sat on the couch not knowing if Rayn, Rose, and I were going to wake up. The day she threw her now-missing bracelet at us.

"Who– Oh, Lauren, dear," Amilia appeared at the railing of the loft. She quickly made her way down the stairs and into the living room. "I'm delighted to see you, and so terribly sorry for the circumstances."

Amilia reached out and gently took Lauren's hand. Lauren let her, and even squeezed back when Amilia comforted her.

"Whit and Rayn said there's another generation." Lauren jumped right to the point. "Someone else like me."

"Yes." Amilia nodded, keeping a tight grip on Lauren's hand. "Warren Edwards. I think you'll like him. Warren is a good balance between ice and fire."

"He seems like a nice guy," I confirmed.

"And they aren't here?" Lauren asked.

"I'm so sorry, dear, they aren't. The Magisters had some business to attend to but they will return in a few days," Amilia replied. "Warren will be eager to meet you."

Lauren didn't hide her disappointment. "So we wait until they come back? What are we doing in the meantime?"

"Finding a way to close the portal," I answered.

Amilia's head snapped towards me. "You girls will wait until the Magisters return. It's not safe for you to be venturing off on your own."

"Where did they go?" Rayn crossed her arms.

Amilia sighed. "There is a book and they are finding a way to destroy it. Getting rid of it will make all the difference for the witches who still support the Elementals."

I scrunched my face. "That's vague."

"I've already told you too much." Amilia turned away from us.

"How is telling us about a book going to put us in more danger than we already are?" Rayn asked, taking a step closer to Mia. "We are Elementals, like the Magisters. We deserve to be in the loop."

"You can't tell us that Elementals were leaders in the past and then withhold information from us." I stated, knowing this reminder was the only way Amilia would agree to tell us anything. Her obligation to serve the generations.

Amilia finally explained, "The Renati keep a ledger documenting all the witches who have lived in Rifton that they know of. They have a DNA sample from all of them, either blood or hair. They use it to track them or worse, threaten them for not joining the Renati. Those who were able to avoid the ledger live in hiding, fearful of being discovered and tracked. The Renati have driven many witches from Rifton with this ledger. If we are going to stand against the Renati, we need to build Elemental support in the Dark Star Forest. The ledger must be destroyed. But it's protected by magic and we haven't quite pinpointed how to break the barrier."

"Sounds like something we should have known about," Lauren replied, furrowing her brow. "Without that ledger, Elemental support will be safe to return to Rifton?"

"Safe until the Renati find them, but it'll be much harder for the Renati to keep track of Elemental support, so yes they will be safer in that regard." Amilia wrung her hands together. "Next weekend is the Founder's Day celebration. Every year the City Council puts together a big event in early December and the ledger is always put on display. To the Elemental supporters, it's a reminder of their power over us. To the powerless in town, they believe it's old records of the families who first founded Rifton."

"Founder's Day? That's the Christmas tree lighting ceremony coming up?" I specified.

Amilia nodded. "Yes, a winter festival of sorts."

"Oh shit, that's what that book is?" Lauren's mouth gaped in response to Mia's words. "I've seen that book a million times! I had no idea it was tied to us and the Renati. I can show you guys where it is."

"We won't be able to do anything to it on Founder's Day," Amilia explained. "It's well guarded under heavy protection spells."

"We should still go." Rayn looked at Lauren in agreement. "Show them we aren't afraid of them or their stupid book."

"Where are these Elemental supporters who have been driven from town?" Lauren asked. "So that when the ledger is destroyed we can bring them home?"

Amilia hesitated, chewing on her lip. "I know how to get in touch with their leader."

"Their leader?" Rayn inquired.

Amilia nodded.

"If you're friends with their leader, why didn't you go with them? Why did you stay in Rifton when everyone else left?" Rayn asked.

Amilia held her head high. "I refused to be bullied out of my home. Once the documented witches left Rifton, I must have seemed less of the threat by myself. The Renati have left me alone for the most part."

Lauren tilted her head. "Are they tracking us too?"

Amilia softened her gaze. "They have your blood, so I imagine so, yes."

I took a step towards her. "Getting rid of that ledger would make a huge difference. I'm glad the Magisters are figuring out a plan. We'll wait until they get back. Maybe once the ledger is gone we can finally close the portal."

Amilia gave a relieved smile. "My thoughts exactly." She turned to Lauren. "Where are you staying?"

"At the inn," Lauren answered.

"You're going to stay at a hotel?" I inquired. "For how long?"

"It's not that bad."

"No, but it's not permanent."

"I'm selling the house."

No one would expect Lauren to live in the house where everything she loved had been taken from her.

"I have an extra bedroom, you're welcome to it," Amilia offered.

Lauren put up her hand. "Oh, I couldn't possibly ask you to do that."

"No one is using it."

"I can't pay for it. I'll have a little bit of money after settling my parent's business but I'll have to get a job. I don't think anyone will buy the house."

Amilia took a step towards Lauren. "There's an opening at the Corner Cup. Olivia put in her two weeks notice a few days ago."

"Did she really?" I asked.

"Amilia, it's too much," Lauren argued.

Amilia chuckled. "Are you not looking for work and a bedroom to rent?"

"I am, but–"

"Then how is it too much? It's not a handout, Lauren. We will draw up a lease and conduct a proper interview for the barista position if it will make you more comfortable."

"It would," Lauren paused. "Thank you."

"Of course, dear. We are a family. We take care of our own."

"Would that bother you?" Lauren turned to me. "Me working at the Corner Cup?"

"Lauren, why would that bother me?" I asked, surprised. "Of course not. I'd love having you there."

Lauren's smile was subtle as she turned to Amilia and thanked her again.

"Mia, do you have any other books we could read? I thought it would be a good idea for us to do some studying while we wait for the Magisters to return." I motioned towards the bookshelf across the room.

"Of course, dear." Amilia snapped her fingers and a stack of books appeared on the dining room table. "I don't believe you girls have read those yet. Take them home and keep them as long as you'd like."

"Thanks, Mia." Rayn headed towards the table and picked up the books.

"Lauren, dear, I'm glad you're home. I want you to know that we will do everything we can to support you through this and we will put an end to the Renati's terror in Rifton and beyond." Amilia reassured.

Lauren nodded. "I want them to pay for what they've done."

"They will, I promise." I stepped forward and placed a hand on my friend's shoulder.

Chapter Ten

STRESS RELIEF

Whitney

Thick leather-bound books sat on the floor of my house that night. We went through the new books Mia sent home with us, looking for something, anything, that would give us additional information but we kept hitting dead ends.

Lauren sat cross-legged on the floor beside me. She glanced over my shoulder, but I couldn't tell if she read or not. The few times I looked at Lauren, she stared off at the corner of the room. I knew how it felt to lose a parent. I knew she needed time to process what she'd been through, but at least she was here with us. Though it was impossible to mend certain cracks in her soul, we could be there to hold her hand through it.

Rose and Brooke sat on the couch with a large book sprawled out across their laps. Dmitri sat on his bed with our spellbook open before him. After everything that had transpired, I felt at peace having everyone in my line of sight on a quiet night.

"I think we deserve a night off, don't you?" Rayn asked, walking into the living room with both hands behind her back.

"We are sort of on a time limit," I pointed out, going back to the leather-bound collection of desperation.

"Whit, the Renati will still exist in the morning. Tonight, we are not witches. We aren't Elementals. We are a group of girls and their brother who need to partake in a rebellious right of passage." Rayn held out a large bottle of vodka and gave it a little shake.

"Not exactly rebellious when Brooke and I are the only minors in the room," Dmitri added, his eyes not leaving the book.

"Actually, Whitney is the only one legally old enough to drink, but I'm listening." Rose pointed out, slowly closing the book in her lap.

"Where did you even get that?" I asked, eyeing the unfamiliar name on the bottle's label.

"Does it matter?" Rose set the book down and stretched out her legs.

"I can't think of anything I'd like to do more than drink a massive bottle of vodka," Lauren muttered beside me.

"It'll be good for us to come back to all this with a clear head," Rayn said. "Think of it as a team-building exercise."

"I think drinking gives you the exact opposite." No one listened to me. Hell, I barely even listened to myself. It's not like these books were giving us the information we wanted anyway. Groaning, I put the potions book back in the stack and turned to my sister's hopeful face. "Did you at least bring a chaser?"

"You think I'm an animal?" Rayn revealed another bottle of bright red cranberry juice.

"Cranberry vodka, classic," Rose laughed.

Rayn giggled, setting the bottles down on the dining table before she rushed back into the kitchen. She came back with a stack of plastic water cups and a few glasses. A mismatched arrangement of drinkware but it represented our little group perfectly. Rayn poured a couple shots worth of vodka in each cup and topped them off with juice before she passed one to each of us.

"Mit?" Rayn offered one of the plastic cups his way.

Without a word, Dmitri slid off his bed and took the cup from our sister.

"Cheers!" Rose held her glass up in the air. The rest of us met her reach and clinked our cups together before we all took a unison drink.

I did my best to hide my sour expression but Rayn made the drinks much stronger than I preferred. I tasted nothing but burnt plastic stinging down my throat. Brooke coughed after her first drink and put her glass on the table to catch her breath.

"Woo, Rayn," Lauren shook her head before going back for another drink. "You aren't fucking around tonight."

"Hell no. This has been long overdue." Rayn took a large gulp from her glass as she headed over to the small closet off the living room. "Do you guys want to play a game?"

Brooke followed behind Rayn to analyze the few board games we had. "Ooo, Monop-oly!"

Rayn looked back at me over her shoulder. "Only if Whitney promises not to get super competitive. She's a shithead when it comes to Monopoly."

"I'm not that bad." I took another drink.

"Yes, you are," Dmitri added.

"Then pick another game," I said, rolling my eyes.

"No, bring out Monopoly. I bet I can beat her." Rose's eyes met mine in a mischievous gaze.

"You can try," I answered but Rose seemed as confident as ever. I smiled back, accepting the challenge.

Forty minutes into the game, Rose and I held most of the properties and half of the bank. Dmitri had already gone bankrupt and now helped Lauren, who surprisingly had never played the game before. Rose took another drink and glanced up at me as she rolled the dice, landing on one of the few unclaimed properties. She handed a wad of colorful cash over to Rayn, who always played as the banker.

"Looks like I'm ready for some hotels."

"About time you caught up." I took the dice and rolled for my next turn.

I woke the next morning to an alarm blaring and a screaming headache. My stomach churned as I attempted to sit up in bed, only to collapse back into my pillow. Pillow. Good, I had made it to bed. Or someone had put me here, but either way I lay under a thick blanket with Lauren passed out next to me. Her blonde hair stuck up around her pillow as she snored lightly into her arm. I turned off the alarm and pulled the blanket up over my head. I began to slip back into a sweet slumber when someone shook me awake.

"Whitney!" Dmitri's voice pounded through my skull. "Whitney, get up. We have that meeting with the school, remember?"

"Huh?" I lifted my head to see a blur that resembled my brother.

"Jesus fuck, Whit, I told you not to drink so much."

"You did?" I held my hand to my forehead, my temple throbbed against my palm.

"What's the last thing you remember?" Dmitri asked.

"Uh...Stevie Nicks and a broken glass?"

"Fuck my life. Get in the shower. We have to be at the school in an hour."

"Mit, I can't. We need to reschedule the meeting."

Lauren groaned loudly, grabbing the blanket and throwing it over her head. "Quit shouting."

"We can't reschedule! You already missed the first one. Whit, please. After this meeting, I can start charter school and we won't have to deal with this again. Get up." Dmitri grabbed my arm and dragged me out of bed.

"I feel sick."

"Go throw up in the shower. I made coffee." Dmitri grabbed my shoulders and looked at me with frantic eyes. "I know you've been trying to stay in the sister lane and not cross over into Mom's territory, but I need you to be Mom right now."

"Okay," I whispered, slipping out of bed and heading straight to the bathroom before I got sick all over my bedroom floor.

Dmitri brought me a cup of coffee, sticking his arm behind the shower curtain. I took the mug and the door quickly opened and closed again. I tried to take a deep breath, hoping the water would cure my hangover but nothing stopped the churning in my stomach. I gave myself a few more minutes under the cool water, not having the energy to actually wash my hair, before I waved my hand and shut the water off. I went back to my bedroom wrapped in a towel, setting the coffee down on my dresser as I dug around for clothes.

"Where are you going?" Lauren asked, still buried in the blankets.

"Meeting with Mit's school," I answered, clenching my teeth to keep the contents of my stomach down. "Is your interview today?"

"Yes." Lauren sat up on her elbows. "Someone poisoned me."

"Sleep it off." I waved my hand at her as I slid on a pair of pants. "Unless you want to go to this meeting and I'll get back in bed."

"He's your kid, not mine." Lauren threw the comforter over her head and nestled back into the pillows. "I'll see you tomorrow at CC if Mia hires me."

"She will."

Dmitri already had the car warming up in the driveway when I stumbled into the living room, searching for my shoes.

"We gotta go." Dmitri grabbed my bag and swung it over his shoulder. "Can you drive?"

"No," I answered, slipping on a shoe.

"Okay," he muttered, kicking my other shoe towards me. "Come on."

I kept my eyes shut tight as Dmitri drove down the windy road into Rifton. Even though I did my best not to look outside, the motion of the car was enough. Dmitri pulled over for me. He stewed silently, his hands gripped tightly around the steering wheel while he waited for me to finish throwing up. I quickly rinsed out my mouth and grabbed a mint from my purse as he got back on the road.

By the time I finally opened my eyes and lifted my head from the cold window, we were pulling into the parking lot.

"Okay," I muttered, sliding out of the car. "I can do this."

I followed behind Dmitri into the building. The school sat in a smaller shopping center, next to a gym. I guess the location of the charter school didn't matter since he'd only be coming in once a week to turn in his homework. I still found it odd to see a school next to a gym and a pizza place. Dmitri sat in a plastic chair up against the wall. I stayed standing, knowing if I sat down I might collapse.

"This is just enrollment. I have all the transfer paperwork we need, you just have to sign your name." Dmitri muttered, his voice sharp and annoyed with me. I couldn't blame him. I had dropped the guardianship ball leaving him alone when we first met the girls, but I had been trying to make up for that.

I nodded slightly, unable to face him. Seeing disappointment in his eyes would have killed me.

A dark-skinned woman opened the door. "Dansley?"

"That's us." Dmitri stood up and walked into her office.

"Hello, I'm Principal Meadows. You must be Dmitri."

"Hi. This is my sister, Whitney, my guardian."

"Nice to meet you." I mustered a smile and held out my hand. I'm sure I looked like a hot mess with my wet hair wrapped up in a bun on top of my head and dark circles under my eyes, but Principal Meadows kindly pretended not to notice.

"Here's my paperwork." Dmitri handed the folder over to Principal Meadows.

She smiled and set the paperwork down on her desk. "Thank you. Tell me, Dmitri, why do you want to start charter school?"

"Um," Dmitri pondered the question. "I've never done well in public school. My grades are fine but the social aspect has always been a struggle. Overwhelming, almost."

"Social anxiety can be difficult, but it's still important for a developing mind to be around people their own age," Principal Meadows replied.

"We have friends," I answered. "Dmitri has friends. Going to charter isn't to get him away from people, just out of the standardized classroom setting. He's the smartest kid I've ever met but he's bored, even in AP classes he's always ahead of everyone else. I think this will give him the opportunity to work at his own pace and stay stimulated."

Dmitri gazed over at me with a surprised gaze.

"Understandable, absolutely." Principal Meadows opened Dmitri's folder and began to scan over the first page. "Your grades are impressive."

"Thanks." Dmitri smiled.

"We are lucky to have you, Dmitri, why don't you go explore the classroom a bit. Whitney, we have some paperwork for you to sign."

"Okay." Dmitri hesitated but slid out of his seat and left the office, closing the door behind him.

"I'm a little concerned that once Dmitri goes into charter he won't have interaction with other teenagers." Principal Meadows jumped right to the point. "I read the notes from his teachers at Rifton High and they share my concerns. His biology teacher noted that the only friend he saw Dmitri with was Abraham Roberts and losing a close friend this close to the passing of your mother...I'm worried he's using this as a tactic to shut down."

"Thank you for your concern. Dmitri isn't the kind of person who needs to be around a bunch of people, he actually hates it. We have friends who adore him and are close to his age, but being at the high school only reminds him that Abe is still missing. I think he'll do better mentally to be removed from the constant reminder."

"As his guardian, I will take your word for it, but I wanted to share my thoughts on the subject." Principal Meadows slid a few documents across her desk and handed me a pen. "And how are you? Taking on a teenager when you're so young yourself could not have been easy."

I blinked a few times before I picked up the pen and signed my name at the bottom of the form without reading it. "I'm fine."

"Just so you have the information, we have counselors available during school hours in case Dmitri ever needs someone to talk to."

"Thanks." I slid the signed documents back across the desk and set the pen down. "We've talked about it before but I'll bring it up again." I mustered a smile and moved to the edge of the seat. I had to get out of there before I threw up again. "Is there anything else you need from me?"

"Uh, not at the moment. We'll send Dmitri home with all his schoolbooks today so we can get started on the weekly assignments."

"Perfect," I whispered, getting to my feet. I turned to leave her office without looking back. "I have to get to work soon. Nice to meet you."

I didn't intend to seem rude. Of course Principal Meadows had concerns after reading Dmitri's file. Hell, I had concerns about my brother's mental health but getting sick all over this woman's office would not help our case.

"My door is always open if you ever need anything, email as well," Principal Meadows called after me as I slowly closed the door behind me.

"Thank you." I gritted my teeth.

Luckily, I found the women's restroom at the end of the hall. I shoved the stall door open and flushed the handle as I emptied the morning's coffee into the toilet bowl. I flushed again as another wave of nausea rushed over me, desperate to drown out the noise. Once I felt the slightest bit of normality return, I went to the sink and splashed some water on my face. Gripping the edges of the porcelain, I did my best to avoid my reflection. I knew I looked like hell. If I had an extra five minutes and a clear head, I might've put concealer under my eyes. With another deep breath, I finally left the bathroom and found Dmitri with his arms full of textbooks.

"Hey," I breathed, retrieving another mint from my purse.

Dmitri shoved his books in his backpack. "We should get going."

He didn't say another word to me as he unlocked the car and threw his backpack into the back seat. He started the engine and waited until I buckled in before he backed out of our parking space. He wouldn't look at me. I waited a few minutes to see if he would break the silence, but his furrowed eyes never left the road.

"Did I fuck up that bad? I thought the meeting went okay," I finally spoke up, leaning forward to see his face. "Mit, I did my best."

Dmitri sighed and relaxed his shoulders. "I know. It wasn't that bad."

"You're still mad though."

"I'm mad I had to drag you out of bed and serve you coffee in the shower. I'm mad because if I didn't go in there and wake you up, you would have missed this meeting. I'm fucking mad that you forgot about it."

"Mit–"

"I cut you a lot of slack, Whitney. Mom died out of nowhere and you never asked for me, but you could have said no. If you didn't want me, you should have said no."

"Of course I want you!" I raised my voice. "You expected me to let them ship you off to Mom's sister? You thought I'd let you go to CPS? You're my brother. I would have died before I let that happen."

"Really? Because beyond signing permission slips you haven't done a fraction of the shit a guardian is supposed to do."

"I dropped out of college." A hot tear escaped my eye as my heart cracked open in my chest. "I got you and Rayn out of a town that wanted to burn you at the stake. I got a full-time job and work hard to keep a roof over your goddamn head."

"You leave me home alone all the time."

"Dmitri, I'm sorry." I choked as the sobs began to build up in my chest. "I'm doing the best I can."

"You wouldn't be able to afford the house if Janice didn't cut us so much slack on rent. You act like this is a burden you carry alone when Ray and I have been pulling our weight since we left Hemston. All you give a fuck about is your powers."

"Fuck you," I cried, turning away from him. "In a year you'll be eighteen and you can take care of your damn self."

"I intend to."

"Dmitri, I'm sorry about Abe and I'm sorry about Mom but that doesn't give you an excuse to treat me like shit."

I turned away from him, crying into the window as he drove us back to Pine's Row. Neither of us spoke another word. We had both already said too much, things we didn't mean. Well, I hoped he didn't mean them. It didn't matter to me if Dmitri was seventeen or twenty-seven, I would always do whatever I could for him. I would do anything.

When we pulled into the driveway, I jumped from the car and slammed the door behind me. Brooke's car was gone but Rose and Lauren's cars were still parked next to the house. I blew through the door without looking up to see who sat in the living room or what expressions they held on their face. I still had a few hours before I needed to clock into my shift but I couldn't be home, I couldn't be in the same room as Dmitri.

I changed into my work clothes and brushed my teeth before I headed back towards the front door. I needed to get some food and pop a few aspirin before I dragged myself into the Corner Cup.

"Whit?" Rayn asked. "You okay?"

"No." I slammed the door behind me.

No one came after me as I started the car and put it into reverse. No one chased me down the porch asking what was wrong or if I needed help. No one stood in the rearview mirror as I left the driveway.

CHAPTER ELEVEN

BROKEN BONES

WHITNEY

I thought going to work on a few hours of sleep had been rough, but going to work with a hangover definitely topped the list. Luckily, I had time to hydrate and try to eat something before I had to fake a smile and serve lattes like my stomach wasn't churning. The nausea was easier to ignore than the fight I had with Dmitri. I began to feel human again towards the end of my shift; only a headache remained.

"Uh, Whitney," Robby said from behind the espresso machine. "I think someone is here to see you."

Glancing up to see two perfectly green eyes in front of the counter nearly knocked me to the ground. His wrinkled white shirt had a marinara sauce stain. His heart pounded in his throat, much different than the giddy nerves he felt when our fingers first grazed. This wasn't the same Bryan who took me in his bed. This Bryan stood before me drained and broken-hearted. The worst part of being able to feel his emotions was knowing he felt that way because of me.

"Can we talk?" I knew the hands in his pockets were trembling. "Somewhere private."

"Um sure, I'm about to clock out," I replied, tossing the damp rag into an empty bin near the floor. My entire body trembled as I found my subconscious spiraling down the rabbit hole. Why was he here?

As Bryan and I stepped out into the night, I barely felt the cold air against my face. I barely felt anything besides two beating hearts pulsing rapidly behind their protective rib cages.

"What did you want to talk about?" I asked, trying not to meet his eyes. I knew I would be done for if I spent too much time floating with lily pads.

"Seriously?" Bryan frowned. Before I could utter another word, he took his phone from his pocket and held it up to me. Within a second, my voice came on over the speaker, drunk and sobbing. A small gasp escaped my lips as intoxicated Whitney betrayed everything I had fought so hard to keep together. That's it, I would officially take an oath of sobriety after this.

"Bryan...Oh, Byn... Everything is so... I'm in over my head. Even though there are people in this town who want us dead and I'm drowning in spellbooks every day, you're still all I think about. I haven't slept since that night in your bed. I haven't breathed since I kissed you last. I'd rather spend a hundred nights locked in the Dragonfly Mystic basement than live pretending that I don't love you."

The voicemail cut out.

"Oh shit," I whispered, covering my eyes with utter mortification. "I was really drunk last night and I don't remember calling you."

"Right," he muttered, nodding slowly. "I'm supposed to write this off as a drunk dial when you say people are trying to kill you?"

"It's not the first time people have tried to kill me." I shrugged. "Probably won't be the last."

"You are infuriating." The sharp, stern tone of his voice made me wince. Bryan peered into my eyes with such intensity my heart nearly fell out of my chest. "And that voicemail was agonizing to listen to."

"I'll delete your number so I don't accidentally call again," I offered a solution but that seemed to set ablaze his already-lit fuse.

"I don't want to disappear and move on like we never happened. Like I didn't fall so hard for you I forgot how to breathe. I can't pretend I don't wake up every morning and wonder where you are or if you're okay. Missing you is the most all-consuming thing I've ever experienced. This whole idea of you pushing me away to protect me from your powers is bullshit. I'm not afraid and honestly, whether I should be isn't up to you." He finally stopped for a breath, closing his eyes to steady himself. "Whitney, do you love me? Or were those drunken words you didn't mean."

"Bryan, I–" I had imagined this moment since he walked out of the cottage. What I would say if I ever saw him again. Would I beg for his forgiveness, fall into his arms and let the rest of the world and all its dark magic fade away with the sunset? That was a fantasy.

As I met his eyes again, movement over his shoulder sent chills through my body. A creeping sway in the darkness cast against the building from the streetlight. The faint clicking of talons on the pavement as subtle as a morning dewdrop on a leaf. Another shift in the shadows caught the corner of my eye. Three of them that I could count.

"What are you–"

"Shh." I held my hand up to silence Bryan, scanning our surroundings for any more threats as my throat closed up. My fingers trembled as I counted two more Shadows. I locked eyes with one of them as they dared step into the glow of the streetlight. Wispy energy raised off the scales on its back. If these demons had lips, this one would have smirked at me, taking another step closer to us. "Don't move."

"Why?"

"Don't move," I repeated through a clenched jaw.

Bryan stood still, but his eyes searched the back parking lot, unable to see what snuck up behind him. As I took a step towards him, the Shadows against the building began to move out like a pride of lions stalking their prey. In one swift motion, I reached out and grabbed Bryan's wrist, pulling him behind me. I threw my right hand towards the Shadows and released icy daggers into the night. The blades of ice cut through the first two Shadows, sending smoke into the dark sky.

My arms tingled from the sudden burst of energy, my skin a sheet of pins and needles. I almost didn't feel Bryan's warm fingers wrap around mine until he spoke.

"Whit..."

The larger of the three remaining Shadows stepped fully into the glow of the streetlight, revealing itself. Its hunched back curved with each step, bony shoulders rising and falling as it sulked towards us.

"What the fuck is that?" Bryan tried to step in front of me but I pushed him back with my shoulder.

"Stay behind me," I ordered, mustering another energy wave as I ran circles above our heads with my open hand. Condensation from the clouds above us began to swirl, quickening as my hand picked up pace. My hair blew into my eyes, slightly breaking my concentration, but I quickly pushed my energy back. Water droplets fell and misted my face as my hand slapped against the asphalt. The vortex crashed onto the Shadows and flooded the parking lot, knocking Bryan and I onto our backs.

I fell on top of his legs, reaching out to catch myself but it only made me stumble against his body. The water from the vortex washed up onto us like an unexpected undertow wave at the beach.

A bobcat snarl from a Shadow echoed behind us and Bryan gasped out in pain. We scrambled against each other as I turned onto my knees to face him at the same time he lunged forward. The Shadow's clawed paw swiped out in front of my face, nearly taking off my nose. I froze my skin as Harmony had taught me to do and threw my clenched fist into the darkness.

My fist went through the Shadow's fanged face, shattering it into pieces.

Crack.

One of my knuckles popped out of place as a cry escaped my throat. My hand throbbed as if I had punched a wall of concrete at full force. A warm tear fell down my cheek as I cradled my injured hand in the other. "Fuck!"

"Are you okay?" Bryan's voice rasped as he reached for me.

"We need to get out of here. Now." I jumped to my feet and searched the parking lot for my car, forgetting Rayn had picked it up halfway through my shift. "Fuck. Rayn needs her own goddamn car."

"I can drive." Bryan panted. "Come on."

We rushed to his Jeep as he fumbled in his pocket for the keys. An eternity passed as he unlocked the car. My thumb pressed the button on the door handle a million times before the passenger door unlocked. Finally, the door swung open and we jumped inside. Bryan started the engine and threw the Jeep into reverse. His foot pressed down on the gas pedal so quickly the engine yelled back at him in protest. He left the parking lot in silence and turned onto a back street, leaving the flooded mess I had made in the rearview mirror.

"Bryan," I began, turning to face him. He didn't look at me, his eyes glued on the road in front of us. "Oh my god, are you okay?"

Bright red stained his left shoulder, blood trickling down his arm and soaking his white dress shirt, ripped in three jagged lines from the Shadow's claws.

"I'm not the one with broken knuckles. You need to go to the hospital," he answered.

"No, take me to the cottage. Turn left up here on Misty Mountain Way," I directed.

"I'm taking you to the hospital."

"No, you are not!" I snapped back. "You shouldn't have been there, Bryan. This is exactly why I broke up with you. You're hurt, and next time it'll be much worse. You're going to take me to Amilia's house where you came to pick up Rose after Halloween. She'll heal your shoulder and then you're going home alone."

"Whitney–"

"Do you hear me?" My voice echoed against the interior of his Jeep.

Bryan's foot slammed on the brakes as he came to an abrupt stop and pulled over.

The seatbelt locked against my chest as my body fell forward. "What are you doing?" I demanded.

"Look at me."

"No, I–"

"I'm not leaving you alone tonight." His voice shook.

"Quit being so damn stubborn."

"Me?" He laughed, rubbing his face. "You're the one who punched that thing in the face and broke her damn hand. You're the one who won't listen to a fucking word I say."

"What is left to say? You saw those things. You saw my powers." My voice cut out as the wave of realization crashed over me. "You saw my powers."

"Yeah," he answered quietly, nodding. "That was terrifying."

"I'm so sorry," I apologized, covering my tear-stained eyes with my good hand. I had never felt so vulnerable. "I understand the powers are a lot to take in. I never wanted you to see–"

"You aren't terrifying, those things were." Bryan reached out and moved my hand from my face, grazing my cheek with his fingers. "You are beautiful."

"How can you say that after what just happened?"

"Because I love you." His words were sharp daggers that warmed my soul and broke my heart all in one fell swoop.

"I'm not who you think I am," I muttered, pulling away from his touch. "You barely know me."

"I wouldn't say that."

"You think I'm a nice girl. I'm not. What you saw back there is the reality of being with me."

"I don't–"

"I killed someone." The words fell from my lips, cutting him off. "Halloween night. It was self-defense, but I wanted to. I wanted him dead so I filled his lungs with water and watched him drown."

Bryan's eyes were hard to read as they peered into mine, but I felt the disappointment swirl around inside of him. His tongue wet his bottom lip before he let out a sigh. "Self-defense."

"But I wanted to. You don't know me."

"I know you didn't tell me about your powers until you didn't have a choice because you were scared. You thought I'd run away or turn on you like that douche back in Kansas. And when I didn't, you pushed me as far away as you could because you can't wrap your head around someone loving you for who you are rather than that front you put up." Bryan's eyes burned passionately into mine as he stripped my defenses down without even trying. "I know you carry all this weight on your shoulders because you feel responsible for everything that happened over the summer. You think you have to do this by yourself but you don't. You don't have to take care of your siblings and save the world by yourself. I'm here and I'm not afraid."

A tear fell down my cheek and I didn't try to hide it. Bryan reached out and gently wiped it away with his thumb.

"If anything ever happened to you..." I choked as more tears followed. "What am I saying? You're already hurt. You don't understand, Byn. It's not as simple as wanting to be together. Of course I want you. Of course I miss you. I don't know if I can keep you safe and that alone is enough."

"Whit–"

"Dmitri's boyfriend is still missing." I sobbed, the words like acid on my lips. "They killed Amilia's daughter. Lauren's mom is dead and her dad is lying in a coma. My mom is dead and I almost lost my sister. We almost lost Rose."

Bryan's shoulders fell. My breath caught in my chest as I swallowed another sob.

"Everyone around us drops dead. I can't handle losing you, not you," I whispered. "Being without you is like having my arm ripped off but at least I know you're alive. At least you're safe if you're far away from me."

Bryan reached out and pulled me as close to his chest as he could with the center counsel between us. He stroked the back of my head and nuzzled his face against my hair. "It's okay, baby," he whispered.

"When this whole thing started, I had no idea what I was getting into. What I got the other girls into. It's terrifying, Bryan. It's bigger than anything I could have imagined."

"I can help."

"If anything ever happened to you, I'd never forgive myself."

"Let me worry about that. I'm a grown man, Whit, I can take care of myself." Bryan's voice was gentle as he pulled away from me, tilting my chin with his knuckle. "Let me ask you something."

My eyelids were heavy from crying and I wanted to protest but it felt so good to be back in his embrace, to have his hands against my skin again. I leaned into him and nuzzled my face into his shoulder, taking in the scent of cedarwood and vanilla.

"Hmm?"

"The night after Halloween, you told me you didn't want to be with me. Did you mean that or were you trying to get me to leave? If you truly don't want this, then I'll take you wherever you want to go and I'll leave you alone. You can block my number and the next time you get drunk and miss me, you can call someone else. But don't end us because of something that might not happen. Don't end us like this."

"I didn't mean it," I answered. "Of course I want you, Byn. That's never been the issue."

"If your powers and the people after you weren't a factor, would we be together?"

"Yes." I answered without missing a beat.

"Because your powers aren't a deal breaker for me. They're kind of a turn on."

I couldn't help but laugh. "I'm starting to think you're insane."

"Me too." He leaned in closer. The tip of his nose brushed against mine.

As our eyes met, I remembered what drew me to Bryan in the first place. Why I was willing to risk everything the girls and I had worked for just to see him. Because this thing between us was the safest I had felt in my entire life. Without a second thought, I closed the gap between us and pressed my lips to his.

The kiss had such force and passion behind it that I had to remind myself to breathe. He tangled his fingers in my hair and deepened the kiss with his tongue. I touched his face, longing to feel his usual stubble under my fingertips. My heart swelling being close to him again. I had ached for him every moment that we were apart. Being back in his arms felt like returning home.

So caught up in the moment, I forgot all about our injuries and reached for him with my right hand. "Ow," I hissed, pulling away from him.

"Oh shit, your hand." Bryan settled back into the driver's seat. "Where do we need to go? Your boss's house?"

I nodded, biting my bottom lip while cradling my throbbing hand. "Brooke should still be there. They'll be able to take care of the scratches on your shoulder too."

"Mia?" I called, opening back the front door of the cottage.

"About time! I know you wanted to walk to clear your head and all, but you got off work a while ago," my sister called from the kitchen as Bryan and I walked into the living room. "I think we found the–" Rayn stopped in her tracks seeing Bryan standing behind me. "What's going on?"

"Where's Brooke?" I asked, scanning the empty living room.

"She and Mia are in the garden," Rayn answered, her eyes still over my shoulder.

"Go get them," I requested.

"Whit–"

"I have broken knuckles and a Shadow fucked up Bryan's shoulder. Please go get them."

Rayn nodded and disappeared into the kitchen. Her voice echoed in my head as the back door opened. *Rose is going to kill you.*

"Your sister's mad," Bryan mumbled, stating the obvious. He stepped away from me and took in the scenery. Something I'm sure he didn't take the time to do the first time he was here.

"Not as mad as yours is going to be." I watched him move around the room towards the bookshelves.

"Let me worry about that." Discomfort radiated through his body. I couldn't tell if he was in pain or if he felt uncomfortable being at the cottage because of the last time he was here.

"Rayn said we have company." Amilia stepped out from the kitchen, silent as a cat. "What can I do for you, Bryan?"

Bryan whipped around and quickly stepped away from the bookshelf, startled by Amilia's voice.

"What happened?" Amilia asked, eyeing the blood stained rip in Bryan's shirt.

"Shadows," I answered, lowering my head in shame.

Amilia gasped, her eyes widening. No one in this house seemed happy with me. Not only had I brought Bryan here unannounced after everyone knew how Rose would feel about it, but he was bleeding.

"Whitney broke her knuckles. She needs help more than I do." Bryan winced in pain as he moved his shoulder.

"Brooke." Amilia waved in my direction as she rushed to Bryan. "May I?"

He nodded. Amilia reached out and pulled the torn fabric back, analyzing his shoulder. She cussed under her breath. "Scale of one to ten on the pain, and be honest."

"Um, like an eight. It hurts to breathe."

"Hurts to breathe?" I moved towards him but Brooke stopped me.

"I'll be fine." Bryan held the end of his breath in and released it with a groan.

Amilia turned and rushed to the kitchen. "Rayn, go to the garden and pick some holy rope. Hurry! Bryan, take your shirt off and keep breathing."

Rayn ran into the kitchen and out the back door. Bryan looked over at me before he began unbuttoning his shirt, leaving his white tank undershirt.

My eyes remained locked on Bryan across the room as he struggled to take another breath. I called into the kitchen. "Mia, what's happening?"

Panic rushed through my veins as Bryan winced again, the adrenaline from our encounter with the Shadows had worn off. He put his hand over the scratches and leaned forward, attempting another deep breath. I pulled my arm from Brooke's grasp and rushed to Bryan, cupping his cheek in my palm.

"Hey, it's okay. Breathe with me. Breathe," I said, taking a deep breath. His eyes locked into mine as he filled his lungs but a sharp pain shot through his entire body. His pulse accelerated and fear took over every inch of him. His eyes widened as he peered into my soul.

"I-I can't breathe," he struggled to whisper.

"Amilia!" My voice boomed through the cottage. "Brooke, do something!"

Brooke rushed to us and put her hands over the wound, the gold rays of her healing magic shined through her fingers but it didn't ease Bryan's pain.

"I think this will help." Amilia rushed back into the room and smeared a green salve against the red tears in Bryan's skin. Rayn rushed back into the room and handed Amilia long green sprouts of holy rope. Amilia chewed on the end of the greenery and took the paste from her mouth, mixing it into the green salve. Bryan cringed when Amilia touched the wound.

"How is he still standing?" Brooke asked Amilia.

"I am wondering the same," Amilia replied, pressing a sheet of white gauze over the salve.

"What do you mean still standing?" I asked, grabbing Bryan's hand. His shoulders tensed in discomfort as Amilia's hands pressed against his chest.

"The Shadow's talons are poisonous," Rayn answered, staying firmly planted in the dining room with her arms crossed. "I told you this."

I had no memory of her telling me anything about this.

"But it didn't have any effect on Brooke or Lauren," I replied, tightening my grip on Bryan's hand. He squeezed mine in return.

"That's because Lauren and Brooke are Elementals. Bryan isn't even a witch. In my experience, this cut should have killed him by now," Amilia answered as plainly as reading a weather report for a sunny weekend. "How're you doing, Bryan?"

He cleared his throat. "The pain is subsiding, but my chest still hurts."

"I don't see any red lines coming from the wound so it doesn't seem like the poison is spreading. Your body is somehow fighting it, and to be completely honest, I'm not sure how." Amilia put her hand on Bryan's shoulder above the wound.

"Is he going to be okay?" I wrapped my free hand around his bare bicep, as if hanging onto him tighter would fix everything.

"I think so. I don't have much knowledge on how Shadows affect the powerless firsthand, but other documented cases have not ended well." Amilia turned to me. "How long ago did this happen?"

"I don't know exactly, maybe twenty minutes?" I estimated.

"Hm." Amilia peeled back the gauze for another look at the cuts. "Bryan, are there many witches in your family?"

"No," Bryan answered, finally able to take a breath. "Only Rose."

Amilia tilted her head. "I find that hard to believe."

"I don't have powers."

"No, but if you were truly powerless, you'd be dead right now. Magic may not have manifested as it typically does, but there is something in your blood."

"Wait, hang on, you think I'm a witch?" Bryan clarified.

"Not necessarily, but there is something brewing under the surface." Amilia held up her hands. "It's the only explanation I have."

"Maybe he's sensitive to energy?" Brooke suggested. "Like, it's there but he can't access it?"

A realization washed over me. "Is that why I can feel his emotions? Mia, you said that witches who are sensitive to one another's energies can feel each other."

"It makes sense to me," Amilia replied.

"So, that isn't a common thing? Whitney being able to feel my emotions?" Bryan asked, seeming to remember everything I'd told him the day after Halloween.

"No, it's not common amongst witches, let alone a witch and someone who is powerless. It's considered the highest connection of souls," Amilia explained.

"You're sure he'll be okay?" I asked again.

"I think so, yes."

Brooke took my still broken hand in hers. "Can I heal you now?"

I nodded, holding Bryan's fingers with my good hand.

"Jesus, Whit," Brooke muttered, covering my swollen knuckles with her palm. "Rose is going to kill you."

"So I keep hearing."

"You know better than to get him hurt like this," she whispered.

"I'm sorry."

"This isn't Whitney's fault," Bryan said, color finally returning to his face.

Brooke closed her eyes and steadied her breath as her powers rippled through both of us. My cold hands warmed in hers and my skin tingled. The throbbing pain lasted for a short moment until the pressure building in my hand released. A gasp of pain fell from my lips as my knuckles snapped back into place, shooting a chill up my spine.

Brooke stepped back. "Good as new. I swear, you two and your libidos are going to get us all killed." She looked back and forth between Rayn and I.

"Hey, I learned my lesson the hard way." Rayn shifted her weight and stepped into the living room. "Whitney is the one who can't let go."

"I came to her. She didn't do anything wrong," Bryan spoke up, tightening his grip around my fingers.

"I want to keep an eye on this overnight in case something changes," Amilia replied, ignoring us.

"What are you thinking, Mia?" I asked, searching her face for clues but she remained unreadable.

"We'll know more in the morning," she answered, turning to leave the living room.

"That's it?" Brooke snapped. "You aren't going to say anything else?"

"What else is there to say?" Amilia asked, calmly. "Whitney is an adult. She knows what could have happened tonight. She's old enough to face the consequences of her actions."

"But it's not just her facing the consequences!" Brooke raised her voice. "We can't lose Rose!"

"I'll talk to her." Bryan's words fell on deaf ears.

"The Renati already have the home field advantage," Rayn added onto Brooke's concern. "The Shadows are getting stronger and we have to close that portal. We can't do it just the four of us."

"My sister doesn't get to dictate whether Whitney and I are together, and neither do any of you." Bryan raised his voice enough that everyone in the room finally turned to him. "Rose talks a big game but this is important to her, just as important as it is for the rest of you. She isn't going to give up on this. Trust me."

"She did before," Brooke replied.

"I will take care of it," Bryan reassured us.

Amilia looked at me with dark circles under her eyes. "What's done is done. Maybe after tonight you'll be more aware of your surroundings, hm?" She pulled a thick afghan blanket from the back of the couch and opened it up. "Whitney, you and Bryan can take one of the spare rooms. I want you to keep an eye on his breathing in case there's a delay in the poison. I'll do some reading tonight and take another look at the cuts in the morning. Maybe I can get a better idea of what happened."

"Okay." I nodded, clinging tighter to Bryan.

"I need to go lay down. Wake me if anything changes." Amilia glanced back and forth between Rayn and Brooke. "And you two are going to let them talk to Rose on their own. This isn't your place to interfere."

"But we only–" Brooke didn't finish her sentence.

"Make sure to add another log to the fire before you fall asleep." Amilia headed upstairs to the loft without another word.

The four of us stood awkwardly in the middle of the living room before I decided to break the silence. "I'm sure you guys are expecting an apology, but I'm not sorry so I won't lie to you. See you in the morning if you're still here." I pulled on Bryan's arm and led him down the short hallway to the guest bedroom.

"Are you okay?" I asked him once the door shut behind us; alone for the first time since we walked into the cottage.

"Yeah, I think so," he answered softly, running his fingers through his hair before he reached out and took my hand in his. "What about your hand?"

"Oh, I'm fine. Not the first time Brooke's mended broken bones. Bryan I–" I took a deep breath and held his hand tightly in mine. "I had no idea about the Shadow's poison, I swear to you. If I did, I would have brought you here sooner."

"I know," he said. "I'm okay."

"You shouldn't be." Tears welled in the corner of my eyes thinking about what could have happened.

"But I am." He took a step closer to me and rested a hand on my hip. "You need to rest."

"I'm fine. You're the one who–"

"You are absolutely not fine," Bryan protested. "I can sleep on the floor, if you want."

"Why would I want that?" I wiped a stray tear away.

Bryan shrugged. "In case you do, it's an option."

"No, it's not." I wrapped my hand around the back of his neck and pushed myself up on my toes, gently pressing my lips to his. The kiss was soft, fragile and vulnerable. The hunger that we felt earlier in the night faded away as the outer layers of strength and hurt melted to the floor.

We kicked off our shoes and lay facing each other on the bed. I gently traced the edges of the gauze bandage on his shoulder, making sure there were no signs of infection coming from his skin underneath. Any traces of something immediately wrong, but all seemed calm.

"I'm so sorry about tonight," I spoke after I traced all four edges of the bandage. "About the Shadows, the voicemail. All of it."

"I wouldn't change a single thing," Bryan whispered, scooting closer against my body. "All of it brought us to this moment, and I've been dying to have you back in my arms."

"Don't say dying," I breathed, my eyes still glued to his shoulder.

Bryan grabbed my hand and brought it to his lips, softly kissing my once-injured knuckles. "We're going to be okay."

"I love you, Bryan," I blurted out. The words had been sitting on the edge of my tongue, waiting for the perfect moment to confess but this was as close to perfect as we were going to get.

A sly smile turned up the corner of his lips. "I love you too, baby."

"If we wake up in the morning and you change your mind, I won't be mad. I want you to know that."

"One day you'll stop giving me an out." He nudged my nose with his.

"One day, maybe," I replied before pulling him in for a kiss; less gentle than when we first got into the bedroom. My fingers slid under his shirt, grazing bare chest. I wanted to memorize the feel of his skin against mine. When I ran my index fingers over the button of his pants, Bryan broke the kiss and ran his tongue over his lips.

He moved a stray strand of hair out of my face. "I want you, but I also don't want you to do anything impulsive you're going to regret in the morning."

"There's nothing impulsive about us," I answered, undoing the button. "Loving you is the most conscious decision I've ever made."

Bryan reached out and pulled me on top of him. Even after weeks without talking to him, my body still naturally pressed into his, absorbing his warmth. His hands slid up the back of my sweater and lifted it over my head. I took his face in my hands and kissed him. I let out a small sigh, moaning against his lips. He rolled his hips against mine, showing me he was already hard.

"I missed you," he whispered, sliding his hands down to the band of my jeans. "Let's never do that again."

"Almost get each other killed?"

"No. I mean, yes, that too. But can we please not repeat the last month? I can't do that again."

"I meant what I said about keeping you safe."

"Well," he chuckled, leaving a trail of kisses down my jaw. "You did a pretty good job at that tonight."

"Those aren't the only Shadows out there."

"Hmm. Good thing my girl can kill them with her bare hands."

I pulled back to look into his eyes. "Your girl?"

"I mean, that's what I want. What do you want?"

I smiled and unzipped his pants, sliding my hand under the waistband of his boxer briefs. He shivered, his breath catching in his throat as I gripped his length.

"I want all of it," I whispered. "All of you."

Bryan flipped me onto my back and pressed his body weight on top of me, his erection hard against my thigh as I wrapped my legs around him. Reaching for the hem of his undershirt, I helped take it off, careful as he slid it over his injured shoulder. His lips crashed back to mine, deepening the kiss with his tongue.

He rolled his hips against me and a soft moan fell from my lips.

"Fuck." He pulled away. "I don't have a condom."

"Oh," I sighed. My heart pounded against my rib cage as I tried to come down from the climbing high. "I'm on the pill. I haven't been with anyone since you, and before you it had been months."

Bryan peered deep into my eyes. "You're the only one since March."

I tried not to wear my relief on my sleeve. His words put me at ease but they still didn't fix our problem. "The thing is though, I haven't been great about taking the pill every day lately. So..."

"We, uh, we probably shouldn't then."

I looked away, not wanting to see the disappointment on his face that echoed in his emotions. "Probably not. But there is something I wanted to do last time, but didn't get the chance."

"Oh?" he asked curiously. His weight still pressed me into the sheets. I never thought I'd be so comfortable pinned under another person but Bryan's weight felt like a security blanket.

"Lay back." I gently eased him off me onto his back.

He watched me with a sultry gaze and I lowered his black dress pants, lifting his hips to slip them down. Bryan's heartbeat echoed through my chest. All his senses heightened as I wrapped my hand at the base of his erection and took him in my mouth.

His groan vibrated in his chest, careful not to alert the rest of the house to our reunion. I watched him as he fell apart before me. Bryan covered his mouth with his hand, muffling a deep moan. His hips rose and fell, gradually at first to test my waters. I welcomed his participation, placing my hand on his hip to mimic his movements. With the green light, his hips thrusted up and his fingers tangled in my hair. He grabbed my hand and squeezed as his muscles tensed under the skin.

I loved every second of it; his whimpering, the way he crumbled at my touch. Feeling everything that flowed through his veins, the fire that ignited in his soul.

"Baby," he breathed. "I'm going to come."

He grabbed his undershirt that hung from the side of the bed and pulled out of my mouth. He covered himself with the shirt as everything tensed and spasmed. He covered his eyes with his forearm as labored breath finally released from his lungs.

"Shit," he whispered.

"I wanted–"

Bryan cut me off, lunging forward as his mouth crashed into mine. It surprised me that he'd want to kiss me after getting head, but I welcomed the affection and ran my fingers through his hair.

I smiled against his lips. "Let's get some sleep."

Chapter Twelve

HARD CONVERSATIONS

Rayn

When I woke up the next morning, the other side of the couch where Brooke had fallen asleep was empty. I stretched my arms and grabbed my phone, reading the text Brooke had left.

Headed home early. Not ready to talk to Whit.

I trilled my lips, letting out a deep sigh. Of course Brooke felt that way. She and Rose were best friends, and Brooke was fiercely loyal. As angry as I had been last night, I understood deep in my core that nothing Whitney could ever do would stick forever. Even after only a few hours of sleep, the anger I felt coursing my blood last night had dimmed. I was less angry with my sister, and more worried about Bryan.

I wondered if he truly knew what he got himself into. Not with Whitney, I knew what he saw in her. But I wasn't convinced he knew how dangerous their situation was. Hell, he could have died last night and it barely seemed to faze him.

I threw off the heavy blanket and left Whitney's car keys on the counter. I laced up my boots and grabbed my bag, gently closing the front door behind me. The crisp autumn hair filled my lungs and fogged my breath as I headed down the sidewalk. I didn't have a long walk ahead of me, but the moisture hanging in the early morning air sent chills into my soul.

Shivering, I buried my hands into the front pocket of my hoodie. I let out another deep breath, watching it fog before my face. When Whitney and I were little, we used to pretend; Whitney would be a dragon and I would pretend I smoked a cigarette. I smiled at the memory and pulled my phone from my back pocket.

"Hello?" Rose's sleepy voice answered on the other end.

"Sorry it's so early, can I come over?"

"Sure, is everything okay?"

"Yeah, I'm good. I just want to hang out," I lied.

"Hm." Rose knew I was being dishonest. "See you in a few."

I took my time, counting the lines in the slabs of concrete that made up the sidewalk. I listened to the birds as they woke up, calling out for one another. I admired the bright, beautiful colors of the leaves above me and how they floated to the ground. There weren't many leaves left on the trees, some of them already nothing but bare branches. The weather had already grown too bleak. I wished I were a bear. I'd eat whatever I wanted and then hibernate through the cold months, emerging only when the temperature rose again.

As I approached the walkway to Rose's house, I hesitated before knocking. Rose was my friend, we had gone through a near death experience together. Nothing bonded people more than shared trauma. Last night, Amilia told Brooke and I to stay out of it. I heard Bryan say he would talk to Rose. It's not that I didn't trust them, I did. But when it came to my sister, I had a hard time leaving her future in other's hands. The stability of my generation depended on this conversation.

"Hey," Rose answered the door after I finally knocked. "Are you okay?"

"Yeah, yeah, I'm fine. I crashed at the cottage last night and uh, didn't want to stick around when everyone woke up," I explained, taking my boots off.

"I've been working on a new potion, come look." Rose led the way up the stairs to her bedroom.

Rose's bedroom was a green witch's fantasy. A large potted fern sat in the corner. Baskets hung from the ceiling with bright green ivy curling down towards the floor. A window bench lay in the back of her room, covered in potted plants with little succulents sprinkled amongst the other greenery. Her walls were covered in various posters with a string of fairy lights around the mirror of her dresser.

Rose opened up her closet and pulled out her stash of a tiny cauldron, a notebook and a bag of various herbs and barks.

"I've been tinkering," she said, putting the stash down on the floor. "I think I've come up with an energy potion, like a Red Bull on steroids. We wouldn't need to take much but it would help with all the magic we've been using. Have you felt the burn out?"

I nodded. "That's a brilliant idea. I have a feeling we're going to need it."

"I want us to be prepared." Rose raised her eyebrows. "But you didn't come here to talk about potions. You're nervous. What's going on?"

I sighed and sat down on the edge of the bed. "First, you have to promise you will not freak out."

"We're off to a great start."

"So?"

"Okay, yes, I promise." Rose sat down next to me.

I had thought about the most delicate approach to this conversation, but when the moment came, beating around the bush didn't feel right.

"It's been a month since Halloween, and Whitney is still miserable. She hides it well, but you're an empath so you know how she is dying inside."

Rose nodded.

"And who else has been dying inside since Halloween? Besides us."

She sighed as if she knew where the conversation headed before I sat down. "My brother."

"He came to the cottage last night. I don't know exactly what happened, but he and Whit showed up there together. He said he came to her." I picked at a rip on my jeans. "He wants to talk to you himself. I'm here because Whitney is a good sister, to me and to you. And I know she went behind your back before and lied, she does that to me sometimes too. But when push comes to shove, she keeps her word."

"Does she?"

"Rose, my question is, with everything else going on...is this really the hill you want to die on?"

"If it keeps him safe, yes," Rose answered.

I shifted my weight. "Whitney and Bryan being together isn't what's going to get him hurt and you know it. I know what it's like to have a brother you want to keep safe, and I know what it's like to have that brother do whatever the fuck he wants anyway."

Rose chortled.

"This is the don't freak out part."

"Oh you haven't gotten there yet?" Rose asked, picking at her fingernails.

I crossed my legs, hiding my trembling fingers between my thighs. "I don't know the details, but somehow Shadows got involved. Whit showed up last night with a broken hand and Bryan had been scratched. He–"

Rose jumped to her feet. "Scratched by the Shadows? But they're poisonous! He–"

"He's fine. Amilia healed him without much trouble." I put up my hands to calm her down. "So, that's something else to unpack, but Whitney had a broken hand because she kept him safe. I don't want to think about what would have happened if she wasn't there."

Rose let out a deep sigh. "Lauren's parents."

"Yeah, exactly. We can't keep him at arm's length anymore. We need to pull him into the fold because if he's in the circle with us, we can keep him safe. Whitney will keep him safe, just like we all look out for Mit."

Rose clicked her tongue. "He's in love with her."

"Yeah, the feelings are mutual."

Rose smiled. "We're going to be sisters-in-law."

I laughed. "I hope so."

"Is he still at the cottage?"

I nodded. "Yeah, Mia wanted to keep an eye on the scratch, but she thinks he's got some magic in his blood."

"Wait, as in not powerless?"

"I have no fucking idea." I shrugged.

"Okay." Rose sat back down. "I'll wait and see what he has to say about it."

"Are you okay?" I reached out for her hand.

"I'm upset he got hurt but I'm glad Whitney was there. I, uh, I probably overreacted. I'm sure I seemed crazy, but..."

I nodded. "Dmitri and I got into some pretty nasty arguments over him and Abe Roberts, so I get it."

"I just...I want him to be happy, I do. I love Whitney, but I'm terrified that my family is going to be next. How would I ever recover from that? I don't know how Lauren does it. I don't know how she gets out of bed in the morning."

"Same way I did, Whitney and Mit, too. It's paralyzing but the world keeps spinning, unfortunately. But listen, no one is working harder to keep them safe than you." I reached out and put my hand on Rose's shoulder. "What's better than just *you* keeping them safe? All of us. Whitney will kill someone before she lets them lay a finger on him."

"I know she would."

"Good. You're okay?"

Rose sighed. "I think so."

"Good." I nodded towards the cauldron. "Show me this potion."

We slid down to the floor and sat cross legged next to one another. "So, I combined these two potions from our spellbook. I started growing phoenix dust by the window and it's actually doing really well. It likes to be sung to, but specifically Michelle Branch. I don't make the rules."

I laughed. "That's where the energy comes from."

"I think so too."

Rose took a sprig of phoenix dust and ground it up in her mortar and pestle, creating a bright green paste. She added the paste to her cauldron with some water and lemon juice.

"It tastes like lemonade." Rose smiled as her powers slithered down my arms. She reached for a small cloth bag. "And now for the secret ingredient, golden root."

"What is that?" I asked, watching Rose sprinkle the ground up powder to the potion.

"Something not easily obtained," Rose answered. "Took me forever to hunt it down."

"Pretty simple potion."

Rose smiled. "The potion is easy to make, the ingredients on the other hand? Not easy at all."

"You're a natural at this. I mean, I'm not surprised because, you know, Mother Earth and all. But, you really are brilliant."

Rose's eyes glimmered as she smiled down at the cauldron. "It takes a while to simmer, but a little bit goes a long way."

A knock at the bedroom door brought us both out of our magical haze. Rose jumped to her feet, barely cracking the door open. I couldn't see who had interrupted us until Rose let out a sigh of relief and opened the door all the way.

Bryan stood in the hallway wearing his glasses and different clothes than he'd had on last night. He looked past Rose and hardened his gaze when he saw me on the floor.

"Hi," he said monotone. I knew that Bryan was smart enough to assume why I'd come over. He could be as angry as he wanted, but I did this with his best interest at heart too. Mostly for Whitney, but he benefited from the conversation all the same.

"Um, I should head out." I got up off the floor and grabbed my bag. "The potion is incredible, Rose, you're a genius."

"Wait, where are you going? You can't walk home from here," Rose told me.

"Uh, I'll be fine. I'll grab the bus or something. You two need to talk."

As I left the house, I put my headphones in and checked the time. After making sure Rose was okay, I needed to check in with my sister. Whitney had probably already left the cottage thinking everyone was furious with her. I needed to fix that. I pulled out my phone and sent Whit a text.

I love you. Everything is going to be fine.

I felt lighter after my talk with Rose. I could guess how things would have gone if I didn't get to her first, but I genuinely felt like I helped. After everything I'd fucked up that year, it was good to feel like I'd helped. Like I was finally able to make up for the whole incident with Jon and the cluster fuck that Tom ended up being.

I heard the voices of my generation in my head, telling me that none of it was my fault and to stop beating myself up, but I couldn't control it.

Chewing on my lip, I scanned over the list of potential Renati hideouts that Dominic had given Whitney. The girls and I had wondered if any of those places held any merit, and there was no time like the present.

Hopefully, a lot of these places would still be around considering how old the list was. The walk reminded me that I needed a car. Rifton wasn't a big town and surprisingly walkable, as long as I didn't need to get to Pines Row. The walk from the community college to Giani's and the neighborhoods was totally doable, but a car would have a heater.

I headed to the first address but it was a vacant lot with a large construction sign out front. Apartments coming soon. I crossed it off the list and moved on. The Post Office? I stared at the list, how deep in the local government were these people?

The location that screamed out at me was a Florist on Mahogany and Violet. According to my phone's map, the florist was a block over from the Corner Cup and I had nothing but time.

The florist was still there and had just opened for the morning. I smiled at the woman behind the counter and took in all the bright colors. Fall and winter themed arrangements took up the front displays. Bright oranges and yellows next to poinsettias and evergreens with glittery red berries.

"Can I help you find anything?" the woman asked.

"Um, yeah. I'm looking for something for my aunt. It's her birthday and I totally forgot. I think she'd like this," I replied, my eye catching a pink orchid planted in a purple pot. It wasn't Amilia's birthday, but she would like the orchid.

"That's a beautiful choice." The woman smiled and picked up the plant. "Is this the one?"

I nodded. "Yeah, I think so. Are you guys doing anything for Founder's Day?"

"We are, actually. We have a booth where we'll be selling wreaths, garland, and all kinds of holiday decor."

"Oh, that sounds nice. It's my first holiday season in Rifton so I'm still figuring everything out. Something about the council?" I asked, trying to pick my words carefully.

The woman's smile faltered a bit but her customer service voice remained. "Rifton is very proud that descendants of the founders still live here, but they're all involved in local politics and have very successful businesses. So, I wouldn't leave either if I was one of them."

The woman did not sound like a fan.

"Sounds a bit silly to parade around the town council members, from an outsider's perspective," I said in my sweetest voice.

"I agree with you there. Founder's Day has always been fun though, despite all that. I think you'll enjoy it. My grandmother loved it, it was her favorite town event." The woman let out a short sigh. "That'll be $14.99."

I pulled out my wallet. "Did she used to own this place?"

The woman nodded. "Yes, she opened it forever ago. She loved plants and I couldn't let the place go."

I took the orchid from the counter. "That's beautiful. Thank you so much."

"Thank you, come back soon."

Okay. Family business targeted as a potential Renati hideout. Loved Founder's Day. That could potentially be Renati members hiding in plain sight. The woman didn't seem to be as enthusiastic about town history though, especially the council. I analyzed every detail of our conversation on my walk back to the cottage.

"It's me!" I called, closing the front door behind me. I set the orchid down on the dining room table. "Anyone home?"

"Hello, Rayn," Harmony said, coming out of the kitchen.

"I didn't know you guys were back."

Harmony nodded. "Late last night. That's a pretty plant."

I glanced at the orchid. "I got it for Mia. Is she home?"

"Just left for the Corner Cup, actually. It's just you and I."

"Oh." I gazed down awkwardly at my boots.

"Um..." Harmony glanced over her shoulder. "Coffee?"

"Please."

Harmony grabbed two mugs from the cupboard and poured our coffee while I plopped down on an armchair. With a wave of my fingers, the flames in the fireplace roared to life. The heat permeated to my bones, warming my soul. I closed my eyes and hummed, taking comfort in the cottage. I hadn't felt this at home since the car accident.

"Here you go." Harmony handed me a coffee mug and sat down on the couch furthest from the flames. "Woo, that is a hot fire."

I smiled. "Sorry, I'm freezing. I've been walking around all over town. Where are Warren and Nic?"

"Warren headed home for a few days but he'll be back. I'm not sure where Dominic went."

I took a sip of coffee. "Does Warren have a family?"

"His father is in an assisted living facility, so he wanted to check on him. Warren's parents were older when they had him and he's an only child. He's a good man," Harmony explained.

"He seems to be," I agreed. "I, uh..." I remembered Whitney telling me that no one knew Nic got into Amilia's old books and found the list of potential Renati hideouts. I'd find Nic later and tell him about the florist. "So what does your life outside Rifton look like?"

"I'm a lawyer in Seattle." Harmony tucked her leg underneath her.

"Wow, that's kind of badass. What kind of law?"

"Family law. So, divorces, child custody, things like that."

"That sounds depressing."

"It sure can be." Harmony nodded.

"I guess we take for granted what you guys are putting on hold to be here with us. This is everything to my generation but you guys have lives away from Rifton."

"Warren and I do, yes. Who knows what Dominic has been up to." Harmony took a sip from her coffee.

I dared to state the obvious. "You really hate him."

"I don't *hate* him. I...Dominic used to be...He..." Harmony tripped over her words, taking a deep breath. "When he and Abbie died...Well, when Abbie died and he disappeared, it destroyed my generation. It destroyed Amilia. We were all broken and for a long time it seemed beyond repair. Knowing he was out there this whole time and let us feel that way? It's hard to forgive. It's hard to forgive him for leaving her behind. Abbie was brilliant and kind, she loved so fiercely. She died and he ran away for *years*. He let us all down."

"I'm not sure if I could forgive that either," I admitted. "I'd be able to forgive Whitney though."

"It's hard to know how you'd react unless you're faced with it."

"No, I'm pretty sure I do. There isn't anything Whit could do that I wouldn't be able to forgive because I know her. I know Whit's moral compass, her integrity. She would never intentionally do anything malicious to our generation. If she had to leave one of us behind like that it would destroy her too. I don't know about Nic, but I know Whitney."

"The twin flames," Harmony muttered.

"What?"

"Everyone always said water and fire are the twin flames of the Elementals. Every generation, those two seemed to have a special bond above all the others. Like you and Whitney, you found one another first for a reason."

"Huh. I always wondered about that, if it was chance or fate. Whitney definitely feels like my twin flame."

"Apparently it can cross generations too, there's just a pull between the two elements that is unexplainable."

"Is that why Dominic is so weird with Whitney?"

Harmony hardened her gaze. "Is he?"

"You don't see it?"

"Honestly, I think Dominic is just clinging onto someone who doesn't see what he does in himself. I don't know how he looks in the mirror. Whitney sees something in him and he is probably starved for that kind of attention. I don't think it's sensual or anything." Harmony raised her brows. "Your sister left here this morning with a very cute blonde on her arm."

"Bryan is a nice guy. She loves him."

"I'm sure but he's powerless and she should leave him alone."

I tilted my head. "You think Whitney should be with Dominic instead?"

Harmony laughed into her coffee. "I think Whitney should focus on the task at hand. She doesn't need any distractions."

"So...if this is intrusive, tell me to shut up, but if water and fire are the twin flames..."

Harmony sighed, staring into the flames of the fireplace. A sadness took over her gaze. "Nicky was my best friend. He used to be fun and loud and brave. He once jumped off a cliff into the lake and I followed without a second thought. I loved him, but that person died a long time ago. I don't know the man who came back in his place."

"I'm sorry, Harmony. That's heartbreaking."

She shrugged, retreating back into her coffee. "I've already mourned him. The important thing now is dealing with Erebus and the Renai. Anything else is irrelevant."

CHAPTER THIRTEEN

MORNING AFTER

WHITNEY

The soft glow of dawn peeked out from behind the curtains as I opened my eyes, taking a moment to remember my surroundings. As warm skin pressed against my back, the night before came rushing over me.

The Shadows. The near death experience. Bryan's clothes in a pile on the hardwood.

I picked up my phone from the nightstand and tapped the screen. 7:36 in the morning. A little less than two hours until I had to clock into work. Unsurprisingly, there were no unread texts waiting for me. Radio silent on all fronts. I couldn't tell if that was reassuring or not.

"Good morning," a sleepy voice mumbled in my ear. Stubble scratched my skin as Bryan nuzzled his face into my neck.

"Morning." I rested my hand on top of his, our fingers intertwining.

He groaned, freeing his hand to pinch the bridge of his nose and rubbed at his eyes.

I turned towards him. "Are you okay?"

"I slept in my contacts."

"Anything I can do?"

"No, it's okay. I have my glasses in the Jeep."

I threw the covers back. "It's time to get up anyway."

"Mmm. I'm not ready," he groaned, pulling me in closer.

"It's almost eight. Amilia needs to look at your shoulder and I have to get ready for work." I tried to get up, but Bryan only tightened his grip. "Wait, it's a weekday."

"Mmmm."

"What time does your class start?"

"It's online, baby, there is no set time."

"I almost got you killed last night, I don't want to mess anything else up for you."

"You're a bad influence." He flashed a tiny smile.

"Come on."

"No." Something unsettled stirred in his gut. It felt like fear.

"What's the matter?"

"Nothing, I just...Nothing."

"Talk to me."

He sighed, unable to look me in the eyes. "It's nothing."

"Baby." I cupped his cheek in my hand and tilted his face towards me.

He looked away from me with heavy eyes. "Last time we were together, you disappeared on me. You didn't even stay the night."

"Oh." I bit my lip as my heart fell into my stomach. "I wanted to stay the night, but Brooke had a Shadow incident."

"I understand, but you can't blame me for being a little apprehensive to get out of this bed."

"I'm sorry. It's different this time, I promise."

He nodded. "We have a lot to talk about, Whit."

"Do we? About what?" I furrowed my brow, confused on what more there was to say.

"Last night," Bryan answered. "The last month...We just, we should talk about it when the threat of death isn't hanging over us. Not right this second, but...eventually."

I opened my mouth to speak but he had already gotten out of bed to search for his clothes. I sat on the edge of the bed, pretending the anxiety over this impending conversation wouldn't be hanging over me for the rest of the day. He slipped his pants over his hips and looked around the room.

"I came here wearing two shirts and now I have none," Bryan sighed, rubbing his face.

"I have an extra hoodie I left here. It's really big on me, so it might fit you."

"I have a change of clothes in the car, it's just getting to the car."

"No one should be home except Amilia," I reassured him.

I was wrong.

"Mornin'," a sly voice greeted us as Bryan and I entered the kitchen. Nic lifted his coffee mug to his lips, raising his eyebrows as he took a drink.

"When did you guys get in?" I asked, ignoring his insinuation.

A half-naked Bryan shifted awkwardly next to me.

"Late," Nic replied.

"And you found what you needed to destroy the ledger?"

Nic nodded. "All we have to worry about is how to nab it." His eyes wandered to Bryan, looking him over from head to toe.

"This is Dominic. He's a witch too, a pyro like Rayn," I explained to Bryan. "Nic, this is Bryan. Um, you want to go get your shirt?"

"Mhmm." Bryan nodded and left the room.

Nic set his mug down and picked up a spatula, moving scrambling eggs around in a frying pan on the stove. He glanced over his shoulder as Bryan closed the front door behind him. "He's cute."

"He's Rose's brother," I answered.

Nic scrunched his brow. "I see the resemblance."

"She's going to be pissed."

"I'm not following."

"You said yourself the Renati would use anyone we care about against us."

"I did." Nic set down the spatula and turned the fire off. Leaning his back against the counter, he folded his arms across his chest.

"He's already in danger of that." I shifted my weight and looked away. "Us being together makes it worse."

Nic laughed, actually laughed at me. "That isn't how it works, Whit."

Bryan came back into the house with a hoodie and his glasses on. Returning to my side, he slipped his arm around my waist.

Annoyed, I mirrored Nic's pose and crossed my own arms. "Enlighten me, Dominic."

"If he's important to any of you, the Renati will exploit that weakness. There's no double whammy because he's important to both of you. Being Rose's brother is what's going to get him killed. You fucking him is a foot note. If anything, *you* should be mad at *her*." Nic waved his hand towards the spare bedroom down the hallway. "Speaking of, you should probably change the sheets before you leave."

"I don't see how any of it is your business," Bryan finally spoke up, his voice sharp.

"I suppose not. Whether the Renati kills you isn't really on my radar." Nic took a plate down from the cupboard.

"Don't be a prick." I resisted the urge to step forward and smack him in the head. I hated how hot and cold Dominic behaved. One moment he seemed so genuine and pure and the next he acted like a total asshole.

"Here, your keys were on the counter." Nic ignored my comment and slid my car keys towards me.

"Oh." I picked them up. "Rayn must have left them."

"She was asleep on the couch when we got home." Nic shrugged.

"I recognize him," Bryan said, leaning towards me.

"From where?" I asked.

"I saw you two together at the Corner Cup," Bryan replied, not taking his eyes off Nic, who pretended not to notice. "Right before Thanksgiving."

"Really? Why didn't you say anything last night?" I asked.

"We were a little preoccupied."

"Bet you were," Nic muttered into his coffee.

"Dominic, that's enough." Amilia walked into the kitchen with Harmony close behind her. "How is your shoulder, Bryan?"

"Still sore but it doesn't hurt like it did last night," he answered.

"May I?"

Bryan pulled up his sweatshirt and Amilia removed the bandage, exposing three pink lines where the cuts once were. Healthy skin healing perfectly well. The mixture Amilia put on the injury last night worked like a charm.

Amilia whispered, "Remarkable."

Harmony scoffed, peering over Amilia's shoulder. "That was not a Shadow."

"It was," I snapped, glaring at her.

"I don't think so. He would be dead right now." Harmony said like I hadn't heard it a million times. Like the weight of that fact wouldn't sink in unless she told me.

"I know what I saw. You weren't there." I brushed Harmony off. "Did you find anything last night in your reading, Mia?"

"Nothing that mirrors this incident, no." Amilia folded the used bandage in half and glanced up at Bryan. She patted his shoulder and he pulled his hoodie back into place.

"You sure he's powerless, Mom?" Nic asked Amilia.

Amilia studied Bryan. "I don't know anything for sure."

"I don't have powers," Bryan answered. "I'm pretty sure I'd know if I did."

"We're clearing his memory after this, right?" Harmony asked as casually as you'd ask someone if they were hungry.

"Excuse you?" I took a step in front of Bryan, looking from Harmony to Amilia. Bryan's heartbeat pounded through his chest.

Amilia turned to Harmony. "Absolutely not."

"But he knows too much," Harmony argued back.

"He isn't a threat." Amilia put her hand on Bryan's shoulder. "He's a good kid. He's been coming into my coffee shop for years. Plus, the girls mean too much to him for any of that nonsense."

"A threat remains whether it's intentional or not," Harmony protested, but luckily Amilia wasn't having it.

"I would never let them do that, Byn." I tightened my grip on his arm.

"Byn?" Nic scrunched his face, stretching out the syllable of Bryan's nickname. *Ben.* "I thought your name was Bryan?"

Bryan ignored him.

"I think you're going to be fine." Amilia smiled up at him. "I can send you home with something for the pain in case it flares up again."

"Thank you, but I should be okay. And thank you for everything you've done." Bryan checked his pockets to make sure he had his things. "We should get going."

"Drive safe," Amilia said.

I turned to Bryan and whispered, "I'm going to hang back for a bit, and then head to work. Is that okay?"

"Oh, sure." Bryan walked to the front door as I followed closely behind.

"Are you mad at me?" I asked quietly.

"No, of course not." Bryan reached out and cupped my cheek in his palm.

"But you still want to talk about us later..."

His thumb swept across my cheek. "It's not a bad talk. I just have things I need to say."

"So say them."

He glanced towards the kitchen. "In private. Don't stress over it, okay? Everything is okay. I love you."

"I love you too," I said, still stressed over it.

"I'll let you know how things go with Rosie. Stop worrying. I'll take care of it."

I pushed myself up on my toes to kiss his lips. "I'm going to have a talk with Ray tonight too, but tomorrow night I'm all yours."

"Sounds perfect." He kissed me goodbye and left out the front door.

Harmony walked into the dining room the second the door closed behind Bryan. "Whitney, powerless boys are fun to play around with but you don't bring them home."

Nic broke into a fit of laughter before anyone could respond, resting his shoulder against the entryway between the kitchen and dining room. "Classic case of pot and kettle."

"Pardon?" Harmony glanced over her shoulder at him.

"You literally did the same thing, didn't you?"

"My choices are none of your goddamn business," she snapped. "Speaking of home life, when are you going to see your mother?"

"I'm not," Nic answered, any trace of humor drained from his face.

"You've been gone for years. If you're going to be home, you need to go see your mother."

"I did come home to my mother," Nic answered, glancing over at Amilia, who had wandered into the living room to flip through another book from the bookcase. With all the years she'd known them, Amilia seemed to have perfected tuning them out.

"It's cruel to let her think you're dead. Seriously, it's the most self-centered thing I've ever seen someone do and that's saying a lot, even for you. I know you have your differences and you like to pretend she didn't bring you into this world, but nothing changes the fact that she's your mother and she deserves better than what you're–"

"Shut up," Nic snapped, his voice booming. "Shut the fuck up, Harmony. I'm not a teenager anymore, you can't boss me around and make me do whatever you want. I'm not putting up with your shit."

Harmony blinked, burning holes into him with her icy gaze. "I suppose that's fair. Your actual mother may not be able to face the man that took both of her children from her."

"Harmony Elizabeth, how dare you." Amilia shot around so fast she nearly dropped her book.

Harmony made her exit out the door attached to the kitchen without another word, leaving it open behind her. Nic didn't move. He stood frozen in place, I studied his chest to make sure he still breathed. His eyes glossed over in a haze of shock and hurt. Whatever Harmony meant, her words cut Nic to his core.

"She didn't mean that." Amilia took a step forward, reaching out for Nic but the damage had been done. He disappeared down the hallway and into his bedroom with his tail between his legs.

"What the hell was that?" I asked Amilia, confused as ever.

"Old wounds that have been allowed to fester far too long." Amilia tossed the book onto the couch with a thud as she marched out the back door after Harmony.

I didn't have a lot of time before I had to clock into work but I couldn't bring myself to leave the cottage until I made sure Nic was alright. I stripped the bedding from the guest room and started a load of laundry, making a mental note to remember Bryan's undershirt was here.

With a deep breath, I gently tapped on Nic's door and listened for the slightest sound to indicate I could come in. Nothing. I knocked again, harder this time but still no response.

"Nic?" I asked, slowly turning the handle. "You okay?"

"Not right now, Whitney." I barely heard his voice.

I pushed the door open anyway. "Nic."

"I said not right now."

"I heard you."

He sat on the floor with his back against the bed, his knees pulled into his chest with his hands buried into his thick hair, hiding his face in his tattooed forearms. That stupid skull ring stared back at me. Nic curled himself into the tightest wound ball of hurt I'd seen in a long time.

I sat down on the floor next to him. "I know you've been out there on your own for a long time, but you don't have to be alone anymore." I reached out and gently touched his arm. "You said you don't have any friends left in this town, but here I am."

"I thought we weren't friends," he muttered, still hidden in his cocoon.

"I could have gone off to work but I'm here, on the floor. Isn't that what friends do?"

Nic finally lowered his arms, wrapping them around his legs. His cheeks were wet, streaks of tears glistening in the sunlight shining through the sheer curtains on the window. His hazel eyes met mine and my heart shattered onto the hardwood.

"Talk to me."

"Remember when I told you that you reminded me of someone?"

I nodded, waiting for him to continue at his own pace.

"I had a little sister, Katie. She would've been around your age. I was supposed to be watching her but I got distracted and she wandered off. She went to the backyard and fell into the pond. By the time I found her..." Nic's voice caught in his throat. "She was only three."

My eyes watered as unimaginable sorrow washed over me. "Nic, that wasn't–"

"Don't you dare say it wasn't my fault," he snapped, another sob caught in his voice. "Harmony knows I've never forgiven myself and my mother never forgave me either."

"Harmony is a bitch," I stated. "How could she use it against you like that if she knew how it would hurt you?"

Nic shrugged. "I'm fine, just caught me off guard."

"Nic, you're not fine."

"Yeah, well, it's been a lot to take in at once. I knew it would be when I made the decision to come back." His heavy eyes met mine. "I don't regret coming back, as difficult as it's been."

"I hope not. We wouldn't have gotten this far without you. We wouldn't have gotten out of Dragonfly Mystic alive without you."

"That's what I'm here for. Daring rescues and witty one liners."

"I'm really sorry about Katie, Nic."

"And I'm really sorry about Audri."

"Guess none of us have had it easy."

Nic rubbed his arm. "Generations of old lived like royalty and we're a bunch of anxious orphans. Punishment for old crimes, I suppose."

"Guess so."

"I'm fine, really. Hey, before you go." Nic hopped up from the floor and opened the top drawer of his dresser. "Here."

Nic handed me a piece of paper with rips on one of the sides from where it had likely been torn out of some book. Across the top of the page was a spell title that made my heart drop.

Portal Travel.

"Will this open the portal in the meadow? Close the Shadow Realm portal?" I lowered my excited voice, skimming over the instructions. "The potion looks too simple. Blood and intent? That's it? How much blood are we talking about?"

"Not much." Nic shrugged. "Magic doesn't have to be complicated."

"Opening a portal feels complicated. Tom had a chalice with black sludge in it and our blood was drawn in a circle on the floor. It was a legit ritual." I shivered at the memory.

"That kid wasn't an Elemental."

"That makes a difference?"

"It makes a huge difference. So how this works is, when someone opens a portal, only they can close it, because it was opened with their life force. This potion should allow you to open the portal in the meadow. Consider it a practice run for the Shadow Realm portal," Nic answered. "You'll have to use your generation's blood on both of them so hope you aren't afraid of breaking the Elemental Code."

Amilia had told us about the Elemental Code, the rules of magic imposed by generations past to protect witches from the darker side of our powers. Certain magic was deemed forbidden, such as blood magic and necromancy.

"Where did you find this?" I asked. "One of Mia's books?"

"Oh, no. Mia doesn't have anything against the Code in her stock. I got this from my recent travels." Nic smirked.

"So Mia knew all along that nothing she gave us had anything to do with the portals." Anger brewed in my stomach.

Nic leaned against the dresser. "I don't know what she was thinking, but portals are against the Code and she has always stuck to that Code. It's like she thinks if she practices any magic the Elementals disagreed with, she'd be no better than the Renati. So, I think we can assume."

"Even though we are Elementals who are saying the Code is outdated?" I tilted my head.

Nic licked his bottom lip. "We aren't *really* Elementals to her though. We're her kids and her best friend's kids. She still knows better than us, don't you know?"

"You actually care," I whispered, my voice getting caught in my throat. "Everyone else is stringing us along but you actually think we can do this."

"I know you can, and I'm not the only one. Everyone else has their own methods."

"You're the only one that doesn't treat me like a child."

"That's because you aren't a child. You're the ones who opened the Shadow Realm portal, you're the only ones who can close it."

I pondered for a moment. "You said you've been through the portal in the meadow a bunch of times. Do you know who opened it?"

Nic's face went pale as he nodded slowly. "Our spirit user, Finn."

"It doesn't take an entire generation to open portals?"

"Little ones, no. But ones between the realms, yes."

"So, Finn is the one who closed it too?"

"No," Nic answered, taking a deep breath. "No, he's dead."

"Then...how did the portal close?"

"I genuinely have no idea, but it's been keeping me up at night."

A chill crept through my body. "Is there any chance he isn't actually dead, like you weren't actually dead?"

"I wasn't around towards the end but from what Warren has told me, it didn't end well for Finn. He had addiction problems and he, uh, he killed himself."

"Oh...that is alarming then."

"Nothing we won't figure out. Don't stress over it, I'm on it." Nic shoved my shoulder playfully. "Get out of here."

"Okay."

Halfway out the door, I heard his voice again. A tone of sincerity that hadn't been there since the first day I met him. "Thank you for listening."

I turned back around and gave a soft smile. "Someone has to keep your big head on straight, Nicky."

That morning when I got to the Corner Cup for my shift, we were busier than usual. The holiday crowd was out in full force, everyone getting their morning fuel before they faced their ever-growing to-do lists. Robby worked with one of the new hires Amilia had brought on a few days ago, helping them make drinks they weren't familiar with. Ashley stood with Lauren at the register, watching over her shoulder as Lauren learned how to input orders. It felt like a lifetime ago that I stood clueless with Ashley behind the counter. I had been so wrapped up in the hectic night, I completely forgot about Lauren's first day.

My phone buzzed in my pocket as I put my bag in my locker. Seeing Rayn's name on the screen sent a rush of relief through my body.

I love you. Everything is going to be fine.

I closed my eyes and let out a deep breath. Regardless of how everything else played out, as long as Rayn and I were okay, I'd be okay.

"Hey, guys," I greeted everyone after I got my apron and clocked in.

"We've been slammed," Ashley said as I appeared behind the counter, still tying my black apron behind my back.

"Where do you need me?" I asked, scanning the line at the counter that almost led to the door.

"Dining room is a mess."

I nodded, grabbing an empty tub and a wet rag. I cleared dirty plates, wiped crumbs and spilled coffee off tables. When I made it back to the counter, the tub was full and my rag was in desperate need of a rinse.

"Here, I'll start the dishwasher." Robby took the tub from me as I rinsed out the rag in the small sink.

"Shit," Ashley sighed, running her hands through her red curls as she glanced at her watch. "We are about to hit five hours. We need to take lunch, Lauren."

"Okay," Lauren said. "Even though it's so busy?"

"Amilia will be pissed if we hit five hours without lunch, it's a labor law issue." Ashley turned to me. "Whitney, can you take over the register?"

"Got it." I squeezed the water from the rag and greeted the next customer with a smile.

"Why do we feel short staffed?" Robby asked Ashley as he came out of the back room.

"Call out," she complained. "I'm going to take a nap in the back."

About twenty minutes later, a gap in the rush came and I nearly collapsed against the counter.

"Holy shit," Robby mumbled, giving myself and the new guy, Luke, a high five. "Good job, guys."

I started tidying up around the register when Lauren came through the employee only doors and sat down on a bar stool at the counter.

"Finally slowing down? Ashley will be relieved, she's been stressed out all morning," Lauren replied, picking at her fingernails.

"Are you doing okay? Hell of a crowd for your first day." I glanced up at Lauren, finally getting a good look at her; dark circles under her eyes. Her blonde hair tied up in a short messy ponytail with small strands sticking up in all directions.

"I'm fine. I actually came out here to see if you're okay. Brooke texted me about last night. What happened?"

"Not here." I glanced around at all the eaves dropping ears. "But I'm okay."

"Sorry I wasn't there. I was up at the hospital and fell asleep. I heard you weren't alone last night. Is *he* okay?"

I nodded.

"Everyone is pissed?"

I shrugged. "I can't stay away."

"I get it. I personally couldn't care less. Not that I don't care about you, I do. I mean I don't care who you bring home, or who they happen to be related to."

"Thanks."

"Have you talked to Rose yet?" Lauren lowered her voice.

"No, he's going to do that today. It's probably better coming from him anyway. She'll at least hesitate before she strangles him." I sighed. "Last night was a mess."

"Yeah, it sounded scary, but you got your man back," she smiled.

"Wait." Ashley appeared from the back room out of thin air, standing next to Lauren at the counter. I didn't even see the doors open. "Wait, wait, wait. Are you and Byn talking again?"

My face heated. "We, uh... He came in last night and we figured some things out."

"That's great!" Ashley squealed. "Aw, he's been such a mess the last month since you guys got into that, whatever it was. He wouldn't tell me shit. *And* that means he'll finally start bringing me lunch again. Wish I'd known this an hour ago."

"Order pizza," Robby added to the conversation. "Seriously, I'm starving."

"I'll chip in," the new guy, Luke, said.

"Saints, all of you." Ashley retrieved her phone from her back pocket and began to dial.

I looked back to Lauren smiling at me, the first genuine smile I'd seen since she came back. I reached out across the counter and rested my hand on hers.

"I'm glad you're home," I admitted. "And not because we need all five of us together. You're the only one who would talk to me the days before Halloween. You didn't hate me then, or right now."

Lauren nodded. "Everyone is too hard on you, including yourself. I've got your back, Whitney, no matter what happens. Founders Day is coming up, so maybe we'll be able to make some headway on this whole mess."

CHAPTER FOURTEEN

'TIS THE DAMN SEASON

WHITNEY

Founder's Day was off to a lively start as the town gathered to celebrate the founding of Rifton and the beginning of the holiday season. Rows of booths were set up; local businesses and independent vendors selling jewelry, baked goods, jarred jams and homemade ciders. Several booths sold homemade remedies as health potions and spell jars. Part of me wondered if these were real witches hiding in plain sight or powerless townsfolk playing into Rifton's niche for a profit. Now that Dragonfly Mystic had burnt to the ground, someone would fill the space it left behind. If these were witches, were they Renati or were they like Mia? How many Elemental supporters remained in hiding after the majority of them left town?

Dmitri and I followed behind Rayn as she shopped through the different vendors, a mason jar of peach cider and one of blackberry jam in her arm. I reached out to feel the soft petals of a poinsettia at a booth where Rayn exchanged pleasantries with the owner.

I turned to Dmitri and smiled. "I bet you'd make bank at a place like this. You're a better artist than that guy over there." I wasn't sure he'd reply. Dmitri and I hadn't necessarily made up after our argument, but at least after a few days we had stopped ignoring one another.

He glanced over at the booth I referred to and shrugged. "Art is subjective."

"Hmm." I hummed.

Dmitri let out a deep sigh and turned to face me. "Hey, I'm sorry about the other day. I think I imploded from holding everything in, and the whole meeting with the school just sent me over the cliff."

My heart melted hearing his apology and I reached for his hand. "I'm sorry that I forgot about the meeting."

"There's been a lot going on." Dmitri shrugged a shoulder. "I miss Abe and I miss Mom. You aren't doing a bad job, I'm sorry I said that."

I pulled him into a hug and rested my head against his chest. "It's easy to blow up on the people who love you, because you know they'll still love you afterwards. I'm guilty of it too. Whatever we have ahead of us, we're going to tackle it together, okay?"

I felt him nod as he returned the hug.

"They're going to be announcing the founding families soon," the woman on the other side of the table said to Rayn.

"Oh, thank you. Good to see you again." Rayn smiled at her before turning back to Dmitri and I. "We better get out there. Where are the girls?"

"I haven't heard from them yet, but we can catch them up when they get here." I stepped out of Dmitri's hug and looked back at the florist Rayn had spoken to. "You know her?"

"I told you I went to those places on Nic's list. Her shop was one of them," Rayn answered.

"Think she's Renati?" Dmitri asked.

Rayn shook her head. "I don't think so, but I'm keeping an eye on her."

Dmitri, Rayn and I left the vendor tables and took our spot in the crowd. My knees trembled, the bones rattling together from the uncertainty of where the night's events would lead. If we were lucky, we'd be able to blend into the crowd and go unnoticed. I didn't feel any Shadows watching us, but the uncertainty still put me on edge. Thinking about how every member of the Renati in Rifton knew our faces yet we knew so little about them made the whole idea of being incognito almost comical but we should be safe as long as we stayed in public. None of them were stupid enough to try and kill us in the crowded town square, right?

It felt like everyone in town was out on the chilly night, even though the cold had arrived in full force. I had grown up in the snow, but this was different. The wet cold of the Pacific Northwest left a bite as the icy breeze blew through the streets. A shiver slithered up my spine as Rayn wrapped her jacket tighter around her body and adjusted her beanie to cover her earlobes. I wore a hoodie with no hat or gloves.

"Hey, have they started yet?" Rose's voice came up behind us.

"Not yet. One of the vendors said they're going to announce the families soon," Rayn replied.

"Every year, like royalty." Brooke nodded, scanning the crowd. "They parade the descendants of the founders around like they built the town themselves with their bare hands."

"Think they're all...you know?" Dmitri asked, watching his words now that we were in a crowd.

Brooke shrugged. "Probably. I can't see how they wouldn't be."

Rayn sighed. "Kind of giving themselves away when you think about it."

"To who?" I asked. "No one but us gives a fuck."

"It's weird watching the town celebrate like nothing is going on," Rose muttered, looking around at the crowd forming around us.

"That's because they don't know the truth," I answered quietly, watching the high school band set up off to the side of a makeshift stage in front of a giant pine tree.

"Mmhmm," Rose answered.

I tripped over my thoughts as the silence fell between us, trying to form the perfect sentence to explain to Rose how I tried to stay away from Bryan. How I agonized for weeks staring at his name on my phone screen, tempted to press call or hit the send button on the million text messages I deleted. I stayed away for Bryan's own good, but I did it for Rose too. For my friend who only ever asked one thing of me and I wanted to honor my word. I didn't fall back into Bryan's arms because I didn't care about breaking my word to Rose.

My thoughts were cut short when a man wearing a heavy dress coat approached the microphone in front of town hall. "Welcome to the 175th Annual Founders Day Celebration! It is my honor to start off by announcing the members of the founding families who serve on our council."

175 years. As the high school band began to play, I wondered if Mom ever came to these when she was younger. If she would stand out in the cold with Amilia and their friends, bundled up with hot chocolate to bring in the holiday season together.

"Greg and Alice Mullins along with their children, Jackie, Janey and Junior."

"All J names," Rayn scoffed. "So tacky."

I laughed with her as the first founding family took the stage, dressed up in their Sunday best. The young girls wore matching dresses and the son wore jeans and a sweater, same as his father. I imagined the hours their mother spent coordinating outfits and settling on a color scheme for the night's festivities.

"Sean and Emily Glover with their son, Connor."

As the second family took the stage, Rayn's hand squeezed mine. I winced at her sudden movement, turning to see panic in her dilated pupils.

"That's Tom's cousin, Connor," Rayn whispered, searching the crowd as if the ghost of Tom Campbell would be amongst the audience.

"You met him?" I asked, putting my other hand over Rayn's in an effort to comfort her.

She nodded. "The day I went up to the lake with them. We went out on Tom's uncle's boat. I had no idea he was on the council."

"Hey, it's okay. They're distracted. They don't even see us," I reassured my sister as the memories of Tom's bulging eyes flooded my memory. The sounds of him gasping for air as he died by my hands. I shook them away as the next founding family was announced.

"William and Tamara Ward."

An older couple walked onto stage next, hand in hand. Older than Mom or Amilia. They could have easily been grandparents. They stood out like sore thumbs next to the younger council members and their families.

A shiver slithered up my spine as the last family took the stage.

"Henry and Bonnie Drake along with their daughters, Emma and Serenity."

The Drakes stood at the end of the stage, smiles plastered across their faces as they waved at the cheering crowd. Serenity and Emma stood close to one another, their smiles fooling everyone. They looked like the perfect family, all beautiful and happy. The kind of family who takes vacations together and posts perfect social media photos. The kind who would sit in front of a well-manicured Christmas tree in matching pajamas with a fluffy dog in the middle.

I doubted anyone knew that their daughters hated one another and their father was an attempted murderer.

Henry Drake sent a chill through my body. The lights above the stage reflected off his black, greasy, slicked back hair. His dark eyes smiled as they scanned the crowd until they finally rested on me. He did a double take at first, but it didn't take long to realize he knew exactly who the girls and I were. He smiled, a genuine pleasantry that made my stomach churn, as he soaked up the reality that we had gone there to see them. As if he got off on the idea of being the center of attention. I wanted to put an icicle straight through his heart and watch him bleed out on that stage, but I took a deep breath. Moments like this were what separated us from the Renati.

"Uh, hey, let's go get some hot chocolate or something. Mit, B?" Rayn nudged Dmitri and Brooke, pulling them towards the food trucks to leave Rose and I alone.

Bryan had let me know that he and Rose talked and everything was fine. He never told me exactly what they said or if they fought. We had yet to have the talk that wasn't supposed to be bad either. In this case, I assumed that no news was good news, especially since Rose still showed up and didn't hit me on sight.

Rose's quiet voice spoke again. "I wonder how many people here are Renati, not realizing who we are. Or how many of them are good-hearted witches who have been led astray. How many of them are hiding their powers because of this ledger."

"I wonder the same thing," I answered, letting her words sink in. "It's hard to tell. The more I learn, the more I realize how much Amilia is keeping from us."

"It's nearly impossible to protect ourselves when we are wearing blindfolds."

"You sound like your brother," I said without thinking.

Rose's face changed. Her smile vanished and her eyes met mine, completely unreadable.

"Um," I stammered. "I've been meaning to bring it up. I swear, I'm not hiding anything from you. I'd never do anything to jeopardize our friendship again. I just–"

Rose stopped me, putting her hand up. "Bryan already talked to me. He came over to the house and we talked for a long time, actually."

"He told me you talked but didn't give any details. Um, was it a good talk?"

"Yes." Rose smiled but the expression didn't match her eyes.

"Be honest with me. I'm not an empath but I can tell you aren't happy."

Rose blinked. "Honestly, I'm not, but Bryan is. I'm worried about everyone. There is so much going on and after what happened with Lauren's parents...I don't like waiting around to see who will be next," Rose admitted, her gaze heavy.

"I know, that's why we need to stay a unified front." I took in a deep breath, the cold air clouding in front of me. "You aren't mad at me?"

I was desperate to clear that up. I didn't want another fight amongst my generation. We had just gotten Lauren back and I couldn't bear to lose Rose.

"Not anymore."

I sighed in relief. "That's nice to hear."

"The truth is, I was so angry over the fact that he got close to you without knowing the truth about what we are that I didn't see how happy he was. I haven't seen my brother smile that much in so long. If you truly make him happy, then there's nothing for me to be mad about. I only want him safe."

"I do too. I would die to keep him safe like I would die to keep Dmitri safe. But they love us, and they aren't going to sit by without trying to help. It's not in their nature. They're good brothers."

Rose gave a soft smile. "You're right. Thank you."

"For what?"

"For caring about him that much. I don't know what you know about Hannah and all that, but he's been hurt. He deserves something good."

"Hannah?" I asked, my heart dropping into my stomach.

"Oh...I've already said too much."

I opened my mouth to reply when Rayn, Dmitri, and Brooke came back with their hands full of hot chocolate. Rayn handed me a warm to-go cup and glanced back and forth between Rose and I.

"You guys good?" she asked.

"Yeah, everything's fine." Rose took her hot chocolate from Brooke.

"Good." Brooke scanned the unfamiliar faces around us. "There's Lauren."

I turned to the direction of Brooke's gaze to see Lauren and Ashley heading our way, both of them wrapped up in coats and beanies. Ashley talked with her gloved hands waving around in front of her telling a story. Lauren giggled, tucking a loose strand of her own hair behind her ear.

"Hey, babes," Ashley greeted as she approached our group.

"Hey, closed up CC early?" I asked.

"Yeah no one was coming in anyway and I didn't want to miss the tree lighting. It's my favorite part." Ashley glanced down at the cup in my hands and turned to Lauren. "Do you want some hot chocolate?"

"Yeah, sure. Thank you. I think I have some cash in here." Lauren reached for her purse but Ashley stopped her.

"My treat. I'll be right back."

"Thank you," Lauren repeated, a soft smile on her face as she watched Ashley walk away.

Rayn and I glanced at each other, knowing without having to say a word out loud. Rayn lifted her eyebrows and took a sip from her hot chocolate. *I saw that coming a mile away.*

"What?" Lauren asked, noticing the knowing glances.

"Ashley is super nice," I replied, taking a quick sip. "The sweetest girl I've met in town."

"That's hurtful," Brooke muttered to herself, playfully.

"Yeah, Ashley is nice. She's really good at her job," Lauren answered.

Rayn winked at her. "She's a lot of fun outside of work, too."

"I bet," Lauren said. "When is this thing supposed to start? It's freezing out."

"The hot chocolate will warm you up," I replied, taking another look around at all the faces.

"Hey," a voice came up behind me. I jumped as two hands wrapped around my waist. My heart leapt up into my throat and I nearly spilled my drink as I choked on it. My powers flared across my skin as I turned to face two wide green eyes.

Bryan quickly let go of me and stepped back. "I'm sorry."

"You scared the shit out of me," I breathed, putting a hand over my pounding heart.

"I'm so sorry. I wasn't thinking."

"It's okay. I'm distracted and didn't feel you coming." I reached out for his hand and stepped into his personal space.

He leaned down and gave me a quick kiss. "I'm too cold to feel anything."

"Here." I handed him my cup of hot chocolate but when he took it from my hands, he frowned.

"This is frozen solid," he said, squeezing the cup.

"Oh..." I laughed. "Oops."

He chuckled. "Guess we'll have to use each other for warmth."

"Guess so." I went in for another kiss as Bryan wrapped his arms around me, pulling me against his chest.

Ashley's voice piped up behind us. "Get a room! There are children here."

Bryan turned to her. "Oh, please. Like you never invite pretty girls to the tree lighting with impure intentions."

"That's enough out of your fat mouth." Ashley's cheeks turned a shade of pink as she cleared her throat and handed Lauren a cardboard cup.

Bryan rolled his eyes and turned to Rose. "Mom called about the car. Troy can look at it."

Rose lowered her voice. "I don't have enough money to fix it and Mom said–"

"Don't worry about it." Bryan cut her off.

"Byn, Mom said Jack will–"

"Jack isn't paying for your car," Bryan said, plain and simple. "I will work something out."

"Mom isn't going to be okay with that. Jack already pulled out some cash."

"She'll get over it."

I wanted to voice my opinion but it didn't feel appropriate. I knew Bryan wouldn't insert himself into a conversation between me and one of my siblings about finances. Bryan hadn't said much about his mom's boyfriend but I got the impression they didn't get along. Why else would Bryan have moved in with Troy and his dad when he was only nineteen?

The high school band stopped playing and the woman's voice came over the speakers, asking for another round of applause for the musicians. I turned towards the large unlit pine tree in front of us. Bryan snaked his arms around me, pulling my back flush with his chest and resting his chin on top of my head. He let out a sigh of comfort. I laced my fingers into his and leaned my weight against him.

"So, what about our talk?" I asked, unable to help myself. I had to know what he needed to say, it was eating away at me.

"I told you not to stress about it," Bryan whispered in my ear.

"I'm stressed."

Bryan sighed. "I'm sorry, I should never have said anything until I was ready to talk. You've had so much going on and I just added to it." He tightened his grip on me. "I just wanted to make sure we were on the same page, that we wanted the same things. I don't want to run into another incident where you push me away. I'm here for you, no matter what is going on. I want to be able to talk things out. Whether it's about you and the girls, or just you."

I turned around to face him, cupping his cheek in my hand. "I still want to keep you as safe as possible, but I will try. I won't push you away, I want to make this work."

"I also want to keep you safe," Bryan kept his voice low. "I know you're capable of taking care of yourself, but maybe you could lean on me sometimes?"

I smiled and turned back around, pressing my body into his chest. "I'm leaning on you now."

As the announcer began a countdown from ten, the rest of the crowd joined in with her. Anticipation and a sense of community flowed through everyone gathered; to share the moment officially bringing in the winter holidays. I looked down the row at our group meeting Dmitri's eyes. I knew he felt miserable in the middle of all these people but Brooke rested her head against his arm. Rose linked her arms with Brooke and Rayn on either side of her, pulling them close as she rested her head on my sister's shoulder. Lauren watched the massive pine with anticipation, counting down with the rest of the crowd. Ashley's eyes were on Lauren, glancing at her sideways but kept her face towards the tree so she could easily look away if Lauren caught her.

It wasn't until the crowd got to the last few seconds of the countdown that I turned back towards the tree in time to see the colored bulbs flick on all at once. The tree looked immaculate in the darkness, the brightly colored lights reflected off the reds and gold of the ornaments that hung from the branches. Handfuls of tinsel twinkled against the lights and a bright yellow star at the top tied it all together. Everyone clapped and cheered as the tree illuminated in front of the town hall.

A warmth spread through my entire being, beginning in my soul and washing down to my fingertips. Bundled up in the arms of the man I loved with good friends at my side. Seeing all the faces of Rifton's community made me want to protect them even more. I felt obligated as a member of this town, as someone whose mother had her roots buried deep in these woods. Rifton was my home and I would do everything in my power to protect it.

Lauren nudged me with her elbow. "I want to show you guys the Founder's Book."

Ashley laughed. "Really? It's kind of corny that they display it every year like the book built the town itself."

"It's tradition. Whit and Rayn are still new in town, they deserve the whole Founders Day experience," Lauren pressed, nodding her head towards a display case in front of the courthouse.

Ashley looked over at Bryan, who shrugged.

"It'll take five minutes," he said.

Lauren led the way through the dispersing crowd. The families who had taken the stage now mingled with the public, shaking hands and giving warm wishes for the holiday season. I scanned the crowd for the Drakes but they were nowhere in sight.

Glittery red bells hung from the streetlights with lit garland twisted down the poles. Wreaths hung from every door, adding the perfect touches to put everyone in the holiday spirit. Bryan reached for my hand, lacing his fingers in mine. He gave it a gentle squeeze as we approached the glass display case.

The ledger laid open on an old wooden pedestal with intricate carvings. The legs swirled into big claws that reminded me of a Shadow's talons. I leaned in to get a better look at the book itself. From the leather cover to the familiar parchment paper covered in old handwriting, it looked almost identical to our spellbook.

The book on the pedestal lay open towards the front, displaying the day the founding families arrived in the valley where they established Rifton. How the town would be a new promised land for their people. Their people. I wonder if the powerless in Rifton who came to Founder's Day and saw this old book knew the people they referred to were the same witches they whispered about.

I glanced back at Bryan, once I had his attention I nodded to Ashley and hardened my gaze.

"Ash, come here. Let's get a pretzel." Bryan put his arm around Ashley's shoulders and led her away from the book. Luckily, she didn't protest.

"So, this is it." Rayn came up behind us. "This is what's holding everything back."

"Even if we do destroy it, who's to say it'll make a difference," Rose mumbled, crossing her arms. "They have a sense of purpose now. They did something they've been trying to do for centuries, they have a cause...something to die for. We haven't delivered."

"How can we?" I turned to her. "We–"

"She's right." Lauren cut me off. "No more excuses. There isn't anyone else. It's up to us. We..." Lauren trailed off, her eyes to the corner, off in the distance. She let her thoughts go and turned to the edge of the festivities.

"What–"

"Shh." She cut me off quickly, turning her head to hear better. We waited in silence until Lauren turned back to face us. "Whispers from the enemy."

One of the first tricks Warren had taught Lauren was to listen. He said if you trained yourself, the wind had all sorts of information to share. It didn't seem like a very useful skill until I saw it in person.

"Vague," Brooke replied. "What did they say?"

A smile curved on Lauren's lips. "It's not safe to repeat here in this crowd, but it's good, don't worry."

"Good timing, because Bryan and Ashley are on their way back already." Rayn looked over her shoulder at the dispersing crowd. "Guess the line was short."

I wanted to press Lauren for more information, unable to wait until we were at the cottage to know what she'd overheard. As Bryan and Ashley approached, I met his eyes. He raised his brow, as if to let me know he'd postponed as long as he could.

"Have we admired this boring book long enough?" Ashley asked, taking a bite of her pretzel.

"Yes," I answered. "Sorry, it's interesting."

"Yeah I know, you're strangely into the history of Rifton. Anyway, Merry Christmas." Ashley wrapped an arm around Bryan's shoulder and pulled his face towards her, planting a kiss on his cheek before she kissed mine as well. "I love you guys."

"We love you. You headed home?" Bryan asked as Ashley wrapped her arms around Rose's shoulders and pulled her into a hug.

"Yeah, probably. I wasn't supposed to close tonight so I worked like a twelve hour shift." Ashley yawned. "The caffeine crash is finally hitting me."

"Thanks so much for all your help today." Lauren's voice shook ever so slightly. "I'd be so lost at that job without you, and Whit, of course."

"Us baristas gotta stick together." Ashley smiled at her. "I'll, uh, see you tomorrow?"

"Yeah, um, I'll be in at noon."

"Cool. Perfect."

I glanced up at Bryan, whose eyes lit up seeing Ashley and Lauren stumble over each other.

"Good night, lovelies." Ashley waved.

"Bye, Ash." We all bid our friend good night.

"I need to go too," Brooke said, pulling her phone out of her pocket to check the time. "Lauren, I need to know what you overheard."

Lauren scanned the remaining pockets of people still lingering from the festivities. Once she determined the coast was clear, we all leaned in towards each other. "They keep the book in Drake's home office when it's not displayed."

My head shot up to meet her gaze. "Seriously?"

Lauren nodded as a smile broke out across her face. "All we have to do is sneak in and take it."

"Easier said than done," Bryan whispered. "He locks the office when he's not in it."

"Good thing I can go through walls." The wheels seemed to turn in Brooke's head. "I'll get it, but I need him distracted."

Rayn glanced over to Bryan. "If you and Emma are really best friends then maybe–"

He cut her off. "No, Rayn, I'm not involving Emma in any of this."

"You don't think she'd do it for you?" I asked.

He shook his head. "I'm not going to ask. We'd be putting her in danger and I'm not doing that to her or Troy."

I nodded. "Okay, I hear you."

Brooke let out a sigh. "Let's meet up in the meadow and get a plan together. I really do need to head home before I miss my curfew."

"She's my ride, so I'll see you guys at the meadow," Rose said. She put out her arms and gave Bryan a hug. "Love you."

"You too." Bryan hugged her back. "Don't do anything stupid."

Rose chortled. "Take your own advice for once." Rose and Brooke left the town square arm in arm.

Rayn turned to Dmitri and asked, "This is pretty much dinner, so do you want to grab a funnel cake before the food trucks leave?"

"Funnel cakes aren't dinner," I heard my mother's words leave my mouth.

"They are tonight. Come on." Dmitri shoved Rayn's shoulder playfully. "You're paying."

"So, Lauren," Bryan spoke once everyone was out of ear shot. "How's your first week at the Corner Cup going?"

"It's busy but I'm so grateful to Amilia for the job. I don't know what I would have done if she didn't take a chance on me," Lauren answered, glancing over her shoulder towards the path Ashley had taken.

"Not to be too forward but you're her type, you know."

"Who's type?" Lauren whipped her head back to face Bryan.

"Ashley has a thing for tall, good looking blondes." Bryan smiled. "I mean, why do you think she's kept me around this long?"

Lauren chuckled, putting her palm over her mouth to hide a blush. "That's good to know, I guess." Lauren took a step towards Bryan and I, pulling us off to the side. "I, um..."

"What's wrong?" I asked, reaching out for Lauren's arm.

"Ashley is great but she's so confident in herself and I'm in such a fucked up place. She...she deserves better than all this." Lauren gestured up and down to herself.

I knew exactly how Lauren felt, exactly where her head was at. "Ashley is a good friend. She's loyal and compassionate. She's always there when you need someone to talk to or a distraction from your demons. Friendship is a really good starting point and if it goes from there, great." I gave her a soft smile. "And if not, you have one of the best friends I've ever made."

"Thank you." Lauren's eyes welled up as she looked over at Bryan. "Could you may be...keep this between us? I know you're her best friend but–"

"Yeah, of course," Bryan replied. "I'm sorry if I put you on the spot."

"No, it's okay." Lauren forced a smile. "You didn't do anything wrong. Ashley told me all about how she set you two up so I'm not surprised you'd try to return the favor."

"I like to think we would have gotten together without Ashley." Bryan glanced over at me, a smile in his eyes.

"She did drag me to that bonfire," I pointed out.

"I would have kept coming into the Corner Cup until I got the nerve to ask you out, bonfire or not."

"You're full of shit." I smacked his stomach playfully.

"Whitney, you had me at 'everything is fucking great, thanks for asking'."

"What?" Lauren laughed, completely lost but I knew what he meant.

"It's the first thing I ever said to him." I peered up into the night sky, the sea of stars above us twinkled in unison with the holiday lights on the buildings.

Chapter Fifteen

PACK OF WOLVES

Whitney

A few days later, Lauren, Rayn and I gathered at the meadow to attempt the portal spell Nic had found for us. We also needed to come up with the best course of action to break into the Drake's house and steal the Renati's ledger without getting caught. So far, we had a vague idea as to how we'd get in, but not how we'd distract Henry Drake. It couldn't be any of us, and we didn't have many people in common with the Drakes. Bryan would be too obvious, even though he was Emma's best friend. Drake knew Rose and I were Elementals, and he knew our connection to Bryan.

"Anything from Brooke or Rose?" Lauren asked, pulling her sweater tight around her chest as the crisp air chilled our bones.

"Rose said they're waiting for B's parents to let her leave." Rayn slid her phone into her pocket, discouraged. "We can't do much without them."

"They'll be here," I replied. "If we get Brooke in more trouble with her parents, then we won't be getting into the Drake's house for the ledger in the first place."

Lauren's head shot up, turning towards the tree line. Her eyes widened as she whispered, "Someone is watching us."

The bushes next to us rustled. The branches on the trees moved as if something large pushed them out of the way. The greenery parted as a large man, well over six feet tall with wide shoulders, stepped out into the clearing. He wore a black jacket with a black ski mask that covered his face. The mask made everything below his eyes look like a skull. The white bones and teeth glared at me as mercilessly as the man's glare.

My blood turned to ice at the sight of a black crossbow on his back and two silver pistols strapped on either side of his waist. Over half a dozen figures in the same black jackets emerged; fully armed with their faces hidden behind skull masks. All eyes on us.

What the fuck.

"Split up!" Lauren's voice carried through the breeze.

She thrust her hand out towards two of the men, creating a wind gust so strong it knocked them both on their asses. Once they were down, Lauren turned and sprinted across the meadow, disappearing into the tree line as her magic still tingled under my skin.

"Bring that one back," the man who appeared to be the leader ordered, his voice deep and angry.

Three of them ran off after Lauren, leaving Rayn and I alone with the others. My heart raced with fear and I reached for my sister's arm. As soon as I grabbed her, Rayn lifted her hand and threw a fireball at one of the men. He cried out and slapped the flames that spread across his neck.

I channeled the moisture in the cold air and shot thick icicles at the man closest to us. The dagger of ice went straight through his boot and he fell to the ground, screaming in pain.

"When the fuck did these abominations learn this kind of magic?" the man pinned to the ground called to his companions.

Rayn ran as fast as she could into the trees, pulling me along. I let go of her hand to jump over a log. I tried to keep up with her long legs, tripping over little things but never completely falling to the ground. Adrenaline ran throughout my entire body, giving me the strength to take the next step as my lungs and thighs protested.

We didn't get far when a sharp pain erupted in my back. Numbness took over my entire body as I let out a small cry and fell to the ground.

"Whitney!" Rayn cried as she collapsed beside me. A dart with a small black feather on it stuck out of her shoulder blade.

I made an attempt to use my magic but nothing happened.

I was trapped within my body.

One of the men walked up to my sister.

"Get away from her!" I screamed with a strained voice. I searched for the rest of them, but he was a lone wolf.

He towered over Rayn. Grabbing her by the neck, he lifted her off the ground and dropped her against an exposed tree root. She whimpered as she hit the ground.

"Rayn!" my voice cracked.

The man looked over at me with honey-colored eyes as he reached up for his crossbow. I stared at his hand, knowing he intended to kill us.

"Rayn!" I shouted again and crawled towards her.

The man froze in place. He stood still with his hand planted on his crossbow, staring down at my sister. The man's hand slowly retreated back to his side. His weapon remained in its holster. Rayn lay on her back, gripping the root of the tree. Her fingernails dug into the bark as she stared up at him with dilated pupils.

He took an unsteady step back. Rayn pushed herself up and leaned against the tree. Tears streamed down her face as the man looked over his shoulder and continued to step away from us.

"Run," he replied with a deep, chilling voice. "Run and never come back."

He turned and jogged in the opposite direction, leaving Rayn and I in the dirt. I crawled towards Rayn and threw my arms around her, using the tree to pull us both to our feet.

"Are you okay?" I whispered to her.

"No." She grabbed my hand and pulled. I looked for the man, but he was already gone.

I had no idea where we were or where to go. I knew we had to move forward rather than wait around to see if he was bringing the others. We got a couple of feet before Rayn tripped and fell to her knees. The sound of footsteps rushed up next to us. Fearful one of the men had returned, I put up my hand in defense but no magic came. I came face to face with strands of copper hair falling into frightened gray eyes.

"Abe?" I breathed.

"Come on," Abe Roberts grabbed my elbow. "We have to leave the forest before they come back."

"Who are they?" I breathed.

He raised his eyebrows. "Is now a good time for questions, Water Nymph?"

Abe took the lead, weaving through the trees, constantly looking over his shoulder to make sure we weren't being followed.

"Where are you taking us?" Rayn asked, putting her weight on me whenever she stepped on her left foot.

"Back to the trail head," Abe whispered.

"I still can't feel anything." Rayn snapped her fingers. "My magic is gone."

Nothing appeared in her hands. Nothing tingled under my skin like it normally did when Rayn used her powers. I tried to use my powers again, but nothing happened. I reached for my back and felt the dart and feather. Gritting my teeth, I pulled the dart from my skin and held it out in my open hand.

"Is that what they shot us with?" Rayn asked, reaching around to feel her back. I helped her remove the dart and closely examined the two of them. The feathers tied to the end were both jet black.

I tried to use my powers again. Frustrated, I closed my eyes and focused all of my energy on doing anything. To feel the water in the dirt below us or manifest it into my cupped hand.

Nothing.

The sound of crushing leaves snuck up behind us and I halted. Reaching out for Rayn, I prepared for one of the men in the masks to return.

Lauren.

"Are you guys okay?" she panted. "No way. Abe Roberts?"

"You took off and left us there." I stared at her in disbelief.

"I said to split up. I knew I could outrun them, and you had three less to deal with. Are you okay?" Lauren asked again.

"They shot us with these." I held out my hand and showed Lauren the darts.

"I can't feel anything and we can't use our powers, at all. We've tried several times," Rayn replied.

Lauren furrowed her brow. "You can't? But that's how I knew you were over here. I felt you use. If I could still feel it, that means you were having some kind of effect. Maybe these darts are temporary."

"We need to get out of the forest before they come back," Abe urged, scanning the forest.

As we moved, I became hyper aware of our surroundings. Every sound felt like one of those men coming after us. Every bird that flew above us warned that they were on their way. Lauren helped Rayn and I under branches and over rocks until we gained full feeling of our bodies again, and with it the aching in our muscles. My entire body trembled and my lungs squeezed in my chest.

Once the numbness completely faded, our powers came back. Rayn snapped her fingers, lighting a small flame, and I created a small pool of water in my hands. I sighed in relief as we trudged through the forest. Finally, we made it back to the car and I rested against the frame, cradling my head.

"What the fuck happened?" Rayn's voice shook. "Who were those people?"

"I don't know." I lifted my head and put my arms around her again, holding my sister close. The thought of losing her broke me. I reached for Lauren and pulled her in as well, and Rayn wrapped her arm around Lauren's shoulder. I couldn't be more thankful that we were able to make it out, that the stranger let us go. But who was he?

Rayn pulled out her phone and called Rose, telling her not to come to the meadow and meet us at our house.

I turned to Abe, addressing the elephant in the room. "Have you been out here in the woods this whole time?"

He looked like he had. His jeans were ripped at the knees and caked in mud. The zip up sweatshirt he wore was stained and wide open as if the zipper had been broken. His copper curls were a mess, sticking up in every direction.

Abe nodded. "Most of it."

"How are you still alive?" Rayn asked. "I don't know many people who can make it alone in the woods this long without some serious survival skills."

"I'm a witch," Abe chuckled. "You think I haven't been exhausting my magic?" He glanced down at his hands, dirt under his fingernails.

"So, what's your plan? Live out here forever?" Lauren crossed her arms. "That's not realistic."

"There's an abandoned hunting cabin not far. It's falling apart but it's a shelter, and no one has found me yet. I'll be okay." Abe blinked away the tears that began to line his eyes. He sniffled and turned his head away.

I reached out for him. "Abe, you have to come home. Your mom–"

"I can't." Abe backed away, shaking his head.

"We can keep you safe."

"No, you can't."

"But Dmitri..."

Abe winced. "I know. I miss him, but the Renati have been out here looking for me. I can't go home. I shouldn't even be talking to you but the hunters changed things up."

"H-hunters?" Lauren stammered. "I'm sorry, like, witch hunters?"

Abe nodded, scanning the parking lot. "I can't stay here. Please don't tell anyone you saw me, especially Dmitri. The less he knows, the safer he'll be."

"I can't keep this from him."

Abe's eyes hardened. "You have to. It's not a request, Whitney."

"You can't stay out here forever. Someone will find you eventually," Lauren said.

Abe's eyes lined with tears. "Yeah, I know, but the longer I stay away from everyone, the safer they'll be."

Lauren's voice caught in her throat. "It doesn't work that way. I ran off thinking I could avoid the Renati and they killed my mother. My dad is still in a coma and the investigation is going nowhere. You want that to happen to yours?"

I put my hands on his shoulder. "Janice is worried sick. She's lost weight and she's–"

"Stop, please." He backed out of my grip.

"You can't stick your head in the dirt and pretend it's not happening." Rayn crossed her arms. "Erebus is back. The Renati have something real to fight for. You're a loose end, Abe, and they're going to tie it up eventually."

He sighed, scanning the empty parking lot.

"No one is watching us," Lauren informed.

Abe shook his head, firm in his decision. "I can't go home."

"That's your choice. I protected your house but I can't do much else." I attempted to ignore the nausea swirling in my stomach.

Abe wiped a tear away. "That's all I can ask for."

"Can we bring you anything? Food? Clean clothes?" Rayn asked, much to my surprise.

He pondered, like his jerk reaction was to say no, but he nodded. "Yeah, I... need help."

"We'll bring you a care package," I offered.

"Shadows could be watching."

I stepped forward. "We'll risk it, for Dmitri."

Abe reached into his pocket and pulled out a light blue stone with lines of white and darker blue through it. He handed it to me as if I should know its purpose.

"What's this?" I asked, turning the smooth stone over in my hand.

"You've never used one?" Abe furrowed his brow in confusion.

I shook my head.

"It's a blue lace agate. It's enchanted. We can communicate through it," Abe said.

Rayn huffed. "Like a walkie talkie?"

"Not exactly. I have the mate in my pocket. It'll glow when I'm trying to get ahold of you and when we get close to one another, it'll vibrate. This way we can find one another and reach out without anyone knowing," Abe explained, pulling an identical stone from his pocket. "Watch."

He rubbed his stone with his thumb and the stone in my hand began to vibrate, a warm glow surrounding it.

"That's incredible," I breathed.

"It'll be nice to have someone...I've been out here alone for...Anyway, rub it when you're ready to meet and I'll come back to this area."

"Thank you, for getting us out of there," Rayn told Abe. "I never thought I'd be saying this, but it's good to see you."

"Don't worry about me, just please keep Dmitri safe." Abe disappeared into the woods.

I had no idea who the witch hunters that attacked us were, but Abe Roberts saving that day was an even bigger surprise. No way in hell I'd be able to keep this from my brother.

"Why didn't they shoot you with those darts?" I asked Lauren.

"They shot *at* me, but they missed. I didn't realize they were shooting magic dulling darts," she replied. "I thought if I went in a different direction, it would split them up, making it easier to get away. I climbed up one of the trees before the three men who came after me finally caught up. They couldn't see me. A few minutes later the others showed up. One of them mentioned he saw where you two had gone and they all followed him. But he took them in the opposite direction I felt your magic coming from."

Rayn's hands trembled as she spoke. "The man who led the group away let us go. I thought he was going to kill us, but he told us to run and never come back."

I clenched my jaw in an effort to keep from getting sick. The meadow had been a safe place; our sanctuary since we moved to Rifton. The place we had opened up and exposed our true powers to Rose, Brooke, and Lauren. Where my siblings and I came to escape. And now those men were there in our sacred place with crossbows and guns trying to kill us.

Why were they trying to kill us?

"Fuck," I muttered, taking the car keys out of my pocket and setting them on the roof of the car. A throbbing shot through my leg where the keys had stabbed me when I fell on them, the numbing dart finally wore off completely.

"Are you okay to drive?" Rayn watched me rub the sore spot on my leg.

"Yeah, I think so," I answered, attempting to ignore the pain.

Luckily, we had a short drive back to the house. A jolt of pain shot through my leg every time I had to press my foot on the clutch but I winced through it. My heart pounded in my throat, throughout my entire body. I leaned into it, focusing on each pulse as we ascended down the winding road into Pines Row. That pulse kept me alive, centered. We wouldn't be safe until we were back in the small cabin with the doors bolted shut.

When Rayn, Lauren and I finally stumbled through the front door, we let the facade fall. Rayn began to cry, her knees hit the floor hard. She held her face in her hands as she sobbed.

"Woah! What happened?" Dmitri jumped up from the couch and put an arm around Rayn's shoulders.

"There were men in the meadow, with guns," Lauren's voice shook. "They chased us and tried to attack but one of them led the others away and allowed us to escape."

"What?" Dmitri shouted in disbelief. "Are you hurt?"

He scanned all three of us up and down. A mixture of fear and concern consumed his brown eyes.

"They shot us with these darts. We could move, but I couldn't feel anything and I couldn't use my powers. I still feel really weak. They knew we were witches." Rayn rested her head against our brother's chest and sobbed. "I'm so scared, Mit."

"I got you." Dmitri gently rubbed her back and led her to the fireplace.

Silence fell over our group. I don't think any of us really knew what to say. There were millions of thoughts racing through my head but I couldn't put any of them in words. I didn't doubt the others were struggling to do the same. My eyes wandered over to the chairs around the table. Holding mom's moonstone ring to my lips, I slid to the floor. I counted the legs of each chair over and over in an attempt to bring myself back down as the reality of what we'd gone through sank in. One. Two. Three. Four.

"He acted like he wanted to hurt us, but when he really looked at me he got the most tender look in his eyes. He told us to run. We made it as far as we could until whatever they shot us with wore off and we could feel and use again. I don't know who they were," Rayn whispered, her eyes staring off at nothing in particular.

"Who was this man?" Dmitri asked.

"I don't know, he never said. They were wearing masks that looked like skulls," I answered.

"What would have happened if he hadn't let you go? You could have died out there." Dmitri's words weighed me down until I stood an inch tall. "How do you keep getting yourselves into situations that nearly kill you? Do you have a fucking death wish?"

I had never seen him so angry. When we buried Mom he had been eerily silent. When Abe went missing, there were cracks in the shell that allowed the tears to fall. Lately, his anger had been a harsh chemical radiation after the blast of an atomic bomb.

"Mit–" Rayn tried to speak but Dmitri stopped her.

"I'm coming with you every single time from now on. I'm not staying home anymore, not when you can't keep yourselves safe."

"Mit, we aren't in danger at the cottage. The meadow is in the middle of the woods, danger comes with the territory."

Dmitri scoffed at me. "Danger comes with the territory. No, Whitney, you go searching for danger."

"That's not true," I argued, resting my back against the wall.

"Say whatever you want but the truth is there." Dmitri shot me a glare.

A knock at the door made all four of us jump.

"I got here as quickly as I could." Brooke brushed past Dmitri as he opened the front door. Her face flooded with worry as she slid her backpack off her shoulder. "What happened? I don't understand."

"I'm so sorry for the hold-up." Rose sat down next to me, pulling me close to her. "Brooke's parents are being dicks. Are you okay?"

Brooke sat down in front of the wood stove next to Rayn, who hadn't left the comfort of the flames since Dmitri sat her down.

"There are men in the forest with crossbows and skull masks," Rayn muttered, holding her knees close to her chest.

"What?" Brooke turned to face me in disbelief, as if she waited for me to tell her this was all a bad prank.

"We were in the meadow," I began with a deep breath. "And these men came after us."

Rose's eyes widened. "Crossbows?"

"Why would anyone want to hurt you?" Brooke put her arm around Rayn's shoulder.

"Isn't it obvious?" Lauren asked from the couch. "They know what we are. They're witch hunters."

"But *how*?" Brooke asked her next question.

Rayn shrugged and rubbed the dark circles under her eyes.

"Maybe the spellbook will have something about them," I replied.

Brooke pulled off her backpack and laid the spellbook on the floor in front of us. "Show us something about these men in the forest."

The spellbook hadn't needed direction or coaxing in the past but it hadn't budged since Halloween night. We all held our breath, sitting and watching the spellbook like it could twitch at any second. Nothing happened. The spellbook sat as motionless as it did at the Corner Cup.

"Maybe it's broken," Lauren muttered under her breath. "We broke it."

"Or maybe it's telling you to stop chasing after things that could kill you," Dmitri leaned up against the wall with his arms folded across his chest.

"But Mit, we–" Rayn argued, but he cut her off quickly.

"No. I wish you had seen the looks on your faces when you came home. The three of you were terrified, you're still trembling."

"We have to at least figure out who they are and what they want with us. Even if we never go back to the meadow, we still need to figure out how they know about magic," Rose said, meeting Dmitri's disappointed gaze. "If they know about witches in Rifton, more people than us are in danger."

"Add it to the list," Dmitri muttered and went into the kitchen.

The spellbook lay open on the floor. I stared down at the aged parchment and the handwritten text when the pages trembled. I shot up as a chill ran through my body. My mind must have been playing tricks on me. I held my breath until the pages trembled again and *finally* the spellbook came to life.

"Look!" I shouted, falling to my knees next to the text.

The pages began flipping towards the back of the book. Dmitri rushed back into the living room. He and the girls crowded around the book, all of us watching with wide eyes as the spellbook decided where to settle. Finally, the spellbook slowed but the page that stared up at us was not a spell.

Brooke leaned forward. "This is from Gabriel's portion of the book, the pages on spirit healing." She turned the spellbook towards her and skimmed the page. "I don't understand, I've read all these entries already. Why would the book want us to see more about mending the soul?"

"Better yet, what does this have to do with the hunters in the woods?" Lauren's gaze met mine over the spellbook.

I shrugged a shoulder. "Maybe this is a way for us to protect ourselves from this?"

"There's only one way to find out," Rayn said, like she had already figured out the answer to all of our problems. "We are going back to the meadow."

"No, you aren't." Dmitri clenched his jaw.

"Yes, we are!" Rayn argued. "We have to. Maybe they left a clue or something. We'll never know until we go and look for ourselves. I left my bag by the trees, everything but my phone was in there."

"Rayn–"

"Dmitri, I love you, but this isn't up to you." Rayn shot him down. "What do you girls think?"

"I think I'm not in a big hurry to get back up there," Lauren muttered.

I could see how badly my sister wanted to get back to the meadow, but Lauren and I were on the same page. After what happened, how could any of us want to rush back up there and search for clues?

"Ray, we need to give it enough time to make sure those men are long gone before we go anywhere near the meadow again," I explained to her. "It's the safest way to go about this."

"It kind of seems like the safest way to go about this is to stay away from the meadow altogether," Brooke spoke up.

Rayn shook her head, not accepting any of it. "No. It's the only way."

"The only way to what? Get us killed?" Rose asked.

"To find answers." Rayn groaned in frustration. Her powers tingled under my skin as the flames in the fireplace danced.

"Let's give it a couple of days, okay? Let the shock of getting attacked wear off. We will decide what to do then." When I saw Rayn's irritation only grow in the fire, I attempted to reason with her. "This is an opportunity for us to sleep on it. If we actually get any sleep, that is."

"That's a good compromise." Brooke linked her arm in Rayn's and nestled against her side.

Rayn sighed and leaned into Brooke. "Fine, we'll sleep on it."

CHAPTER SIXTEEN

SHARED TRAUMA

RAYN

I hadn't thought being a hostess would require much work. Greet people at the door and walk them to their table. But Giani's was a different ball game. The restaurant was packed every night for dinner as if it were the only one in town. Every single night.

And I was already pissing people off. Not intentionally, I genuinely wanted to keep this job. I didn't realize I had been playing favorites by keeping Bryan's tables full instead of spreading the wealth. After one of the servers came at me, claiming partiality, I realized I had actually been doing it. Oops.

Even unintentionally, I wasn't surprised. Of course I favored Bryan over the other servers. Beyond his relationship with Whitney and his relation to Rose, I had grown to care for him in my own right. A feeling I'd never felt for any of the idiots Whitney messed around with back in Kansas, but Whit had been able to keep her past in the past and I...well, I wasn't.

Now the servers at Giani's barely spoke to me, but that didn't matter. I didn't work to make friends, I worked to make money. But my feelings were still hurt and my feet were still sore. Sighing, I dragged myself through the front door of the cottage. I should have gone home, but Whit was at the Corner Cup and Dmitri was dropping off his weekly homework at school. And I didn't want to be alone.

"Hello?" I shouted into the seemingly empty house. "It's Ray, is anyone home?"

"Hey." Lauren came out of her bedroom with her cellphone hanging limp in her hand.

"You okay?" I asked her, noticing the metaphoric rain cloud above her head. The air felt thinner in the house, making it hard to take a deep breath. "You feel off."

Lauren wet her lips. "I just got a call from the funeral home...they want me to stop by."

"Oh," I whispered.

"Pick up my mom...her urn."

I closed the space between them, moving across the living room to pull Lauren into my arms. I was the only one in our generation even close to Lauren's height and I pulled her in with ease. Lauren welcomed the embrace and rested her head on my shoulder.

"I don't know what to do," Lauren muttered against my jacket.

"I'll come with you, if you want," I offered. "This isn't something you need, or should, be doing alone."

Lauren nodded. "Yeah, come with me, please."

"Right now?"

"I think if I put it off, I'll never go."

I released Lauren from the hug and linked our arms. "I understand. Want me to drive?"

"I can drive. It's not far from here."

Lauren remained quiet most of the drive, the radio playing quietly in the background to fill the silent void that had fallen between us.

I had a million things to say, a million little pieces of advice. I knew how it felt to go to the funeral home to pick up the remains of your parent, all too familiar with the consuming emptiness. The disassociation. Pretending to be literally anywhere else because acknowledging being at a funeral home made it real. I stayed silent, unsure if any of my words would bring Lauren comfort or not. Did I need to speak or was my presence enough?

"Did you have to do this with your mom?" Lauren finally broke the silence.

I nodded. "Yeah, we have our mom's urn in Whitney's closet."

"The closet?"

"That's just where we put it. I was terrified it would be broken on the drive. I wrapped it up in a blanket and kept it in the backseat of the car." I cleared my throat. "When we got to the new house, Whit put it up in her closet to keep it safe and we just haven't touched it since. I don't know, it feels weird because it's her, but it's not her. The photos on the wall feel more like her than a box of ashes."

"I didn't know that," Lauren answered softly as we pulled into the parking lot. "It doesn't feel real."

"It won't. It still doesn't for me either. Especially when you're blindsided with it." I paused. "I know it doesn't take any of the pain away, but I know how you feel. You aren't alone."

"Thanks." Lauren gave a faint smile as she stared down the building. "I guess we should go inside."

"Whenever you're ready."

We sat in silence for another moment before Lauren got out of the car. I followed her, taking in the eerie quiet of the waiting area. Low, peaceful music played in the background of the room covered in delicate colored flowers; soft pink and white arrangements in neutral-tone vases. This was only the second funeral parlor I had ever been in, but they both felt the same.

Lauren checked in and we were told it would only be a moment. I sat down in the closest chair and Lauren sat next to me, letting out a deep sigh.

"I'm so sorry," I apologized, not knowing what else to say.

Lauren didn't reply for a minute. "Do you remember me saying my parents are actually my biological aunt and uncle?"

"Yeah, I remember."

"My biological mother is my dad's sister. He's lying in a hospital bed, and his wife is dead, and you know where *she* is?"

I shook her head.

"Me either." Lauren sniffed, wiping a stray tear that fell down her cheek. "Not that I want to see her. I don't. But her brother is in a coma and she's off doing...I don't know what. Probably drunk on someone's couch. She doesn't care. Not about him, or me. I know this has nothing to do with her, but it's like she's giving me up all over again." Her voice quivered as she spoke. "The first time she left hurt, but the more she did, the less I cared. I had my parents and so it didn't feel so isolating, but now...Now my mom is gone and my dad may not wake up, and the woman who birthed me is still choosing her addiction over me. And now I don't have anyone."

I took Lauren's hand in mine and said the only thing that came to mind. "Moms are complicated."

"Doesn't sound like yours was very complicated."

"She was." I offered her a small smile. "She kept secrets and lied. She feels like two different people. The mom that we knew, and the woman she actually was."

"I feel like two different people sometimes," Lauren admitted.

I sighed. "I think when we are kids, we forget that our parents are just people too. They have flaws and make mistakes. This is their first time living life too, and I always thought my mom was perfect because she was my mom. I didn't realize she was a human being until she was gone."

Lauren stared across the room, biting the inside of her cheek. "I understand why your mom did what she did, keeping things from you guys. I kept all kinds of things from my parents. But in the end, it didn't protect them. And your mom keeping stuff from you didn't protect you, either."

"She tried." I tightened my grip on Lauren's hand. "*You* tried. The Renati would have come either way and if you had been there at the house, who knows what would have happened. You can convince yourself that you would have been able to protect them, but we will never know for sure. None of this was your fault. The car accident that took my mom wasn't my fault, it wasn't Whitney's either, but we all still carry the guilt around."

Lauren didn't speak. She sat quietly, wiping tears away as they fell.

I continued. "Sometimes things just happen."

"This wasn't a car accident. This was deliberate, this was calculated," Lauren sobbed. "They came for the bracelet *I* left behind. They came for my parents that *I* left unprotected."

"Lauren, I don't know how many of them came to the house, but you wouldn't have been able to fight off all of them alone."

"I could have tried."

"And I could have gotten a ride home, but I didn't. Your mom wouldn't want you to beat yourself up over this. She would have wanted you safe. She was your mom. I know she isn't the mom who gave birth to you, but she's the mom who chose you, and I, better than anyone, understand the gravity of that. Our moms would have given themselves in our places a million times over. No matter what you and I could have done differently, our moms would not have changed a thing. You know that in your heart."

Lauren leaned in, resting her head on the crook of my shoulder. Her back bobbed as the tears took over. I held her as the shield of anger and revenge Lauren had built crumbled. Lauren's heart cracked open and I clung to her. Even though I had more time to process losing my own mother, and more time to begin healing, the thin scab formed over my broken heart ripped open and I felt the heavy loss of my mom all over again.

When I closed my eyes, memories flooded through me; the impact of the truck slamming into the side of our car whiplashed me against the window. Glass shattered around me all over again, but it never touched me. The glimmer of the shield my mom had put up surrounded me and the shards bounced off. It wasn't until the car skidded to a stop and I looked over to my mother that I realized the shield only surrounded me.

It took me a moment of deep breathing to bring myself back into the funeral home. My vision cleared as I clung to Lauren's sweater. I wiped my own tears from my face and cleared my throat.

"Miss Thaner?" A voice startled both of us as it filled the silence that had fallen over us.

Lauren pulled herself away from me and sat up straight. "Yes?"

"We are ready, if you are."

"Yes. Yeah, I'm ready." Lauren stood up from the chair with shaky hands, following the woman.

I wasn't sure if I should go with her or not, but Lauren didn't say a word or look over her shoulder. I stayed in my chair, trying not to look around the waiting room. It had been set up differently than the one back in Kansas, but the vibes were there all the same. The thickness in the air weighed down on my shoulders and sunk my heart into my stomach. A lump formed in my throat as I tried to imagine myself anywhere but there. But no matter how hard I tried, I was back in Hemston sitting in between Whitney and Dmitri, waiting to retrieve our mother's remains.

This shouldn't be something for Lauren and I to share. No one should have to go through this as young as us. We should have been older. We should have already lived long lives, maybe with partners and children when we buried our mothers. Our mothers deserved to be there for the milestones and the mundane moments. The weddings and the quiet dinners on a random Wednesday night. The graduations and trips to the movies.

I shook my head. I would do whatever I could to support Lauren, just as Whit and Dmitri had been there for me. As absolutely infuriating as my siblings could be, they were my grounding force.

Lauren came back into the waiting room, holding a small wooden box in her hands. She stared down at it like she carried a bomb ready to detonate at any moment.

I stood up from my seat and met her across the room. "You okay?"

Lauren barely nodded. "Let's go."

I followed her out to the car, a million words on the tip of my tongue, but I wasn't sure what to say. I didn't know if there *was* a right thing to say. We climbed into the car, and Lauren held the box in her lap. She stared down at it, her face unreadable.

"Thank you for coming with me," Lauren finally said.

"Of course." I smiled at her, but the smile faded as my question came out. "What are you going to do with the urn?"

"I don't know," Lauren admitted. "It's not my decision alone to make right now. I think I'll just hold onto it until my dad...If he wakes up, then we will decide together, and if he doesn't..."

"You don't have to make that decision alone either, you have us," I reassured her. "You're one of us, and we will be here through all of it."

"Thank you. I'm not sure I deserve it after the way I acted in the beginning."

"Oh, please, you think I'm never a brat?" I forced a laugh, trying to lighten the heavy air that hung around us. "We all have our moments, Lauren. That doesn't make you any less deserving of love and forgiveness. That's what friendship is, giving people space to be all the different versions of themselves."

"You are really wise, Ray." Lauren started the car and backed out of the parking space.

I smiled, hoping I had made this difficult event easier for Lauren. It didn't take the pain away, and it didn't bring either of our mothers back, but we were able to go through it together. I knew the hard times would keep coming, but we would be able to face anything if we leaned on one another.

"I'm going to change the subject for my own sanity because there's something I want to talk to you about," Lauren said, turning to face me at the next red light. "What happened in the woods with the hunters?"

"You were there," I replied.

"Not when that guy let you go. Why would he do something like that?"

I paused. I had been wondering the same thing. I played the events of that day on repeat in my head over and over, trying to pick it apart. None of it made sense. One moment, the hunter loomed over me, ready to draw his weapon. And then he wasn't. The moment our eyes met, he halted. Like a switch in him had been turned off. His eyes had been so vicious, full of hatred, and the next...honey. Rich pools of amber.

"Rayn?"

"I can't explain it."

"You know, if you wanted to keep anything between us, I wouldn't tell Whitney. I love her but I understand."

I paused, chewing on my bottom lip. "I'm not trying to keep anything from Whitney."

"I know...I don't think we should either." Lauren shifted in her seat. "I guess what I meant to say is, if you wanted to talk but weren't ready to talk about it with her, I understand and I'm here."

"I can't stop thinking about why he let us go...I keep feeling the pull that we should go back to the meadow."

"The pull?"

I turned to face her. "Yeah...You know, when something yanks at your gut to send you one way or another?"

"Intuition."

"Yes, exactly. My gut is screaming at me to go back, even though I know it may not be safe. I know those men could come back, but I can't ignore the pull. Part of me is hoping they are there, that *he* is there, and we can finally get some answers. So we can figure out who those men truly are and why he let me go." I glanced out the window, watching the world pass us by. "Why he looked at me like I was too precious to kill. I know it sounds crazy."

"You don't sound crazy," Lauren said in a soft voice. "I don't know if Whitney will go back to the meadow, she is pretty traumatized."

"Then I'll go alone."

"Absolutely fucking not," Lauren snapped. "We will all go together, all five of us. We're stronger together. No way in hell are you stomping up there alone when there are witch hunters running wild."

"And if the girls refuse?"

Lauren sighed. "I will help you convince them. We'll follow the pull."

Chapter Seventeen
The Hallow
Whitney

I wasn't expecting to see Bryan's Jeep parked in front of my house when my shift ended. I double-checked my phone to make sure I hadn't missed any texts from him as I opened the door.

Bryan and Dmitri sat side by side on the couch playing video games. They stared intently at the screen, pressing buttons and pulling triggers on the controllers. I didn't recognize the gaming console sitting on the floor or the game they played. Bryan must have brought it over.

"Hi," I greeted the house, closing the door behind me.

"Hey!" Rayn called from the kitchen.

"Hey, baby." Bryan smiled. He set the controller down and met me by the door.

"You died!" Dmitri called, moving to the edge of his seat, focused on the task at hand.

"Worth it." Bryan gave me a kiss. "How was work?"

"Long. I didn't know you were coming over."

"Oh," Bryan paused, rubbing the back of his neck. "Is that okay?"

"Of course! It's a pleasant surprise."

"Mit mentioned he's been wanting to play Halo." Bryan motioned towards the television.

"I like coming home to you." I smiled and gave him another kiss. "Let me get changed and I'll come hang out."

By the time I changed into sweats and a long sleeve, Bryan and Dmitri were back to their video game. Dmitri's shoulders relaxed as he reclined into the couch. He laughed, actually laughed at whatever Bryan leaned over to say. I had almost forgotten what Dmitri's laugh sounded like.

A knock at the door pulled my attention as Rose's magic tingled in my stomach, letting me know who was here. I opened the door to let her and Brooke in. "Hey, guys."

They kicked off their snow covered shoes and Rose slid a backpack off her shoulders, scanning the living room.

"Fancy seeing you here," Rose smiled at her brother, plopping down on the couch between him and Dmitri.

Brooke settled on the floor at Dmitri's feet. "Are you winning?"

Dmitri laughed. "Trying to."

"Did you bring the spellbook with you?" I sat down on Bryan's other side. His hand quickly found its way to my thigh.

Rose reached for her backpack and slipped the spellbook out. She handed it over across Bryan's lap. I ran my fingers along the familiar parchment. It had become a comforting feeling, like a safety blanket. I flipped the book to the familiar map I kept opening up to every time I got my hands on it.

"You and that damn map." Rose shook her head, watching me take solace in the book.

"I can't help it."

"What's the map of?" Bryan asked, kissing my shoulder as he glanced at the pages.

"Wait, you can see the map?"

He nodded. "It's ripped in half though."

I side glanced at Rose, both of us wide-eyed and confused.

She looked at her brother. "Byn, you shouldn't be able to read that."

"Why not?" he asked.

"It's cloaked," I explained. "Powerless people are supposed to see an old encyclopedia."

Brooke turned to face us. "You aren't powerless, Bryan. You can see the spellbook *and* survived the Shadow poison."

"I don't have powers," Bryan argued as a hint of fear swam through him. "I've never had a spark of magic."

"Maybe he just needs some training?" Dmitri suggested.

"Amilia asked if you guys had any other witches in your family? Maybe there is magic in the bloodline or something," I said, looking at my friend for any answers.

Rose sighed. "If there were, they never told us. Grandma always had that weird insight, now that I think about it. Always knew when someone was coming over before they got there."

"You think Grandma was a witch?" Bryan shifted his weight.

"She could've been, we don't know."

I studied the mountain line on the map, like the ink on the parchment would answer all of my problems. As if this map would tell me who those men in the forest were, where the Renati were hiding, or how to close a magical portal.

Closing my eyes, I took a deep breath; a feeble attempt to center myself and use my intuition like Amilia always talked about. She said the answers were inside of us but lately, I felt microscopic.

"What happened in the basement of the Dragonfly broke our spirits. Maybe that's why the spellbook hasn't shown us anything useful since," I muttered.

"I'm sorry I haven't been there to help when these big things happen. My stupid parents and their fucking grip on me. I feel like I'm failing you guys, like I'm never there to help protect you," Brooke admitted, hanging her head.

"That's not true, B." Dmitri put his hand on her shoulder.

"I'm glad you weren't there," Rayn said, leaning against the wall.

"I wish none of us had been there." Rose stood up from the couch, stretching out her back.

"Me too." I turned back to my map.

Lauren burst through the front door without knocking, sending a chill through my body. Everyone in the room leapt to attention as a cold breeze hit us.

"Guys!" Lauren shouted, closing the door firmly behind her. "You'll never believe—"

"Jesus, Lo, you scared the shit out of us." Rayn put her hand over her heart and hunched over.

"Oh, come on, I texted you that I was on the way." Lauren flung her bag off her shoulder and rummaged through its contents. She pulled out a folded piece of paper and rushed to me, handing it over. "I was left alone in the cottage and decided to take advantage of it. Look what I found in Warren's bag."

"You went through Warren's bag?" Brooke clarified, her voice full of surprise.

"Of course I did. Look at it!" Lauren waved her hands at me.

I unfolded the aged parchment carefully. Half of a page with a sketch of a mountain ridge sat before me. The tip of the tallest mountain had a sharp edge that resembled a bird's beak and two wide peaks next to it, like wings spread wide open.

"Wait...is this?" I'd recognize the jagged edges of the page anywhere. I'd only been staring at the other half for weeks.

Lauren nodded with a smile. "Yeah, I think so."

"What are you two talking about?" Dmitri leaned in close to see.

I placed the torn page Lauren found along the ripped edge of my favorite map. A golden light outlined the jagged edges as the two pieces of parchment fused together. The completed map looked less like a map than it did before.

Ink bled through the bottom of the page, showing two words. A title.

The Hallow.

Everyone huddled around me, watching the page come to life before our eyes.

"Oh my god! This place on the map is called the Hallow. I think we're supposed to find it." My heart raced in my chest.

"I know Rose recognized a few of the maps are in Europe, how are we supposed to find our way to the Hallow?" Rayn asked. "What if it's not on this continent?"

"I'm a bit more concerned with why this half of the map was hidden in Warren's bag," Lauren replied. "They wouldn't be hiding it from us if it wasn't important."

I let the realization of our discovery wash over me. "If Amilia's daughter's ghost led us to the book in the first place, their generation must have known it was there."

"And they never told you?" Bryan asked.

Lauren huffed. "There's a lot they hide from us. As if things aren't hard enough."

Bryan leaned over my lap, taking a closer look at the finished map. "Kind of looks like Falcon Ridge."

"Falcon Ridge?" I asked.

He nodded, looking over at the girls who had also grown up in Rifton. "Doesn't it?"

"Oh, shit!" Rose exclaimed. "It does!"

"Falcon Ridge is a peak in Falcon Bay, it kind of looks like a bird, hence the name. It's been worn down over the years but I imagine when this book was made, it looked more like this." Bryan explained.

"Wait, so this is only a few hours away?" I clarified.

"Falcon Ridge is. I don't know about the Hallow," Bryan said.

Brooke crossed her arms. "We should ask Warren why he hid this map from us."

Lauren scoffed. "So he can find out I went through his things? Amilia would kick me out of the cottage for sure. We'll get to your map, Whit, but we have other things to deal with first."

"That's right, we have a potion to make." Rose hopped up from the couch. "You have everything, Rayn?"

"Yep, all here in the kitchen." She paused. "We should, uh, do this in my bedroom. The five of us. Easier to focus, you know?"

Bryan and Dmitri looked at each other. "Another match?" Bryan asked, reaching for the controller.

I pressed a kiss to Bryan's cheek and grabbed the spellbook, following behind the girls to Rayn's bedroom.

This time when we made the unwanted guests potion, we made sure to set our intention to all Renati members *and* the witch hunters. Hopefully this time we'd avoid what happened with Tom Campbell. The potion was intended to keep out unwanted guests, but Tom had pulled Rayn in close enough that he was not an unwanted guest.

Rose poured the bright blue liquid into a glass bottle as Rayn grabbed a folded map from her dresser.

"We haven't tried scrying for the Renati hideout," Rayn suggested.

"Do you think that'll work?" I asked.

"Only one way to find out," Brooke replied.

Rayn laid out a map of Rifton on the carpet. We had read about scrying in one of Amilia's books, it was about time to test these extra abilities she talked about. Rayn unhooked a clear crystal at the end of a thin silver chain from around her neck and dangled it above the map. She let the crystal swing in its natural pattern. Back and forth.

Rose closed her eyes. "Everyone focus."

Taking in a deep breath, I ran my fingertips along the scar on my forearm. I closed my eyes and focused on the Renati. My body began to warm with anger as hatred came over me like a thick black sludge. I didn't think it possible to despise someone as much as I did Serenity Drake. I breathed deeply, trying to center myself and overcome these emotions but it felt hopeless.

The crystal made a noise as it touched down on the map. I barely opened one eye, enough to see through my eyelashes as my heart pounded in my chest.

The crystal had landed on the gated community of Diamond Gate. Rayn's crystal sat on top of the Drake's house.

"I doubt they're hiding down the street from me," Brooke muttered.

"Sorry, I was thinking of Serenity," I admitted, turning my arm over to hide the scar she'd given me.

"Why weren't you looking for Erebus?" Rayn asked.

"I got distracted," I whispered.

Rose let out a deep sigh, her brows heavy with concern. "I'm distracted too. I heard about something today."

"What's going on?" Lauren asked.

"The missing girl, the one from the flier? They found her body. I've heard people talking, they think it's a mountain lion but–"

I rubbed my face with my hands. "These Shadows are getting worse."

"Shadows or hunters?" Brooke asked.

"We have to do something about the portal," Rayn said. "We have to go back to the meadow and practice that spell Nic gave us if we stand any chance of closing the portal at Dragonfly. The longer we wait, the more Shadows are getting out."

"You're right," I agreed. "But what about the hunters?"

"We are going to be prepared this time. We know what we are up against."

"They have weapons, Rayn. They have darts that can keep us from using our powers..."

"So we won't get hit. We have weapons too, Whit."

"Before you say no," Lauren spoke up, turning towards me. "We made this potion to keep unwanted guests out of the meadow. We need to practice on that portal anyway. We'll all go together, it's safer that way."

I looked around at the girls. "You all want to go?"

"Yes," Rayn answered too quickly.

Brooke nodded, but remained silent.

"For the portal, yes," Rose said. "We'll go back to the meadow."

I trilled my lips, defeated. "Fine."

The girls and I tried scrying again, this time all of our attention focused on Erebus. The crystal spun around the map in circles, never landing on one specific spot. Wherever the Renati were hiding him, it was well cloaked.

When I left Rayn's bedroom to walk the girls out, Dmitri lay passed out on the arm of the couch. Bryan sat on the other side with a pen and notebook in his lap. He glanced up and quietly waved to Rose, Brooke and Lauren as they left.

"Mit," Bryan reached over and gently shook his shoulder. "Get in bed, dude."

"Hm?" Dmitri lifted his head before he stumbled to his bed in the corner of the room.

I walked over to Bryan, glancing down at the familiar gray journal in his hands. "Whatcha writing?"

"Just brain dumping," he answered, closing the notebook with the pen holding his place.

I offered him my hand, pulling him to his feet. "I'm exhausted, let's go to bed."

He followed me to my bedroom and closed the door behind us. I flopped down on the bed, hugging my pillow. Defeat was a feeling I'd frustratingly grown used to.

"Guess whatever you were doing in there didn't go well?" Bryan asked. He set his notebook down on my nightstand and pulled off his shirt.

"It'll be fine. Can I read what you were writing?"

He chewed on his lip and opened his notebook to a different page. "No, but there is something I wanted to show you."

Loving her is like seeing color for the first time. I had been living in a world of black and white, admiring the shades of gray. Never realizing I missed out because I had never seen the rich browns of her eyes or her dark red lipstick. The soft blush of her cheeks when she comes undone at my touch. The warm honey of her skin and the brightest aqua dangling from her neck. I never saw the color inside myself either, never appreciated the green in my eyes or the blue sadness that lived under the skin until she fell in love with it, simply and all at once. As if loving me were as easy as breathing when I spent years feeling like a burden.

Woah.

"You were never a burden," I said to him, closing the notebook.

"I know that now."

I grabbed his face and pulled him into a kiss, trying to somehow show him how precious he was to me. His words made me ache for the hurt he experienced before me, because of me. I ached to prove to him that nothing in my life had ever been as good as him, that nothing could ever compare. He kissed me back, pulling me close against his bare chest. We made out lazily, slowly admiring each other's bodies with my leg wrapped over his hips and his thigh pressed against my center.

Bryan broke the kiss and let out a heavy sigh. I nuzzled into him as he traced my spine. Bryan hesitantly tapped his fingertips against me. Even if I hadn't been able to feel his emotions as my own, I could tell from the way his chest rose that he wanted to speak, but let it deflate instead.

"Byn." I kissed his collarbone. "Say it."

His breathing steadied as he mumbled into my hair, "I really can't hide anything from you, can I?"

"What's on your mind?"

"Christmas," he finally admitted.

For some reason, that caught me off guard. Of course he would be thinking about the holidays. Christmas was less than two weeks away, and we had yet to discuss it. I didn't want to think about it, mostly because I had very limited resources to get presents for anyone. Rayn, Dmitri and I were skipping out on gifts this year anyway, none of us particularly feeling the spirit of the holiday.

"What about Christmas?"

"What do you usually do? I mean, I know this year is probably not..." He sighed again. "Do you have anything planned?"

"Not really. Amilia wants to have a Yule dinner for the Solstice at the cottage but if it's anything like Thanksgiving, I don't know if I even want to go. It was all family drama and too much wine. Though the girls will be there this time so that may ease the tension, I think."

"Hmm." His chest vibrated under my ear. "The Solstice. I guess I didn't really think about you guys not celebrating Christmas. I assumed."

I lifted my head to look at him. "We still celebrate Christmas. I think Amilia is happy to have some of her loved ones back after so long and Dmitri is finally coming around so she wants everyone to be happy. She's like everyone's surrogate mother."

Amilia had collected quite the gaggle of orphans.

"That's a lot of big personalities in one room. I caught a glimpse of it that morning when I was there. I can't imagine an entire day of that."

"It's self-indulgent," I answered.

After Bryan fell quiet, I realized I hadn't been reading between the lines. I should have known better by now. "What do you have planned?" I asked.

"Oh. Christmas is a big deal for my mom. Christmas Day is pretty laid back, but she always has a party on Christmas Eve. It's usually pretty big, secret Santa and eggnog. She puts a lot of effort into it."

"Wow," I whispered, a bit mystified hearing about it. It sounded like a Hallmark movie. The ones I would always put on around this time of year and pretend I had that kind of life. Thinking about it, I realized I hadn't watched a single Christmas movie yet this season. If it wasn't for the Christmas tree lighting downtown, I wouldn't have done a single festive thing.

"It would mean a lot to me if you came." Bryan's heart pounded in his throat as nerves tingled under his skin.

"To your mom's big party?" I clarified.

"Yeah. I want you to meet her." He bit his lip. "I want to sit with you by the fireplace and introduce you to all of the family friends. Sneak out back after a while with some spiced rum and kiss you in the snow. I want to show you off," he whispered, lifting my chin so he could gaze into my eyes.

"I don't have any nice clothes that fit."

"Whit, you can wear whatever you want."

"I can't show up to your mother's Christmas party in Vans and a Bad Religion t-shirt."

"Why not?" he smirked.

I let out a small laugh. "Bad Religion and your Catholic mother? Great Christmas mix. We'll go to mass together afterwards."

"Then I'll buy you a dress."

"What if she doesn't like me?"

"My mother?" He tucked a loose strand of hair behind my ear. "She's going to love you."

"How do you know?"

"Because there's nothing to dislike. She's my mom and I've told her how important you are to me. She wants you to come. You can bring Rayn and Dmitri too if it'll make you more comfortable. Emma and Troy will be there. It's always a lot of fun."

"Ash?"

"She'll be out of town, I'm sorry."

"Okay," I whispered, my nerves completely consuming my body.

"Don't be nervous," he said as if he was the empathic one. "I promise you'll have a good time. Bring Rayn and Dmitri."

"I'll talk to them."

"Good." He smiled and kissed my lips softly. "Now get some sleep before I'm tempted to keep you up all night."

"I'm awake now." I let my fingertips wander down his chest, taking in every inch of bare skin.

He let them move as far down as I wanted to go. "You were so sleepy a moment ago."

"How am I supposed to sleep when you're so handsome and write so beautifully?" I scrunched my nose and leaned into him.

He laughed, pulling me into another deep kiss. For the rest of the night, the hunters and the Renati all cease to exist.

CHAPTER EIGHTEEN

THE HUNTSMAN

WHITNEY

When Rayn, Lauren, and I pulled up to the trailhead of Eagle Loop the following day, Rose and Brooke waited inside Rose's parked car. I waved to them as we got out of the car.

"We figured it would be safer if we all went in there together," Brooke explained. "Plus, it started snowing."

"I'm glad you did," I told them.

Tiny flakes of snow fell from the sky, floating to the ground. The trees around us were dusted white and the cold seeped into my bones, sending a comforting chill up my spine. I looked up into the sky as a snowflake landed on my cheek. A soft smile swept across my lips as I took in a deep breath, centering myself.

"Let's go secure the meadow from these hunters and then we can see if this portal spell from Nic actually works," Brooke announced, turning down the trail.

I breathed in the fresh mountain air and took off after her. As we got closer to the meadow, tension rose as a lump in my throat. The meadow looked so different in the snow. Powder dusted the ground with blades of grass peeking through.

"Where did you drop your bag?" Brooke asked Rayn.

"Over there, by these trees." Rayn walked across the meadow, her footprints exposed more of the greenish-yellow grass. We looked around for a while, moving snow off of piles that looked like it could have been Rayn's bag, but we found nothing.

"Do you think the hunters took it?" Rose asked.

"They might have," I answered.

"Ugh! That had my wallet and everything in it! If they took it then they have our address and my name and my debit card!" Rayn panicked. "I'm going to have to get a new license."

"We'll keep looking," I offered, reassuringly.

Rose opened her bag and took the vials of the protection potion out. Unwanted guests would no longer be able to enter the meadow once we secured the perimeter. The meadow would officially be ours again.

"Do we have enough for the entire meadow?" Lauren asked, watching Rose carefully.

"We should." Rose transferred the vials into two spray bottles, careful not to spill a single drop. "It doesn't specify how much you need so maybe a spritz will be enough."

"That's genius," I remarked.

We broke off into two groups, each taking a side of the meadow. Lauren sprayed the tree line with the perimeter potion as Rayn and I dug in the brush for her bag. After Rose and Brooke finished protecting their side, they came to help us look.

A groan of pain echoed behind the trees and I turned my head towards the noise.

"What was that?" I asked, taking a step back.

The groan sounded again.

Rose took a few steps towards the moaning pile of snow as I reached for Rayn's arm. Rose used her powers to move the leaves and earth to reveal a body. The snow around it was stained black and dark red. Brooke gasped and looked away.

I recognized the black jacket and empty holster. One of the men from the attack. I grabbed Rayn's arm tighter and stepped in front of her, not knowing if he was still strong enough to attack us.

"Watch out," I said, loudly. "It's one of them."

Lauren looked down at him. "This one has a face."

"What?" I stepped towards the body, and instead of the terrifying black and white skull mask, I looked into a human face. His eyes were closed and his long dark hair pushed back, exposing a cut on his forehead. "How long has he been here?"

"Not long, I don't think," Rose replied, kneeling down next to him and examining him closer.

"Be careful, Rose," I warned again.

"Is he alive?" Rayn moved forward.

I put out my arm and stopped her, making her step back. My heart raced as fear swam through me. I couldn't let anything bad happen to anyone, especially after the close call we had with our first encounter. I wouldn't hesitate to end this man's life if it meant protecting my generation.

Rose moved more dirt and leaves to reveal another empty holster on his other thigh. "He's unarmed."

"This could be a trap." I looked around to make sure this wasn't a decoy and the others weren't out there somewhere, watching us. Waiting for us to come back and make their final attack.

"What's wrong with him?" Brooke asked, coming up behind me. "Maybe I could help."

Rayn came up on his other side. "They left him behind, abandoned him."

The man moved his fingers before the rest of his body shifted. Leaves rustled and crunched under him.

"He's waking up." Rose jumped to her feet and backed into my chest. I took a few steps back with her, holding onto her shoulders.

The man slowly opened his eyes and looked around. He closed them and winced in pain as he tried to move the lower half of his body.

"Who are you?" Rose demanded. The stern tone of her voice made the man fall still.

I readied my hands, feeling all the energy around me from the ice and snow. I knew I could protect us against him now, especially in his condition.

The man opened his eyes again and slowly moved his head to look at Rose, then me. I looked into his eyes. My own widened in recognition.

Honey.

The man who let Rayn and I live during the attack looked so different without his mask but those honey-colored eyes...I couldn't mistake them for anyone else's. He must have recognized me too, because the next person he looked to was Rayn.

She slowly backed up, until their eyes locked. He seemed almost relieved to see her standing before him.

"I–" he tried to speak, stopping to take a deep breath. "I p-prayed that...You'd come back." His head fell to the side and his breathing steadied.

"It's him!" Rayn shouted. "He saved our lives. We have to help him!"

"How?" I asked, looking down at the cuts and bruises, the dried blood on his forehead.

"Take him somewhere, anywhere!" Rayn ran to his side and fell to her knees.

Brooke knelt down beside her and examined a larger cut on his leg.

"Where do you suggest we take him? Your house? The cottage? We'd lead the other men straight to us," Lauren protested.

"This one doesn't look too good. We need to get him out of the cold before these cuts get infected," Brooke replied, clearing more debris from his body.

"Whitney, Lauren," Rose said in a hushed voice, turning to us. "We are obviously the only ones thinking clearly. He could have killed you guys, I know he didn't but he was with other men who wanted to."

"We don't know anything about him," I agreed. "Brooke heals him and then what?"

"I know," Lauren replied. "But I don't think we should leave him here to die in the freezing cold either. The Renati are the ones who leave others for dead, not us. Besides, Rayn felt the pull."

"What do you mean?" I asked.

"I think this is why she felt the pull to come back." Lauren glanced down at the man. "For him."

I looked over at Rayn and Brooke, who examined his wounds.

Brooke turned to us. "He'll freeze to death if we leave him out here."

Rose sighed. "Fine, but we keep him guarded the entire time. I don't want him to recover and kill us all in our sleep or run off and tell the others where we live."

"Maybe once he's better we can get some information," I said.

"Interrogate him?" Lauren asked.

"Basically," I answered.

"And after we get our information?" Lauren asked. "What are we going to do once he gets better?"

The tingle of Brooke's powers danced inside my chest like I had swallowed a pack of pop rocks and it all went down into my rib cage.

Brooke's hands pressed against his bare stomach. She had unzipped his jacket and lifted his undershirt to see how bad his injuries were. A slight glow of light appeared under her hands. She used more power than I had felt before, more than when she fixed my hand the night the Shadows attacked Bryan and I.

At first, Brooke had wondered if she truly belonged in our generation, but she turned out to be just as powerful as the rest of us.

Once the golden light disappeared, Brooke lifted her hands and exposed freshly healed skin.

"Did Amilia teach you that?" Rose asked, moving closer to inspect Brooke's work.

"No, Gabriel did." Brooke smiled, astonished at her own work.

"The spirit user from the spellbook?" Lauren clarified.

Brooke stood up. "He was brilliant. He could cure almost anything, heal almost anything by transferring his own health."

"Don't hurt yourself," I said. "He isn't worth your own health."

"Don't say that! He saved us." Rayn snapped.

"It replenishes on its own in time. I'm fine," Brooke reassured me.

"Whit, he needs some water." Rayn looked up at me. "Please."

I stayed still for a moment, looking down at his body. He had a muscular build. Athletic and massive like he could snap me in half over his knee.

I knelt down next to my sister. The moisture from the ground soaked the knees of my jeans. I cupped my hands together and used my powers to fill them with water. Holding my hands to his chapped lips, Rayn opened his mouth enough for me to pour some water in. He choked at first, but soon woke up enough to drink a little.

"We'll take him back home," Rayn said, her mind already made up. "We can hide him in the tool shed in the backyard. The Roberts never go in there anyway."

"Someone will have to watch him at all times." Rose clenched her jaw.

"Good thing the semester is officially over," Rayn replied, pulling the man's shirt back down and zipping his heavy black hunting jacket. Out of the three of us who were attacked by these men, Rayn was the only one in a hurry to bring one home like a stray dog. "Help me lift him."

"Your classes may be up but we still have jobs. We can't sit at home with him all day and I'm not letting this man near Dmitri," I argued.

Rayn looked up at me in disbelief. "He saved us and led the others away. He could have killed us, then what would have happened? They would have eventually found and killed Lauren. Help me get him up."

I went to his other side and grabbed under his arm, using all my strength to lift him up. Brooke came up behind him and pushed. The man let out a groan, but kept most of his pain behind tightly shut eyes and clenched teeth. Brooke quickly moved in front and grabbed his legs, holding one in each arm until Rose and Lauren finally gave in.

It took all five of us to carry him back to the trailhead. The huntsman's leg slipped out of Brooke's hands and hit the ground. He let out a loud groan of pain and I froze. Rose and Lauren gently set his other leg down and stepped back. Rayn and I almost fell over from his weight and we were forced to set his shoulders down too.

"Are you sure we aren't making it worse?" Lauren asked, wiping her forehead.

"We're almost to the car." Rayn crouched so he could hear her more clearly. "We're going to help you, but we have to go a little further."

Why did my sister feel so sympathetic to this killer, and more importantly, why wasn't I stopping her?

"Come on. Once we get him back we can question him." I grabbed under the man's shoulder once again.

"Okay," Brooke nodded.

"We have to blindfold him. We can't take him back to your house and have him know where you live. Then there's a chance he'll go back to his crew and they'll all come," Rose said.

"That's if they don't have my bag, which we never found. You know, the one with my license and address in it." Rayn grunted as she and I both lifted the huntsman once more. Rose, Lauren and Brooke grabbed his legs again, and we continued to carry him back to the cars.

Once we got back to the trailhead, we decided to lay him in the backseat of Rose's car, since that was the only place he would fit. We opened up the back door and did a quick count to three before we lifted him into the seat. When we couldn't get him up the first time, Rose went around to the other side and pulled on the back of his jacket. Eventually, we got him inside.

"I'll ride in the back with him," Rayn announced.

"Are you sure? There's hardly any room." Rose asked.

"Yes, I'll be fine."

"Blindfold him."

"I think that's a bit too far," Rayn protested.

"It might not be," I said. "Just in case this is a trap."

The huntsman's eyes fluttered open as he woke, and he lifted his head. Rose's hand clenched into a fist and the vines that kept him tied to the chair tightened. He looked down at the plant around his wrists, waist, and ankles before his gaze came back up to us.

"Who are you?" Rose demanded. "What's your name?"

He didn't reply. Instead, he looked around at the various items the Roberts stored in their tool shed.

"Where did you come from?" I asked him.

"More importantly, why were you trying to kill us in the woods?" Rose asked, tightening her vines. The man clenched his jaw as small thorns on the vines pierced his skin like needles. Not enough to injure him, but get the message across.

"We deserve an explanation." Rose kept the vines around him tightly.

"Rose, stop!" Rayn turned to Rose with pleading eyes. She returned her attention to the hunter, gently putting her hand over his. "What's your name?" When he looked away, she spoke again. "My name is Rayn, and yours?"

"Aden," he whispered in a deep, gravelly voice.

"Aden, why were you in the forest?" Rayn asked.

"I..." He paused and took a breath. "I was hunting with my pack."

"Hunting what?"

"Abominations," Aden whispered, looking down at the concrete floor.

"You hunt witches," I clarified. "You were in the forest to kill us because of our powers?"

"Is that true, Aden?" Rayn asked him, backing away a little.

"Yes." He nodded.

"Why did you let us go?" Rayn asked.

"I couldn't hurt you. You were so..." He paused. "I didn't have it in me. They had already taken a witch a few weeks ago, but they didn't shoot and kill like we normally do. They kept her and took their time. Left her body to be found."

"Oh," I muttered. "The girl from the flyers? The one missing around Falcon Bay?"

"You could kill that poor girl, but not us?" Rose's voice was ice cold.

"It's the world I was raised in," Aden answered.

"Where are you from?" Rayn asked him. He didn't answer, he looked away and shook his head.

I felt invisible, like Rose and I weren't even there. Just Rayn and the huntsman.

"What are you going to do with me?" Aden asked, looking up at Rayn. "You want information? Revenge?"

"Information would be nice," Rose mumbled.

"Suppose I don't have much choice," Aden replied.

"You had plenty of choices." My shaky voice surprised even myself. "You had a choice when you pulled the trigger on an innocent girl. You had a choice on all the countless witches you sacrificed for something they were born with, something they didn't choose. You are a monster."

Aden's honey-colored eyes met mine. "I spared you, didn't I?"

CHAPTER NINETEEN

GUILTY CONSCIENCE

WHITNEY

Aden didn't give us any information after that. He accepted food and water when we offered but otherwise kept his mouth shut. We left him in the toolshed with a charm on the door. Only Rayn, Dmitri, and I would be allowed to open it, which gave Rose and I a bit of freedom to go to the cottage.

Amilia walked into the room with a thick book in her hands. The cover wasn't nearly as worn as the older books in her collection, and the blank spine gave no indication of the title. She handed the book to Rose and smiled. "I found this while going through some of my old things. I think you'll get use out of it."

Rose took the book from Amilia and opened the cover. The old text had been hollowed out with little wooden drawers inside. When the book closed, no one could tell anything was hidden inside.

"I used this as a mobile apothecary when I was younger," Amilia explained. "It's enchanted. You can keep much more in this book than meets the eye."

Rose pulled the tiny wooden handle on one of the drawers. When I expected the little drawer to stop, it kept going. Rose pulled it out to the length of her arm before looking at Amilia in awe. "Thank you, this is perfect!" Rose smiled warmly at her.

"You're very welcome, dear. Would you two care for something to drink?" Amilia shuffled into the kitchen.

"Coffee would be great, Mia, thank you." I headed over to her bookshelves in the corner of the living room, skimming over the collection to make sure I hadn't missed anything. There had to be something in one of these books about the hunters.

Rose set her mobile apothecary on the table and joined me at the bookcase. She stood in front of the books and closed her eyes, taking in a deep breath.

"What are you doing?" I asked quietly.

"Following the pull." Rose reached out and ran her fingers down the spines, stopping at a dark green book near the bottom. "This one."

"I doubt Mia would keep anything out here that gives us any real info." I crossed my arms. "If she even knows the hunters exist."

Rose glanced up. "There is no possible way she doesn't. I know she's your mom's best friend, but–"

"I know." I cut her off. "Let's keep digging and see if we can find anything."

Rose nodded, running her fingers over the edges of the book. A thin layer of dust floated to the floor as she opened it. We must have missed this one. I leaned towards the kitchen, listening closely for Amilia. Sounds of the faucet running and dishes clinking together indicated we had a few more minutes of privacy.

"Whit, I think I found them." Rose tilted the book towards me so we could both read. "This powerless group originated in Europe centuries ago after a fight between Elemental supporters and Renati burned down a local village. The fighting...it killed a lot of people."

"That's awful." I skimmed down the page to see what else the book said about hunters. "There isn't much here. They don't actually call them hunters."

"No, unfortunately not." Rose sighed, her voice lowering into a whisper. "But this is a good start. I wonder why Mia never told us about the hunters."

I shrugged. "I wonder all the time why she keeps things from us. I know she's trying to protect us, but–"

"Are you girls hungry?" Amilia walked back into the room with two coffees.

"I don't think I could eat, honestly. Not with this knot in my stomach." I barely glanced up from the book.

"You still need to. You have to take care of yourselves." Amilia mothered us like she longed to care for someone.

"Thank you for the coffee." Rose smiled at Amilia.

Amilia smiled back and peeked at the book in Rose's hands. "Find anything interesting?"

I considered brushing it off as nothing, but what the hell. "Yeah, it's kind of interesting. There's this group that started hunting witches when a fight burned down their village?"

"Oh, yes, unfortunately when some powerless discovered magic, they feared it."

"I would too if it destroyed my entire family," Rose replied.

"Their reasons certainly seem justified in the beginning, but it morphed into something bigger. Remnants of the group still exist today."

"Are there witch hunters in the forest?" I asked.

Amilia took a sip from her own coffee mug. "There used to be. The only good thing the Renati did was to drive the hunters away from our part of the forest with protection wards. There haven't been hunters around Rifton for a long time."

I glanced at Rose side-eyed as she watched Amilia carefully. "Is there any way the wards could wear off eventually?"

"Oh, no not on their own. They would have to be broken," Amilia explained.

I studied Amilia's face. "Do you know anything about them?"

"From my understanding, they all participate in a joining ceremony where they are injected with a sort of enhancement serum." Amilia winced as she shook her head, as if disgusted with the practice.

"They alter themselves?" I asked, thinking back to how big the hunters who ambushed us in the meadow were.

Amilia nodded. "They must have believed it would give them an edge over our magic. Gives them the ability to sense when a witch is nearby."

"How does that work? How does that make them any different than us if they are purposefully changing their genetic makeup?" Rose questioned.

"I'm not sure how they justify it, to be honest. The forest used to be a much more dangerous place. The hunters were like a pack of wolves but luckily they have moved on from here. I hope wherever they wander, the witches in those areas are taking similar precautions to keep themselves safe."

"Wow. I hope so," I muttered. I knew exactly what I would interrogate Aden on next.

Amilia watched me closely. "Your wheels are turning. Is there something else you'd like to ask?"

"Actually there is." I shifted my weight. "Do you know anything about the Hallow?"

"The what?" Amilia asked as if she knew nothing about it, but I knew this act already. This wasn't the first time Amilia hid information from us.

"The Hallow? I found it in our spellbook on one of the maps, but the map is torn," I explained.

"That's peculiar."

"Yeah, I thought so too." I watched her facial expression, her body language, but nothing gave me any clues. "So you've never heard of it?" I asked again.

"I'll be honest, my dear, I truly have no idea where the Hallow is," Amilia admitted. As much as it pained me, I believed her.

"But do you know *what* it is?" Rose asked, listening carefully to the way Amilia worded her sentences.

She sighed. "It's rumored there is a colony of witches living off grid in the forest."

"Why would they be out in the middle of nowhere?"

"The Renati are not kind to Elemental supporters. Which is why we must burn the ledger."

I thought back to when I had asked Bryan's friends about the history of Rifton at Acoustic Night. "Wait," I paused. "I heard about a group of people who disappeared. Some people say they moved away, but others say they were dragged off into the woods by the witches. Are these those same people?"

"I'm not familiar with the stories the powerless tell one another for entertainment," Amilia answered.

Rose and I gave each other a knowing glance, deciding to leave our inquiries at that. We finished our coffees and said goodbye to Amilia.

On the way to our cars, I turned to Rose. "Is she telling the truth?"

Rose nodded. "Surprisingly, yeah. She didn't lie about any of it, but she knows I'm an empath. She's probably wording things in a way that she isn't technically lying but still not giving the whole truth."

"Like how she said she didn't know *where* the Hallow is," I pointed out.

"Yes, that's why I asked her specifically. It's all about asking the right questions." Rose ran her fingers through her hair.

"Troy told me the story about the people who disappeared. He believed they were killed by the witches in the forest, but what if they *are* the witches in the forest? The ones who live at the Hallow?"

"Nothing is too far-fetched anymore. I do think Amilia didn't say anything about the hunters because she doesn't think they're an issue anymore."

"Someone must have broken the wards that were keeping the hunters out of Rifton," I agreed.

Rose gave a defeated nod. "Another puzzle piece."

"So, you haven't exactly said why we are going to the meadow alone," Dmitri said from the passenger's seat later that afternoon as I turned towards Eagle Loop Trail.

I tapped the steering wheel with my thumb. "I have to show you something."

"Just me?"

"Yes."

"Could you be any more vague?"

My knees rattled with nerves. It was ballsy bringing Dmitri with me to the supply drop for Abe after he made me swear not to tell Mit anything, but how could I keep this from him? If the roles were reversed and Bryan hid alone in the woods, I'd kill whoever withheld that kind of information from me. Still, I didn't know how Abe would react. If he turned and ran at the first sight of us, that would hurt Dmitri even more. If Abe truly cared about my brother, now was the time to prove it.

I parked in the far corner of the lot and Dmitri eyed me as I retrieved an old backpack from behind my seat. "Promise me something." I glanced over at Mit. "Don't freak out. Stay calm and don't make a lot of noise."

"What the hell is going on?" Dmitri's eyes grew as he followed me off the path in the opposite direction of the meadow.

I didn't answer, not wanting to draw any attention. We hadn't seen any more of the hunters but I didn't want to push our luck. The blue lace agate vibrated in my hand as we came closer to the meeting place. We stood in silence, waiting for Abe to show himself. I listened carefully to every sound that echoed through the trees: the birds chirping, the wind blowing the branches, the brush rustling. Finally, Abe emerged from the trees.

I watched Dmitri closely; his face blank and his body motionless as his lips parted slightly. They stared at each other for what felt like a lifetime before Dmitri blurred, crashing into Abe. Their arms flew around one another as a sob escaped my brother. Abe grabbed fistfuls of Dmitri's sweatshirt, pulling him close as Abe buried his face into Mit's neck.

"I'm sorry. I'm so sorry," Abe whispered, running his fingers through Dmitri's hair as they both cried.

"How?" Dmitri turned to look at me, tears streaming down his cheeks.

"Abe helped us get out of the woods when the hunters attacked," I answered, keeping an eye on the perimeter.

"And you didn't tell me."

"I begged her not to," Abe replied, glaring at me. "I'm trying to keep you safe."

I shrugged. "I couldn't keep this from him. He's my brother."

Dmitri looked at the backpack in my grip and turned to Abe. "For you?"

Abe nodded.

"You can't stay out here. It's not safe. The hunters and the Renati...one of them is bound to find you."

"What other choice do I have?"

"Come with us. Come home."

"Mit," Abe groaned. "You live on my parent's property."

"We can keep you safe." Dmitri turned to me. "If the roles were reversed, we'd never leave Bryan out here."

"Bryan is powerless," I pointed out. "At least Abe has some kind of defense. He's kept himself alive so far. I brought nonperishables, a blanket, and clean clothes." I unzipped the backpack and pulled out a plastic wrapper, handing it to Abe. "I found this water purification straw at the store."

"Thank you." Abe nodded.

I cleared my throat. "There's something I want to ask."

"Okay..." Abe shifted awkwardly.

"Can you tell us anything about the Renati? Or is that spell they used on you still active?"

Abe opened his mouth to talk but nothing came out.

"Okay, so how do we break that?" Dmitri asked.

Abe let out a deep sigh. "I don't know if we can."

I stepped towards him. "We need to know where the Renati hideout is and where they could potentially be keeping Erebus. They stole something of ours and we need it back."

"Even without the spell, that's not information I'd have." Abe shook his head. "I was never anyone important, knowing just enough that I was a risk but never so much I could ever do any damage. I think they only tried to kill me because it's a blood in, blood out kind of thing."

"A cult," I replied.

"Sure," Abe said. "If you wanna put a title on it."

"Is there anyone else in the Renati like you? Someone who doesn't want to be there, who got trapped?" Dmitri asked.

"Not that I know of," Abe answered. "The D—" His voice cut out, catching in his throat.

"The Drakes." I answered for him.

He nodded. "They are all fiercely loyal to him."

"To Henry Drake or Erebus?"

"Both," Abe whispered. "Even if you were able to take one of them out, it would only turn them into martyrs."

The Martyrs.

"There's an old Elemental generation called the Martyrs, the ones Erebus killed before he was trapped in the Shadow Realm."

"I know the story, only they tell it a bit differently on the other side of things." Abe said. "It's viewed more as a sacrifice."

That sparked a hatred in my blood, thinking about the generations before me being used as a blood sacrifice. Not only killed for nothing, but that the Renati spun the tail as a necessary means to the end goal. The Renati celebrated the death of the Elementals.

"This fight is going to burn the entire fucking forest to the ground," Abe muttered as he watched the wheels turn in my mind.

"I'm trying to prevent that from happening," I answered. "I don't want anyone who isn't guilty to get hurt. The Renati are the ones willing to burn everything."

"Whitney, if they wanted Rifton to burn, they would have lit the match long before you showed up."

"So this is our fault?" Dmitri asked.

"I'm not saying that, but I'm not *not* saying that. It's complicated, guys." Abe ran a dirty hand through his messy copper hair. "It's not like this all wouldn't have eventually happened, but you showing up definitely kickstarted things."

"No, I get it. We're the only reason they were able to resurrect Erebus in the first place. I'm trying to clean up the mess we made. To send the demon we unleashed back to hell."

"Easier said than done," Abe muttered. "I know it doesn't seem like it, but I'm doing what I can. I don't sit in the woods all day. I'm watching them, but they're watching you."

Dmitri wrapped his arm around Abe's shoulders. "Don't risk your safety for us. It's not worth it. We'll figure it out, okay? You focus on keeping yourself safe."

Abe nodded, pulling my brother close.

"We're all doing the best we can," I said.

"Let's hope it's enough," Abe replied, cupping his cheek. "It won't be like this forever, I promise."

"I thought you..." Dmitri's voice trailed off.

I cleared my throat. "I'm going to wait by the car. Dmitri, don't run off with him. I'm not leaving that parking lot without you."

Dmitri gave a slight nod. When I got back to the car, I leaned against the hood and pulled out my phone. Bryan answered after the first ring.

"Can I see you after work?"

He chuckled. "Do you even have to ask? I just got to work so I have to go, but I'll see you soon."

"Okay, have a good day. I love you."

"I love you too." A smile shone through in his voice.

I let out a deep sigh, taking in every little sound the forest had to offer. Every bird that sang above me, every rustle of the breeze through the branches put me on edge. My mind struggled to differentiate between a harmless forest dweller, a masked man, or a lurking Shadow watching from afar. Dmitri took too much time with Abe, right as I pushed myself off the hood of the car to go after him, he emerged from the trees alone.

"Are you okay?" I asked, studying his wide eyes and raised brows for any indication of what he thought.

Dmitri cleared his throat, choking on his words. "I can't believe he's been out here this whole time. An abandoned hunting cabin? He can't stay out here."

"I'm sorry I didn't tell you sooner. Abe made it very clear he didn't want you to know, but...but I couldn't keep it from you. I should have told you sooner."

"I'm not mad at you. I think I'm in shock, honestly." Dmitri's voice quivered as he ran his fingers through his hair. "I'm so relieved to see him and I miss him." He wiped a tear from his cheek. "If Abe won't come with us, I can't do anything about it. Let's go home."

"Are you sure?" I asked as Dmitri opened up the passenger door and climbed into the car.

He nodded, burying whatever he felt deep inside his stomach. I got in without any protest and the two of us drove home in silence.

CHAPTER TWENTY

THE PULL

RAYN

I sat on the floor of my bedroom organizing my bookshelf. There weren't many books in my collection but I alphabetized them by author's last name and genre. A stick of incense released a long steady line of smoke into the air and the scent of dragon's blood filled the room. I had already gone through my dresser and taken out some clothes I wanted to donate, matched up all the pairs of socks, and narrowed down my massive hoodie collection. I had swept the floor, made my bed, fluffed the pillows, and dusted every surface.

Leaning back, I admired how clean my bedroom looked. Chewing my bottom lip, I wondered if I should move onto the bathroom. When was the last time someone had scrubbed out the shower?

I didn't actually care about the cleanliness of every square inch of the house. While I enjoyed having things neat and put in their places, I couldn't deny why I was stress cleaning.

The pull.

I wanted to slip out of the house and walk the short distance to the tool shed. I wanted to break the spell keeping Aden locked inside. I wanted to talk to him. Maybe he would give me more information without Rose and Whitney there. I had been the only one he was willing to talk to, and maybe he would be more comfortable with just the two of us.

Should I feel comfortable with just the two of us?

My voice of reason echoed Whitney's concerns, but my gut told me that Aden would never lay a finger on me in anger. I didn't know which to trust. My own intuition had been wrong before, *so* wrong. I questioned if this feeling in my belly was actually the pull or me once again ignoring red flags.

But this wasn't the same. I was not the same person who met a cute boy in class and trusted whatever he said as fact. I knew my worth and I wasn't afraid to use my powers against anyone who challenged that. I was strong enough to do this on my own. Plus Whitney was at work for another hour or so. It was now or never.

With a wave of my hand, I extinguished the candles on my dresser and tiptoed out of my bedroom. I was unsure of how Dmitri would react if he saw me sneaking into the backyard. My brother wasn't stupid. He'd know where I headed the moment he saw me. But much like Dmitri didn't care about my warnings against his sneaking around with Abe Roberts, I didn't care about anyone else's cautionary words.

I peaked my head around the corner. Dmitri's curtains were half open, but his head was down, buried in his sketch pad. Headphones in his ears. I could hear the faint music from across the room. Dmitri appeared to be in his zone. He wouldn't notice me unless I started jumping on his bed. I scurried across the living room to the kitchen, as quickly and quietly as I could. I stopped as I put my hands on the counter, looking back at Dmitri. He hadn't moved an inch.

The cold night air rushed me as I opened the back door, sending chills through my body. I missed summer. The holiday season could not go by fast enough. I tried not to think about how different the holidays had been as I walked across the dew-covered lawn. The Roberts' tool shed was closer to the guest cabin than the main house. I didn't think much of it when we first moved in, but I couldn't be more thankful for it now.

I paused at the door, my fingers barely grazing the door knob. I ran over all the things I would say, all the questions I would ask. We needed a better understanding of the hunters if we were going to keep ourselves safe. Know your enemy and all that.

With a breath of courage, I turned the handle. A faint golden hue glowed around the door, breaking the spell that locked Aden inside. I slipped in and closed the door behind me. Then I met his gaze.

Aden sat up when he saw me, his back straight as a board. His breath caught in his throat as he spoke. "Is everything all right?"

I nodded. "Yeah, um, nothing is wrong. I just wanted to come check on you."

"I'm fine," Aden answered simply.

"Good, good." I wrung my hands together. "Are you feeling better? Better than you were when we found you at least?"

Aden nodded.

"Good. Um, do you want to talk about what happened?"

"No."

"Hmm. Okay, then I'll talk and you can listen." I leaned against the tool bench mounted to the wall. Aden shifted his weight and I tried not to stare at his bare arms. I noticed he wore a black tank top the moment I walked into the tool shed, but it felt impossible to carry on a conversation with his muscles out in the open. "Aren't you cold?"

Aden shook his head. "I don't typically get cold."

I rest my hands on the wooden bench behind me. "I sure do. I hate the winter months."

Aden turned his head to gaze out the window. Black lines in his skin peaked up at the base of his neck from the top of his tank top. The jagged lines could've been a tattoo, but the coloring seemed off. It wasn't pure black like ink would have been. The possible tattoo resembled something in between tree roots and a bolt of lightning. He turned back to me and caught my gaze on the back of his neck. Aden straightened his posture and leaned against the wall.

"Is that a tattoo?" I dared ask.

Aden glanced down at his hands. "No."

"Um, what is it, then?" I furrowed my brow.

Aden cleared his throat. "It is my hunter mark."

"Hunter mark?" I tilted my head and chewed on my lip. He spoke as if the mark was something I should be familiar with.

"Every hunter in the community, when they come of age, goes through a, uh," he paused. "Well, we are marked. It happens when we are given our abilities. I'm not sure what it is exactly, but it's not a tattoo."

Whitney had told me about the brief bit of information Amilia had spilled about the hunters. That they went through some sort of ritual to alter themselves, to give them abilities that helps them hunt the witches.

I blinked at him before I asked my next question. "Is it your veins?"

Aden shrugged. "I don't know."

"Did it hurt?"

"Yes."

"Can I see it?"

"No."

Oh, okay then.

"The hunters are a complete mystery to us. I had no idea you guys existed until a couple of days ago. I thought the issues we were having with the other witches in town was bad enough, but this..." I let out a deep sigh and gazed into his honey-colored eyes. "We have been up at that meadow countless times before. Just when I feel like I'm starting to wrap my head around things, the world shifts."

"The older I get, the less I know," Aden replied.

"What?"

"Something my father used to say."

"Oh. That makes sense. A couple years ago I thought I had everything figured out but now? I'm...I feel so lost." I surprised myself with how easy it was to admit that to Aden.

"I know a thing or two about having to dismantle everything you've been taught," he said.

"My mom didn't prepare us for any of this," I whispered.

"I can't imagine she did it on purpose."

"No, I don't think so either but it doesn't change anything. Why will you only talk to me?"

"What do you mean?"

"You won't talk to my sister or the other girls. Why?"

"I spoke to them after I woke up."

"Not really."

He glanced at me with heavy eyes. "It's not easy to have people you were raised with, people you considered family, try to kill you for going against the pack leader, and then wake in enemy territory."

"We aren't your enemy. We saved you."

"Yes, but I don't know your motives. I don't understand why you came back. I told you not to come back."

"I felt the pull," I said simply.

"What is that?"

"Your intuition, the little voice in your head. My gut told me to go back, so we did. And we found you barely hanging on."

"I was ready to let go."

I raised my brows. "You said you were praying I'd come back?"

"I did not."

I scoffed. "I remember it clearly. You said you prayed we would come back and then you passed out."

"Well, I don't remember that," Aden huffed.

"Do you pray often?" I asked, genuinely curious for his response. I wanted to know if he believed there was a god in the sky, or if his parents dragged him to church. Did he want to go?

"Sometimes."

"Do they ever answer? Whoever you're praying to?"

Aden glanced up and met my gaze, sending a warm heat through my body. "Sometimes."

"I always wondered what that was like," I admitted. "To have something to believe in?"

"What do you believe?" He tilted his head.

"I don't know anymore. No one has ever answered any praying I've done...or manifesting or hoping or whatever. My mom made a point to raise us without religion, without any of that. She thought it was all bullshit."

Aden nodded. "And you agree with her?"

"I don't know what kind of god would have let her die like she did, so yeah, I agree."

"Oh," Aden paused, shifting his weight. "I'm sorry."

"Me too," I whispered. "Are both of your parents still alive?"

Aden shook his head. "Only my mother. My father passed away years ago on a hunt."

"A...a hunt? Was he..." I stopped myself. "Sorry, I shouldn't be asking such personal questions."

"Yes, he was killed by a witch."

"I'm sure they were only defending themselves."

Aden didn't reply.

This was too easy, talking to Aden. The words fell out of my mouth like I had known this man my entire life. I completely forgot he had chased me through the forest, that his fingers wrapped around my throat. The man who sat before me looked nothing like a killer. His shoulder-length brown hair fell around his face as those honey eyes glistened in the single light bulb hanging in the tool shed. I wasn't a witch and Aden wasn't a witch hunter. We were two people having a conversation.

"It's easy to forget that a person trying to kill you is someone's parent or someone's child." I bit my lip. "Like it's easy to forget that witches are people too, I imagine."

"We aren't taught that witches are people. We are taught that they are demons."

"Do I look like a demon?"

Aden's gaze slid down my body and I suddenly became aware of every little detail about myself. My messy curls tied into a quick braid. The rips in my jeans that showed hints of my long, pale legs.

Aden's eyes slowly moved back up to meet mine. "No."

I cleared my throat. "I mean, I'm sure to someone who is afraid of magic, my fire powers probably look straight from hell."

"Are you sympathizing with those who tried to kill you?"

"I'm trying to understand, that's all. I'm wrapping my head around it." I slid down to sit on the cold concrete. I didn't like towering over Aden while I questioned him. It gave off the impression that I was his captor. I didn't want him to feel like a prisoner, even if that's what the other girls intended.

"Why are you here?" Aden questioned, resting his hand on his knee.

"I already said, I wanted to check on you."

"And you have. Why are you still here?"

"Are you asking me to leave?"

"I'm only curious. I'm wrapping my head around it."

The corner of my lips curved into a smile as Aden used my own words against me. "Because you let us go," I admitted. "You saved me, and my sister, and I owe you. You may have been born a hunter but you're still a human being and you're still deserving of kindness."

"You...you are unlike any witch I've ever met."

I chortled. "I bet you twenty bucks you've never actually *met* a single witch in your life."

A small smile graced Aden's lips. "I forgot my wallet at home."

I laughed. "You can owe me, then."

Chapter Twenty-One
Narrow Escape
Whitney

That night after work, I watched the soft multicolored lights reflect off the fresh rain on the sidewalks. All the shops downtown were decorated for the holiday season. Lights strung across all the rooftops. Windows painted with snowmen, reindeer, and big sacks of presents. The businesses were all closing up and the last of the shopping traffic made their way home. A calming presence lingered in the air as tiny snowflakes danced down from the sky. I held out my palm and caught one, holding it close to my face to try and see the unique pattern.

The planters along the sidewalk that once held blooming wildflowers were now filled with bare branches and dirt. The paths in front of the shop doors were shoveled and salted but a thin layer of ice formed as the chill of the night air set in. I stood there frozen, taking it all in.

This time last year, Rayn and I were in downtown Hemston, looking for a particular comic book Dmitri wanted. Mom had a stash of gifts hidden in her closet. It had been her hiding spot of choice because she thought we didn't know about it, but we found them on our first Christmas at home. None of us felt the holiday spirit last year. We were all annoyed with each other. Rayn had spent Christmas Eve with an ex-boyfriend. Dmitri had sat in the corner doodling. Mom and I got into an argument over something stupid and I spent the evening locked in my room. I spent the last Christmas Eve I'd ever have with my mother angry at her.

Now we were in Rifton, and amongst all the things to deal with, part of me wished I could go back to the holiday season last year and appreciate what I had in the moment. A wave of concern washed over me, serene feelings that weren't my own crept in and settled next to my nostalgic sorrow.

"Baby, you okay?" a deep, tender voice asked behind me.

I turned to face Bryan's worried gaze. He reached out and gently wiped a tear I didn't realize was there.

"Uh, yeah. Yeah, I'm good," I answered, sniffling. "Just a rough time of year."

He nodded with understanding and wrapped an arm around my shoulders, pulling me against his chest. "Are you hungry?"

I shrugged.

"What do you need, baby? We can talk about it or we can go get tacos. Both?"

"I told Rayn and Mit I'd bring something home for dinner," I answered.

"Okay, so tacos to-go, then. Come on." Bryan turned to head down the sidewalk, but I stopped him.

"I only have like, ten dollars until payday."

He reached for my hand. "I'll get dinner, don't worry about it. I'm hungry too."

"Bryan." A sob lodged in my throat when I tried to say his name. "You're always paying for everything."

"I'm your boyfriend," he answered, confused.

"I'm not a charity case."

"No one said you were." He rested his hands on my shoulders and leaned down to meet my eyes. "I'm sorry. I know your first Christmas without your mom is painful, but let me try to ease it a bit. Let me be here for you."

"What would I do if we weren't together? How could I feed my family on ten dollars for the rest of the week when I still have to get gas?"

"You'll never have to worry about that," Bryan answered softly.

"What was she thinking of leaving him in my custody?" I covered my face with my hands. "How am I supposed to take care of us?"

Bryan pulled me into a hug. "You're doing fine."

I wiped another stray tear away with the back of my hand and tried to steady myself with a deep breath. "It makes me feel like I'm failing when you pay for everything."

Bryan sighed. "I'm sorry. That's not my intention."

"I know it's not. You do so much. You got Ray that job, and you buy us food all the time but–"

"That's what family does, Whitney. We take care of each other." He wiped the next tear away with his thumb.

His words echoed in my soul. "Family."

"When I told you I'd always be there, I meant all of you. You, Ray, and Mit are a packaged deal. I knew that going into this."

I sniffled and smiled up at him. "I don't deserve it, but I'm really thankful for you."

"Of course you deserve it." Bryan put his hand on the small of my back and steered me down the street to a Mexican restaurant at the end of the block. "Do you want me to crash at your place again? Since you're having a rough day."

I took a moment to think up a good excuse. "I want you to, but another time, okay?"

Bryan let out a disappointed sigh. "What else is going on?"

"What do you mean?"

Bryan shifted his weight, his brows lifting with concern. "Something is off. You're all acting weird. You and Rose are always both somewhere else mentally. Someone came up behind Rayn at work the other night and she was so startled, she cried."

I looked up at him. "She didn't tell me about that."

"Whit, come on. Don't push me away."

I let out a puff of air. "We were in the meadow last week and..." My voice trailed off as I choked on the knot forming in my stomach. It moved up into my throat with each word. Bryan's soft eyes encouraged me to keep going as he lifted my hand to his lips and gently kissed my knuckles. With another deep breath, I started again. "We were in the meadow last week and we were attacked."

His eyes widened. "By the Renati?"

"No," I paused. "There are witch hunters in the forest." Bryan remained silent, so I continued. "Lauren was able to hide in the woods but one of them let Rayn and I go. They had darts that numbed our powers and–"

"Whitney, never go back to that meadow again." Not a plea, but a demand.

"We already protected it with a potion," I answered, feeling the mix of anger and fear course through his body.

Bryan shook his head. "That's not good enough."

I grazed my fingers against the stubble on his cheek, attempting to calm him. "It's safe now. I promise."

Bryan's arms wrapped around me, pulling me close to his chest. I nuzzled my face against his unsettled heartbeat and took in a deep breath of safety.

"Darts that numb your powers?" Bryan clarified into my hair.

I nodded against him. "It was the strangest thing. My powers came back after a while but I couldn't feel anything. It wasn't magic though, it was...something else."

"Like what?"

"I have no idea." I shook my head.

Bryan huffed. "So now we have to worry about the Renati and fucking witch hunters?"

"Luckily, I don't think the hunters discriminate between the two of us. I think they want us all dead."

"That's comforting," he muttered sarcastically. "You seem to know a lot about these guys."

"Rose and I found a book at the cottage. There wasn't much in there, but enough to know they started when a village burned in the crossfire of a fight between Renati and Elemental support. They were scorned by magic, not a side. It seems they see all witches the same. Amilia said there are supposed to be wards in place around Rifton keeping them away from here but someone must have broken them."

Bryan pulled away and furrowed his brow. "I'm sorry but why the hell wouldn't Amilia warn you about witch hunters?"

"It seems she genuinely didn't think they were an issue anymore?"

Bryan frowned. "You actually believe that's true?"

"I don't know." I shrugged.

"I don't." He rubbed his face, quickly returning his hand to my back. "I wonder if Emma knows anything about these guys."

"I'd be curious to know," I admitted. "But we agreed to keep her out of things."

"We did. I'm just talking. I wish we could pull our allies together but it's not safe for Emma to do so."

"The Drakes aren't allies."

"Emma is," he insisted.

"We don't know that." I gazed into his worried eyes. "You really think she would choose us over her family? Her own blood?"

"She has no love for Henry."

"And Serenity? Her own twin?" I crossed my arms. "I don't know, Bryan. No matter what Rayn did, I'd never be able to turn on her like that."

"Even if she killed people?"

"I'd help her bury the bodies." I answered without a second thought. "She's my sister."

Bryan nodded. "I'd do the same for Rosie, but I also like to think I know Emma better than that."

"We don't need to worry about all that right now." I rest my hand against his side. "I really do need to get home. I don't want to leave Ray and Mit alone after what happened."

"Let me come with you." He stepped towards me.

I took his hand in mine and smiled. "We'll be okay, babe."

"Did you think you could tell me all that and I'd let you go home without me? You're never leaving my side again."

I didn't want to tell Bryan about Aden in the toolshed. Telling him about the hunters went far enough but to let him know we had actually brought one home? That would not have gone well.

I reached out and cupped his cheek in my other palm. "I promise we have defenses up on the house, okay? I'll be okay and if anything happens, you will be my first call."

"Okay," he gave up with a short, disappointed sigh before he kissed my palm. "Text me when you get home."

"I will. I promise."

Quietly, I unlocked the front door and set a bag of tacos down on the table. "Dinner!" I called out, my voice echoing through the house.

I went to Rayn's room to let her know I'd gotten home. Her door had been left cracked open, but she wasn't there. At least this time her room wasn't thrashed.

"Hey, are these all the same?" Dmitri asked, digging through the bag of tacos.

"Some are chicken and some are shredded beef," I answered, peeking into the kitchen. "Where's Ray?"

"I thought she was in her room."

A chill ran up my spine. "She's not."

"I've had my headphones in but I didn't see her leave." Dmitri glanced over his shoulder.

I walked into the kitchen to the window that looked over the backyard. After seeing the dim light shine through the small window of the tool shed, my face fell flat.

"She's with *him*," I muttered.

Dmitri nearly dropped his taco. "Why?"

"I'm going to find out."

Once I got to the tool shed, I pressed my ear against the door and listened. I could make out two voices and what they said. Sure enough, one of those voices belonged to my sister.

"I'm sorry everyone has been so rough on you," Rayn replied softly. "They don't understand."

"My fate would be much worse if I had stayed with my pack," Aden said. I pressed my ear harder against the door. "I wouldn't have made it another night in the woods with those injuries."

"I can't believe they tried to kill you." Rayn sounded surprised, even though we had found him half dead in the trees, left behind by his own family.

"Were you never punished? I can imagine you've run into some mischief with fire magic," Aden said.

Fire magic. The biggest question, did Aden see Rayn use her powers in the meadow or did she tell him? Aden had saved us and hadn't given me any reason not to trust him. But still, this could be a cover. I honestly didn't know what to believe anymore.

"Oh, no. My mom never did anything like that. She grounded us and stuff, but she was always forgiving when it came to our powers," Rayn explained. "I got into a lot of mischief, but Whitney was always there to step in before things got too out of control." She laughed, giggled almost.

I opened the door back, and the laughter stopped immediately. "Hi."

Rayn jumped up to her feet. "I didn't know you were home."

"Here, I brought you a taco. Hope you like chicken." I handed the wrapped soft taco to Aden.

"Thank you." He took the offering and set it on his lap.

"I have some questions for you," I said to Aden, leaning against the wooden work bench. "I need honest answers."

"I have nothing to gain from lying to you," Aden replied.

"I hope not. How long have you been hunting around Rifton?"

"Not long," Aden answered. "A little over six months."

"And why not longer?"

Aden shrugged. "I didn't think to ask. A while back, my pack leader told us we would be hunting south and moved into the forest around town. He explained the town had become overrun with witchcraft."

"It's not overrun." Rayn put her hands on her hips. "Rifton was always intended to be a safe haven for witches."

"There used to be wards up around the forest surrounding Rifton to keep the hunters out, do you know anything about that?" I asked.

Aden shook his head. "No. My pack is based outside of Eugene, so I didn't think we had reason to be down in this part of the forest."

I cleared my throat. "How does the hierarchy work? Is your hunting pack the only one?"

"We are all part of the same community made up of four different hunting packs." Aden shifted his weight, staring at his hands. "There are dens scattered throughout the state, several different ones. My community are the only hunters here, multiple dens but we are all under the same umbrella of leadership, if that makes sense."

"So you don't know anyone who could have been in Rifton to break the wards before you moved south?" I clarified.

"I don't know who could have broken the witch's wards. I wasn't very far up in the chain of command." Aden rubbed the back of his neck. "Those sorts of things are a need to know, and I didn't need to know."

"Okay." I accepted his answers. "Thank you for being honest. I'm sure it's not easy to go against your pack."

"They left me for dead," Aden answered coldly. "I have no love for those who wished to kill me for disobeying sadistic orders."

I decided to continue my questioning while Aden was willing to answer them. "How much do you know about when and how the whole hunter thing started?"

"It's an old story they tell us as children. The devil plagued our world with witches to lure the faithful from their path of righteousness, to turn the world black. That witches are abominations and hunters are the chosen warriors to eradicate them. It's our entire purpose in life, a family right. My father was a hunter and his father before him. My family have been hunting since before they came to this country."

"So there's a joining ceremony?"

Aden narrowed his gaze. "How do you know about that?"

"Tell me about it."

"No," Aden answered, his voice cold. "It's sacred."

"Sacred? What happened to no love for those who tried to kill you?"

"The members of my pack may have tried to kill me but my family is still in the community. I still have people I love with them. I won't go back to that way of life but I also won't betray my blood."

"Fair enough..." I took a step away from him.

"I owe you a life debt and I will repay it, but I won't betray my family to do so."

"I understand." I nodded.

"We'll let you eat and get some rest." Rayn met my gaze and motioned towards the door. "Goodnight, Aden."

He nodded at us as we left and sealed the charm around the door.

"What are you doing?" I asked Rayn once we were outside.

"I...we were only talking."

"About what?"

"I'm an adult, Whit, you aren't my guardian." Rayn crossed her arms.

"I'm still your sister. I'm curious which secrets about our powers you shared with the witch hunter," I replied. "Did you tell him anything about us, or just your own shit?"

"He doesn't want to hurt us. Why can't any of you understand that?" Rayn defended. "You were there, you saw him lead the others away. He got us out of there alive."

"Don't tell him things he doesn't need to know," I replied. "Don't forget he's a hunter. That's all I'm asking."

Rayn curled her lip in anger. "You're in absolutely no place to pass judgment on me. We're all still pissed at you for bringing Bryan to the cottage covered in Shadow gashes."

"It was one scratch and Bryan isn't a hunter," I argued.

"He still almost died!" Rayn threw out her arms. "You don't trust me anymore." She stormed past me back to the house.

"It has nothing to do with that!" I shouted across the lawn.

Rayn didn't turn around. She walked into the house and closed the back door with a thud that echoed against the trees. I didn't go after her. Instead I went back to the huntsman.

I didn't get nervous until my hand touched the knob, breaking the charm. I took a deep breath before I twisted my hand and pushed open the door. Aden sat in the corner of the tool shed with one leg tucked under him, his food untouched. He looked up as if he expected me.

"She's barely nineteen, she's still figuring herself out," I snapped at him. "It's all too risky, Aden, you can't stay here anymore. We have enough on our plates without worrying about hiding a witch hunter in our tool shed and putting everyone in danger. What if they come after you?" I asked.

"For all they know, I'm dead," Aden answered calmly.

"Well, you aren't dead and you can't stay here. You saved our lives and we saved yours. We're even and I expect you to be gone by morning." I crossed my arms.

"I respect your decision," Aden replied.

Though there wasn't much emotion on his face, his eyes looked disappointed. But he couldn't expect to stay here forever, especially if he's going to be up all night talking to my little sister.

I turned to leave out the door when Aden stopped me. "Wait."

"What do you want?" I snapped back, ready for a rebuttal.

Aden put his finger up to his lips. A cold chill went up my spine and I stood still as a statue, looking around to see what he referred to.

"Is Rayn back inside the house?" Aden whispered, standing slowly. He winced as he put pressure on his left ankle, but he still stood tall as a mountain.

"Yes."

Aden nodded, calculating a plan silently.

My heart pounded in my chest as I demanded, "Tell me what's going on. Now."

"Go inside, lock the doors and hide. You'll know when it's safe." Aden's eyes locked with mine. "And for the love of God, do not lock me in here."

That was all he had to say? "Not until you tell me what is happening."

"Little witch, this is not the time to argue with me. Go." Aden stepped away and quietly rustled through the Roberts' tools. He looked over to see I still hadn't moved. "Go!"

"Don't make me regret this."

I closed the door to the tool shed behind me as quietly as I could and swiftly moved up the porch steps. When I got inside of the house, I locked the deadbolt on the doors and turned off the porch light. My heart raced in my chest as I threw back the curtain of Dmitri's room, finding him and Rayn sitting on his bed. They fell silent when they saw me. I didn't care that Rayn vented to Mit about what an asshole I was.

"Turn off the light. Now." I ordered, leaping across Mit's bed to flick off his lamp.

"What are you doing?" he asked, confused.

"Shhh." I put my finger to my lips as Aden had done to me. "Aden heard something, or I think he did. I don't know. He told me to come inside, get you, and hide. He said we would know when it was safe to come out."

"What's going on?" Rayn asked, fearful.

"I don't know," I admitted. "He didn't say."

Dmitri crept to the window and peeked over the edge of the windowsill.

"Do you see anything?" I whispered, kneeling down next to him. I was afraid to let too much of me show in the window. The tops of our heads would give away our spot. Aden told us to hide, not stare out the windows.

A crescent moon showed brightly in our backyard. The branches of the trees that lined the property began to shift and the leaves brushed together like the wind blew through the yard. None of us breathed, our heartbeats echoing against our ribs.

A large man in all black stepped out of the treeline and I recognized him instantly. Four more hunters followed behind the first; only a handful but more than enough to kill all of us with their power-numbing darts.

Dmitri, Rayn and I all shot down out of sight. The last thing we needed was one of the hunters to look up and see us peeping out the window.

"They came for Aden," I whispered.

"Goddamn it, I told you this would happen," Dmitri hissed through his teeth.

"How did Aden know they were coming?" Rayn whispered, her hand over her chest in an attempt to calm her pulsing heart.

"He's in on it," Dmitri said.

"No, he would never," Rayn snapped back.

"Shut the fuck up," I whispered to both of them.

Rayn was the first one to peek out the window again.

"What are you doing? They're going to see you." Dmitri grabbed Rayn's arm, but that didn't stop her.

"To see if Aden is okay."

"Forget Aden."

Rayn ignored him.

"What do you see?" I asked, curiously.

"Nothing yet. I can't see where they went," Rayn replied. her breath fogging the cold glass.

"They are probably breaking into the house to come and slaughter us," Dmitri muttered.

"I deadbolted the front door," I whispered.

"Like that's going to stop them."

"Shhh, look," Rayn replied, her fingers curled over the edge of the windowsill.

"What is it?" I asked.

"Just look."

"I don't think–"

"Ezekiel!" A loud voice thundered outside, making me jump and grab Dmitri's arm so tight my fingernails dug into his skin.

"It's Aden." Rayn gripped the edge of the windowsill.

Aden stood proudly in front of the pack; his head up and his back straight as if he had never been injured at all. He held a hammer in his hand.

"I knew we would find you with the witches. You smell like them," the man who I assumed to be the leader of the pack seethed.

Aden shook his head. "You can kill them, but it will only risk exposing the den. Like when you killed that girl and left her body for the authorities to find. You're sloppy, Zeke."

"And you've betrayed your family."

"Then come and give me the punishment you see fit." Aden held his arms out. "If you can catch me."

Surprisingly, none of the men reached for their guns or their crossbows but instead took off running after Aden as he disappeared into the trees.

"What just happened?" Rayn sat up on her knees, peering out the window in the direction Aden had gone.

I took in a shaky breath, still clinging to Dmitri's arm. "I have no idea, but the hunters officially know where we live."

"Do you really think they're gone?" Even in the darkness, tears welled clearly in Rayn's eyes.

"I don't know…either way, I'm not sleeping tonight." Dmitri tensed as I clung to him. "We can't stay here."

"Where are we supposed to go?" Rayn asked quietly.

"The cottage," I answered, jumping up. "It's the only safe place we have right now."

My hands trembled around the steering wheel even after we entered downtown Rifton. Rayn sat in the passenger seat, her head against the glass as she gazed out the window solemnly. I glanced at Dmitri in the rearview mirror, he looked like he might be sick.

"This is wild." Rayn threw her head back against the seat.

"Well, that's what people do. They surprise you." I tilted my head against the window, hoping the cold glass would help subside my growing headache.

"Yeah, that's for sure...Um, excuse me. What is this?" Rayn grabbed the collar of my sweatshirt and yanked on it, exposing my neck.

"What are you doing?" I pulled my clothing back into place with one hand as I gripped the steering wheel with the other.

Rayn looked at me like I had eaten the last cookie. "More like what have you been doing? You have like three hickies on your neck."

"Ugh, of course I do." I huffed, suddenly feeling self-conscious.

"You are an addict. Obviously Bryan isn't any better. He left his mark all over you."

"He loves me, Rayn," I explained. "He knows everything now, and he still wants me."

"Well yeah, he would be stupid not to."

"No, Ray, I mean...He knows about Tom. About what I did."

"Sis, you can't keep moping around like you're some monster. You were protecting us." Rayn reached out for my hand. "You really think the world isn't better off without scum like Tom Campbell crawling around? You are a hero."

"I killed someone."

"An evil someone. You did humanity a favor."

"He was still a person." I rubbed my aching temple.

"How are we going to begin explaining all of this to Mia?" Dmitri asked.

"Uh, I don't know, maybe she'll learn that keeping shit from us is dangerous?" Rayn raised her voice in irritation.

"Does she know we're coming over?"

"I text Nic."

"You text him but not Mia?" Dmitri asked me, confused.

"Yes. He and Ray could do some serious damage. If the hunters come back, light 'em up."

Rayn chuckled. "I love you."

"I love you too, both of you." A tear streaked down my cheek. "More than anything."

Chapter Twenty-Two

RUSHING THINGS

Whitney

We didn't tell Amilia about the hunters, or why we showed up to her house in the middle of the night. I had every intention to, but when the moment came and I looked into her blue eyes, I couldn't speak.

Amilia didn't push us for information, she simply put her hand on my shoulder and gave it a gentle squeeze. "You three are welcome here anytime, for whatever reason you chose."

Dominic, on the other hand, didn't stay quiet. He stood by the fireplace with crossed arms and flames in his eyes after Amilia made her way upstairs for bed. "Well? Something you'd like to share with the class?" he asked.

"Not to you," Rayn answered quickly and headed down the hall to Lauren's bedroom, Dmitri on her heels.

Nic's demeanor softened as he sighed. "Talk to me, kiddo."

"Hunters," I whispered without a second thought.

Nic's brow furrowed. "In town?"

"At my house."

He stood silent for a moment, as if gathering his thoughts. "Okay, okay, start at the beginning."

"They ambushed us in the meadow and then found out where we lived. Rayn left her bag up there after the attack, so they probably found our address on her license," I answered, conveniently leaving out key details.

"And how exactly did you get away?" Nic pushed his back off the mantle to take a step towards me.

"Magic," I whispered.

"This isn't a game, Whitney. Fucking talk to me," Nic snapped.

"I already told you more than anyone else. Stop being so greedy. I'm going to bed, I have to work in the morning." I started to turn away.

Nic gently grabbed my shoulder and turned me to face him. "You don't understand, the hunters don't come into town. They've never been this close to Rifton in my lifetime."

"And how do you know so much about them, yet failed to mention their existence to us? Now I have to worry about hunters hidden in the crowd with the Renati too? You guys aren't doing anything to help us!"

"Because the meadow is supposed to be protected. They were never able to get to it, not the hunters, not the Renati. There are supposed to be wards around the forest."

"A lot has changed since you faked your death."

Nic took a step back, glaring at me. "Goodnight, Harmony," he hissed and retreated to his bedroom.

All the information Nic had shared with me, and he conveniently left out that there were witch hunters in the woods potentially tracking our every move. He wasn't any better than Amilia for that, but I couldn't control their choices. If Mia and the Magisters were going to lie to us, we would have to figure this out on our own. But there wasn't anything else I could do about it that night. Hopefully Aden had survived his pack and they were far away from here. We were in a safe place, and that alone eased some tension in my shoulders.

A lingering silence hung over the Corner Cup the next morning. Everything went on with an unsettling normalcy as if my siblings and I hadn't been forced from our home the night before. Luckily, the morning rush had faded and the stragglers were quiet. We were only a few days away from the solstice, the first day of winter. The streets were crowded with holiday shoppers and those already on break.

The jingle of the opening door echoed through the dining area as a rush of excitement came over me. I knew who had walked in before I laid eyes on him. I waved to Bryan as he strolled to the counter.

"Hey, baby," he smiled, sitting down at his usual seat next to the food display case.

"How does it feel to be officially done with the semester?" I asked, meeting his beautiful green eyes.

"Relieved," he answered, stretching his arms out over the counter. "I, uh, I couldn't get all online classes for Spring like I did this semester though."

I froze in place. "Oh...what is that going to look like?"

Bryan sighed. "I couldn't get all my classes in two days either, so I'll have to be in Falcon Bay Monday through Thursday. I'll come home Thursday evening and head back Sunday night."

My heart sunk, weighing me down. "Oh."

"I'm not very happy about it. My hours at Giani's are getting cut in half, but it's only for a few months. I'll be done with college all together come June."

"We'll make it work." I smiled, genuinely meaning my words. A customer came up to the counter and I stepped away to take their order. Lauren was on her break and I didn't want to call her back just to make a quick americano, so I made the drink myself and returned to Bryan.

"Hey," Bryan reached across the counter for me as I returned. "I'm really sorry, I tried. Things are finally official with us and I didn't want to force you into a long distance relationship. I can tell you're upset."

I let out a deep breath and took his hand. "I'm going to miss you, but I'm not upset about you going to college, Byn. Besides, is an hour and a half even considered long distance?"

"Then what's going on?" His eyes searched mine for an answer.

I hesitated. "If I tell you, you can't freak out."

"That's a great way to begin a conversation." His fingers tightened around mine. "Seriously, Whit, what happened this time?"

I skimmed the dining area. The remaining customers were minding their coffee, not paying attention.

"The hunters from the forest came to the house last night," I whispered before someone interrupted us.

"What?" Bryan's voice echoed through the shop.

"Shh." I leaned over the counter, desperate for him to keep his voice down.

"I'm sorry," he whispered, leaning into the counter to meet me halfway. "You dropped a bomb on me. Is everyone okay?"

"We're fine, they didn't get inside. We stayed at the cottage last night."

"I knew I should have gone home with you. You can't stay in your house, they know where you live."

My shoulders fell. "Even if we leave, they can track us somewhere else, I'm sure."

"You still have to try to protect yourself, and not just you but Ray and Mit." Bryan sighed, nerves accompanied his worry. "I'm not saying this because of the hunters…There's something I've been thinking about."

"What do you mean?" I asked, tilting my head.

His eyes softened as his voice took a serious tone. "Move in with me."

"Oh…" I paused, not sure how to respond.

"We spend most nights together anyway. Troy's dad is taking a job promotion in Portland and leaving the house with Troy and I. I already talked to them and they're both okay with it."

"Bryan…I don't know. It feels really sudden."

"Does it though?" he asked, putting his other hand over mine. "I want this. It's more than wanting to keep you close to protect you. I want to wake up to you in the morning. Make tea while you drink coffee and get ready for the day." He ran his thumb across the back of my hand. "We'll have two extra rooms, you and I can have the master. Dmitri and Rayn can have their own bedrooms. The house is paid off and Troy and I already pay the utilities so all you have to worry about is food." Bryan smiled. "And I don't know, maybe this will help us put some money aside to buy our own place someday."

"Our own place," I whispered, allowing the day dream to wash over me as if we had a real future together past Erebus and the Renati.

He smiled. "With a porch swing. What do you think?"

"I think you've put a lot of thought into this." I imagined what living together would look like. Waking up to the same alarm, falling asleep every night without the looming decision of staying or going so I wasn't leaving anyone home alone. Two toothbrushes on the bathroom counter. My books on his shelves. I smiled at the thought when reality washed over me. "How is this going to work if you're in Falcon Bay all week?"

"I don't start classes until the end of January."

"I know, but what does this look like if you're gone and I live at the house without you?" I chewed on my bottom lip. I didn't want to admit to Bryan that it could potentially be awkward living at the house without him. I got along with Troy fine, but we never hung out just the two of us.

He paused, as if he hadn't actually come up with a solution yet. "We'll figure it out."

"That simple?" I raised an eyebrow.

Bryan nodded. "I know in a typical relationship, this is rushing things but you and I are not in a typical relationship. Promise me you'll think about it."

I smiled, squeezing his hand. "I'll talk to Rayn and Dmitri."

"So you guys will stay at the cottage until you figure everything out?" Bryan leaned back in his seat.

I shrugged. "I don't know. We're going to stay there until the Solstice dinner but haven't discussed after that. It only happened last night."

"Okay." Bryan sighed, his emotions unsettled. I imagined they were mostly from hearing we were staying at the cottage and not with him.

"Are you sure you can't come to Solstice dinner?" I asked, wanting to ease his stress.

Bryan shook his head. "I have to work, baby. It's okay though, I wouldn't want to intrude."

"You're not intruding if you're invited."

Bryan reached across the counter and covered my hand in his again. "Try to relax. You need a night off."

Solstice dinner looked much different than Amilia's Thanksgiving spread. Instead of lavish side dishes, the table was filled with a variety of hors d'oeuvres and a massive pot of stew. Apple tarts and a tray of fudge sat at the edge of the table. A Yule log decorated with small candles atop pine branches and bundles of red berries all foraged from the woods sat as the centerpiece. Amilia had gone all out for the holidays, making me wonder how she ever lived in solitude for so many years. The holiday itself felt different than Thanksgiving too; the air lighter with less tension. It may have had something to do with Harmony's absence, since she went back to wherever she lived for Christmas.

I watched Dmitri gently wave his fingers as ornaments floated up from his hand onto a large fir tree in the corner of the living room. Warren and Rayn hung strands of garland across the top of the fireplace. It reminded me of how Mom would decorate the house during winter. The smell of cinnamon and clove wafted in from the kitchen, mixing with the scent from the dried oranges hanging from the mantle.

Unlike Christmas Day, there would be no exchange of gifts. Amilia requested we celebrate the solstice together "as a family" rather than "under obligation". I wish I could explain to her that I still felt obligated but I appreciated her attempt to maintain some sort of normalcy during this time.

With a sigh, I leaned against the wall. No matter how hard I tried, I couldn't muster a shred of holiday spirit. It felt like I watched a movie. There were no swells of joy that ran through my body, no smile on my face as I watched my siblings and friends mingle by the decorated fireplace. As if I wasn't actually here, just observing.

I wandered across the room to the bookshelves, running my fingertips along the spines. Maybe the holidays gave me nostalgia but I wanted to see those photo albums Dmitri had seen on Thanksgiving. I slipped one out from the shelf and opened to a random page, my mother's young face immediately smiling up at me. Tears welled in the bottom of my eyes, blurring my vision as my heart swelled. My chest ached seeing her but I missed her enough that the pain felt worth it.

I flipped the page to see my mom and a man with Dmitri's eyes. My breath caught in my throat as I ran my fingers over the photo.

"Ah," Amilia's voice came over my shoulder. "I believe that's the only photo I have of them."

"Is this Kyle?" I whispered, glancing over at Dmitri who still decorated the tree.

Amilia turned to look at me, a glimmer of surprise in her eyes. "Yes."

"Mom wrote about him in her journal," I lied, not wanting to throw Nic under the bus. "Dmitri doesn't know anything about him."

"Whatever fantasy he has created in his mind about his father is better than the reality," Amilia replied, a hint of sadness in her voice.

"He still deserves to know," I argued. "It's half of who he is."

"Did you ever go digging for your birth parents?"

Amilia's question hit me in the chest like a sucker punch. "No. This isn't about me, this is about Dmitri."

Hearing his name, Dmitri turned his attention to Amilia and I. "What about me?"

Amilia sighed, clearly irritated with me. She probably didn't plan on heavy conversation during the Solstice, but I wanted Dmitri to at least have the option. If he told me himself he was uninterested in knowing about his father, I'd drop it.

"Whitney found an old photo of your father," Amilia said.

"My father?" Dmitri crossed the room to look at the photo. He took the album from my hands and held it close to his face. "Wow...that's him?"

"Have you never seen a photo of him?" Amilia asked, watching Dmitri's face carefully.

He shook his head. "Everyone tells me how much I look like Mom, but...he's in here too, isn't he?"

No one spoke as Dmitri processed, the gears turning in his head as he stared off into the corner. He looked over at Amilia and asked, "Can you tell me about him? Like, why he and my mom didn't stay together?" He paused, chewing on his bottom lip. "Because of–?"

"No." Amilia answered before Dmitri finished his thought. "No, their separation had nothing to do with you. Kyle and Audri had their own differences that they weren't able to work through."

Unsatisfied with her answer, Dmitri pushed on. "Like what?"

"He, um, Kyle and your mother had different ideals."

"Mia, just tell me."

Amilia sighed. "Kyle was a member of the Renati."

Dmitri blinked at her, his face unreadable. "Was? As in he isn't anymore?"

"He passed, years ago."

"Oh." Dmitri's shoulders fell and he handed the photo album back to me. "Okay."

"Mit, are you okay?" I asked, worried I had made the wrong choice.

Dmitri nodded. "Yeah, I'm kind of surprised, honestly. He's a stranger, so it's not like his death means anything." He gave me a small smile. "Either way, I became an orphan the day Mom died. Did my mom know he was Renati when they got together?"

"She didn't know until after." Amilia shook her head. "It's the reason they broke up."

"That makes more sense," Dmitri said, going back to the tree ornaments.

Amilia looked at me sideways before she joined Dmitri by the fireplace. I put the photo album away, staring into the flames. Maybe Amilia had been right, maybe whatever fantasy Dmitri made up about Kyle was better than knowing the truth.

Where is Dominic? Rayn's voice asked inside my head, drawing my attention from the fire.

Outside. Why? I answered.

Come with me.

Rayn made eye contact with me before she slipped out of the living room through the kitchen. I made sure no one noticed us before I followed Rayn through the back door. The crisp winter air chilled my lungs as I took in a deep breath, watching the small cloud form in front of me as I exhaled. Rain was on its way, I could feel it in the atmosphere. I could smell it lingering.

Nic leaned against the railing with his back to us. The smell of cigarette smoke hit me in the face and I turned my head away.

"Those things are going to kill you," I said, gagging on the overwhelming smell.

Nic looked over his shoulder and took a final drag before he put the cigarette out on the railing. "What can I do for you?"

Rayn stepped towards him. "I looked into your list of potential hideouts. Most of them were busts but I went into the florist and it's still there. The owner doesn't feel like she's Renati though, she openly talked about how annoying the council was at Founder's Day," Rayn jumped right in. "I just wanted to update you. There's something about the florist. I felt the pull."

"Not Renati?" Nic crossed his arms and leaned his back against the railing. "Something might come of it, though. Thank you for doing all that, Rayn." He looked back and forth between us. "While I have you both, I talked to Warren about the portal closing in the meadow."

"What did he say about Finn?" I asked.

"Definitely dead. Open casket and everything," Nic sighed in frustration.

Rayn shook her head. "There's no possible way someone else could have closed the portal? It had to be him?"

"Yes, unless I didn't understand portal magic as well as I thought I did. A lot of knowledge has been lost over the years." Nic ran his fingers through his hair. "I'm starting to question things I accepted as fact."

"Welcome to the club." Rayn buried her hands into the pocket of her hoodie.

"Kind of like hunters roaming around the forest? Seriously, I didn't keep that information from you intentionally. They genuinely weren't supposed to be an issue." Nic's eyes locked on mine. "Do you honestly believe I'd let you get hurt like that?"

"No," I answered softly. "I'm sorry."

"Don't apologize. We have to figure out who broke the wards." Nic crossed his arms. "The Renati are intense but they aren't stupid. Hunters are just as much a danger to them as they are to us."

"Who else besides the Renati would have broken the wards though?" Rayn asked.

"Someone powerful," Nic admitted. He glanced over my shoulder and smiled. "I'll pay your florist a visit, Rayn. Try not to stress tonight, have a drink."

Nic walked past us into the house, scooting past Lauren, Rose and Brooke in the doorway.

"Are we interrupting?" Rose asked.

"Nope, just chatting. What's up?" Rayn asked, eying the wine in Lauren's arms.

Lauren set two bottles of Rosé on the ledge of the deck. "I wanted some time for the five of us to say thank you." She cleared her throat and steadied herself. "You guys have been there for me in ways that I didn't deserve...after the way I treated you...I wanted to show how much I appreciate you. How much you girls mean to me. I wasn't sure what to expect when I came back to Rifton. I was in shock about what had happened and I worried about seeing you again. I wasn't even sure you'd care if I came back. So, thank you for caring."

"Lo." I wrapped my arms around her and pulled her in close. "You can't get rid of us that easily."

Lauren chuckled and stepped back, twisting off the top to one of the bottles. "Shit, I didn't grab any glasses."

"Oh, who needs a glass." Rayn reached for the second bottle and took off the cap, taking a quick swig before handing it to me. "Happy Solstice, girls."

"Happy Solstice!"

The five of us drank to one another, to our generation and the bond we shared. A bond so strong that nothing thrown at us thus far had been able to break us. It had bent and swayed but we were flexible, and we would remain so against whatever else the Renati had planned for us. But in the meantime, we were safe at the cottage. The perimeter spell held strong, and for one night we could relax and drink without looking over our shoulders.

"I made you guys something," Brooke announced, pulling four little wrapped packages from her bag. "It's not much, but I wanted to do something more sentimental than buying gifts."

"B, you didn't have to do that." Rose took the package from Brooke.

The wrapping all matched our powers. Rose's present was covered in cartoon cacti. Rayn's had an orange ribbon tied around red paper. Lauren's was shiny with golden swirls and mine had little blue and purple mermaids.

"Open them." Brooke smiled watching us all take in the time and effort she'd put into the wrapping. Inside the little box lay a string of buttons tied together. "They're bracelets."

"These are adorable!" Rayn pulled her orange and red button bracelet from the box and held it up.

I took my bracelet from the box, buttons of different shades of blue all strung together.

"I know we already have matching jewelry but those are kind of heavy, metaphorically. Everyone calls them the Shepherd's lost talismans, like they aren't actually ours. But these bracelets I made are ours, to symbolize our bond. Because of everything we've been through, not because of a past generation." Brooke pulled up her sleeve to show the purple and black buttons tied around her wrist.

"I love them so much." I smiled.

"Here, let me help you." Brooke tied the bracelet around my wrist.

Rose smiled, putting her arm around Brooke's shoulders. "The sentiment is beautiful. I love that we have something just for us."

Lauren sat down, leaning her back against the railing. She picked up the bottle and let out a relaxed sigh; the first time I'd seen Lauren's shoulders free from tension since she'd returned to Rifton.

"So, now that we're alone." Rayn glanced over at me. "Uh, we're okay, obviously, but the hunters found our house."

"What?" Rose startled towards us. "What happened?"

"They followed that man there, didn't they?" Brooke linked her arm in mine.

Rayn nodded. "Aden led the pack astray and we left as soon as we could, in case the hunters came back to the house to finish us off."

"So, this huntsman from the forest...he saved you guys again," Lauren clarified, taking another drink from the bottle before she handed it to me.

"They know where you guys live now either way," Rose replied.

"I know." I sighed, taking a drink of wine. "So much for having our own place."

"I can't sleep in that house." Rayn looked off into the distance as she spoke. "It's been too much, too many bad memories."

"If Abe doesn't come home, Dmitri thinks Janice and Jeff might sell. We would have to move anyway." I handed the bottle to my sister.

"And he's just hiding out in the woods?" Brooke looked up at me.

I shrugged. "He won't come home."

"Will you guys stay here?" Lauren asked.

"I don't know where else to go," Rayn answered. "It's getting crowded here though."

"Yeah…" Lauren chuckled. "Too bad Mia can't magically create another bedroom, or a bathroom at least."

"Bryan asked me to move in with him," I announced while I still had the nerve to do so.

Rose's head whipped towards me. "What?"

"I know." I slowly nodded. "It's a big step."

"He did? When?" Rayn asked with wide eyes.

"After I told him about the hunters coming to the house," I answered. "Not just me, but you and Mit too."

"How are all three of us supposed to move into his house when he already lives with Troy and his dad?" Rayn lifted an eyebrow and crossed her arms.

"I guess Troy's dad is taking a promotion in Portland so they'll have two open bedrooms."

Rose remained silent. I couldn't tell by her face if she had an opinion on the matter, or if she pretended she didn't care. She took a drink from the bottle Rayn handed her and cleared her throat.

"I'd rather stay here," Rayn said. "No offense. I like Bryan and Troy, but I'll never live somewhere that I can't openly be myself. Home has been a place where we can use magic without thinking twice and I'm not going back to how things were in foster care."

I was disappointed in her answer, but I understood. She brought up a point that I had yet to consider. "I get it."

"What are you going to do?" Lauren turned to me.

"I want to move in with Bryan," I answered honestly. "I stay there a lot anyway, but I don't want to split the three of us up."

"I mean, we're all pretty much adults. We were never going to all live together forever." Rayn's words caught me off guard.

"Dmitri is not an adult." I furrowed my brow.

"Then if you're going to tell him where to live anyway, what does it matter? Move Mit in with Bryan and I'll stay here."

I didn't know what to say. I had lived under the same roof as Rayn since I was eight years old. For thirteen years I had my sister across the hall. So many things in our lives had been uncertain but she remained a constant.

Rayn offered a reassuring smile. "Whit, I had a feeling this would happen when you and Bryan got serious. I'm not mad."

"I know..." I paused. "I didn't think it would happen this soon."

"I did." Rayn chuckled.

Rose finally spoke. "I definitely did."

"What do you mean?" I turned to her.

Rose shrugged. "I'm surprised he waited this long, to be honest. He's been wanting to move you into the house since you got back together."

Rose handed me the bottle and I took a long drink.

Chapter Twenty-Three

Uninvited Guests

Whitney

I stood frozen on the sidewalk. A statue out in the cold as I peered through the windows of Rose's house. The Christmas Eve festivities were in full swing. People conversed with small cups of what I assumed was spiked punch in their hands as they laughed amongst themselves. I didn't recognize a single one of them. Rayn had already rung the doorbell before she realized I was incapacitated with anxiety, my lungs collapsing in my chest.

Dmitri stepped towards me. "Whit, you gotta take a deep breath. Your hands are literally frozen."

I glanced down at my bare hands, glistening against the porch light. A thin sheet of ice covered my bright red fingers. Doing my best to steady myself, the ice melted from my fingers.

"Hey, guys!" Rose greeted from the front door as she opened it, stepping back to let Rayn in. Rose noticed Dmitri and I in the middle of the yard and stepped out onto the porch, pulling her thin sweater tightly around her purple dress. "Are you guys coming inside?" she asked, no doubt feeling the freight train of emotions that ran through my body. "It's supposed to start raining any second."

"I'm nervous," I admitted softly.

"Don't be." Rose reached her hand out and motioned for me to come with her. I climbed the porch steps and she took my hand in hers. "Every time the doorbell has gone off, Byn's jumped to see if it's you. He's nervous too."

The house felt too warm. A fire roared in the brick fireplace in the corner of the living room with stockings hung picturesquely on the wall next to it. Garland adorned the mantle and every railing in the house. A huge pine tree with bright white lights sat in the far corner with red and gold decor. Christmas music played quietly in the background; the same radio station all the stores downtown used to put everyone in the spirit to spend money. Trays of finger foods covered the kitchen counter with a separate table for drinks. Everything about the room felt warm. The guests were thrilled to see one another; hands on elbows, tight hugs and kisses on the cheek. I scanned all the unfamiliar faces, begging to see blonde hair and green eyes and home.

I finally found him by the staircase talking to Emma and Troy. My breath caught in my throat at the sight of him. Bryan wore a pair of nice jeans with brown dress shoes and a navy blue sweater. He hadn't seen the dress I bought but we still ended up matching. I wanted to call out for him from across the room. I wanted to push past everyone standing between us and collapse into him.

As if he could hear me, Bryan's attention turned to the entryway. When our eyes locked, a smile broke out across his face. He quickly excused himself from his friends and made his way across the room. One. Two. Three. I counted his footsteps as he came within reach. Bryan grabbed for me and pulled me against his chest.

"You look incredible," he whispered in my ear, placing a gentle kiss on my neck.

I hugged him tightly, letting the fear and nerves melt away. "We match," I replied, rubbing his back.

Bryan chuckled. "Blue is your color."

He pulled away and laced his fingers in mine. His warm skin thawed the ice that still lingered on my palm. His eyes wandered down to my freezing skin, knowing what it meant. "You want something to drink? Something strong?"

"Yes," I answered without a second thought.

"Hey, Mit." Bryan rested his free hand on my brother's shoulder. "Hey, Rayn."

"Hey, thanks for the invite." Dmitri smiled.

"Of course."

"Oh, Bryan, don't let me forget." Rayn turned her attention away from Rose. "I have something to tell you later."

"About?" Bryan tilted his head.

"I heard some shit in the breakroom at work. You want to hear about it."

"Katie and Dustin?"

"Wait, you already heard?" Rayn's shoulders fell.

"Bits and pieces." He shrugged.

"Okay, well this is juicy so remind me."

It was odd that Bryan and Rayn had their own insider knowledge. Rayn had never been close with anyone I'd dated in the past. I hadn't been serious with any of them, but Rayn never had her own relationship with them beyond common courtesy and small talk.

"Eggnog or cider? Maybe punch?" Bryan asked, pulling me away from our siblings and towards the beverage table.

A dark green tablecloth sat underneath a large punch bowl with a clear ladle hanging off the side. A glass jug full of eggnog sat next to a beverage dispenser full of apple cider. At the end of the table sat a collection of liquor bottles.

"Um, I've never actually had eggnog," I answered, eyeing my options.

"Here." Bryan grabbed a glass and made himself a drink. He poured some spiced rum in first before filling the rest with the eggnog. He swirled it around and handed it to me. "I usually put cinnamon in it, but this'll give you an idea."

I lifted his glass to my lips and took a sip. The rum slapped me across the face as it burned my throat on the way down.

"Woah." I coughed, handing it back to him. "Oh my god, how do you drink that?"

"Too strong?"

I cleared my throat, thinking back to his buzz from the bonfire. "No wonder you get drunk so quickly."

Bryan laughed. "Do I?"

"Just thinking about the bonfire."

"Psh. I wasn't that drunk at the bonfire. Maybe cider, here." He grabbed the bottle of bourbon and handed it to me. "I'll let you pour."

I made myself a drink and turned to take another look at the guests. Emma and Troy were still tucked by the staircase; Emma up on her toes for a kiss that Troy had to lean down to give her. I couldn't help but smile at them.

Even amongst the happiness that filled the room, I felt someone's gaze on me. As I locked into a pair of all too familiar dark eyes, a chill ran through my body. Henry Drake had appeared to tower over everyone on the stage at Founders Night but he was tall up close too. He wore a nice tailor-made black suit. His dark hair had been styled nicely but the dried gel still made him look greasy. It was surreal being this close to him. Too close for comfort.

My eyes stopped at his hands, covered in scars. He wore long sleeves so I couldn't see how far up the scarred skin went but his hands had been severely burned. The memory of Nic in the forest outside of that burning house flooded my memory. Seeing with my own eyes that Henry Drake had been in that house and tried to kill Nic made my stomach churn.

I waited until Henry Drake glanced away before I turned to Bryan. "Is Serenity here?"

"No," Bryan answered quickly. "She knows better."

"Does she?" I looked back at Henry Drake, glad his attention wandered elsewhere.

One of the key leaders of the Renati in Rifton. The demon that spawned Serenity and the man responsible for the horror Nic went through thirteen years ago. I swallowed the urge to put a spike of ice through his chest.

"Hey." Bryan's warm fingers tilted my chin towards him to get my attention. "My mom is in the kitchen. I'd like to introduce you while she's alone."

"Oh, okay," I answered, putting all my focus into not letting my body freeze over again.

Bryan took my hand and led me into the kitchen. I had seen photos of Rose and Bryan's mother from when I'd been at the house before, but she seemed different in person. She stood on the shorter side with broad shoulders and wide hips but she held herself like she stood seven feet tall. Her dark brown hair pulled up into a bun with loose curls hanging down around her face.

"Bynie, do we need any ice?" she asked, not looking up at us from the oven to see if the man in her kitchen was her son. She just knew.

"No, everything's fine." Bryan cleared his throat and wrapped his arm around my shoulder, squeezing me gently. "Mom, I want you to meet Whitney."

"Oh." His mother dried her hands off on a kitchen towel and turned to face us. She tried to hide that she looked me up and down but I felt her eyes linger before she put out an open hand. "Nice to finally put a face to the name."

"Thank you for having me, Mrs. Mc- Um..." I reached out and shook her hand before she pulled away a bit quicker than I expected.

"Please, call me Nancy." She smiled but her eyes didn't match her lips. "Did you bring your family?"

"Um, yeah. My brother and sister are here."

"We adore Rayn. She's such a sweetheart."

"Yeah, she's everyone's favorite sister," I answered before I realized the words left my lips.

"Not mine," Bryan whispered.

Nancy cleared her throat and wiped her palms on her maroon dress awkwardly. "So, Byn told me you work with Ash at the coffee shop. We're missing her tonight but it's a busy time for everyone."

"Yeah, I've been there four months now." I forced a smile.

"And do you go to school here in town?"

"Oh, um, no. I'm working full time."

"Oh." Nancy turned to Bryan, surprised. As if picturing him with someone that wouldn't one day have a degree pained her.

"Whitney just got a promotion at work, actually," Bryan replied, giving my shoulder another gentle squeeze. "She's a supervisor."

"Well, good for you." Nancy gave a soft smile. Her attention quickly pulled away when a man entered the kitchen holding a bottle of brandy.

"I brought your favorite," the man said, giving Nancy a quick kiss on the cheek before he retrieved a glass from the cabinet and poured her a drink. "Oh, Bryan, I have a check for you."

Bryan's gaze hardened before he turned to face the man, not bothering to hide his annoyance. "Jack, I already paid for Rose's car."

"Yeah but I know you had to pull the cash out of your savings. There's no need for you to put yourself in the hole over something your mother and I can gladly help with. Your best friend may be a mechanic but you're not responsible for Rose's car," the man answered, handing Nancy her glass of brandy, which she quickly took a swig of.

"Technically neither are you," Bryan muttered.

Jack pulled a check out of his pocket and handed it over. Bryan stared down at it, irritation swirled through his body.

"Stop being so stubborn and take the damn money, Byn," Nancy snapped at him.

Bryan let out a huff and shoved the check into his pocket. His fingers dug into my skin. He didn't realize until I squirmed, scrunching my shoulder. He quickly released me and whispered, "I'm sorry, baby."

"Is this her? Whitney, right? I'm Jack, Nancy's other half. Rose told us all about you, which is great because Bryan likes to keep his love life a secret." Jack put his hand out and gave mine a sturdy shake.

"I wasn't keeping her a secret," Bryan answered monotone.

"Well, all I'm saying is if I knew you were bringing home a woman, I wouldn't have wasted Becca's time," Jack said as Nancy finished off her glass of brandy.

"Hmm?" I turned to Bryan, confused as to what Jack meant.

"Nothing," Bryan answered softly, letting his fingers graze down the side of my body until they rested on my waistline.

"My buddy's daughter was so smitten with this guy, but he had his sights set elsewhere. Nance and I didn't even know he was seeing someone until he told Becca he was hung up on some girl. Hannah all over again." Jack spoke like a faucet with a broken handle; no turning it off once he got going.

Who the hell was Hannah and why did everyone keep bringing her up?

Nancy poured herself another drink and finally rejoined the conversation. "Byn wants what he wants and if he can't have it, then he won't have anything at all."

I wasn't sure what to do with that.

"Bryan is an absolute catch. He has no reason to settle when he can have whatever he wants," I answered, my knees beginning to tremble. I planted my feet onto the laminate floor so they couldn't see my nerves.

"Hey, Whit," Rayn's voice filled the kitchen. She stood by the dining room table close to the beverages. "Can I borrow you real quick?"

"Yes," I answered too quickly and slipped out of Bryan's arm.

Rayn took my hand and we weaved through the guests to a small half bathroom by the staircase. She swiftly closed the door behind us and turned to face me, her pupils dilated.

"Are you okay?" she asked.

"They hate me. Nancy hates me." Tears welled in my eyes before I could get the words out.

"Don't cry, you'll mess up your makeup." Rayn wadded up some toilet paper and held it under my eye, catching a stray tear before it should stain my cheek. "And Nancy doesn't hate you. I'm sure she's stressed from throwing this big party."

"She told me how much she adores you and didn't bother to hide her disappointment when she found out I'm a college dropout. She thinks I'm not good enough for him."

"That is bullshit because you are way out of his league, do you understand me? Fuck what Nancy or anyone else thinks about it. Bryan is damn lucky to have you."

"You're biased," I answered, taking the toilet paper from her and wiping away the last of my tears.

"So? It's still the truth."

I changed the subject. "Henry Drake is here."

"I saw him. Luckily I think we're in a public enough place that he won't try to kill us here. It would expose him."

"Where's Mit?"

"With Rose. We're going to stick together and get through tonight, okay? Henry Drake can't touch us and you're going back out there with your head held high because you don't give a fuck what anyone thinks about you. You know your worth."

I sighed, letting her pep talk sink in enough that I started to believe it. "Thank you," I whispered.

"Oh, dude, the moment I heard Jack's big ass mouth going off I knew I had to come get you." Rayn put her warm hands on my shoulders. "He's a nice enough guy but he doesn't have a filter."

"I noticed."

She gave my shoulder a comforting rub. "Bryan has been really nervous about tonight. He told me at work."

"Because he's worried about impressing his mom."

"No, quite the opposite. He's worried about *you* liking *them*."

"Really?"

"Yes." Rayn smiled, taking out a bobby pin that had fallen from my hair. She held it in her mouth as she fixed the rogue strand. "Jack pisses him off and Nancy is completely non confrontational. He's been stressed over how you'd take them, not how they will take you. Bryan is proud of you and he loves you, college dropout and all."

I sniffed, swallowing all those feelings of self-doubt as Rayn pinned my hair back up.

"Come on," I said, reaching for the door handle. "Let's get back out there."

When I opened the door, Bryan leaned against the wall with his hand in his hair. He was a bundle of nerves, wound so tight he might snap from the pressure. A small spark of relief relaxed his shoulders when he saw us. Rayn slipped past, giving us a moment of privacy.

"I'm sorry," he said, taking a step towards me. "That's why I wanted you to meet my mom alone."

"It's okay, everything is fine." I rested my palms on his chest and leaned up for a kiss, pressing my lips to his. Bryan's hands wrapped around my back and returned the kiss with an eagerness that wasn't there earlier. Relief with a hint of desire coursed through me.

"You're gorgeous every day but you really do look exceptionally stunning tonight," he whispered against my lips. "That dress."

I let out a soft laugh as my fingertips caressed down his chest, hooking into the belt loops of his pants. "These jeans look great on you."

"Thank you." He eyed my hands carefully.

"I bet they'd look even better on the floor."

A jolt of electricity shot through him and he cleared his throat, caught off guard. "That's an interesting theory. We should test it."

I laughed and gave him another kiss before we were interrupted by the sound of Nancy's voice echoing through the living room.

"Thank you everyone for coming tonight. Every year we look forward to this gathering of our family and friends," Nancy announced, clasping her hands together. "Now it's time for my favorite part of the night, secret Santa. If you signed up, please come over to the gift table and find the package with your name on it for the reveal."

Bryan pressed his lips to my forehead. "I gotta partake in that."

"Yeah, of course." I grabbed his hand and pulled him back, wiping away the maroon lipstick I'd left behind on his bottom lip with my thumb.

He smiled slyly and leaned into my ear. "Afterwards, we'll slip away with a bottle."

"It's a date."

He joined the crowd gathering at the gift table, slapping Troy on the shoulder. Troy wrapped his arm around Bryan and pulled him into a sideways hug.

Emma picked up a poorly wrapped gift with her name on it and a messy bow. She held it up in the air and announced. "This is from Byn! I can tell by the wrapping."

Everyone laughed as Bryan shrugged. "Merry Christmas, Em."

"Shut up! I pulled your name too!" Emma squealed with glee as she handed Bryan a gift bag with perfectly curled ribbons and a reindeer tag.

Bryan and Emma stepped off to the side to unwrap their gifts as everyone else participating in the exchange searched for their present, Rose among them. Rayn and Dmitri crossed the room to join me at the base of the staircase.

"Where did Drake go?" Dmitri asked quietly, scanning the room.

Rayn shrugged. "I lost track of him when Whit and I were in the bathroom. He couldn't have gone far."

The party dwindled down as the hours went by, and soon only a handful of us remained. Emma and Troy gave us hugs before they left. Bryan grabbed my hand and gently pulled me towards the back of the house, a half empty bottle of wine under his arm.

We were the only ones in the backyard and the rain made a musical pattern on the covered patio. The sound of holiday music muffled by the barrier of the exterior walls. Bryan took a drink from the bottle before handing it to me. The wine tasted sweet and went down easily. Bryan smiled as he pulled a narrow, neatly wrapped box from his pocket. "Merry Christmas." His voice was soft as he placed the gift in my hands.

"I didn't bring your present." I met his gaze.

"Open it."

"This is wrapped much nicer than your secret Santa gift," I teased, breaking the tape seal.

"Rose wrapped it for me," he admitted, a slight pink tint flushing his cheeks. "I wanted it to look nice."

I didn't have jewelry that wasn't purchased from vendor booths at craft fairs, but I knew a jewelry box when I saw one. I opened back the lid and shiny silver stared at me. Swirls of sterling silver wrapped around a long row of little diamonds. My heart dropped into my stomach.

"Baby." I breathed. This was too much, too nice. I would never be able to get him anything that compared to this. How could I possibly give him the books I had picked out after he had given me a diamond bracelet?

"It's our first Christmas together. I wanted to get you something special." His deep voice soothed my anxiety as he gently took the bracelet from the box. "May I?"

I held out my arm and watched as he carefully clasped it around my wrist. A perfect fit.

"Bryan..."

"I initially thought of getting you a necklace but your talisman is the star of that show." Bryan ran his fingers down the silver chain of my aquamarine that hid strategically underneath my dress. He pulled on the chain and revealed the blue gem, white ink swirling around it. "Do you like it?"

"I love it." A tear escaped the corner of my eye, overwhelmed with how cherished and adored I felt. "I love you."

"I love you too." Bryan brushed his lips against mine, pulling me close to his body.

My lips parted, welcoming his tongue against mine. His fingertips trailed up my thigh, lifting my dress. He ran his fingers along my skin, leaving goosebumps. Once he hooked a finger into the band of my panties, I pulled my lips from his and gazed into his eyes.

"Our families are inside," I whispered.

"I don't see anyone out here."

"Babe–"

"Everyone is gone. I tried to wait until we ended up in one of our beds, but I couldn't." He inched his fingers into the seam of my panties and I didn't stop him. Once he felt how wet they already were, he smiled against my lips. "Thought so."

He slid his index finger into my core and I melted. I bit my lip, attempting to take a deep breath as his thumb rubbed lazy circles around my most sensitive area. My thigh muscles clenched as sparks of heat ignited through my body. He smiled at how I responded to him, pressing a kiss to my neck.

He began to pick up his pace when a scream erupted from inside the house. Bryan and I startled apart. I didn't recognize the scream, but Bryan did. He rushed into the house without a word. I quickly straightened my dress and chased inside after him. The rush of endorphins from having his fingers inside of me mixed with the sudden rush of his fear overwhelmed my system as I followed Bryan into the living room. Rose and Rayn's backs were to me, with Dmitri hidden behind them. I shoved my way past Bryan and grabbed Dmitri, pulling him close as the cause of the scream came into sight.

A massive Shadow hunched over on all fours with large wings sprouted from its back. I had never seen a Shadow this large or with fucking wings before. These creatures were evolving faster than I could wrap my head around. It snarled a hiss at us, attempting to take another step forward, but a thick vine sprouted out of the floor held its back right paw in place. As the Shadow tugged against the vine, the plant began to fray. Rose would only be able to hold it for so long.

Nancy stood in the kitchen, her hand over her quivering mouth. Another scream came from her lips as the vine holding the Shadow finally snapped.

"Bryan, get her out of here." I shoved Dmitri towards the back door. "Get them out. Now."

Bryan didn't hear me, his eyes frozen on the Shadow. Fear pulsed through him as his stomach churned, witnessing a true waking nightmare. "Bryan!" I snapped him out of it. "Get them out. Now!"

He startled back into reality and met my gaze briefly in acknowledgement before he dashed to the kitchen and grabbed his mother's arm.

"Wh-What is that thing?" Nancy stammered, cementing herself to the floor.

"Mom, come on!" Bryan yanked on her arm, pulling her towards the door into the back yard with Dmitri behind them.

I released an ice spell at the Shadow, briefly freezing it into place before I allowed my attention to divert. I made sure Bryan and Dmitri got Nancy out of the house before we unleashed our full power onto the monster.

Several more vines broke through the ground, wrapping around the Shadow and yanking it to the floor. I thrusted my hand at the winged demon, releasing sharp icicles but none of them penetrated its stone skin. The Shadow yanked its back paw up, breaking free from a vine.

"Ray!" I called out, waiting for my sister to help Rose and I.

"I don't want to burn the house down." Rayn surveyed the room in a panic.

Rose threw her other hand out as more vines crashed through the living room window, knocking the Christmas tree over. Glass bulbs and ornaments shattered against the hardwood floor. The vines wrapped around the Shadow's legs and yanked it backwards, pulling the winged beast towards the window. Rose strained, tightening her fists as blood dripped from her nose. With the next tug, the vines pulled the Shadow through the window and into the front yard.

Rayn, Rose and I rushed out the front door to the porch. The Shadow lay on its side on the lawn, struggling against Rose's vines. Now that we were out of the house, Rayn seemed more confident in her abilities. She snapped her fingers, setting her hands ablaze and threw a fireball at the Shadow. Her flames made the beast whine in pain but they also burnt Rose's vines. Rose desperately tried to sprout more to hold the Shadow back but Rayn's fire burned too hot. The vines barely broke through the ground before they caught fire.

"Shit!" Rose cussed. "We're canceling each other out!"

Rayn stepped forward and threw another fireball at the Shadow, striking it in the face. The Shadow stepped backwards, crying out in pain as the fire singed its scales. Rayn quickly conjured another, grunting as she threw the fire with all her might. The winged

Shadow backed away from us slowly, its long, thin tail hanging low behind it. The Shadow flapped its wings, lifting off the ground as it flew into the night sky.

"They're flammable, good to know," Rayn muttered, extinguishing the fire that danced from her fingertips.

We watched the Shadow until it disappeared from sight, blending into the rest of the darkness. My heartbeat pounded in my ears as I attempted to wrap my head around what had happened. That Shadow not only had a fully formed body, but massive wings. It could have easily killed all of us. The Shadow gave up.

"If that thing wanted to kill us, it would have tried harder," I said, turning to Rose and Rayn.

"I agree." Rose nodded, her eyes wandering off into the distance. "My mom..."

"Are you okay?" Rayn asked her.

"No, absolutely not," Rose marched back up the steps into the house. "Can you fix the tree before my mom comes back in?"

I nodded even though Rose wasn't looking. I walked back into the living room, my body trembling with adrenaline as I waved my hand over the Christmas wreckage, putting the tree back on its trunk and mending the broken decor.

Bryan, Dmitri and Nancy came in through the back a moment later. Dmitri shoved his way past everyone, throwing his arms around me. I pulled him close, thankful that they were able to get away from the Shadow. Dmitri let go of me to hug Rayn and Rose as he let out a deep sigh. The moment Dmitri let go of me, Bryan was right behind him, pulling me against his chest. His heartbeat accelerated and his fear washed over me as if it were my own.

"I've never seen anything like that," I admitted into his sweater.

Bryan didn't speak, just gently rubbed his hand against my back.

"I-I don't understand," Nancy stuttered, wringing her quivering hands. "What is going on? What was that thing?"

Bryan broke his hold on me and went to his mother's side, putting his arm around her shoulders. She gripped his sweater sleeve with white knuckles, her face was pale as a ghost.

"I think we should go?" I asked, glancing over to Rose. "Give you guys some space."

Rose nodded. "Yeah, I'll call you."

Rayn put her hand on Rose's shoulder as she and Dmitri headed out the front door.

"Let me walk you out." Bryan left his mother's side as she loosened her tight grip on his arm. Bryan followed us to the car before he spoke again. "The fuck happened?"

"I don't know," I answered honestly. "But my guess is Henry Drake."

Bryan shook his head. "Henry has been at the Christmas parties for years and they've never ended like that."

I stopped and turned towards him, reading between the lines of his words. "You think this is *my* fault?"

"I never said that."

"You didn't have to."

"Whitney." He sighed, running his fingers through his hair. "This isn't about placing blame. It's about a gargoyle in my mother's house."

"They're Shadows."

Bryan shook his head. "Not anymore. That isn't the same thing that came at us after work."

"I know," I admitted, looking back at the front door. "I never meant to put your mom in danger."

"You didn't. You're right, things are different now. I don't know why I thought we could take a night off for Christmas." Bryan opened the car door for me. "I should get inside and see how Rose's talk with my mom is going."

I nodded, attempting to hide my disappointment. "I love you."

Bryan gently took my chin in his hand, tilting my head up to look at him. "I love you very much. I hate that we aren't seeing each other tomorrow."

"You should be here, especially after what happened tonight. Besides, I think Ray, Mit and I should be alone. At least for a bit."

Bryan faked a smile as his fingers slid from my face. Without another word, he headed back up the pathway into the house. My breath turned to smoke in the cold air as I watched him walk away, counting each step.

Chapter Twenty-Four
Holiday Spirit
Whitney

There were no Christmas lights hanging from the Roberts' home. No wreath on the doorway. I would have assumed they were out except for the small light coming from the living room window.

Dmitri knocked on the door then stepped back next to me. He cleared his throat and fidgeted with his hands as if he tried to mask his nerves. Now that the mini mart had officially closed down, I wasn't sure how often he had seen Janice. The door unlocked and opened slowly as Jeff poked his head out.

"Oh, hello." Jeff opened the door further.

"Merry Christmas. We wanted to bring you something." I gave a soft smile as I held out the casserole dish. "It's lasagna. Rayn made it."

Jeff glanced down at the dish and blinked.

"We can come back later if now is a bad time," Dmitri added.

Jeff took the dish from my hands. "Sorry. No, this is fine. Thank you. You're good kids."

"Is Janice home?" I glanced over his shoulder into the dimly lit living room.

"She's upstairs, but I will let her know you brought this by. She'll appreciate it. She likes the three of you a lot." Jeff sighed, shifting his weight between his feet. "I've been meaning to come talk to you kids, Janice has been putting this off but I don't think it's fair to drop it on you at the last minute." Jeff glanced down at the porch. "We're thinking about selling."

"The house?"

Jeff nodded. "If my son...I don't know if we can stay here."

Dmitri let out a breath. "We understand."

He had called it. The longer Abe stayed missing, the harder it would be for the Roberts to stay in this house. How many times could Janice walk past Abe's empty bedroom before the heartache became unbearable?

"We haven't decided, but just in case. We'd never put you kids out." Jeff blinked down at the casserole dish. "Thank you again."

"Thank you for the heads up. Merry Christmas." I grabbed Dmitri's elbow as I turned to leave the porch.

Mit followed quietly until we were halfway across the field. "Now what?"

I sighed. "They haven't decided yet."

"Yes they have," Dmitri replied. "I could see it coming a mile away. I guess we'll be moving into the cottage?"

"Rayn wants to." I chewed on my lip.

"What other choice do we have?"

I paused., curious to see Dmitri's reaction to Bryan's offer. "Bryan wants us to move in with him."

"Seriously?" Dmitri's voice rose with excitement.

"Is that something you'd consider?"

He nodded. "I like Bryan, he's a good guy."

I smiled. "He is. He likes you a lot too. Rayn doesn't want to live anywhere she would have to monitor her magic, and since Troy lives there too, we'd have to watch ourselves."

"I get that," Dmitri said, stopping in front of our porch steps. "The cottage is crowded, and I want to go wherever you go. Not just because I legally have to, but maybe Bryan can help me keep an eye on you, make sure you eat three times a day."

I gave his shoulder a playful shove. "You'd have your own room at Bryan's. Troy's dad is moving out and leaving them the house, so there's an empty bedroom. I guess Troy already said he's okay with us moving in if we wanted to."

"Rayn would only be across town," Dmitri offered, knowing I hated the idea of Rayn not coming with us.

"I know, but I've grown used to having her across the hall."

"Me too. I'm okay with whatever you want to do." Dmitri sighed, his breath smoking in the cold. He squeezed my hand and pulled me towards the house. "Come on, it's Christmas."

When we walked inside, Rayn sat cross legged on the couch, staring at her phone.

"You guys want to watch a movie or something?" I asked, eyeing Rayn's intent texting.

"Actually, I think Mit and I are going to go for a drive." Rayn slid her phone into her back pocket as she jumped up from the couch.

I glanced back and forth between them. "Oh, just the two of you?"

"Yeah, give you some space." Rayn motioned for Dmitri to get his shoes on.

"Um, but we agreed that none of us would stay here alone..."

"Trust me."

After Rayn and Dmitri drove off, I grabbed some wood from the overstock next to the woodstove and attempted to keep the fire alive. I clicked the lighter several times before it finally sparked a flame, but the newspaper I lit disintegrated instead of catching to the wood. I sighed in defeat as I fell back on my ass. Rayn and Mit were off who knows where and I was alone on Christmas. By the time my siblings returned, the house would be freezing cold. I barely noticed the chill that began to fill the house, but they certainly would.

It wasn't long before I gave up on bringing the fire back to life and poured myself a glass of wine. As I began to put the wine back in the fridge, I glanced at the half empty bottle and shrugged, carrying it back to the living room with me. I plopped down on the floor, staring at the diminishing embers when a knock at the door made me jump. Rayn or Mit must have forgotten something.

I opened back the door, surprised to see perfect green eyes smiling back at me. "Bryan, what are you doing here?"

"Dinner wrapped up early." His breath visible in the cold air. "So, Rose called Ray and Mit to see if they wanted to come over for dessert and I snuck off with half an apple pie."

He held up a pie dish wrapped in plastic wrap.

My face broke out in a smile as I let him inside, closing the door behind him. "I thought I'd be spending the rest of the night alone," I admitted, watching Bryan as he set the pie down on the table and stripped off his jacket.

"Have anything special planned?" he asked.

I glanced back at the dark fireplace. "No, I tried to save the fire but I realized I've never had to without Rayn before."

"I can fix that." Bryan grabbed the poker and knelt down in front of the wood stove. He rearranged the wood and added more newspaper in between the logs. Bryan got the fire roaring in no time, making the entire process seem effortless. He leaned back on his heels, admiring his handiwork.

I grabbed two forks from the kitchen and the pie from the table, sitting down on the floor next to him. I handed him a fork. "My hero."

He chuckled, snaking his arm around my waist to pull me close. "Anything for you."

"Did you guys have a good Christmas?"

"Um, yeah," Bryan paused, staring into the flames. "Jack officially proposed to my mom this morning. They want to get married in a few months."

"Oh, wow. That is a quick engagement," I replied, not sure how to react.

"They've been together for years so I guess they don't want to wait. They already booked a venue in Falcon Bay." Bryan frowned at the fireplace.

"Already booked a venue?"

"I guess they started planning a while ago, but didn't tell us. Jack's daughter is an event planner. She already has a spreadsheet."

"And we're happy about this?"

Bryan shrugged. "There are worse men out there, I suppose. It doesn't really matter how I feel about it, she said yes and seems happy. Which is fine, she needed a distraction after how the party ended last night."

"How did everything go after we left?"

"I think my mom is still in shock. She's pretending like nothing happened which is her typical coping mechanism. She'll probably never bring it up again if we don't either."

"After what happened with Lauren's parents, I'm not sure she's safe regardless."

"Rose is brewing something in her room. She won't let anything from the Shadow Realm in the house again. Though with the spell she already put in place, the Shadow shouldn't have gotten in to begin with."

"Henry Drake got in..."

"He was invited." Bryan sighed, sliding his fingers under my sweater to gently caress my skin. "I don't know. If Henry wanted to hurt my mother, he would have done it already."

"No, Byn, that's not how this works." I paused, chewing on the inside of my mouth. "Harmony wanted to wipe your memories at the cottage."

Bryan furrowed his brow. "And?"

I met his gaze, hoping he would guess the thoughts swirling in my mind. Bringing Nancy into the fold didn't make sense when she didn't have any powers to protect herself.

Bryan blinked. "You want to wipe my mother's memories of last night?"

"I mean..." I let out a short sigh, choosing my next words carefully. "Her knowing certainly complicates things, don't you agree? She probably has a million questions and things are hard enough as it is. I'm only trying to protect her, I hope you know that."

Bryan's brow softened as he closed his eyes and nodded. "How would that work exactly?"

"I don't know but I can ask Harmony."

He cleared his throat and shifted. "Let me talk to Rosie first. Did you eat today?" he changed the subject.

"Yes."

"Good. Eat some pie."

I took a bite of pie, closing my eyes as the delicious taste of cinnamon and apple filled my senses. "This is amazing."

"You're amazing." Bryan took the pie from my hands and placed it on the floor. "I thought about you all day. I couldn't stay away." He gripped the back of my neck, pulling me into a kiss.

"I'm glad you came," I smiled against his lips.

Bryan pulled his head back and smirked at me. "You know, I have this vague memory that we were in the middle of something last night, something I very much intend to finish."

I waited for the spark in my soul to ignite, for the passion and excitement to build. While I also intended to finish what we started the night before, my heart wasn't in it tonight. I sighed, not wanting to let him down. "It's been a long day."

"Oh, yeah, that's fine." He tucked a strand of hair behind my ear and kissed my cheek. "We'll make up for it next time."

"Are you sure? I feel bad. You came all the way here and–"

"I came up here to see you on Christmas," Bryan cut me off. "Anything else would've been a bonus." His fingers feathered down my arm, smiling at the diamond bracelet around my wrist.

"You're not mad?" I asked, needing reassurance even though I could feel in my own bones he wasn't the least bit upset.

"Why on earth would I be mad?"

"Just making sure."

"Whit, eat more pie." Bryan gave me a quick kiss before he scooped up a fork full of pie and took a bite. He put his arm around my shoulder and gave a gentle squeeze.

"Oh! Wait!" I jumped up and rushed to my bedroom. Sliding back my closet door, I grabbed the wrapped books I'd gotten for Bryan. I stared at the diamond bracelet for a moment, knowing how sad these gifts seemed in comparison. I let out a short sigh before I headed back to the living room. I handed the wrapped books to Bryan. "Merry Christmas."

A smile swept across his face as he began to unwrap them. "You didn't have to get me anything."

I watched him closely, pretending nerves weren't rattling my core. It's not that I didn't think Bryan would enjoy the books, I knew he would. I only wished I was in a different financial position, able to get him something deserving of a first holiday together. He flipped one of the books over to see the cover and smiled up at me. "I've been wanting to read this."

I smiled back and sat down next to him. "It just came out, so I was hoping you hadn't bought it yet."

He pressed his lips to mine and held the back of my head, pulling me close. "I love them. Thank you so much."

Warmth spread through me as his admiration and joy washed over me as if it were my own.

"I'm glad." I took another bite of pie and settled in against his side. "I talked to Dmitri about moving in."

"Oh yeah?" Bryan nervously shifted his weight. "And?"

"He wants to. So do I." I paused, taking a deep breath. "Rayn wants to move into the cottage. It's not you or anything personal, she just doesn't want to hide her powers from Troy."

"That's completely understandable. So, you and Dmitri want to?"

"Yeah, but there's a conversation we need to have first." My heart pounded in my chest, making my stomach swirl. I swallowed my nerves but they rose back up.

Bryan sensed my anxiety, putting a gentle hand on my hip even though his nerves peaked at my sudden shift in emotion. "I'm listening."

"It's, um, it's not something we've discussed yet but we should be on the same page about it. Especially before I move in, before we take that next step in our relationship. I don't know how you feel about it but, um, my mind is made up on the issue."

He slowly nodded. "Okay, and that is?"

I took in a deep breath, knowing that once I spoke the words there was no putting them back. This conversation could go one of two ways and it would either end in us finishing this apple pie or Bryan leaving without looking back.

"I don't want kids."

"Oh," Bryan whispered, surprised. Whatever he anticipated, I didn't think the subject of children was what he had in mind. "Okay."

"Okay?"

"Yeah, I mean, if you are certain you don't want kids, then we won't have kids."

I blinked at him, processing his words but still unsure if he had heard me. "But is that what you also want or are you saying that because it's what I want?"

"Both?" Bryan chewed on his bottom lip. He turned so that we faced one another. He reached out and gently stroked my cheek with his thumb. "I mean, kids are definitely something I've thought about but to be completely honest, the idea of being a parent is paralyzing. It scares the shit out of me."

"Why?"

"I have a shitty father. I don't want to ever make anyone feel the way he's made me feel over the years." He stared off into the corner of the room before his eyes met mine again. "Then there's the flip side, I can be better than what I had, like Troy's dad has been to me. But, I don't feel strongly about it one way or another. If it's something you have strong feelings about, I'll default to your preference."

"Hmmm." I leaned back, still unsure how I felt about the conversation. "This feels too easy."

Bryan chortled. "Were you expecting a more theatrical response from me?"

"I don't really know what I expected, to be honest."

"Can I ask why you don't want kids?"

"I think the years I spent in foster care did it," I answered, reaching out to grab his hand. Bryan's thumb grazed the back of my hand as I continued. "Most of the foster parents weren't kind. Some of them were, but we got passed around a lot. Not that our kids would end up in the system if we ever had them but it really turned me off to the idea seeing how unloving so many parents could be." I let out a sigh. "The older I get, the more I like the idea of focusing on me, on us. Especially with all this impending doom on our doorstep. I think if we get to the other side of this fight, I want to make up for lost time. I want to go to Europe and Africa. I want to see polar bears and drink out of coconuts on a beach. I want to live." I kissed his hand. "My mom kept us so well protected. We only ever left

Kansas twice in all the time we lived with her. I don't want to be tied down by anything except you."

Bryan smiled, the light of the fire reflected in his eyes. "Yes."

"So, we're on the same page?"

He nodded. "Yeah, we'll go see the polar bears. Maybe get a dog or something. We can take a dog with us when we travel. We'll get one of those little RVs and drive."

I smiled and cupped his cheek. "I love you so much."

"I love you too. So you and Dmitri are moving in?"

"Yes." I smiled, kissing his other cheek. "Dmitri and I are moving in with you."

His heart bloomed in his chest as he threw his arms around me, tackling me to the ground.

"This is going to be great, I promise. Mit can paint whatever he wants on the spare room walls, and Troy is actually a really decent cook so dinner will be taken care of most of the time. And I know I'll be gone a lot but I'm going to do what I can to make sure it's not awkward for you guys."

"I'm excited."

He kissed me again. "I can't wait."

I smiled at him and though I meant it when I expressed my excitement, something else had been looming in the back of my mind. I let out a soft sigh and turned away from him.

"What is it?" he asked.

"Nothing." I forced another smile.

Bryan's shoulders fell. "Just tell me, please."

I let out another sigh, preparing for the worst as jealousy overwhelmed my system. "Who is Hannah?"

He chewed on his bottom lip again. "Who told you about her?"

"No one, really. Rose mentioned her at Founders Day, saying you'd been hurt before, and Jack made a comment last night about you hiding a relationship. He said, 'Hannah all over again'. It's okay if you don't want to talk about it."

"Of course they would." Bryan cleared his throat. "Hannah is a girl I used to date, obviously. She's a year older than me. We started seeing each other in high school and when she graduated it became on and off. It, um... it wasn't a healthy relationship in hindsight."

I furrowed my brow. "How so?"

"We fought a lot. I picked her over everyone and looking back, I feel like such an idiot for holding on so tight. She cheated on me and I kept forgiving her because I wasn't always faithful to her either, as hard as that is to admit to you. I was so determined to make things work that it took me a long time to see it wasn't worth saving." Bryan tightened his grip on my hand. "We used to see each other over holiday breaks when she'd come back and visit from Boise State but we called it quits for good last spring break."

"Like, this year's spring break?" I clarified.

Bryan nodded.

"How long were you guys together?"

"Like I said, it was a lot of on and off, but over the course of five years."

"Holy shit." I shifted back, holding myself up with my palms firmly on the floor.

I tried to picture it, tried to imagine how it all went down. I did my best to wrap my head around someone who could treat Bryan in such a way that caused this wave of sadness to wash over him when he spoke about it. Bryan, the most loyal and understanding person I'd ever met. Bryan whose eyes lit up like fireworks when he smiled, who had accepted me fully for everything I was, everything I'd done because he loved me. How could someone know Bryan so well, probably be his first love, and break him into pieces?

"It wasn't five straight years," Bryan reminded me.

"That's still a long time," I whispered.

Bryan let out a sigh. "If I could go back, I'd definitely do things differently. But then again, everything that happened in the past brought me to this moment, right here with you." Bryan wrapped his arm around my waist and pulled me closer to him. "And I wouldn't trade what I have with you for anything." He kissed my cheek. "I'm sorry if you feel like you're being compared to her."

"I was going to let it go when Rose brought it up but when Jack mentioned her again last night... I got curious."

"I would be curious too if the roles were reversed." Bryan kissed my cheek.

"You said you two used to hook up over the holidays. Has she tried to get in touch with you over Christmas?" I watched his gaze dart to the floor.

"Uh, yeah she sent me a text earlier in the week but I ignored it."

"Why didn't you tell her about us?"

"I didn't want to get into it, to be honest. There is already so much going on that I figured if I ignored her, she'd get the hint. Which she did." Bryan tightened his grip on me. "I'm not hiding us."

"Kind of feels like you are."

"Okay," Bryan whispered. "I can see how you'd feel that way. I'm sorry."

He pulled his phone out of his pocket and unlocked the screen, bringing up his texts. He tilted the screen towards me so I could see. He opened up a text from a number, Hannah's name no longer saved in his contact list. Her most recent message was the only text bubble on the thread.

Hey Bryan Allen, I know it's been a while but just in case you wanted to see me, I'm in town for the week.

Bryan began to type out his reply, moving his thumbs across the keyboard on the bottom of the screen.

I hope you're having a good Christmas, but no I don't want to see you. I'm spending the holidays with my girlfriend.

He clicked send and glanced over at me. "You okay?" he asked in a whisper, his heartbeat pounding through his entire body.

I let out a deep breath, trying to let go of the jealousy coursing through my veins. I leaned into him and pressed my lips to his. "Thank you."

"I love you," he said against my mouth, pulling me in for another kiss.

Before I could reply, a knock at the door sent a chill up my spine. The door cracked open and Rayn's voice filled the living room. "Are you decent?"

"Oh my god, Ray, yes." My cheeks heated in embarrassment.

"Hey, you can't blame me for asking." Rayn pushed the door open, Dmitri and Rose following behind her.

"Are we okay?" Bryan whispered as our siblings came into the living room.

I nodded with a genuine smile and gave him another kiss.

"I can't believe the holidays are already over with." Dmitri plopped down on the couch, hugging his legs to his chest. "They went by so fast this year."

"Technically we still have a few hours of Christmas left. It's only eight thirty." Rose pointed out.

"Let's take the kids to go look at Christmas lights," Bryan whispered, sweeping a strand of hair from my face. "We'll take the Jeep and drive up to Diamond Gate. The houses by the lake are always decked out this time of year."

"That sounds perfect."

"Keep your shoes on, we're going to see the lights," Bryan announced, jumping up off the floor.

Fifteen minutes later, we were pulling into Diamond Gate. The community was illuminated with holiday lights, glowing brightly against the night sky. We weren't the only ones out enjoying the sights either. Lines of cars drove slowly through the neighborhood admiring the view. Almost every home was decorated. Every roof, every tree in the yard had lights strung across them. Wreaths hung in the doorways and brightly colored bulbs outlined windows and garages.

Bryan leaned forward onto the steering wheel, his chin resting on his folded arms. Those bright green eyes lit up at the rows of glowing lights strung across the mansions. His inner child beamed through and a smile swept across his face. I couldn't take my eyes off of him. I didn't see if the lights on the house were white or multi-colored. If they hung down like icicles or lined the gutters. None of those Christmas lights shined nearly as bright as Bryan did.

"Ooh, look at that one!" Rose leaned forward, pointing to the house across the street with giant lawn decor out front. "B said her mom paid this company to come out and decorate their house all up. We should drive by and see her."

"Sure," Bryan replied, taking one last glance at the light show before he continued down the road.

I reached out and rested my hand on his thigh. "I love you."

He winked at me, his eyes leaving the road only for a moment.

Initially I had been dreading this holiday. I didn't know what Christmas would be like after losing my mom. I remember what Christmases were like before her; donated presents and impersonal gestures. But after Mom...well, that was still being written. I had convinced myself that the holidays needed to be canceled. I didn't feel an ounce of holiday spirit, and when I tried to let myself enjoy the festivities, a winged Shadow crashed into the living room. But sitting here in the Jeep next to Bryan with Rose, Rayn and Dmitri in the backseat, that warm glow of belonging sparked in my chest. My heart felt less heavy than it did the day before. Even though we were experiencing our first Christmas after losing the most important person in our lives, we had gained so much and I wouldn't change it for the world.

Chapter Twenty-Five

CHARMING

WHITNEY

"Man, it's been a long time since we were up here." Warren turned in a circle as he took in the details of the meadow. He and Nic had brought Dmitri and my generation into the forest a few days after Christmas for a reason they had yet to divulge.

"A lifetime," Nic added quietly as he scanned the tree line.

"Why did you want to meet here?" I asked, watching them both relive old memories.

Nic smirked. "Because we have something to teach you that Harmony and Amilia wouldn't approve of."

"Why wouldn't they approve?" Rayn looked back and forth between them.

"The Elemental Code," Warren teased in a deep, foreboding tone. "Plus, we wanted to see if your protection spell actually worked against the hunters."

I crossed my arms. "Amilia mentioned the Code. You want to teach us forbidden magic?"

"Sure do," Nic answered. "Charming is pretty basic compared to some of the spells forbidden by the Code. It doesn't actually hurt anyone. It's just...invasive?"

"Charming is the ability to project your thoughts on other people, get inside of their heads, and make them do things you want," Warren clarified.

I tilted my head. "Like mind control?"

"Almost. It's typically short-lived and requires a lot of magic. The stronger witches can charm the powerless pretty easily, but only an Elemental can charm another witch."

"If this is something Amilia doesn't support, how did you guys learn to charm?" Brooke asked.

Warren crossed his arms. "Amilia was only one member of her coven. There were other women we grew up around, and not all of them were as righteous as Mia and Audri."

"Amilia doesn't talk about the other members of the coven. She barely talks about my mom," I answered as Nic cracked his knuckles.

He shrugged. "Not everyone likes to dig up the past. Audri isn't the only one Mia lost too soon."

"So, how is charming going to help us close the portal into the Shadow Realm?" Lauren asked curiously.

"It probably won't, but it's a good self-defense skill." Nic nodded. "It's gotten me out of a lot of sticky situations over the years. We want you girls to have all the weapons in your arsenal. Who knows what's waiting for us in the future."

Rose crossed her arms and swayed back and forth. "Could we use charming to make someone forget they saw something?"

Warren nodded. "You can manipulate whatever you want."

Rose's eyes met mine as she gave a slight nod. It appeared she and Bryan had made their decision on how to handle their mom seeing the Shadow on Christmas Eve.

"Can Elementals charm other Elementals?" Brooke asked, taking a step forward.

Warren shook his head. "No."

"Ah," Dmitri kicked a lump of dirt. "Guess that's why I'm here?"

"Yes...and no. We're going to teach you to charm too."

"Little good that'll do when I won't be able to use it against the people who are actually trying to kill us," Mit murmured. "I'm an inferior witch."

"Hey." Nic's stern tone made Dmitri freeze. "You are Audrianna Dansley's son. You are anything but inferior."

Dmitri blinked at him. "No one here is powerless for me to practice on."

Nic shrugged. "Practice on Whit's boyfriend next time he babysits you."

"Watch your mouth, old man," Rose shot at him. "Now make good on your word and teach us something."

Nic smiled. "Charming is all about confidence and eye contact. You have to believe that you can get into their minds and believe in what you're saying. You gotta sell it to yourself."

"Guess that makes sense," I muttered.

"Give it a whirl." Warren motioned towards my brother. "Dmitri, you don't have to do anything special."

Dmitri and I locked eyes. "Clap your hands." I ordered with false confidence.

Dmitri chortled. "That's what you came up with?"

"Shut up, it's the first thing that came to mind." I cleared my throat and took another deep breath, repeating myself with more force. "Clap your hands."

Dmitri glanced around awkwardly, trying not to laugh again.

"I know he's your brother, but you can't hold back. It isn't going to hurt him. Watch." Warren grabbed Dmitri's shoulders and turned him so they were face to face. Warren stared into Dmitri's eyes and lowered his head. "Dmitri, clap your hands."

Dmitri looked back at Warren with furrowed brows until the spell took over. Dmitri's face softened and his head tilted to the side. He slowly raised his hands and clapped them together. Warren turned towards me and smirked like he'd performed the easiest magic trick in the book. The moment Warren broke eye contact with Dmitri, he shook his head free of the spell.

Mit rubbed his eyes and cleared his throat. "I did not like that."

"What did it feel like?" I asked Mit before turning to Warren and Nic. "You two said it wouldn't hurt him."

"He isn't hurt," Warren answered. "People can't tell they've been charmed."

"I could," Dmitri replied. "I could feel you take over."

"Huh, that's new." Nic raised his eyebrows, impressed. "See? You aren't inferior at all."

Rayn crossed her arms. "If people can't tell they've been charmed, how come Dmitri could?"

"Probably because he's stronger than he's given credit for," Warren answered. "I didn't realize Audri hindered you guys so much."

"She was trying to keep us safe," I defended my mother.

"I wonder why," Warren said, side-eyeing Nic. "Probably trying not to repeat the past of losing kids."

Nic must have pretended he didn't hear, because he moved on like Warren never spoke. "Whit, try to charm him again. Dmitri when you feel her tugging on your consciousness, fight it."

I tried again with the same results.

"Use your energy to search for the cracks." Nic's voice came up behind me.

"I don't know how to do that."

He cleared his throat. "Okay, so imagine your magic is a flood. The water pours down over rock beds and seeps into the cracks in between the rocks. Emit your energy over Dmitri's and feel for the spots in between the rocks."

I steadied myself before I looked into Dmitri's rich brown eyes. With a slow and steady breath, I released my magic, feeling it wash over us. This time, I followed it. My magic swam into Dmitri's space, pushing against the walls of his mind in search of those weak spots. The space between the rocks. I pushed again and this time his wall gave a bit, but he shoved back.

My energy returned, like the flood against a wall of sandbags. I pushed harder this time, seeing the shift in Dmitri's eyes as he tried to resist but I remained persistent. With one final shove against his mind, I got in. Dmitri's brow softened, his shoulder lowered and the tension left his body.

"Clap your hands," I ordered.

He did.

The moment Dmitri's hand came together, I left his mind. I hated the feeling that I intruded in his most personal spaces. A stranger would have been much easier to practice on, but I suppose that was the point of this exercise.

"Hell yeah, Whitney!" Warren cheered me on. "That's how it's done. The more we practice, Mit, the easier it'll be for you to block them. Rose, your turn."

Dmitri nodded and hardened his stance as if determined to succeed this time.

"How was Christmas at the cottage?" I asked Lauren, watching the next charming lesson.

"Better than I expected. Amilia passed out early so we got drunk," Lauren answered. "Nic and Warren aren't that bad. Warren is teaching me to float."

"Float in the air?" I clarified.

Lauren nodded with a smile. "It's so cool."

"That's a badass power!" I smiled. "I'm sorry if you feel like we left you out. I didn't plan for Rose and Bryan to come over."

"I didn't feel like being around everyone anyway. It was real low-key, and that's what I needed. I spent time at the hospital, so afterwards I just needed a drink."

I put my hand on her arm, unsure of what to say.

Each of us took a turn attempting to charm Dmitri. We all felt intrusive and dirty getting into Dmitri's mind but the more we tried, the harder it became. Dmitri quickly perfected pushing us out. Nic and Warren swore that only Elementals can charm other witches and none of the Renati in town would be able to charm him, strengthening his mental fortitude would make it easier for him to charm the powerless. If he ever needed to.

Nic approached me after the lesson, pulling me away from the others. "I want to ask you something about your visions." He moved into my personal space. "Abbie was our Seer, as I've mentioned before. She, uh…well, okay, can you get into memories yet?"

"Memories?"

"That answers that." Nic crossed his arms. "So, Abbie could get into other people's heads. Like charming, but instead of taking control of them she could view their memories. I was always curious if it was a Seer thing or an Abbie thing."

"I'm not sure, I've never tried."

"Try on me."

"I thought Elementals couldn't charm one another."

"They can't, but Abbie used to be able to get into my head when I let her. Here." Nic grabbed my shoulders and positioned me so we were facing one another. I looked down at his hand, the skull around his thumb stared back at me.

"I hate that ring," I said.

Nic glanced down at it and laughed. "It's sentimental."

"It's stupid."

His eyes lit up. "Shut up and focus. Accessing memories is essentially the same as charming, only there won't be a wall."

"I'm confused." I stopped him. "How is it the same as charming when Elementals can't charm each other?"

"I said *essentially* the same. The Seer, I think, can get into people's heads to see their memories but they cannot take control of another Elemental's mind. I think you already did without knowing it. I don't know how else to explain you seeing the fire."

"You think I accessed your memories without trying?"

Nic nodded. "I do. I was already back in town when you had the vision of the fire. It's the only thing that makes sense to me."

"But I didn't even know you existed, how could my mind find yours?"

"The magic calls to one another. Especially water and fire. Why do you think you found Rayn so young?" He smiled at her over my shoulder. "Okay, now my mental block is down, get in here."

"What are you going to show me?" I asked hesitantly. If Nic's other memories were anything like the fire, I had no interest in seeing them.

"Something happy, I promise."

"Okay," I whispered, letting my magic reach out and wash over us both.

I got into Nic's mind with ease, not a trace of a mental block remained. I essentially opened the door to his head and walked right in.

Teenage Nic sat in the back garden of the cottage. Amilia's backyard had not changed much in the last couple of decades. Garden beds and rose bushes covered the ground. Nic sat on the dirt with his back resting against the tool shed, smoking a rolled-up paper that I knew wasn't a cigarette. A rustling noise came through the flowers and Nic quickly hid the joint behind him.

Abbie emerged through the greenery and laughed at Nic's wide eyes.

He let out a sigh before lifting the joint back to his lips. "I thought you were Mom."

Abbie sat down next to him. "You think she doesn't know what we're doing back here?"

Nic handed the joint to Abbie. Her blue eyes lit up when she looked at Nic, full of love and admiration. She looked at Nic like he was the center of the universe.

Abbie turned to face him. "Hey, do you think Mom will let us go out of state for college?"

"I haven't thought much about it."

"I wanna go to California."

"Yeah?"

"Yeah, let's go." Her smile beamed at him. "Let's get the fuck out of here."

Nic smiled back at her. "Let's do it."

Abbie put the joint between her lips and tilted her head, listening. "Mom and Audri are talking on the porch."

"I hear them," Nic whispered. "Come on."

The two of them crept through empty garden beds, getting as close as they could without being detected. The usual lush greenery of Amilia's garden was sparse, definitely towards the end of winter. Once they got close enough to the porch, they stopped. Abbie handed the joint back to Nic and they sat in silence.

"How do I tell him? This wasn't planned...we haven't been together that long. I don't know how he'll react..." My mother's voice. Her tone shook with uncertainty and fear, but it was her.

Nic shifted in the dirt, peeking around the apple tree and she came into view. Her brown hair was pulled up in a messy bun and she wore a thick flannel and black pants. Looking at Amilia, my mom chewed on her fingernails.

"Hey, this is fantastic news and I am extremely excited. If he's half the man you think he is, he will be too." Amilia put a comforting hand on my mom's shoulder.

"But what if–"

Amilia didn't let her finish, pulling her into a bear hug. Amilia smiled and a tear rolled down her cheek. "We're having a baby," she whispered.

My mom let out a laugh that ended in a sniffle. "I think it's a boy."

The memory ended as quickly as it began. Nic's mental wall came back up, swiftly blocking me from his mind. I rushed back into my body, my heart pounding as if I had dreamed of falling off a cliff.

"I'm guessing it worked since your eyes clouded over?" Nic asked as I put my hand over my pounding heart.

"It worked," I whispered as a tear slid down my cheek.

"She found out she was pregnant with Dmitri." Nic smiled softly.

"Thank you." I pulled Nic into a tight hug. "Seeing her again…" I choked on another tear. This had been such a gift, one I never expected. I never thought I'd see her face outside of a picture again.

"You're welcome," he muttered into my shoulder.

I pulled away from him and wiped my tears. "Abbie loved you. She looked at you like–"

Nic cut me off. "I know."

"I'm sorry."

Nic shook his head. "My theory was right. Now you know how to charm and access memories. That trick should work on anyone, witch or powerless. Use it wisely."

"Is that where you've been the last thirteen years? California?"

Nic nodded.

I hesitated, but asked anyway. "Nic, what happened with the fire?"

"I don't…I don't want to talk about it."

"I think you need to, though." I stepped towards him. "You said Henry Drake tried to kill you thirteen years ago. I saw the burn marks on his hands. He was in the house?"

Nic let out a deep sigh and nodded. He swallowed the lump in his throat but didn't speak.

I pressed on. "What were they doing? Why did the Renati have you and Abbie there?"

"Hindsight, I think they were trying to open a portal to the Shadow Realm. I think they were trying to bring Erebus back."

"Holy shit." I breathed.

Nic nodded. "Holy shit."

"You stopped them."

"I killed my best friend in the entire world and somehow Henry Drake got out alive. I fucking failed, Whitney." Nic's eyes grew heavy.

"Where was the rest of your generation when this happened?"

"At a bonfire. They didn't realize we were gone until it was too late. When I came to, I ran. I left before anyone showed up."

"Why didn't you go back to the bonfire? Why didn't you go to them for help?"

"How was I supposed to face them knowing what I'd done? They didn't want me around anymore, anyway."

"Warren seemed to miss you when you reunited at the cottage."

"Well, he was the only one." Nic let out another sigh and shook his head. "I went into the woods to run away, to get the fuck out of this town. Abbie followed me and...and everything that happened that night is my fault. I carry that guilt with me every day. It eats away at me and helping your generation kill Erebus is my redemption. It's how I'm trying to make up for it."

"Nicky..." I reached out for his hand but he pulled away.

"Let me make up for it."

"Okay," I whispered, understanding the gravity of the past. "Okay."

"Woah, I have a massive headache," Rayn said a few yards away. I turned around and she held her forehead in her open hand, wincing in pain.

"Did you do a lot of magic this morning before we came up here?" Warren asked, putting a concerned hand on her shoulder.

Rayn nodded. "Yeah, Rose and I were replenishing some of our potion supply." She winced again and rubbed her forehead. "Ow, I've never had a headache this bad."

"Magic hangover?" Warren asked, looking at Nic.

Nic sighed. "Sounds like it, yeah. You girls have to be careful not to stretch yourselves too thin or your bodies will start to crash."

"That's a thing?" Dmitri tilted his head curiously.

"You're damn right it's a thing. You think magic doesn't come with a price? It can pay a hell of a toll on your body," Warren explained. "If you push too far, you could go into cardiac arrest."

"Oh shit." I turned to Nic. "Thanks for the heads up."

"I'm telling you now," Nic replied.

Warren took a step towards us. "We don't know what you girls know, Whitney. We are learning as we go, being teachers is new for us too."

"Assume we don't know anything," Rose said.

"Okay, I see that." Warren shot another worried look at Rayn. "That's enough for now. None of you do any magic the rest of the day unless you absolutely have to. Give your magic time to replenish."

On our way out, Nic stopped at the massive tree Rayn found when we first discovered the meadow. He ran his fingers along the carving, tracing the circles of the elemental symbol. He stood so still, I almost couldn't tell if he breathed as he took in every little detail. How the bark had healed itself, how weathered it had gotten over the years.

"Was that there when you guys used to come up here?" I asked, startling him.

"Of course," he whispered, pulling his hand back. "We're the ones who carved it." Nic took a deep breath and stepped away from the tree. "It's funny. When we were growing up, we were made to believe we were so special. The generations hadn't been seen in centuries, and then there we were like beacons of hope, but we fucked that all away. Maybe that's why the talismans went to you and the girls. The five of you are much more put together than my generation ever was."

"It's not like your powers are useless or anything," I replied. "Every generation serves a purpose, doesn't it?"

Nic nodded. "Yes, you're right. It's a trip sometimes to look at how much has changed since we carved this, that's all."

Nic turned back to Warren, who talked to Dmitri and the girls. As if Warren could feel something brewing within the connection between their powers, he turned towards Nic and dug his feet into the ground. Nic shot a wave of energy towards his Elemental brother, the ripples of magic cutting through the air as it hurled across the meadow. The others jumped back from Warren as he stepped into the path of destruction. Warren thrusted his powers back at Nic's strike, countering the blow as the two waves of energy crashed into one another, nearly knocking the rest of us over.

Warren thrusted his hand out once more, quickly and almost unnoticeable as Nic smirked at me. I saw the energy wave cut across the air towards Nic but didn't say a word. I simply smiled at him and waited for the blow. As it struck, Nic stumbled backwards onto his ass, feet flying up into the air. Warren burst out into laughter, leaning forward to hold his stomach.

I chuckled, offering a hand to help Nic onto his feet. "Do you use your other powers more than your elements?"

"There's more to being a witch than elemental magic." Nic pulled on my arm as he stood.

I scoffed. "Not if you asked my mom. She never taught us half of the things we could do."

Nic paused. "You and Rayn are powerful. Audri was probably afraid of you."

Those words cut into my soul. No, that couldn't be true. My mother loved us, she took us in off the streets and gave us a real home. She taught us about family, helped us control our magic, slept outside under the full moon with us.

Still, I'd often imagine the distressed look on her face if she lived to see the burn marks on Rayn's ex's body.

"Probably," I answered, masking how deeply the words affected me.

"Don't take it the wrong way." Nic must have seen through my facade. "Everyone is afraid of us, they always have been. The generations in the past did not receive the respect of the people because they were kind and loving all the time." His voice softened. "You cannot respect something you don't fear."

"No wonder Erebus killed us," I whispered, letting the reality of my past sink in.

Nic shrugged. "Let's try to make sure he doesn't do it again, hm?"

He placed a warm hand on my shoulder before he headed down the trail after the rest of our group.

Moving day was upon my siblings and I. *Again*. Even though we'd been staying elsewhere at night, we kept our belongings in the Roberts' rental after the hunter's discovered our home.

Janice didn't seem surprised when I told her. She faked a smile and gave me a hug, but her eyes were void of any inkling to how she truly felt on the matter. Her eyes had held that same vacancy since the day the police told her they'd found Abe's bloody sweatshirt in the forest. I wished Dmitri could convince Abe to stay with us instead of sleeping in that abandoned shack, but Abe seemed set in his decision.

"Didn't we just pack all this shit up?" Rayn muttered under her breath as she took a photo of Mom off the wall. "Hey, how are we going to split this up?"

"Oh, I don't know…" I paused, looking at the photos. "Which ones do you want?"

"This one." Rayn smiled down at the photo she held. "It's always been my favorite."

Packing up our stuff this time around felt more emotional than when we left Kansas. Coming to Rifton had been a whirlwind of emotion, we were scared and panicked. Everything packed in a hurry and whatever didn't fit in the truck we left behind. It didn't matter because we'd never see it again, but this hit different.

I knew we were staying in the same town, but for some reason this felt like a break up. For the first time in years, Rayn wouldn't be under the same roof. If I needed to talk, I'd have to call. I wouldn't be able to shout her name across the hall. Not only would I be away from my sister, but moving in with Bryan completely changed the dynamic of our relationship. Excited to take this next step with him, part of me wondered, what if… I guess there were a lot of what if's I could drive myself crazy with. I needed to trust the process. Rayn would be safe at the cottage, and Mit and I would be safe with Bryan. The financial burden was off my shoulders. On paper it sounded like a win win.

I blinked my thoughts away and smiled at Rayn. "I love that photo too. Amilia has storage, we can keep a lot of stuff there."

"We're ditching this old couch though." Rayn nodded her head to the worn brown couch in the corner of the room. Stained and used up, a token of our old life.

I laughed. "So, you and Lauren will be sharing a room?"

Rayn nodded. "I'm kind of excited. It'll be nice to have more time with her." Rayn grabbed my hand. "This will be good, Whit, I promise."

"Yeah, you're right." I squeezed her hand back.

Bryan and Troy showed up shortly after with Troy's truck to help us move. The first load of Rayn's belongings went to the cottage. Rayn and I drove behind them in my car with Dmitri staying back at the house to finish packing. Nerves rattled my core leaving him alone at the Roberts', but I took comfort in the fact that the hunters wouldn't come to the house in the middle of the day. At least I hoped not.

Lauren was the only one at the cottage when we pulled into the driveway, waving at us as we pulled in. "You should've left him behind. We could've had all this unloaded in seconds with our powers," Lauren whispered, watching Bryan and Troy carefully lower Rayn's dresser from the truck bed.

"I know," I answered quietly. "But I didn't have a good excuse for Troy not to come."

"Mia put an enchantment on the closet." Lauren told Rayn with the boys out of earshot. "Doubled the size so it's a walk in now."

Rayn smiled. "We're going to need it."

"Are you sure you'll be okay without a car?" I asked Rayn, turning to face her.

"Yes," Rayn reassured. "I'm in town now, so walking to Giani's won't be bad."

"Plus, I have a car," Lauren chimed in. "And Giani's and CC literally touch. I'll get her back and forth."

"Thank you." I watched Troy give a thumbs up that everything had been unloaded.

"You sure you don't need anything taken inside?" Troy asked, approaching us. "We really don't mind setting the heavy stuff up in the bedroom."

"We got it covered. Thank you for letting us use the truck, I owe you one." Rayn smiled at Bryan and Troy.

Bryan put his hand on Troy's shoulder. "Hey, let's head back up the hill and start loading the rest of it. Give the girls a minute alone."

Troy nodded and smiled at me. "See you at home."

Home.

Bryan mouthed "I love you" to me as he and Troy got into the truck and pulled out of the driveway.

As the reality sunk in that I would be driving away from the cottage and leaving Rayn here for good, my vision blurred with tears.

"Please don't." Rayn pulled me into her arms.

"I'm going to miss you."

"I don't like splitting up either, especially right now with everything going on. But you'll be here all the time, and you can crash whenever you want. Not much is going to change, okay?"

"You're right."

"See you at work." Lauren put her arm around my shoulders and gave a quick squeeze before she went into the house.

"Do you think we're close enough to talk telepathically?" I muttered into Rayn's shoulder. We had never been far enough away from one another to even test it.

"We'll find out," she answered, giving me a tight squeeze. We held onto one another, neither of us wanting to let go first. "Enjoy Ashley's birthday this weekend. When you and Lauren get back, we'll get some shit done. The Renati can't hide from us forever. We're going to get Lauren's bracelet back and kill that mother fucker once and for all."

I nodded. "While we're in the bay—"

"We won't be sitting on our thumbs, things will get done." Rayn held me out at arm's length and smiled. "You're the best sister, now go pack the rest of your stuff so you can move in with your boyfriend."

Dmitri and I's stuff went to Troy and Bryan's house. Our new house. I watched as Bryan and Troy did all the heavy lifting, carrying Dmitri's bed, dresser, and desk into Bryan's old bedroom. Seeing the room empty felt bizarre. All of the galaxy posters off the walls and the carpet bare, vacuum lines across every inch. Bryan must have scrubbed the place clean in preparation for our arrival.

I didn't have much to take with me. I left my bed tucked away in the corner of Amilia's garage and sold the bookshelf. Bryan's bed was already bigger than mine and though the master was larger than his old room, I only brought my dresser. He had been so thoughtful, going through his things and downsizing to make room for me in the closet and the bookcase.

"Thank you," I said to Bryan, putting my arms around his waist.

He smiled and hugged me back. "You know I'd do anything for you."

"I know, but this is a big deal. It's more than I could have asked for."

Bryan rested his head atop mine. "Even when all three of you worked, I know money was tight. It'll be an adjustment, but maybe this will take some of the stress off those perfect shoulders." He kissed my forehead before he pulled away to pick up a box of books. "Can I help you unpack?"

"Yes." I smiled, opening back the flaps to see all my hardcovers neatly stacked inside. "Was it hard to get rid of some books?"

"Nah," Bryan replied, taking out my worn copy of *Tides of Time* with a grin. "I had plenty of books that I didn't plan on reading again. Plus, it's kind of nice to purge through everything. You don't realize how much stuff you hang onto that you really don't want."

"I can't believe everything I own could fit in the back of my car."

"That's not a bad thing though." Bryan slid another book into place. "Means you aren't weighed down with junk. What do you want to do for dinner tonight?"

"Oh, whatever sounds good," I answered, looking around the bedroom, noticing he'd left an entire wall blank in case I wanted to hang anything up. A smile swept across my face as my chest tightened, overwhelmed with the reality that it had been years since someone had done anything on this level for me.

Though so many things were uncertain, I had an optimistic feeling. Our living situation would work out. The girls and I would get Lauren's bracelet back and kick the Renati's ass.

Everything would work out.

It had to.

CHAPTER TWENTY-SIX

RESOLUTIONS AND REVELATIONS

WHITNEY

That weekend we went to Falcon Bay to celebrate Ashley's twenty-fourth birthday and New Year's Eve. Emma and Troy sat on one of the couches in the living room of Emma and Bryan's apartment. Bryan and I sat on the other couch as we waited for Ashley to finish her hair.

"Babe, can I paint your nails?" Emma asked, looking up from the bright red polish she coated on her fingernails.

"Yeah, sure." Troy reached his hand out, spreading his fingers without a second thought.

Emma squealed, tightening the cap on her polish and grabbing a bottle of dark blue from her collection. "Byn, can Whitney paint your nails?"

Bryan glanced over at her sideways before he faced me. "Which one of you is asking?"

"Whitney, paint his nails. He'll let you do it if you pick a darker color."

"Hmm," I leaned over the coffee table, analyzing Emma's collection. "Black or olive green?"

"If those are my choices, black." Bryan didn't protest.

"Why are you painting their nails?" Lauren raised her brow.

"Because it's fun and they're good sports." Emma lightly blew on Troy's thumb. She leaned towards Lauren and whispered, "Between you and me, I think they like having their nails done."

Bryan chuckled and put his hand on my knee, spreading out his fingers as I unscrewed the top of the polish bottle.

The Falcon Bay apartment sat on the third story of the complex with a large balcony overlooking the city. Though the walls were painted white, Emma's interior design taste was more feminine. The living room had bright and colorful decor with soft pink area rugs and decorative throw pillows on the furniture. The kitchen had a large bouquet of mixed flowers on the counter and most of her small appliances were mint green. Incense burned in front of a row of candles on the coffee table and mirrors shaped like the moon phases hung on the wall.

"Everyone ready to go?" Ashley asked as she came out of the bedroom. She wore a short black dress with a plastic tiara on her head. Her curly red hair stood more voluminous than usual and earthy tones highlighted her eyes.

"You look fucking gorgeous!" Emma called out, jumping to her feet to pull Ashley into a hug. "We're almost ready. The boy's nails have to dry."

Lauren stood up as Ashley walked across the room, letting out a shallow breath. Her eyes lit up as she whispered, "You're beautiful."

"So are you." Ashley smiled back, her gaze following Lauren's short red dress down to her legs that went on for miles.

"Finished," I said, blowing on Bryan's black fingernails.

"The polish is quick drying so we can start heading out." Emma grabbed her black clutch from the counter. "The Lounge is a short walk."

"I can't believe you guys got reservations at the Lounge on New Years Eve," Lauren remarked, slipping on her coat.

"It's all about who you know." Emma winked as she headed out the front door.

The line outside the Lounge wrapped around the entire building with most of the crowd dressed up. High heels and short dresses covered by heavy coats. Collared long sleeve shirts and fresh haircuts. Instead of getting in the back of the line, we followed Ashley to the front door and straight to the bouncer. A tall man wearing all black and dark glasses stood guard by the door.

Emma looked up at the bouncer's face and smiled. "Six under Drake."

The bouncer scanned down his list and gave her a small nod. He checked each of our IDs and stamped our hands. I knew the ID that Lauren handed him was fake, but he didn't comment on it.

"Happy birthday, Ashley," the bouncer said as he unhooked the rope and let us in.

"This place is packed," I whispered to Bryan before the bass of the next song took over, vibrating against the dance floor.

Bryan leaned in close, his lips against my ear sent a chill up my spine. "It's not usually this crowded." He kissed my earlobe before he pulled away and scanned the room.

The bar top took up one side of the room, with bottles lining the entire wall. Rainbow lights shone under each shelf to highlight the liquor labels in the darkness. Bartenders were bustling back and forth from the bottles to the crowd of patrons ordering drinks. It reminded me of the Corner Cup on steroids. The crowded dance floor had multicolored lights flashing above everyone's heads as they moved to the beat.

"Lana is bartending!" Ashley clapped her hands together and bounced towards the bar, searching for an opening.

I turned to Lauren, who watched Ashley leave with a glimmer of sadness in her eyes.

"You okay?" I asked, linking my arm in Lauren's.

She turned to me, blinking the disappointment away as she nodded. "Come on, I'll buy you a drink."

Lauren and I walked arm in arm to the crowded bar. Ashley stood at the other end chatting with Lana, the bartender. Both of them beamed with excitement to see one another. The two male bartenders were much too busy with the girls they poured shots for to notice us at the other end waving for their attention.

"This is annoying!" I shouted over the commotion around us.

Lauren smiled slyly. "If only we had, like, magic powers or something. Hey!" She waved her arm in the air and got the attention of one of the bartenders. The moment their eyes locked, his face softened and his stare focused onto Lauren. "Serve us."

The bartender left the girls he entertained and came straight to us, quickly pouring six shots. The moment he set them onto the counter, Lauren dropped the charm, releasing him back to his job. She turned and waved the rest of our group over.

"First round is on me," she smiled as they approached the bar.

"Aw, thanks Lauren." Emma took the drink. "Where's Ashley?"

"Other end of the bar," I answered. "She and the bartender are chatting."

"I love Lana, she goes to FBU with us. She and Bryn are both bookworms so they end up with a lot of classes together. She's fun. Plus, it's always handy to have a bartender in your corner." Emma nudged me with her elbow playfully.

Ashley spotted us and came over, Lana trailing behind her from the other side of the bar.

"Hey, friends!" Lana smiled, reaching across the bar to grab Emma's hand. "A toast!" she grabbed a shot glass and filled it before she held it into the air. The rest of us held up our glasses as we toasted to Ashley.

"Bryan, is this the new girlfriend?" Lana asked, nodding her head towards me. "You're gorgeous."

"Oh, thanks," I blushed.

Bryan put his arm around my shoulders. "Whit, this is Lana. Lana, this is Whitney."

"And my friend Lauren." I gestured to Lauren.

"Hi! I've heard a lot about both of you actually." Lana winked at Ashley.

Lauren turned away, hiding a smile.

Emma pulled a black credit card from her wallet and handed it to Lana. "Open a tab?"

"Sure!" Lana took the card. "Let me buy a round for Ash's birthday real quick."

Lana poured various liquids into a shaker and rattled it around. She poured the contents into a row of glasses and set them on the counter. I smiled in thanks to her as I took a drink and sipped. It tasted like pineapple and rum, warming my throat as I swallowed. The next song took over the speakers.

"Hey, grab Byn and I a beer before you go?" Troy yelled to Lana over the music.

She turned around and grabbed two dark brown bottles, twisting the caps off. Lana blew Troy a kiss before she went back to mixing drinks for the masses.

Emma started bouncing on her heels. She grabbed Troy's hand and pulled him towards the dance floor. "Dance with me!"

A popular song I didn't much care for came over the speakers accompanied by a squeal that echoed through the bar.

"Byyyyyn!" Ashley threw her hands in the air. "It's our song!"

Bryan met my eyes and smiled as he removed his sweater. He handed it to me and took a long swig of beer before he joined Ashley.

Their energy was infectious. I felt the pulse of the music flow through Bryan's veins as the alcohol heightened his senses. Watching them jump around reminded me of how little I'd drank but they were having fun and I enjoyed the show. Emma and Troy danced close together, her back against his chest. His hands on her hips, pulling her close as they swayed to the music. Ashley and Bryan were sporadic. Jumping around with their hands in the air, not worrying about who saw them or what anyone thought if they did. I was jealous of that kind of self confidence, the way they moved their bodies.

As Ashley jumped into the air, her drink tipped over and spilled all over Bryan's chest.

"Ah!" he yelled loudly as the cold liquid soaked his shirt.

"Shit, I'm so sorry, Byn!" Ashley shouted over the music, reaching out to help him.

"Gross," he complained, undoing the buttons.

My eyes wandered down his bare chest, unable to control myself as I drank him in like a shot of liquor. My gaze followed the line of chest hair down the trail past his belly button. Bryan returned to my side and took his sweater back. My heart thudded loudly in my ears as the path of body hair met his jeans, slightly lower than usual as his arms lifted again to put his sweater on.

Another song came over the speakers and drowned out all the background noise. Troy and Emma moved together once more. They were so in love and in sync with one another. This was clearly their group's thing; their way to unwind and forget about their troubles and responsibilities. The way their bodies moved and how they laughed at top volume showed their bond. I wondered how many nights they had spent with alcohol and a loud stereo to recharge their batteries with a smile.

Lauren bounced on her heels watching the dance floor. The next song brought a change in her energy like she itched to get out there herself and join in on the fun.

"You don't dance?" Lauren asked me loudly over the music.

"Not really, no," I answered awkwardly.

"Well, I want to."

Lauren grabbed my hand and spun me around, determined to make me relax. She dragged me away from the bar to join our group on the dance floor. Lauren's narrow hips swung with the beat as she sang lyrics I didn't know. I let the music guide me and moved my shoulders and hips to the beat. I wasn't on their level of intoxication since I didn't pregame with them back at the apartment but I knew how to dance somewhat.

"Hell yeah, Whitney." Troy threw his hands over his head and jumped into the air, the most theatrical of the bunch. Everyone fed off of his energy, egging one another on to let go of their insecurities and be young.

A smile swept across Bryan's lips when he saw me and his hand found my hip, pulling me against him as he let the beat take over once more. The moment Bryan's body met mine, an electric spark shot through me. Every time I looked up at him, his eyes peered into my soul, drinking me in. His hand tightened around my waist as he took a step back, shimmying his shoulders to the beat. Laughter erupted from my lungs. He laughed deeply too, his cheeks turning a brilliant shade of bright pink but he didn't stop dancing.

Bryan and his friends threw their hands into the air as instructed by the lyrics right before the beat dropped. With a new drink in one hand that I didn't see him grab, his other hand slowly came back down and traced my spine, finding its home on the small of my back. His fingers gently grazed against my dress. His touch set my skin on fire.

I reached for him, pulling him close. I wanted to be as close to him as possible. I wanted to stay right here with his arm around me and his heat radiating into my essence. I wanted to watch him dance and hear his laugh echo into the night. He was fearless and unapologetically himself and it made me want to be that bold.

It made me believe I could be so bold. Everything else faded into the background, irrelevant because nothing existed in that moment but the two of us and the pulse of a pop song. His eyes poured into mine and I pushed myself up on my toes, bringing him in for a kiss.

Bryan broke the kiss, quickly pecking my lips again before he began jumping around Lauren. Lauren threw her arms into the air, spinning around and moving her body in perfect sync with the beat. Bryan grabbed her hand to twirl her. They both laughed, their stance sloppy from the alcohol. I loved seeing Bryan like this, the tension in his shoulders and the uncertainty of the world I'd dragged him into were gone.

As happy as I felt to see Bryan so carefree, seeing the joy on Lauren's face is what brought the tears to my eyes. I had known Lauren for months now and I'd yet to see her genuinely happy. After our fights with the Renati, losing her mother, her father lying unconscious in a hospital bed, her entire childhood ripped away from her... After all of that she smiled and danced in a crowded club like she didn't have a care in the world. As much as others told me that I needed to get out and clear my head, this night was for Lauren.

"It's almost midnight! Are you ready to count down into the new year?" a voice shouted into a microphone from the DJ booth.

The crowd shouted in unison. "3...2...1...Happy New Year!"

The bar erupted in cheers as confetti and balloons rained down from the ceiling. I looked up at the falling glitters of rainbow with a smile as the moment warmed my core. I'd never seen anything like this in person.

Bryan snaked his arm around my waist and pulled me against his chest, lowering his lips to mine. I met his kiss with hunger as I grabbed his sweater and yanked him closer. His tongue swept across my lower lip as they parted, gliding my tongue with his. The first kiss of the new year. Someone bumped into us, causing Bryan to jerk away as my power stirred under my skin.

After assessing that the guy who bumped us was innocent, Bryan turned back to me with a smile. I laughed as I reached up and removed pieces of confetti from his hair. I lifted myself up on my toes for another quick kiss before I slipped the confetti pieces into my small purse.

"Happy birthday, Ashley!" Emma's voice rang against the still roaring crowd as she threw her arm around Ashley's shoulders and pulled her in for a hug.

"Happy birthday!" We all shouted and joined in, forming a big group hug around Ash.

Ashley smiled at all of us and quickly downed the rest of her drink. "Can we go get pizza?"

"Fuck yes!" Troy punched the air and grabbed Emma's hand, leading the way to the front door.

We picked up two pizzas to go from a 24/7 parlor and took them back to the apartment. Troy put the boxes on the coffee table as Emma and Ashley plopped down onto the floor, immediately taking off their heels.

"That was fun but I'm glad to be back here," Ashley said, stretching out her legs before opening up the pizza box and taking a slice.

"Mmm, babe, before I forget." Emma waved her hand around, getting Troy's attention. "Grab some paper and pens."

"Oh, yeah, I almost forgot." Troy rummaged through a small bookcase in the corner of the room and passed out a piece of paper and a pen to everyone.

Lauren looked up at Troy, puzzled. "What's this for?"

"On New Year's Eve, we write down the things we want to leave behind and burn them. Kind of like a resolution." Ashley sat up on her knees.

Lauren smiled. "I love that idea!"

I thanked Troy as he handed Bryan and I each a pen and a piece of paper. I drummed the pen against my thigh, thinking about what I could write down. There were plenty of things I didn't want to carry with me into the new year, but nothing I could write down and share with the group.

As if he could read my mind, Bryan leaned over and whispered in my ear, "Nobody reads these before we burn them, you can write down anything you want."

Oh. That changed things.

I clicked the pen and jotted down the first set of things that came to mind.

Hesitation

Not taking charge

Not being in control

The Renati

The hunters

Officer Grady

Fear of letting Mom down

Fear of losing Bryan

As I folded up my paper, I noticed Bryan had been reading over my shoulder. "Hey!" I nudged him with my elbow. "You said no one would read it!"

"Sorry." He pulled away.

"Let me see yours, it's only fair." I leaned against him, glancing down at his page.

Bryan chewed on her cheek and turned his paper, allowing me to see what he had written down.

Weakness

Holding back

Feeling powerless

Letting Whit feel inadequate

"You don't make me feel that way." I turned to him, guilt flooding my body.

"No," Bryan whispered. "But I'm going to do everything I can to make you feel as incredible as you are."

I pulled him into a kiss and folded up our papers. Emma folded up her paper and hopped up from the floor, retrieving a large abalone shell and a lighter from her bedroom.

"Who wants to go first?" she asked, holding up the lighter towards Ashley. "Birthday girl?"

Ashley took the lighter and placed her folded up piece of paper into the abalone shell. She lit the corner of the page and we all watched as it caught fire. The paper took to the flame quickly and soon chunks of ash fell apart and sat at the bottom of the shell. We took turns, burning our papers one by one. Lauren closed her eyes and took a deep breath, taking a moment of meditation before she lit her baggage on fire.

I was the last to go.

Bryan handed me the lighter and kissed my cheek before I got on my knees before the coffee table. I did the same as Lauren, closing my eyes and centering myself before I took part in this ritual. I took care and set my intentions like I would have done with any other spell. My mind went down every item on the list; the things that would not serve me well in the future. I said goodbye to my insecurities, the things that had been holding me back, and lit the paper on fire.

"I love how seriously you two are taking this. What great sports." Emma smiled as she carried the bowl of ashes to the bathroom and flushed them.

"Since my birthday is almost over, I have one last request." Ashley took another slice of pizza from the box and snuggled under a thick blanket. "Put on that bake off show."

"This has been such a great day." Troy smiled at Emma as she walked back into the room. He lifted his arm and welcomed her under their own blanket.

I snuggled into Bryan's chest, listening to the steady rhythm of his heartbeat. My body felt lighter after burning those fears, like I had been carrying them around with me for too long. Bryan felt lighter too; his carefree spirit seeped into mine as we intertwined ourselves.

Two episodes later, I began to fall asleep against Bryan's warmth.

"I'm ready for bed." Troy yawned, stretching his long arms up over his head. He looked down at Emma, noticing she had passed out, her head resting on his thigh. He smiled at her, carefully standing up. Troy slid his arms under Emma's petite frame and lifted her up. "Night everyone," he said, carrying her to their bedroom.

Ashley watched them with a smile in her eyes. "I'm ready for bed too."

Bryan grabbed my hand and stood up, leading me down the short hallway to the other bedroom. "Good night, girls."

I turned my head back, ready to ask Lauren where she was sleeping that night when Bryan's fingertips caught my chin, turning my attention back to him.

"Shhh, just let it happen," he whispered, pulling me into the open doorway of his room.

I scanned the bedroom, a bit disoriented in the pitch black. My eyes adjusted as the door clicked closed behind me. Bryan's hands wrapped around my waist, slowly sliding up my sides. I closed my eyes as his lips found the crook of my neck. I tilted my head, giving access to his mouth's exploration of my skin. Every touch left goosebumps behind, awakening my senses from their slumber.

His fingers found the zipper of my dress, slowly pulling it down. A chill ran through my body as the straps fell from my shoulders.

"I thought you were ready for bed?" I asked as the dress dropped to the floor.

Bryan's lips peppered kisses across the back of my shoulders, gently moving my hair out of the way. He kissed up my neck and took my earlobe between his teeth. His warmth seeped into my naturally chilly body, gathering in my core.

"I never said that," he purred in my ear, turning me to face him. A glimmer of mischievousness sparked in his chest. He undid my bra and ran his hands down my curves, giving attention to every soft detail. Without warning, he grabbed under my thighs and lifted me against his chest. My legs wrapped around his waist as he took us to the bed.

I ran my fingers through his hair and pulled him into a kiss. Bryan pecked my lips as we fell onto the bed together, his weight pressing me into the blankets. He ran his fingers down my bare skin, pausing at my rib cage to tickle me.

"Stop!" I squirmed under him, laughing loudly into his shoulder. I let out another playful scream before his mouth covered mine, stifling my laughter.

"Don't worry, I'll have you screaming again soon," he whispered against my lips and he trailed kisses down my neck.

All the heat in my body pooled between my legs. Bryan's excitement bubbled through us both, mixing with the alcohol from the bar. I undid his belt quickly, moving onto the button and zipper. He moaned against my lips as I slipped my hand down his pants and grabbed his erection.

Bryan hooked his fingers into my panties and pulled them down my legs. He barely threw them to the side before he slid his fingers against my slick core. He smiled in satisfaction as he slid a finger inside and began rubbing me with his thumb. Every muscle in my body tensed as endorphins rushed through me. He knew exactly what to press and how to stoke against me to set me ablaze. As if he had mapped out my body and committed every little hitch in my breath to memory.

"You're so beautiful," he whispered.

He slid in another finger as I lifted my hips. I felt his heart swell in his chest as my body climbed towards climax. Both of us burned at his touch and the way I crumbled under it. My breath quickened and my heart sped as I clung to the sheets under me. Bryan leaned down and took one of my nipples into his mouth, taking it gently between his teeth. A shock of pleasure coursed through my body, sending me to the edge.

I gripped onto him, digging my nails into his skin. He lifted his head from my chest and his eyes met mine.

"Look at me when you come," his voice was soft but commanding.

His demand sent me over the edge and I fell apart, locked into his smoldering gaze. The tension left my body and I slowly came down from the high, both heartbeats pounding in my head. Bryan pulled his fingers from me and into his mouth, tasting me. My breath caught in my throat watching him.

He leaned over me, pressing himself against my thigh. Biting my earlobe again, he hummed, "Get on your hands and knees."

The longer my relationship with Bryan went on, the more I learned about him. His ticks, his dislikes, the little things that made him smile. In that moment, I learned something new about myself. I loved getting a drunk, demanding Bryan into bed.

I rolled into my stomach, getting up on my hands and knees while he put on a condom. Bryan ran his fingers up my spine and kissed the backs of my shoulders. I barely felt him at my entrance before he grabbed my hips and yanked me towards him. He thrust inside of me and I gasped at the quickness of his actions, the way he filled me without a word. The way he pulled out to the tip and thrust back in before my mind registered his presence. I fell forward and a deep moan escaped my lips.

More. I needed more. I angled my hips up and his next thrust hit deeper. He groaned and cussed under his breath, digging his fingers into my skin.

I reached down between my legs and rubbed myself as Bryan picked up his pace. His breath came in deep labored pants as everything in his body tensed. His orgasm crashed through my body and I came with him. Neither of us were able to keep our voices down as his chest met my back and we both collapsed onto the bed.

"Woah," he whispered and rolled to my side.

I panted, my mouth dry. "Remind me to get you drunk more often."

Bryan let out a deep laugh and kissed my cheek. "I'm just deeply, profoundly in love with you."

A wave of warmth and comfort crashed over my own adoration of him, two oceans meeting in the middle of the sea.

That morning, I gripped my hot coffee mug and took in a deep breath as I gazed out the window over the kitchen sink. A beautiful rainy morning with clouds covering the sky, kissing the tops of the majestic mountains. The mountain directly in my line of sight towered above the town; a pointed peak in the middle angled sideways with two smaller peaks extended out on either side. An eagle spreading its wings.

"So, this is Falcon Ridge?" I asked Lauren as she joined me at the window.

She nodded. "It does look a lot like your map."

"That's the gate to the Hallow." I nodded towards the mountain. "It's on the other side of the mountain."

Lauren crossed her arms. "But it's pointless to go until we've taken care of the ledger. Our support won't come back until we make Rifton somewhat safe again."

"You're right, one thing at a time," I agreed.

"Morning. What are you guys looking at?" Emma asked, strolling into the kitchen for a cup of coffee.

Lauren glanced sideways at me, moving only her eyes. I tilted my head, wishing she could telepathically tell me what buzzed around her mind. Lauren peered back at Emma over her shoulder and widened her gaze as she turned back to me. I shook my head and Lauren let out a huff of irritation. Lauren narrowed her eyes. Something in her hardened gaze told me she was going to confront Emma with or without me. I wanted to protest. I had promised Bryan I wouldn't involve Emma, but we needed to destroy the ledger in Drake's office.

Lauren and I turned around to face Emma, who furrowed her brow. "You two okay?" she asked cautiously.

"We know, Emma." Lauren dove in, fearless of the consequences.

"About?"

"All of it. Your sister, your dad. The Renati. Dragonfly Mystic. Everything."

Emma laughed nervously. "Is all that supposed to mean something?"

"We know they're hiding Erebus somewhere."

Emma's pupils dilated as she took a step away from us. "I'm powerless," she said quietly. "I don't know shit."

"Yeah but we aren't," I spoke up.

Emma took another step, her back against the wall. "You're not Renati."

"No," Lauren agreed simply.

"Then how do you know about Erebus?" Emma whispered, not wanting to alert the rest of the house to our conversation. I still had no idea what Troy knew but Ashley was clueless.

I rolled up the sleeve of my sweater, showing Emma the scar on my forearm. "We involuntarily helped bring him back."

Emma's breath caught in her throat. "You're the Elementals."

Not a question, but Lauren answered anyway. "Yes."

"Does Bryan know?" Emma asked me.

I nodded.

"Why are you telling me this?" Emma kept her distance. "I'm no one. I'm a disappointment born into an ancient bloodline that serves no purpose."

I let out a deep sigh and bit my lip. "We need to get into your dad's home office."

"No, absolutely not." Emma's voice echoed through the kitchen.

"What's going on?" Bryan asked, walking into the room. His hair stuck up in a sleepy mess and he had yet to change out of his sweatpants and t-shirt.

Emma met his eyes, fear and surprise written all over her face. Who knows what lies and stories she has been told growing up about the terrors of the evil Elemental generations.

"Are you serious?" Bryan frowned at me with a furrowed brow.

Emma grabbed his arm. "Do you have any idea what they're asking of me? My father won't show mercy because I'm his daughter if he catches me snooping in his office. Not if he thinks I've switched sides."

"You won't get caught. We need him distracted. Our friend can get in, take what we need and leave. Five minutes tops," I assured her.

Emma was hard pressed to listen. "Byn, Serenity told you about all this to keep you out of it."

"I know," Bryan said softly. "But I can't stay out of it when Rosie is caught in the middle. I can't..." He looked over at me briefly before he turned back to Emma. "I can't stay out of it. We haven't found another alternative. As long as the Renati are tracking witches in Rifton, none of the Elemental support will be safe."

Emma waved her hand towards Lauren and I. "Do you have the faintest clue what they are capable of? They're dangerous. There's a reason they were eradicated."

"Well we came back," Lauren shrugged. "And we have a score to settle."

"See? Vengeance doesn't lead anywhere good, Byn."

"They killed my mom." Lauren choked on her tears.

"I'm sorry, I truly am," Emma whispered. "But I can't help you."

Lauren cleared her throat, seeming to harden herself and bury the emotions back down. "Sorry won't bring her back. But destroying that ledger will buy us time to take

Erebus out for good. Our followers have been run out of town and we need them. Doing this will ensure their safety."

"That's easier said than done. He's worshiped and under constant protection. You can't take him down."

"I'm not asking for your advice. I'm asking you to have a five minute conversation with your father and not ask questions," I snapped.

Bryan peered at me, his brow furrowed.

I eased up the tension flowing through me and took a deep breath. "Emma, we wouldn't be asking if we had another option. *Please...*"

Before Emma could answer, Troy strolled into the kitchen rubbing his eyes. "Is there coffee?" he asked sleepily.

"Uh, I don't know. I just woke up," Bryan mumbled, his disappointed gaze still on me. He didn't understand why I didn't respect his wishes to keep Emma out of this. I knew he wanted to keep her safe and I did too, but this was life and death for us.

Lauren stood solid next to me, supportive and strong. Exactly what I needed in that moment to remind Bryan that it wasn't me being obsessive but my entire generation desperate to end this war before it truly began.

"Yes, honey, there's coffee." Emma glanced up at Troy, doing her best to fake a smile.

"You're a queen." Troy bent down and kissed the top of Emma's head before he went for the cupboard behind Bryan and got himself a mug. "We should go to that pancake place for brunch. Where's Ash?"

"She's passed out," Lauren answered.

"Oh, is she?" Troy teased. "Did you two sleep well?"

Lauren blushed, hiding behind her coffee mug. She saw everyone's eyes on her and turned around. "Stop looking at me! Nothing happened."

I playfully nudged her with my elbow, but even Troy's light hearted energy couldn't ease the tension lingering between Emma and I.

"Go wake her up so we can get some food," Troy said to Lauren. "I'll call ahead and get us a table."

"Thanks babe." Emma smiled as Troy and Lauren left the kitchen.

"I'll go get dressed," Bryan mumbled and left without looking my way.

I sighed and turned around to the window, taking in the sights of the mountains once more. I had never imagined the map from our spellbook would be this close to Rifton. Right in front of our noses.

Emma came up next to me, her voice still and quiet. "This is a one time thing, do you understand?"

"Wait, are you agreeing to help?"

"Don't make me regret it." Emma hissed through her teeth.

"I won't."

"If you do anything that hurts Bryan, I will hand you over to my father without a second thought. Do you understand?"

"I'm not going to hurt him."

Emma sighed, turning to face me. "My sister has turned into a heartless bitch, but she's done more to keep him out of harm's way than you have. Chew on that."

Emma pushed off the counter and left before I had time to reply.

Chapter Twenty-Seven

STOLEN GOODS

Whitney

"Byn, I'm sorry," I apologized to Bryan a few days later at the Corner Cup.

He huffed and leaned into the counter. "You knew I wanted to keep Emma out of this. It feels like I talk but you never listen."

"I do listen." I reached for his hand. "Lauren was going to confront her whether I stood by her or not. Dealing with that book is too important, and Emma agreed to help at the end of it. She could've said no."

"She feels obligated to help because of my involvement," he pointed out.

"Does it matter why she does it as long as we get what we need done?" I chose my words carefully since we were in a public place with customers sitting at the far tables of the dining area.

He pulled his hand away and glared at me. "Of course it matters why. I'm not happy about you and Lauren cornering her like you did."

"That came out wrong. Of course it matters and I'm sorry our approach lacked tact. I didn't plan on it happening like that, I just meant that she's really the only person who can help us with this." I stared down at his hands, wanting them back in mine but he had leaned back out of reach.

Bryan rested his elbows on the counter. "So it's okay for Emma to be in the middle, but not me. I want to be more involved too. I want to help you and Rosie."

"I love you. You're a good man, and I appreciate your enthusiasm but it's best if you aren't involved. Keeping you safe, remember?"

"I already know what's going on, that makes me part of this. You involved one of my best friends, that pulls me in even more." Bryan pointed to his chest as he spoke.

"No," I repeated. "Rose and I both agree that this isn't what we want. Telling you the truth and having you charge head first into the fight aren't the same thing. The latter doesn't keep you safe."

"Then why tell me in the first place?" Bryan asked, folding his arms across his chest.

"That wasn't up to me. Your sister led that crusade. I planned on taking all this to my grave with you." My shoulders fell thinking back to the night after Halloween.

"Lauren, help me out here," Bryan begged, turning to face her.

Lauren shook her head and put up her hands. "No way, dude, I'm staying so far out of this one."

"*Now* you want to stay out of it." Bryan huffed and turned back to me. "I guarantee I could be useful if you'd trust me."

"Trust has nothing to do with it."

"You dragged Emma into this but I'm the only reason she agreed to help." He hardened his gaze. "You two cannot bring her into this and tell me to fuck off. I don't work that way. That is not how my friendships operate. On top of all that, my sister is part of your generation. Whit, I love you more than anyone on this planet, but this isn't up to you."

I sighed, knowing he was right. "We are all meeting at the cottage tonight. You can come, but tell Rose before we go. I don't want her upset when you walk in the door with me."

"I'll text her right now." Bryan pulled his phone from his pocket.

The bell above the door chimed, bringing in another customer. A cold chill came up my spine as an unwelcome sight entered the Corner Cup. Officer Grady stood in the doorway, scanning his surroundings before he strolled up to the front counter as if he wasn't there to watch me. Again. I couldn't help but scoff and roll my eyes watching him strut over.

"Douchebag alert," Lauren muttered under her breath.

"What's wrong?" Bryan asked, turning to look at the police officer.

"Nothing," I whispered as Grady approached the counter. "Welcome to the Corner Cup, what can I get started for you?"

"Large black coffee," Grady ordered with no pleasantries. No please, no thank you.

"2.75." I smiled, burning holes into him.

"Keep the change." Grady handed me a five dollar bill and walked over to an empty table by the window.

I asked Luke if he would mind delivering the kind officer his coffee and turned to Bryan, who nodded his head towards Grady. "What was that?" he asked, not accepting my original response.

"Honestly?" I leaned closer to him. "Officer Grady comes in here to watch us because he thinks we had something to do with Abe Robert's disappearance."

Bryan's eyes widened and his pulse accelerated. "Did you?"

"No." I hissed in a sharp whisper

"I'm sorry... It's not an unreasonable question to ask."

I hated that he had a good point. "I know, but I swear I had nothing to do with it."

"Then you have nothing to worry about. He's a douche with nothing better to do." Bryan reassured me, but surprisingly his words didn't make me feel any better.

"Yeah," I muttered, watching Grady. He sat in the corner glaring right back at me with no shame. He didn't care if I knew he was there to stare at me, but Bryan had a point. I'm not the reason Abe hadn't come home.

As Luke came back from delivering Grady's coffee, he tripped on one of his shoe laces and dropped a bright yellow ceramic mug onto the tile flooring. It shattered into several pieces and everyone in the coffee shop jumped, including Grady. His head shot to the left like a watch dog who heard a strange sound in the night. Everyone looked at Luke and the broken mug but my eyes were glued on Grady. My heart raced and my hands trembled at the sight of a thick, nasty burn scar on the right side of his neck. I knew the texture of those scars. No normal fire gave him that souvenir. That burn was from Elemental fire. Nic had either forgotten to mention that he and Grady had history, or there was only one person Rayn had burned since we moved to Rifton.

A witch hunter in the meadow.

"Fuck," I whispered, not taking my eyes off the burn. Not even when Grady turned back to me with worry in his eyes. I reached down the counter and grabbed Lauren's arm, turning her towards the dining room.

"What?" Lauren asked, looking down at my grip. "What's wrong?"

I widened my eyes, attempting to nod towards Grady without giving too much away. She furrowed her brow, moving only her eyes to glance in Grady's direction. I reached up and rubbed the side of my neck. Lauren's eyes finally slipped to the burn mark and I watched realization wash over her. Her jaw tightened as she clenched her teeth and her lips curled into a snarl.

Bryan turned to look at Grady but he didn't understand the intensity of Lauren and I's gaze. Officer Grady left his coffee and exited out the front doors.

Slowly, I pulled my phone from my pocket to message Rayn, Rose and Brooke to meet at the Corner Cup immediately.

"That mother fucker," Lauren whispered, watching Grady rush down the sidewalk.

Bryan looked back and forth between Lauren and I. "Care to fill me in?"

"The hunters from the meadow," Lauren began. "Rayn burned one on the neck."

"And Officer Grady has a fat burn mark in the exact same place...I always thought he was Renati," I added.

"Wait, that cop is a witch hunter?" Bryan whispered, leaning across the counter. "And he comes in here to stare at you?"

I nodded. "We have to–"

A ding from Bryan's phone interrupted me. He opened up the message and locked eyes with me, his pupils dilating. "It's from Emma. It's go time."

"Today?" I lifted my brow in surprise.

Bryan nodded. "She's saying she can do her part if you get up to Diamond Gate within the hour."

Luckily, the rest of the girls came through the front door all together. Rose sat on the stool next to Bryan and nudged him with her elbow.

"What's the emergency?" Rayn asked. "Could I have an oat milk latte, by the way?"

Lauren glanced around the empty dining room and groaned. "We don't have time to socialize over coffee. Emma said if we can get up to Diamond Gate like right now, she can keep her end of the agreement."

"Today?" Brooke jumped. "That barely gives us any time to prepare. Why didn't she give us more notice?"

"I think she saw an opportunity and decided to take it." I answered.

"Risky," Rose replied, drawing out the syllables as she looked at her brother. "I can't believe you're okay with this."

Bryan shrugged his shoulders. "I wasn't given a choice."

I interjected. "We have our chance today and we have to take it. We burn the ledger, weaken the Renati, and steal back Lauren's bracelet."

Brooke sighed, rubbing her face. "Okay, I can do this. Let's go."

"We'll call Mia and the Magisters on the way so they can get the spell ready to destroy this thing." Rayn pushed off the counter.

"And Grady?" Lauren whispered, leaning in close to me.

"After." I took off my apron. "We need to find coverage. We can't leave the place empty."

Bryan stood up from his seat and looked around at the rest of us still motionless. "The place is already empty. I'll call Ashley and see if she can figure something out. Go!"

The girls and I scrambled to the door.

"This is taking too long," I whispered to Brooke as she and I huddled in the woods behind the Drake's home. It felt like hours, but it had only been about ten minutes since Emma texted that she'd give us a signal when her father was out of his office and distracted enough for Brooke to work her magic. Serenity and their mother were out of the house. It was now or never.

"We trust this girl, right?" Brooke asked quietly, shifting her weight between her feet.

"Bryan does." Nerves bubbled inside me, churning my stomach.

"Good enough, I suppose." Brooke closed her eyes and took in a steadying breath. "If this is going to work, we'll have to get closer."

"We will, but we need to wait until the risk of being seen is gone."

Brooke nodded. "Get the ledger and get out. That window up there is the office?"

"Yeah, the one next to the lattice going up the side of the house."

"I doubt Drake is stupid enough to keep it laying out in the open. I'll have to dig around for it. It'll probably be cloaked."

I scanned the back yard once more. "Yeah, but that's what the dust is for."

Brooke patted her pocket where a small cloth bag Amilia gave her hid. A magic dust that would give away cloaking spells when blown on them. "He'll know it's gone the second he walks back into his office."

"It should be burned by then. Rayn and Rose are across the way keeping watch and Lauren is down the street with the car. It'll all go as planned."

Suddenly a flickering light in the distance caught my eye. A mirror shining in the sunlight. The signal.

"Let's go."

Brooke and I trudged through the last of the forest before we set foot into Drake's backyard; officially in enemy territory. The chill in the air seeped through my skin and into my bones as I scanned the area looking for any sign that we were being watched.

"Close enough." Brooke crouched down behind the gazebo and scanned the backyard. I knelt down next to her and leaned my back against the wood, watching her closely as she mentally prepared. "Keep watch."

I nodded. "Be careful."

Brooke dashed across the backyard and climbed up the lattice on the side of the house up to the second story. Her powers rushed through me as she passed through the wall and inside Drake's office.

I sucked in a deep breath and kept my head on a swivel, watching the backyard like a hawk. Any moment, a Shadow or a member of the Renati could spot us. I stayed well hidden behind the gazebo from anyone inside the home, but still exposed to the yard.

It felt like an eternity passed. My thighs ached from crouching down, so I rested on my knee. Every second that ticked by took a decade off my life as anxiety riddled my bones. I had no idea how long Emma would be able to successfully keep her father occupied, but Brooke needed to hurry up.

The leaves in the tree line rustled and a chill crawled up my spine. My head shot towards the direction of the noise but nothing seemed astray. I looked back to the window, hoping Brooke remained aware of the ticking clock.

Out of the corner of my eye, a black wispy paw stepped out from behind a thick tree, followed by a large set of wings. The Shadow from Christmas Eve.

"Fuck," I muttered.

This Shadow would not wait patiently until Brooke finished digging through Drake's office.

Rayn, the winged Shadow is back! I mentally shouted out into the universe, hoping Rayn and Rose were still close enough to come to my aid.

I positioned my feet in a battle stance and covered my body in my second ice skin. I took a quick glance down at my hands to see ice glistening in the sunlight. A quick sigh of relief left my lips as I looked back up at the charging fully formed Shadow.

It tackled me, and we fell hard against the ground. My back hit the dirt and my hands flew up to grab the Shadow's face as its jaw snapped at me. Large stone teeth mere inches from my face.

Help! I mentally screamed out for Rayn again.

Footsteps behind me sent another chill of terror through my core as an energy wave knocked the Shadow off balance. Enough for me to wiggle away from it. Brooke appeared above me, her hand extended out with a thick, leather bound book secured in the other.

She did it.

Emma actually helped us.

The winged Shadow charged again, snapping at my nose.

I cast out my magic and froze the Shadow as best I could as another energy wave washed over us. The Shadow staggered back on his back paws. I kicked the Shadow in the jaw as my second skin of ice hardened my body to the blow. Luckily, my bones didn't break this time.

Whit! Rayn's voice filled my head as more shuffling came through the leaves.

Vines broke through the ground around us and wrapped tightly around the Shadow, pulling it to the ground. Rose tightened her fist in front of her as the Shadow struggled to break free.

"Not today, big boy," I said to the Shadow, ignoring the pain from kicking it that pulsed deep in my bones.

"We gotta go!" Brooke rushed to my side, cradling the ledger. "Drake was on his way up the stairs when I finally found this stupid thing."

We had less time than we planned for.

The four of us sprinted through the woods, taking what we hoped to be a short cut back to the car where Lauren waited with the engine running. We had to get this book back to the cottage.

"Those vines won't hold long," Rose huffed over her shoulder. I nodded, but didn't dare look behind us, fearful of what I might see.

Our feet finally hit pavement as we turned a sharp corner to see Lauren standing next to the car, driver's door open and emissions coming from the back tailpipe. She perked up as she saw us sprinting and quickly opened the back doors of the car, running around the car until she was back at the driver's side. Her eyes widened as she pointed behind us.

"Hurry the fuck up!" she shouted, jumping inside the car.

The heavy footsteps of the Shadow echoed behind us as I pushed myself until I could fling my body into the back seat. We all piled in on top of each other, not bothering to take the time to sit up or buckle in. Once we were all inside, Lauren slammed her foot onto the gas, speeding off from the curb before the tires had time to grip the pavement.

We were yards down the road before Rose had time to grab the door and close it, but as she did the door caught on the Shadow's head. She let out an ear piercing scream and jumped back. The Shadow's jaw snapped up, attempting to take a bite out of Rose's arm.

"Drive faster!" I ordered, throwing myself across Rose. I grabbed hold of the door handle and pulled with all my strength.

"I'm going as fast as I can!" Lauren shouted as she took a sharp corner. The car tilted and I feared we would tip over and wreck before we made it to safety.

Luckily, the sharp corner caused the Shadow to trip over its feet and its head slipped from the door, allowing us to slam it shut. Rose fell into me as Lauren finally got us back into town. I sat up, looking out the back window as the Shadow shot into the air, its wings flapping hard against the wind. Now that we were in town, the Shadow turned and flew back into the trees clearly not wanting to risk being seen by powerless eyes.

"You okay?" I asked Rose.

She nodded, remaining against my side.

We pulled into the driveway of the cottage and tripped over one another as we scrambled to get into the house. Mia and the Magisters were waiting eagerly as we piled in. Mia closed the door firmly behind us and locked all four of the bolts.

Brooke ran to the fireplace and threw the ledger in without a second thought. The thud of the book disturbed the burning wood, shooting ash up into the air. The book remained untouched.

I rushed to the table and grabbed the bowl Amilia had waiting for us. We had combined salt with dried nettle leaves and ground wormwood. Whatever spell the Magisters found said this mixture combined with the hot fire of a Flame Elemental would break the spell protecting the ledger. I tossed the salt and herb mixture into the fire where the book lay. The flames hissed and turned a bright yellow.

"Salt puts fire out so we need to jump in." Nic gestured to Rayn in a hurry.

Nic and Rayn lifted their hands, both of them adding to the intensity of the flames. Heat burned my face as the fire grew, both of the Flame Elemental's full focus on their task.

Lauren fell into an armchair with her hand over her heart. A tear escaped her eye as she watched them both carefully. "I thought we were going to die."

"That Shadow has to be attached to Drake somehow. They follow one another around too often for it to be a coincidence," Rose said, intently watching as the ledger still didn't catch fire.

"What the fuck," Rayn whispered, looking over at Nic. "What the fuck?"

"Stop doubting yourself," he ordered. "Elemental magic is stronger than whatever protection spell they put on this thing. Focus."

Rayn clenched her teeth and furrowed her brow, her fingers trembled as she poured her focus into her magic.

Finally, the corner of the ledger caught to the flame and the leather began to curl against the heat. The pages quickly turned black. I sighed in relief, running my fingers through my tangled hair, finding a leaf stuck to the back. I removed the foliage as we watched the ledger burn to ash together. Rayn fell to her knees and rubbed her face.

"You kids did good." Nic put a hand on Rayn's shoulder, turning to look at me. "This is huge."

"That Shadow almost took my face off," I muttered, finally taking a moment to assess the throb in my head. I pulled my hand from the back of my head to see blood trickle down my fingertips. My head spun and my vision blurred. "Oh."

Someone's arms flew around me as I folded towards the floor.

"Mia!" Rose's voice echoed against the walls of the cottage.

Chapter Twenty-Eight

GHOSTS OF THE PAST

WHITNEY

I opened my eyes to the ceiling of the cottage and Rose shaking my shoulders.

"Whitney!" she shouted, her voice trembling. "Whit!"

I tried to sit up on my own but Rayn stood at my other side, easing me upright. "Slowly."

"What happened?" I asked, rubbing the back of my head.

"Honestly, I don't know," Rose answered as I used her and Rayn to stand up. "I never saw you hit your head, but Brooke got you healed up."

"Thanks, B." I sat down on the couch, still a bit unsteady. "It must have happened when the Shadow tackled me. Adrenaline rush, I guess."

"You okay, Whit?" Lauren put her hand on my shoulder as I snuggled in next to her.

"Yeah, I'm okay."

"Think they followed us here?" Brooke peeked outside through the sheer curtain in the window.

"Yes." Nic paced the dining room as he answered. "But they can't come onto the property. We're safe here."

Rayn groaned and rubbed her face. "I think that's all the fuckery I can handle for one day."

"Well hold onto something, because Grady is a hunter," I announced, slumping over the arm of the couch. If the furniture didn't hold me up, I'd be on the hardwood floor.

"He came into the CC today and I saw a fat burn scar on his neck. He's the one you burned in the meadow the day we got attacked, Ray." I turned to look up at Nic. "Unless you have something to tell us?"

Nic shook his head. "I have no idea who Grady is."

"He's a cop here in town." Lauren put a comforting hand on my back. "We think he's the hunter that Rayn burned when we were attacked."

"Hunter?" Amilia shrieked from the dining room.

Rose cussed under her breath. "We are way over our heads, girls."

"You said hunter?" Amilia clarified, unable to grasp our words. "A witch hunter? In Rifton?"

I nodded. "I don't know how, but the wards are broken. Hunters came into the meadow and they used Rayn's driver's license to find our house. That's why we left Pines Row."

"And you withheld this information from me because...?" Amilia took a step towards me.

"Mia," I chuckled, unable to keep my composure. "That's bold of you to assume you're the only one keeping secrets in this room."

"Is this why you asked about the hunters?" Amilia stood before me with her arms crossed. "You should have said something, we all deserved to know hunters had returned to Rifton. The Magisters deserved to know."

"I knew," Nic announced.

Harmony glared at me, knowing I had told Nic. "Of course you did," she hissed.

Nic ignored her. "We can't trust anyone in this town."

"Well perk up because Dmitri and Bryan are on their way over," Rayn announced, rubbing my back.

Nic scoffed. "Why?"

Rose stood up. "My brother is the only reason we got our hands on that ledger. Show some respect."

"Okay." Nic chortled.

Not even ten minutes later, the front door opened. Dmitri rushed in, looking around the room to take inventory of everyone. He let out a sigh when he saw Rayn and I on the couch. "Is it done?"

"Yeah," Rayn answered. "The ledger is nothing but ash in the fireplace."

Bryan walked across the room and planted a kiss on my forehead. "Emma messaged on our way here. Henry knows it's gone."

Lauren shrugged. "Who cares? It's destroyed now."

"He's suspicious of Emma now." Bryan put his hands on his hips. "That was our only favor we're getting from her."

I looked up at Bryan. "She already made that very clear."

"Now all we need is the location of the Renati hideout," Rose said. "Without the ledger, we can take them by surprise."

Rayn turned to our brother. "Abe doesn't know anything useful?"

Mit sighed and leaned against the wall. "Even if he did, they put a spell on him. He can't even say their names. He said they never took him to the main hideout. Plan B anyone?"

"Hold Serenity Drake down and charm her until she breaks," Lauren suggested, picking at the loose strands of her jeans.

"We can't torture people," Brooke sighed. "But we can't exactly ask her nicely either."

"I can do it." Everyone in the room turned to Bryan. "I can get Serenity to tell me where it is."

"I highly doubt you can." Harmony crossed her arms, saying aloud what I had been thinking.

"Not directly but she'll let something slip," Bryan insisted.

I tilted my head. "And why would she talk to you at all?"

"Because Serenity and I have history. She'll talk to me."

"Years ago maybe but she knows you picked a side, Byn," Rose said.

"I can do it," he repeated.

Rayn let out a sigh. "We don't really have any other options at the moment. While Bryan is talking to Serenity, we'll try and come up with an alternate plan."

Everyone nodded in agreement but I couldn't take my eyes off Bryan. The way he took in a deep breath before he paced the room. How his nerves slithered through his body, increasing his heartbeat, making his fingers tremble. Why would he volunteer for this if it made him so unsettled? Whatever *history* Bryan and Serenity had, it made my stomach churn.

Harmony met Bryan near the door. "What exactly do you have planned?"

Bryan shrugged. "I'm still working on that part."

Harmony scoffed. "Well, I admire your confidence."

"I need to talk to you." I stood from the couch and followed Bryan out the front door, my knees trembling with every step.

Bryan spoke as we walked to the driveway. "I know it sounds far-fetched but I'm positive I can get something useful. A hint or an idea. I'm not naive enough to think Serenity would come out and tell me where it is, but she'll–"

"Did you sleep with her?" I asked, my knees beginning to tremble as Bryan turned to face me. "Is that why you think she'll talk to you now? Why she told you about her powers in the first place? Because the two of you were together."

Bryan looked away towards the trees, nerves taking over his entire being. He licked his bottom lip before he finally met my gaze and nodded.

Nausea crept through every part of my body. I tried to swallow the lump in my throat but the knot in my stomach wouldn't allow it. Tears overwhelmed my eyes as the question struggled to leave my lips. "When?"

"I was twenty, so almost four years ago."

The thought of Bryan and Serenity in bed together put a crack in my soul. I didn't want to imagine it but my brain betrayed me as images of them tangled in bedsheets overwhelmed my mind. Their lips pressed together. His head between her legs. I wanted to scream.

"Were you in love with her?" I dared ask aloud.

"No, baby. It wasn't like that." Bryan reached for my hand, but I pulled away. "Not like you and I. It was a short-lived casual thing we did when we were both in bad spots. Serenity wasn't always like she is now."

I couldn't look at him, not without seeing her wrapped around him.

Bryan stepped towards me but I backed away. "Baby, I'm sorry. I should have told you sooner but it was a long time ago. You and I never really talked about our pasts like that and I knew it would upset you."

"You're damn right I'm upset!" Tears streamed down my cheeks. I clenched my jaw to keep the nausea at bay before I unleashed on him again. "You know what she did to me. You know what happened Halloween night and all this time you've been in bed with me hiding the fact that you've been inside of the girl who gave me this." I held up my arm, putting the scar in my skin on full display.

Panic flowed through him. His heartbeat pulsed through his veins and his breathing accelerated as he stepped towards me again. "Whitney, I'm sorry but I didn't know at the time that it was going to turn out the way it did. Serenity didn't tell me about the witches in Rifton until after. I can't predict the damn future."

"Don't be a dick. I'm upset that you didn't tell me the moment you knew that Serenity had abducted my sister and tried to kill us. I deserved to know before you and I got serious."

"Would that have changed the way you feel about me?"

"I don't know." I answered without thinking, letting the hurt overshadow any consequence of my words.

Bryan's heart sank into his stomach and he stepped away from me. "You want to break up with me because I have a past? This happened before we met."

"Maybe if the girls you fucked wouldn't try to kill me, it would be different."

Bryan ran his fingers through his hair, grabbing the roots in his fists before he rubbed his face. "Whitney, if I knew you were out there, I would have behaved differently. I would have waited for you, but I didn't know. How could I? I'm sorry that I didn't tell you about Serenity sooner. I should have."

"You should have told me the moment you found out what she did."

He threw his hands in to the air. "You fucking broke up with me in the same breath that you told me what happened on Halloween! Sorry I didn't immediately tell you that I hooked up with her years ago in the middle of that intense conversation." How dare he think sarcasm was appropriate right now.

"Don't try to turn this around on me! I didn't do anything wrong."

Bryan's shoulders fell. "To be completely honest, babe, neither have I."

My head spun with a million different thoughts. I hated Serenity Drake. The mere thought of Halloween night made my entire body tremble. The bruises and marks on Rayn's body, chains wrapped around her wrists. The memory of Rose clawing at her throat, gasping for air. Serenity lifting Rose into the air with magic and slamming her against the brick wall. The terrifying realization that we could have died in that basement. Bryan knew his own sister had been in that basement, that Serenity wanted to murder her. How could he possibly think I was overreacting when Rose and I had both been on the receiving end of Serenity's fury.

"Fuck off, Bryan." I turned away from him and headed to the car. I was too hurt to care that we were yelling at each other outside of the cottage. I didn't care that everyone inside could hear. Hell, the neighbors halfway down the street could probably hear us.

"Don't do this." Bryan came after me. "Don't push me away. I want to talk this out."

"I have nothing left to say." I dug around in my purse for the car keys as Bryan gently grabbed my shoulders.

"Baby, don't. Don't do this," he begged. "I'm sorry. I'm so sorry. I know you hate her, but I never lied to you. I never deceived you. If you had asked me at any point for a list of every girl I've been with, I would have told you about her. But you never asked and I didn't know how to bring it up."

"I don't need a list, Bryan. Who knows how long that would take to compose, but I deserved to know that my boyfriend had slept with my nemesis."

"I know," he whispered. A tear escaped from the corner of his eye. "I don't want to lose you."

"Let go of me." I shook my shoulders and turned away from him, putting the car key into the door handle to unlock it. "I don't want you to touch me with the same hands you've had on her."

"Whitney," he sobbed, letting his hands slip to his side. "I'm sorry. I love you so much and I never wanted to hurt you. If I could go back and change things, I would."

I opened the car door and Bryan took a step back. I threw my bag into the passenger's seat and got inside, slamming the door behind me. I didn't look back at him as I started the car and left the driveway. I didn't want to look at him. I didn't want to see him cry. Hearing the tears in his voice broke me in a way I couldn't explain. Part of me wanted to turn around and go back to him, but every time I blinked, I saw Bryan and Serenity in bed together.

Instead, my foot pressed harder on the gas pedal.

I pushed everything to the back of my mind the next morning when I met my generation in the meadow. The time had come to see if the portal spell Nic found would be enough to open the portal in the meadow and close the one under Dragonfly Mystic's ashes.

Rayn and I were the last ones to arrive. Rose, Brooke and Lauren stood in the middle of the clearing with a backpack at their feet.

"What happened with you and Byn yesterday?" Rose approached me with her arms crossed. "I heard you two arguing. When I asked him, he told me not to worry about it, but I'm worried."

I crossed my arms. "He slept with Serenity."

"When?" Rose furrowed her brow. "Like when you guys were broken up?"

"No." I shook my head. "It was a while ago, but he didn't tell me until yesterday."

Rose blinked at me for a moment. "This happened before you moved here?"

I stopped her. "Listen, I'm not saying he cheated. I'm mad because he knows Serenity tried to kill us and he didn't tell me they had that kind of history. He intentionally kept it to himself."

"I know you hate her, Whit, but I don't think that warrants you sleeping at the cottage."

"I'm not asking." I hardened my gaze.

Rose lifted her brows. "Wow. You can act like it's none of my business but he's still my brother and you're being unreasonable."

"I can't turn off how I feel. I'm mad and I don't know how long I'll be mad for."

Rose shook her head, disappointment echoing in her gaze. She bit the inside of her mouth before she spoke. "Your feelings aren't the only ones that matter, you know."

"Rose, we can argue about this later. We have bigger things going on." I turned to the other girls. "You guys ready?"

Lauren nodded, taking another look around the meadow. "No one is watching us, so we are good to go."

Rayn picked up the backpack and slung it over her shoulder. "Time to see if Dominic found anything useful."

"I have to get home right after we finish up here," Brooke said as we all walked over to the closed portal. "My parents are starting to get antsy about me being out after they found that missing girl's body."

I nodded. "It shouldn't take long to know if we were successful or not."

The girls and I surrounded the closed portal like we had done before. Hopefully this time would yield different results.

Rayn turned to Rose. "What do you think of the potion?"

"I had all the ingredients. You'd think something to open a portal would be more complex." Rose pulled a dagger from her bag and stared down at it before she glanced across the way at me. Her gaze still narrowed with irritation. "Are you sure about this?"

"They used our blood to open the portal to the Shadow Realm. It makes sense that we would need blood to open this one. That's how portals are opened and closed, with blood magic. Since Elemental magic is stronger, the potion is simpler. But blood magic is against this Elemental Code so people stopped using portals. Well, except the Renati, obviously." I bit my lip. "Are you guys okay with this?"

"Yeah, it makes sense that we'd have to use blood after everything on Halloween. Plus, we need to think outside the box. Nothing else has worked," Rayn agreed.

"I don't care about the Elemental Code." Lauren waved it off with her hand. "I do think the Renati push the boundaries, but we have to close the portal. If I have to shed a little blood to do so, I'm fine with that."

Brooke nodded. "Me too. Let's hurry up and get this over with. I'll heal everyone when we're done."

Rose pulled the cork off a potion bottle with her teeth and poured it into the grass. She took a deep breath before she pressed the knife to the meaty part of her hand with a wince. Pain spread across her face as she looked over at Rayn.

"Are we going to all use the same knife?" Rose asked. "Kind of gross."

"Do we have a choice?" Rayn took the knife. She wiped it off on her jeans before slicing her hand.

By the time the knife had been handed to me, nerves overtook my entire body. But the girls were already bleeding and I needed to hurry up. I cut my palm without a second thought and let the blood drip onto the portal area.

We all grasped one another's hands and closed our eyes, letting our magic pour into the ground. I pictured the lake, the section of beach that extended out into the water that I'd seen from Dmitri's memory. I imagined the splash from where he'd fallen in. I saw the gentle ripples of the lake surrounded by pine trees, overseen by a gray winter sky.

The energy around the portal shifted and swirled. I opened my eyes to waves rising up from the earth like steam.

"Did we do it?" Rayn asked, looking around at all of us.

"Only one way to find out." I took in a deep breath of courage and dropped my bag at my feet.

I stepped forward into portal.

A ripple of energy dispersed around me as I passed through. My stomach churned as I reached around me for anything solid but there was nothing to grasp. A pang of fear rushed through me, wondering if we opened the portal to the lake or if our intentions may have skewed and prepared to spit me up somewhere entirely different.

Luckily, I splashed.

I hit the water before I could hold my breath. Opening my eyes, I looked up to see beams of light shining through the water. I swam up, gasping for air the moment my head reached the surface. Droplets rained down on me from the sky, bouncing off the lake and creating little ripples around them.

Holy shit. We did it. We opened the portal.

I laughed, running my hand over my wet hair as I treaded water. A sting of pain jolted through my hand and I hissed. I'd nearly forgotten the cut on my palm or the nausea in my stomach. Nothing could outweigh this victorious feeling. We were finally getting somewhere.

The cold didn't usually bother me, but we were still in the middle of winter. Even though it hadn't been cold enough for the lake to freeze over, the water still seeped under my clothes and chilled my bones. My teeth rattled and I began to swim towards the shore.

A large splash behind me pulled me out of my head. I spun in the water as Rayn surfaced, gasping for air. Her red curls slicked back as she turned to me.

"I feel like I'm going to throw up," she said, clenching her jaw.

I nodded, my own stomach unsettled. "Come on."

We swam to shore and squeezed out our drenched clothes, which seemed to be pointless with the rain. I plopped down on the rocky shore of the lake, stretching out my legs. I closed my eyes and took deep, steadying breaths waiting for my insides to stop swirling. Once my stomach stopped doing flips, I turned to my sister.

"Why'd you follow me?"

"You wouldn't let me go after Mit when he fell and I always regretted it. Maybe if we went in with him, Serenity wouldn't have gotten away," Rayn replied. "We could have stopped all this before it began."

"Yeah, maybe," I sighed, looking around at the deserted lakeshore. "Are the girls meeting us here?"

"Yeah, they were running out of the meadow when I jumped through. Luckily the lake is a short drive from the trailhead." Rayn took a deep breath. "That was like a roller coaster on steroids."

"We did it though. The spell worked and now we know how to close the portal to the Shadow Realm." I smiled as tears welled in my eyes, blurring my vision. "We're going to pull this off, Ray. We're going to make it through this."

Rayn reached out and took my hand in hers, giving it a gentle squeeze. "Are you okay?"

"Yeah, we opened the portal, why wouldn't I be?"

"I'm not talking about the portal." Rayn paused. "I'm not dismissing what happened. I totally understand why you're mad, but he's really sorry."

Oh. Him. My heart constricted in my chest. "He should be."

"Whitney, Bryan is not a bad guy. Don't toss him aside over ancient history."

I scoffed. "How ancient is the history if he thinks he can convince her to slip the hideout location in conversation?"

Rayn let out a deep breath. "I don't know about that. I'm always on your side and I understand why you're upset. I'd be jealous if I found out my boyfriend hooked up with Serenity Drake too, but have you considered that you're overreacting?"

"Did he ask you to say this?" I turned to look at her.

Rayn shook her head. "No, but we work together so obviously we've talked."

I chewed on my bottom lip as anger brewed through my blood. "It's not him sleeping with someone else that got to me. If it had been literally anyone else..." I met my sister's sympathetic gaze as my eyes welled with tears. "Why couldn't it be anyone else?"

"Whit." Rayn reached out for me but I shook my head.

"I don't want to talk about it." I wrapped my arms around my trembling body.

"Okay." Rayn left it at that.

Soon, Lauren's voice carried through the breeze and she came into view, jogging over from the parking lot.

"Where's Rose and B?" I got up from the ground. The rain hadn't let up since we landed in the lake and my clothes had no opportunity to dry, but the water helped my stomachache. Rayn, on the other hand, shivered with her arms wrapped tightly around her body.

"Rose took Brooke home. Her dad called all pissed off. They have her on a short leash." Lauren offered out her hand and helped Rayn to her feet. "You okay?"

"I'm f-freezing." Rayn's teeth chattered.

"I'll turn the heater on in my car. Let's go back to your car. I grabbed your bags too." Lauren headed up the trail towards the parking lot next to the lake. "I'm so glad that worked out the way it did. Driving down here, I started to worry myself that you two got spit up in another dimension."

"Me too," I admitted. "Why are Brooke's parents so mad?"

"I only heard bits and pieces from the phone call, but they don't want her out and about." Lauren shrugged. "She lied to them about being at a study group? I don't know, they seem very overbearing. I heard something about medication?"

I remembered back to a conversation I'd had with the girls months ago. "I know her parents tried to medicate her when she told them she saw ghosts, but I didn't realize it was a recent thing too."

Lauren shook her head. "Rose is worried they're going to try and check her into the mental ward again."

"C-can they d-do that?" Rayn asked through her shivers.

"She's a minor, so I imagine they have some sort of control over those sorts of things," I answered, wrapping my arm around Rayn's shoulders.

She shoved me off. "I appreciate you, but you're ice c-cold."

"Sorry." I turned back to Lauren. "Is that something we need to worry about? Brooke's parents going insane?"

"I don't know, I sure as hell hope not."

Chapter Twenty-Nine

PLAN OF ATTACK

Whitney

Three days passed without a word from Bryan. Dmitri and I slept at the cottage, crammed into Lauren and Rayn's already crowded bedroom. I sent Dmitri over to Bryan's house while he worked to get some clothes to hold us over. I hadn't slept. I had no idea how much being against Bryan at night helped me relax. Now my stomach churned and my head spun. Everything that kept me grounded had been turned upside down. Rose hadn't said another word on the subject since she confronted me at the meadow. No one else commented on the dark circles under my eyes or the food I didn't eat.

Rose came over to the cottage that afternoon, but she hadn't heard from Bryan since the day before and last she knew, he had yet to speak to Serenity. At that point, I didn't know if he still planned to. I wanted to call and hear his voice, to have any excuse to see if any resentment echoed in his tone. Whenever I picked up my phone, the anger resurfaced and I shut myself down again.

Rose sat down on the couch next to me and shifted her weight. "So, I've been thinking about magic in my family line. It got me thinking about my grandma and I asked my mom about her."

I turned to face her. "What did she say?"

"She said that my grandma was always very intuitive. I remember she had a massive garden, my mom always said that's where I got my green thumb. Now that she doesn't remember what happened on Christmas Eve, I can't ask her about it directly. Whatever is going on with Bryan being powerless or not, we're on our own to figure it out."

I got up from the couch and wandered into the kitchen where Amilia heated a kettle on the stove. "Mia?"

"Everything all right?" she asked, turning her attention to me.

"I have a question. It's about Bryan maybe not being powerless."

Rose followed behind me, leaning against the kitchen counter. "I think my grandmother was a witch. She died years ago but looking back, there were signs. Is there a way to test someone? Their sensitivity to energy or something?"

Slowly, Amilia shook her head. "Not that I've ever read about, no. Usually you have to wait until the powers manifest and show themselves. If Bryan had any sort of abilities, they would have come by now."

Rose took a step forward. "We all know he doesn't have powers, but there's something there."

"I agree, but I don't have any answers for you," Amilia said. "My best guess is there's enough magic in his blood to protect him from the Shadow's poison. Enough that you can sense, Whitney, but not enough for anything more. Whatever energy is active in Bryan, your magic can sense it." She covered her mouth and sighed through her fingers. "Like I said before, witches who are sensitive to one another's energy can sense each other's magic. Since you can feel his emotions and his body helped fight off the Shadow's poison, I definitely believe something is there."

I glanced at Rose sideways. With a slight nod, Rose confirmed Amilia told us the truth.

The front door of the cottage opened without a knock or a warning and we all jumped to attention, ready to strike whoever imposed into our safe space. But it wasn't an intruder at all.

Bryan walked into the living room like he lived there. His eyes scanned the room, glancing right over me before his gaze settled on Rose.

"They're keeping Erebus at the old hospital outside of town," Bryan announced.

"What?" Rayn jumped to her feet.

Harmony scooted to the edge of her seat in shock. "Wait, is this trustworthy? It could be a trap."

"It's not. He's there."

"Serenity Drake told you where they're keeping Erebus? I don't believe it." Harmony shook her head. "You just casually asked?"

"She was venting about her dad, saying he'd been spending all his free time at the old hospital." Bryan crossed his arm like he'd done something as simple as strolling through the park.

"Son of a bitch," Nic muttered. "Maybe you're more useful than I thought."

"Nobody listens to Serenity, they never have. It's not hard to get her talking when she feels like someone actually gives a fuck about her." Bryan shrugged. "Do with that what you will."

He turned his back to us and headed towards the door without another word. Without so much as glancing in my direction. Bryan didn't even acknowledge my existence.

"Byn, wait!" Rose went after her brother, following him out of the cottage. The front door closed behind them.

Tears welled in my eyes but I quickly blinked them away, swallowing any shred of emotion I'd been carrying. I pretended I hadn't been dying to see him, that the very thought of being in the same room as him made my entire being tense with anticipation.

"I don't believe it. It's too easy." Harmony paced across the living room, turning to Warren. "I'm not putting the girls at risk. How do we know he isn't playing both sides?"

"He's Rose's brother!" I raised my voice, turning to Harmony.

"That doesn't mean anything," Harmony shot back. "If any of the Drakes trust him, I don't."

"It means everything. He would never do anything to put Rose in danger."

"Henry and Serenity Drake are two different people," Warren offered. "Maybe the girl isn't as loyal to her father as it appears."

"It doesn't have to be this complicated," Nic spoke up. "Whit can get into his head and see their conversation for herself. If there's any foul play, she'll be able to know before we burn the old hospital to the ground. Remember that trick I taught you in the meadow?"

"No. I'm not doing that," I snapped.

Nic's shoulders fell with a sigh. "I won't argue, but I think you should. Last time your generation ran blindly into a building, Erebus was resurrected and you almost died. Learn from your mistakes, maybe?"

I groaned, knowing Nic was right. I wanted to hear Serenity's words for myself, but I didn't know if my heart could handle seeing her and Bryan together. Whatever he did to convince Serenity that he cared about her. What if he didn't have to pretend to convince Serenity she was safe with him? What if he didn't want to talk to me in the first place?

Nic took a step towards me and lowered his voice. "Go talk to him."

I chewed on my bottom lip. "He doesn't want to see me."

"Of course he does. Go after him."

I left the house, hoping to catch Bryan before he left. Luckily, he and Rose were still talking in the front yard when I walked outside. Rose stopped mid-sentence, sensing the tension before I even spoke.

"I need to see your conversation with Serenity," I told Bryan, getting straight to the point.

"Why?" he asked, monotone.

"I don't trust her. I need to assess the situation before the girls and I follow her word blindly."

"I didn't lie."

"This isn't about you. I need to see it." My words came out harsher than I intended.

Bryan glanced over at Rose for a split second before he came back to me. "I don't know how to show you."

"I don't need help getting into your head." I cleared my mind, focusing on the two heartbeats pounding in my chest. Bryan already thought about his conversation with Serenity. No defenses kept me out of his head and I got in with ease. I stood in the employee parking lot behind the Corner Cup within a matter of seconds.

"Hey, Byn," Serenity greeted, walking up to Bryan standing next to his Jeep. Her steps were slow and hesitant like she wasn't completely sure if she should be there.

Bryan glanced up at her, his heartbeat accelerated. He answered casually, "Hi."

"Heard there was trouble in paradise." Serenity took another step closer before she stopped a few feet in front of him.

Bryan crossed his arms. "Come here to gloat?"

"Kinda." Serenity chuckled, looking down at her hands. "Partially. You know, when I told you about magic, I did it to make sure you knew who to stay away from. Not who to jump into bed with."

"I didn't know what Whitney was until after," Bryan answered.

"Not the first time maybe, but you do now and you're still fucking her."

"I haven't talked to her in days," Bryan snapped. "If you came here to talk about my love life, you can leave. I don't want to hear her name right now."

"Ooh, Bynie is mad." Serenity widened her eyes. "I saw the fight. I wanted to make sure you were okay," Serenity admitted.

"You saw the fight?"

"You fought out in the driveway, Bryan. It's a small town. We've been monitoring the old crone's house for a while now. Of course I saw it." Serenity paused, checking her surroundings for any intruders before she continued. "She treated you like shit. Figured you'd be tired of that kind of abuse by now."

Bryan narrowed his gaze but didn't say a word.

"What I'm trying to say is, are you okay?" Serenity asked, her shoulders fell as her body seemed to release some tension.

"Not really," Bryan answered, honestly. "This whole thing has me conflicted. I should hate you for what happened on Halloween, and part of me does, but it hasn't overshadowed that part of me that still cares about you."

"Because I'm Emma's sister."

"Because you'll always be that girl covered in yogurt on the first day of school."

Bryan wasn't acting. I couldn't keep watching this. I wanted to snap out of it, but I had to see this through to the end. It hurt enough knowing there were other women that Bryan cared for, that he was such a sensitive and loving person that he carried a bit of everyone he's ever loved around with him. Such a Pisces. Watching this had been overwhelming enough, but seeing how Bryan still cared for Serenity Drake was torture.

"It's been a long time since then," Serenity said, leaning forward like she intended to take a step closer to Bryan but stood her ground. "A lot has happened."

"You're telling me. It's funny that you show up here worried about me when I've been doing the same for you."

She blinked in surprise. "You worry about me, Byn?"

"All the time," he admitted. "I know what kind of pressure your dad holds over you. I know that you've always carried the brunt of it between you and Emma. Your shoulders have to be getting tired."

Serenity paused, chewing on her bottom lip before she finally did take that step closer. "He expects a lot from me, but in times like these I don't have a choice."

"You always have a choice."

"Don't give me that shit about how I used to be a sweet girl and that she's still in there somewhere. You don't know me anymore."

"Don't I?" Bryan pushed back. "You think it's easy for me to see Emma every day without thinking about how much I miss having you around? I never told a single person the secrets you shared with me, even after we cut each other off. You know why? I knew doing so would put you in danger and I'd never do that to you."

Serenity froze, staring into his green eyes. "You know, when I found out the Elementals were back, I was enraged. I was ready to kill every single one of them, no hesitation. And then I saw Rose and I...I hesitated for a second."

"I didn't know that."

"I think you did, though. You're a good guy, Bryan, one of the best I've ever met, but you're mixed up with dangerous people. You picked the wrong side."

"Maybe." Bryan looked away for a split second before his eyes locked back into Serenity's. "I don't know how I'm supposed to feel anymore."

"I get that. Now that He has returned, there is so much tension. Even after I did everything I could to prove myself to my dad and the others, it wasn't enough. I don't know if it will ever be enough."

"You're enough. They aren't seeing you."

"No, they aren't. They don't see everything I've given up for this. Everyone that I've given up."

"Emma."

"You," Serenity admitted. "No one ever put up with my shit like you did."

Bryan laughed softly. "You feel like they take your dedication for granted?"

"Yes, sometimes. Especially lately. I'm exhausted. I spend most of my time with busy work, like it was my fault Tom Campbell got himself killed. He was weak. I got Him out alive. Tom wouldn't have been able to do that. I've given so much of myself and yet they give the important assignments to everyone else."

"You've always been one of the most capable people I've ever met. Remember biology class in high school? You ran circles around Mr. Johnson."

"Oh, that idiot. Sometimes my father reminds me of Johnson. Spends all his nights at the old hospital and wonders why everyone thinks he's benefiting from favoritism. My father is the only one allowed at His bedside. They all treat him like he's the one who brought Him back instead of me. I did that," she stopped. "Sorry, I'm venting. I came here to check on you, not dump all my shit."

Bryan shrugged. "Sometimes all you need is someone to listen, Ren."

"Will you go back to her?"

"I don't know if she wants me to."

"You're an idiot too, then. I hate that abomination but even I see how she looks at you." Serenity paused for a moment. "I guess I wanted to remind you that you're better than that.

You deserve better. You don't understand what the Elementals are underneath those pretty faces."

"And what's that?" Bryan asked, tilting his head.

"Corruption. Tainted magic. They will burn this world to the ground to put themselves back in power."

"That was hundreds of years ago."

"Bryan, the Elementals are reincarnated. They're literally all the same. They're the same greedy, manipulative fucks that they've always been. Do you really think an entire faction of the magical world would rise up against them for no reason?"

Bryan stood silent, his head spinning.

"Don't fall for everything you hear." Serenity sighed and gazed around the parking lot. "I should go. Don't tell anyone about this."

"I won't." Bryan's voice turned soft as he watched her turn and walk away. Serenity was almost out of the parking lot when he called after her. "Take care of yourself, Ren. No one over there is going to do that for you."

Serenity stopped and gazed over her shoulder. "I could say the same to you."

I snapped out of his head as quickly as I strolled in. When I came back into my own mind, a pair of wide green eyes watched me with an uneasy mixture of confusion and fear. Bryan had never seen my eyes cloud over before, but my work here was done.

"I needed her to think I was mad at you," Bryan explained, but I didn't have time for this conversation.

"See you inside," I said to Rose, turning back to the cottage without another word. "Serenity is pissed at her dad," I announced as I walked back into the house. "They're at the old hospital. Serenity let it slip in a rant. That's probably where Lauren's bracelet is too. We're going tonight before Serenity realizes her mistake."

"We're coming with you," Harmony informed, not an offer but a demand.

"Tonight? Goodness." Amilia jumped up from her seat. "I'll stay behind and make sure we have everything we need when you get back. Healing potions and herbs, just in case. I hope we don't need them."

Nerves rushed through my unsettled bones at how quickly this all happened. Everyone dispersed, getting ready.

"I'm coming too," Dmitri announced.

"No," Rayn and I said in unison.

Dmitri glared in our direction. "I wasn't asking."

"He'll be with us," Nic said, reassuringly. "We will cause a distraction around the perimeter. There will be someone keeping watch, I'm sure. We'll draw them away so you can get in without alerting anyone inside."

Warren nodded. "Dmitri will be safe. You're the ones who need to keep your heads on a swivel while you're in there."

"Wait, wait, wait." Harmony put up her hands. "Are we letting the girls go in there alone?"

"You're not letting us do anything, it's our responsibility," I snapped back.

"Lauren needs to be in there, she'll be able to sense if her talisman is nearby. And the girls have to go with her so they can sense one another's powers. We won't be able to keep track of them like they can with one another," Warren explained to Harmony. "Plus we will be right outside if anything goes sideways."

"They'll be okay, I have faith in them." Nic looked over at me and smiled. "This is one of the moments we've been preparing them for."

"Okay." Harmony nodded reluctantly. "Let's head out."

Chapter Thirty

BREAKING AND ENTERING

WHITNEY

As the sunset behind the mountain, Rifton prepared for a good night's sleep. Our group, however, prepared for infiltration. I had no idea how much time we had or if Serenity even realized the consequence of her conversation with Bryan, but it was imperative we catch the Renati off guard. For once, we needed to be a step ahead.

The old hospital stood on a hill at the outskirts of town. Lauren told us it closed down over a decade ago when the new hospital had its grand opening. We parked down the road and hid the cars behind some trees. The rest of the trek to our destination happened on foot. The hospital had been boarded up and blocked off by a chain link fence around the perimeter. Men that I assumed were members of the Renati strolled the property, carrying firearms on their hips.

We'd known we couldn't waltz in through the front door, so we found a weak point in the back near the woods.

"What are the chances they're powerless dudes with guns?" I whispered to my sister as we assessed our surroundings.

"Slim," Rayn answered.

One of the guards whipped their head to the side, something in the distance catching their attention. I held my breath as the guard alerted their battle buddy and they both approached the noise to investigate.

"That's the signal." Lauren lifted herself off the dirt. "I can hear Warren's voice in the breeze."

I turned back to the guards but they had vanished. I quickly pushed myself up from the ground and led the way down the hill towards the fence. When we reached it, there was no gate in sight. I glanced up at the top of the chain link to see rolls of barbed wire like a prison.

"We can't go over," I said, searching down the fence line.

"Then we go under." Rose waved her hand at the ground as the tingle of her powers rushed through me. A chunk of the earth scooped up and moved to the side, creating enough space for us to move through.

I crawled under first, watching carefully for anyone to notice us as the girls came through one by one. "Dmitri?" I whispered into the crystal Amilia had charmed into a communicator. A similar blue lace agate that Abe and I used to find one another. I waited impatiently, desperate to hear my brother's voice before the girls and I made our way into the old hospital.

"Only three guards left," he whispered back. "They're on the south side. Harmony is moving that way."

I glanced around trying to get a sense of direction. "South?"

Dmitri huffed. "The one with the big parking lot."

I scanned the back of the building, finding the parking lot Dmitri referred to. There were only a few cars parked there, one of which was private security.

"Be safe." I followed behind Lauren as she led the way towards the main building. She held her head to the side, listening closely for any whispers in the wind she could pick up.

"It's too quiet," she replied after a second.

Brooke stopped in her tracks. "Are we walking into a trap?"

"Even if we are, I have to get that bracelet back." Lauren kept on but I grabbed her elbow to slow her down.

"What about Erebus?" Rose asked.

I paused, my mind running a mile a minute. "I don't feel like tonight is the night. Our main objective right now is the talisman. In and out. Hopefully undetected."

Brooke nodded in agreement. "In and out."

Rose looked around the grounds as the remaining security guards' voices echoed in the distance. "You say that like it's going to be easy."

"We should split up," Rayn announced, causing us to all turn towards her. "We'll cover more ground and find the bracelet easier."

Lauren nodded. "Let's go."

"Wait, who's going where?" I asked. "I don't want to run in there without a plan."

"We have a plan. It doesn't matter who goes where, we need to go. We're running out of time."

"Okay," I whispered as Lauren took off towards the building.

"Come on, Lauren," Rose followed after her. "Let's get your talisman back and maybe burn the place down for your mom."

Lauren gave a small smile as the two of them snuck off to the side opposite the remaining guards.

"Let's go take care of the last few guards while the Magisters distract the rest," Brooke replied. Rayn and I followed close behind.

We snuck up to the corner of the building and peaked around. The three guards seemed to be oblivious to their missing counterparts. They stood huddled together looking at each other's phones over their shoulders, laughing at a stupid video.

"Perfect." I waved my fingers as the pavement below them turned to a solid sheet of ice.

The guards jerked to see what had happened and their sudden movements caused them to slip. One went down right away, smacking his head on the ice and remained on the ground. The other two tried to stay upright as they slid and flailed but eventually they hit the ground too.

Rayn giggled and shrugged. "They'll be fine, probably."

Brooke waved her hand over the locked door to the side of the building and it clicked open. The three of us crept inside. Lights flickered above our heads. From the outside, the hospital looked dark and unoccupied. Inside only certain areas were lit up. We must have walked into the main hallway.

"You guys check these rooms and I'll go further down the hall, we'll meet in the middle," I said to Rayn and Brooke. "The talisman has to be close. They wouldn't keep it somewhere they couldn't easily get to."

I intended to start at the end of the hall and work my way back to the girls, but voices on the other side of the door caught my attention. I held my ear to the door and listened closely, trying to make out what they were saying. Suddenly the door creaked under my hands. I had put too much weight against it. The voices stopped and my blood ran ice cold.

I searched over my shoulder but Rayn and Brooke were in one of the other rooms searching for the bracelet.

"Who's there? Will?" a male voice on the other side of the door asked.

I bit my bottom lip, taking the few precious seconds I had to calculate my next move. Remaining incognito was out the window now that they knew someone stood on the other side of the door. While I still had the courage to do so, I swung the door open and flung sharp icicles at the voices. I struck two Renati members and both men fell to the floor in screams of pain. I recognized the remaining woman in the room.

The owner of Dragonfly Mystic.

Tom Campbell's aunt.

"Elementals!" she screamed, her voice echoing off the walls. She threw a wave of energy at me as I dodged out of the way.

I turned quickly, throwing my hand out to strike back but she made an evasive maneuver to the right.

"Henry!" Her shrill voice filled the room once more as she called out for Drake's help. She levitated a chair and threw it at me, but I ran across the room. I threw the other door open and sprinted down a foreign hallway.

She followed, screaming as she raced after me. I didn't know where I headed, but I knew I led her away from Rayn and Brooke, hopefully giving them time to find Lauren's talisman and get out.

A blast went off above my head from a burst of magic. I ducked as chunks of the ceiling fell around me, narrowly missing my skull. I dodged the blast as best I could but still took a blow to the shoulder from falling debris. I hissed as pain flew through my body but I kept pushing.

I turned a sharp corner, trying to remember how I got into that corridor to retrace my steps. I threw myself into a door, but it didn't budge. Locked. I turned in time to see Tom's aunt throw another spell at me as I waved my hand over the door, but it didn't budge. I dodged the spell and threw a wave of energy in her direction aimlessly. I missed. I tried to unlock the door again. Nothing.

I pounded my fist on the glass but it didn't shatter. Another blast went off next to my feet, making me jump. I turned to face her, covering my skin in ice in preparation to fight. I gritted my teeth as adrenaline ran rampant through my body.

As Tom's aunt sprinted down the hall towards me, an arrow shot through the back of her skull. Blood splattered on the walls as she collapsed to the ground.

Aden stood behind the dead witch, his crossbow aimed at me.

My powers swirled around my fingertips, preparing to put the hunter down when he lowered his weapon.

"You're alone," he stated.

My heart pounded in my throat. "So are you."

"Where are the others? I doubt you decided to storm the castle alone."

"Hopefully close by."

"Then let's get out of here." Aden ripped the arrow from the Renati member's skull and put it in the quiver strapped to his back.

Aden and I went the opposite way, knowing there had to be more than one route to get out of the hospital. His heavy boots echoed through the halls with each step.

"How did you know we were here?" I asked, looking down a hallway before we made our next move.

"I followed you," he answered. "I came back into town once the pack was led astray."

"Why?"

"I have a debt that I intend to repay."

"Us saving your life *was* repaying the debt."

Aden shrugged. "Maybe I wanted to come back."

An explosion in the other room caught our attention and we both sprinted in its direction. Aden kicked the door in and I ran past him to find Lauren and Rose back to back, surrounded by Renati members. Lauren and Rose jumped, turning their attention to us. One of the attackers had a vine around their neck, desperately scratching at their throat while Lauren levitated another in the air, but they were outnumbered.

Aden lifted his crossbow and shot a Renati member in the chest. I blasted the other two with ice, knocking them unconscious. With our help, the Renati members lay motionless on the floor.

"The hunter is back?" Lauren asked, walking over to us.

"Where's Rayn?" I asked, my heart pounding in my ears.

"Hopefully having better luck than us," Rose answered. "The talisman?"

"Nothing," I sighed. "We need to find Ray and Brooke."

"There can't be that many left," Rose stated. "We've knocked out half a dozen already."

"Me too, including those guards." I replied, keeping my head on a swivel. "Drake is here. Tom's aunt screamed for him before Aden killed her."

"My bracelet is close by. I can feel it." Gracefully, Lauren strolled down the hall, running her fingers along the wall. She halted at a door with a large padlock. "Bingo."

Lauren waved her hand over the lock but it stayed firmly in place.

I watched Lauren try a second time to undo the padlock. "I couldn't unlock half of the doors in this place."

Aden scrunched his nose, closer analyzing the lock. "Are you not powerful enough?"

"We're Elementals," I stated in irritation.

"Then unlock the door."

Suddenly, the padlock unclasped and fell to the floor, clanging at our feet as if the door welcomed us inside. I looked over at the girls. Rose's eyes were on the floor, glaring at the padlock.

No one's powers tingled under my skin.

Lauren reached out and pushed the door open, only darkness greeting us as we stepped inside with Aden close behind.

As my eyes adjusted to the darkness, a chilling voice crawled up my spine.

"We meet again."

Rose, Lauren and I jumped to attention, ready to strike. Henry Drake stepped into view, though the voice didn't belong to him. A light flipped on above his head, revealing Drake was not alone in the cold room.

Erebus lay on a hospital bed dressed in a white gown. Cords hung from monitors and tubes kept him hydrated and nourished as his body adjusted to this new plane. His pale and wrinkled skin revealed more color than when he was resurrected but he had clearly not seen sunlight since leaving the Shadow Realm. Dark circles sat under his eyes. His once-red irises now a deep brown though his eyes remained bloodshot.

Without hesitation, Lauren struck. Her powers bounced off an invisible energy shield surrounding Erebus and kicked back towards us like a rogue bullet. We ducked as the energy wave exploded above our heads.

Henry Drake clicked his tongue, tisking at our naivety. Before he could speak, a dart shot across the room and struck him in the side of the neck. Drake winced in pain and pulled the dart from his skin, analyzing it with a puzzled look. His eyebrows furrowed as he ran his fingers along the small feather at the end. He threw the dart across the room and shoved his hand at us angrily.

Nothing happened.

I sprinted across the room to the metal shelving unit, desperately digging through the boxes and bins. Shuffling boots and a low grunt sounded behind me but I didn't look back. I wasn't leaving this room until we got what we came for. I knelt before the shelves, going through the last of the boxes when defeat hung over my head.

I opened the last bin when Lauren shouted from across the room.

"I found it!" A sob caught in her throat as she clung to the yellow bracelet.

"Let's go!" I jumped up and started for the door, looking over my shoulders to see Aden had Drake pinned to the wall. His elbow in Drake's throat and a handgun aimed for his head.

"Should I kill him?" Aden asked as the girls and I sprinted for the door.

"Yes," I answered without hesitation.

The moment Aden's finger squeezed the trigger, the dart wore off. The gunfire erupted against an energy shield Drake mustered at the last minute, absorbing the blast.

"Aden, run!" I screamed as the hunter turned on his heel and followed us down the hallway. "That dart wore off fast!"

"It must have gotten damaged in my travels." Aden huffed behind me.

The door of Erebus' room blasted off the hinges as Drake came sprinting after us. Aden fumbled with his other gun, loading a second dart into the chamber and shot over his shoulder. I couldn't see if he hit Drake or not as I sprinted towards the exit. I let my power surface and drip water down my fingertips, signaling Rayn and Brooke to our whereabouts.

As we turned a corner, I collided into Brooke.

"Go, go, go!" Rose grabbed my sister's hand and sprinted down the first hall we'd come in through.

We burst through the exterior door, running into the parking lot where Serenity and another Renati member waited.

"Well, look what we have here," Serenity snickered. "We gotta stop meeting each other like this...you thinking you'll walk away from me unscathed."

Serenity enjoyed the cat and mouse game; eerily calm as if we would be intimidated.

"Get the fuck out of our way," I shot back, fully prepared to leave her blood stained on the pavement.

Serenity's eyes lingered on Aden and the crossbow he pointed in her direction. Her chest rose in an uneven quiver watching his finger kiss the trigger.

"We walked away from you before, and we'll do it again." Rose's powers flared under her skin.

"You think I don't have people around the perimeter hunting your brother as we speak?" Serenity asked, studying my face for a reaction but I wouldn't give her the satisfaction.

"Good luck, he's with three Elementals," I stated.

Serenity chortled. "You think that poor excuse for a generation can protect him? My father destroyed them."

I smiled back. "And walked away with some nasty scars."

"How did they know we were here?" the taller redhead asked Serenity.

I shrugged. "Sometimes all you need is someone to listen, Ren."

The wheels that seemed to be turning in Serenity's mind halted at my words as a fire took over her gaze. She grit her teeth and hissed. "I'm going to kill him."

"Touch him and it'll be the last thing you do." A ball of ice formed in my hand and I chucked it as hard as I could at Serenity's face. I caught her off guard and stuck her in the eye.

She cried out as a blast came from behind us, blowing chunks of pavement into the air.

"Are you going to let them stroll past you again, Serenity?" Henry Drake sneered at his daughter, emerging from the old hospital. "Did I raise you to be weak?"

"No!" she shouted back at him, holding her bleeding face with one hand.

Snarls echoed as claws tapped against the pavement. I knew that sound. A pack of Shadows crept out into the light with the biggest demon at the front, winged spread open. They didn't hesitate before they rushed towards us.

"Go!" Rayn shouted as flames erupted from her hands, throwing fire in either direction at both of the Drakes.

Her flames gave the Shadows pause, but didn't stop them.

Serenity and Henry jumped back to escape the burns as the rest of us took off to the escape route Rose had left under the fence. The sound of the Shadow's talons filled my ears, growing louder with each step. I flung myself onto my stomach and crawled under the fence, turning to see Rayn running after us, the Shadows hot on her heels. I grabbed Rayn's hand and yanked her under the fence as Big Boy snapped his jaws at her ankle, barely missing.

We ran down the road to the cars where I hoped Dmitri and the Magisters were waiting for us. I glanced over my shoulder as my lungs constricted from sprinting, my body fighting against me.

Not a single Shadow left the perimeter fence of the old hospital.

When we emerged from the bushes, Dmitri and the Magisters were on high alert, ready to strike until they saw us. I ran to my brother and pulled him into my arms, holding him close. I knew the Magisters would keep him safe but bringing him on this mission only heightened my anxiety. Dmitri patted my back, reassuring me silently as I pulled away.

Aden emerged from the bushes last, his crossbow hanging limp at his hip. The moment he came into view, fire flew at his face. He ducked, rolling out of the line of fire. He landed on his knee with his pistol already drawn, pointed straight at Nic.

"Stop!" Rayn screamed, throwing herself in between them, holding out a hand in each of their directions. "Stop! Aden saved us!"

"He's a hunter," Nic stated, flames dancing through his fingertips.

"He's the same hunter who let us go in the forest, who led the pack away from our house. He came back to help us," I explained, grabbing Nic's arm and forcing it down but the flames did not extinguish.

Rayn turned to Aden. "Please lower your gun."

Aden let out an angry sigh that growled in his throat as his gun slowly lowered towards his holster.

"We have to get out of here. The Renati are pissed," Lauren explained, opening one of the car doors. Moonlight reflected off the golden bracelet secured on her wrist. "Let's go!"

CHAPTER THIRTY-ONE

PROJECTION

RAYN

"Mia!" Nic called as he opened the door to the cottage. "The girls befriended a rogue witch hunter and brought him home."

"That's not funny, Dominic." When Amilia laid eyes on Aden, she leapt up from the safety of the armchair. "What is going on?"

"He saved our lives, twice. He wants to help us." I stood firm in front of Aden, refusing to let any of them touch him.

"You know what he's done, right?" Harmony asked as if we had never encountered a hunter before.

I stood my ground. "I also know what he didn't do. He stormed the old hospital and helped us. We trust him, and if you have any faith in us as the only complete generation, you will trust him too."

Aden sat down on the edge of the couch, fully aware that everyone's eyes followed his every move. Harmony paced the room, never turning her back to the hunter. Amilia slowly sunk back down in her chair.

Dmitri and Lauren moved to the dining room table while Brooke, Rose, and Whitney stood in the entryway of the living room. There wasn't enough seating for so many people in the same space. I sat down on the couch next to Aden, ready to strike out at anyone who spoke up against him.

He had come back. A fact that I struggled to wrap my head around. When I first saw him as we escaped the old hospital, I fought the urge to throw my arms around him. I had reminded myself a million times since that Aden did not come back for me. He returned because he felt like he owed us. But we were only repaying his kindness from when he let Whitney and I go in the first place.

Aden didn't actually owe us a life debt, but that still didn't mean he came back for me.

"What's your name?" Harmony asked him.

Aden hesitated before he spoke. "Aden."

"How exactly did you come across the girls?"

"My pack hunted in the forest where we picked up a large amount of magical activity, but I'm no longer part of the pack. Their mission isn't mine anymore," he answered.

"Did you spare them because you know how valuable they are?"

Aden's lip curled in confusion. "No. I spared them because the previous witches we had captured hadn't been killed...humanely. I didn't want to see it happen again and I figured they were young girls, how much damage could they do?"

"A lot." Nic raised his brow.

"Apparently." Aden nodded.

Nic paced across the living room. "Okay, we can work with this. We can use this to our advantage. He can give us insight into the hunters, maybe keep them off our backs until we deal with the Renati."

"There is inner fighting amongst the witches?" Aden asked, resting his elbows on his knees.

Harmony scoffed. "You hunt us but don't bother to learn our culture?"

"All we learn is how to defend against spells. None of the pack leaders care about your politics," Aden answered.

"Yes, there is inner fighting, there has been for centuries," I informed him. "Our plates were already full with their leader coming back into power and the Renati wanting to kill us, but your pack added a whole new level of stress."

Aden nodded slowly, taking in the information. "I see."

"So, you'll help us nip this hunter shit in the butt?" Nic turned to Aden.

Aden glared up at him. "My allegiance is to the girls. I will do as *they* ask."

Nic looked at me, waiting for me to step in.

"Thank you, Aden." I smiled at him. "We could use your help."

Those honey colored eyes softened at my gaze, sending flutters through my entire body. "I'll do what I can."

"Aden, what can you tell us about those darts? The ones that dull our powers." Whitney moved towards him.

Now that the shock of the night's events began to wear off, we needed to get answers out of Aden while he sat before us. I hoped he wouldn't disappear again.

"I don't know how they are made, I am not part of the process. I do know they cut off the witch's ability to access their powers, making them easier to kill." Aden paused. "Temporarily."

"If you aren't part of that process, who is?" Nic asked, crossing his arms firmly.

"They aren't scientists, per say, but we call them alchemists. They tinker with ways to give us an edge over magic users. I never stopped to ask how they do it. I didn't start asking questions until recently, and it nearly got me killed," Aden explained.

A chill ran up my spine hearing about the alchemists. If they found a way to cut off a witch's magic, what else were they capable of?

"Are they the ones who created whatever you guys do to alter yourselves?" Whitney asked.

Aden narrowed his gaze and nodded.

I turned to Amilia with a hopeful heart. "Mia, Aden needs somewhere to sleep."

"No." Amilia spoke sternly without hesitation.

"He can't sleep out in the cold!" I raised my voice.

"He's not staying in this house." Harmony chimed in, backing up Amilia.

"You have a garden shed. Right, Mia?" Whitney asked. "At least give Aden shelter from the cold. We're supposed to be better, aren't we?"

"He's a hunter. He's killed people." Amilia argued.

Whitney took a step towards her. "You let Nic come home."

I widened my eyes. I never expected Whit to throw Dominic under the bus like that for Aden. I smiled at her sister, thankful that at least someone in the room had my back.

Nic's jaw clenched as he turned to Whitney, betrayal echoed in his gaze.

Amilia crossed her arms. "I've known Dominic since he was a little boy. These two things are not the same."

I jumped in. "Her point is, you've made it clear that you don't let people's pasts define their future. You forgave Nic's past. You act like we are better than the hunters, but you overlook the girls and I killing Renati members as if the ends justify the means, as if our hands are any less bloody." I motioned towards Aden. "You can't forgive a man who saved your last chance at defeating the Renati for good because he *has* killed? Who in this room has clean hands?"

"Me," Brooke answered quietly.

Rose reached out and put a hand on Brooke's shoulder.

Amilia sighed, crossing her arms. She shook her head before answering. "Fine, but I'm putting a spell on the lock."

"Aden?" Whitney looked at him for his approval of the situation.

"You live here now?" Aden turned to me. My heart skipped a beat as I nodded. Aden continued to Amilia. "Thank you. I won't be any trouble."

"Rayn knows where everything is," Amilia huffed and headed towards the stairs. "We were successful in retrieving the talisman?"

"Yes." Lauren held up her wrist, showing everyone her bracelet.

Amilia nodded. "I'm very proud of you girls." She excused herself without another word.

I caught Whitney finally turn her gaze to Nic, who burned holes into her with his eyes. Without a word, he went down the hall to his bedroom and firmly closed the door.

"I'll show you to the shed," I offered to Aden, standing up from the couch and heading to the back door.

"I'll come with you." Dmitri shot up from his seat.

"Why?" I hissed under my breath.

Dmitri clenched his jaw. "Because I'm your brother and I don't trust him."

I glared at him as I opened the door, motioning for him to lead the way.

The three of us headed into the backyard. Amilia used her gardening tools more than the Roberts' did, but we also weren't hiding Aden here either, so this was probably a better arrangement. Aden set his crossbow down on a plastic tub and unhooked his holster.

I mustered every ounce of courage left in my exhausted body. "You came back."

Aden turned to me. "I came back."

"Because of the life debt?"

He glanced awkwardly at Dmitri over my shoulder. "Thank you for offering a place to stay. I won't be in the way."

I let out an angry sigh. Aden obviously wouldn't talk to me openly in mixed company. Dmitri stood in the doorway with his arms crossed showing no intention of leaving.

"Goodnight." I turned on my heel and shoved past Dmitri, hitting him with my shoulder.

"The hell was that for?" Dmitri followed behind me across the lawn and up the porch steps. "Are you seriously pissed right now?"

I turned around to face him but swallowed all the words on my tongue. I wanted to be angry with my brother, I wanted to take everything out on him, but he hadn't done anything wrong.

"No," I answered.

"Hey, I'm just looking out for you, okay?"

"I was only looking out for you with Abe Roberts too, you know."

Dmitri turned away, facing the herb garden that grew along the back deck. He nodded, barely moving his head enough for me to notice.

I ran my fingers through my hair. "I know you and I have always fought the most, but that doesn't mean I love you any less. I know it's easier with Whitney, she's your favorite sister, but I care too."

He turned back to me at that. "I don't have a favorite sister."

"Shut the fuck up." I marched up the porch steps, convinced he was lying. Dmitri stopped me.

"Ray, stop." He let out a deep breath. "Listen, I know how it looks on the outside, okay? I know Abe has made some questionable decisions, some that I don't even agree with. But my heart still tugs when I'm around him. I can't...I didn't just wake up one morning and decide I would crush on the landlord's son. Falling into the lake that day, it changed things. So, I can empathize that what happened in the meadow with the hunters changed things. But you can't blame me for being overly cautious."

"Because I have a history of making bad decisions."

"Because I don't know that guy well enough to determine that he's not a piece of shit. It has nothing to do with your decision making."

"It feels like it."

"Well you're projecting because no one is holding your past against you but yourself." Dmitri's words rattled me to the core. "I didn't come back here because I don't trust you. I'm out here because you're my sister and that man in the shed is trained and altered to kill us. He's still a stranger and you're too important."

I nodded. "Okay."

"Okay," Dmitri echoed and brushed past me into the cottage.

The rest of my generation stood by the front door talking amongst themselves. Lauren held tightly onto the bracelet around her wrist as if someone would try to steal it from her any moment.

I turned to Whitney. "Are you staying here tonight?"

She reached for the doorknob with trembling fingers. "I hope not. I have someone to apologize to."

I smiled as Whit closed the door behind her. "About fucking time."

Rose let out a deep sigh. "I try to stay out of it, but..."

"But Whitney deserved to know about Bryan hooking up with Serenity before now. She shouldn't have found out this way," Lauren argued.

"I'm not defending his hoe phase." Rose put her hands up. "I'm just saying, she makes it hard for me to stay out of things, because I can't fight with Whit and keep the generation together, but he's my brother. He's the only sibling I have and he does a lot for me, more than our own father."

"Bryan had a hoe phase?" Brooke laughed. "I've always thought he gave off hermit vibes."

Lauren giggled. "Nah, I've seen him dance. He's no hermit."

Rose let out a sigh and turned to me, changing the subject. "Things okay with Aden?"

I nodded. "I think he's going to stick around this time. I hope so, at least."

"A rogue witch hunter isn't a bad card to keep in your back pocket," Brooke said.

I shook my head, a blush warming my cheeks. "Not bad, at all."

Chapter Thirty-Two

FORGIVENESS

Whitney

My heart pounded in my chest, beating louder with each step up the walkway to Bryan's house. I took a long pause at the front door, contemplating whether I should turn around and go back to the car. Did Bryan even want to see me? He hadn't sent a single text since our fight. Our first real fight. The first time he'd ever raised his voice or cussed at me. The first time I'd ever seen him cry. I needed to stop being a coward and face this. I opened the front door and stepped inside. It felt like I had barged in, even though I lived there. Even though all my things were still there.

Troy sat in the living room, silent and unreadable.

"Hi, Whitney," he said, monotone.

"Is Bryan here?" I asked, even though I had seen his Jeep parked on the street.

"He's in *his* room," Troy answered.

His room. Not ours.

"Thanks." I took a step towards the hall when Troy's voice stopped me.

"Look, Whitney, I try to stay out of Bryan's relationships. I haven't confronted Hannah or anyone else about their fights because it's not my place. But I feel like I need to say something this time, because he's like my brother and I'm concerned."

"Troy–"

"I don't know all the details and I don't need to, just...do better."

I didn't say another word as I headed down the hallway. It wasn't Troy's business anyway. Bryan's friends didn't know why I ended things with him after Halloween or why I had felt so betrayed when we fought about Serenity. It didn't matter if they approved of me. All that mattered to me was the person on the other side of the door I stood in front of.

I knocked gently, taking in a deep breath as I waited to hear his voice.

"What's up?"

I froze with my hand on the knob but I didn't open it. I just listened.

"Come in?" Bryan said again.

I turned the knob and pushed the door back, staying in the frame. If he told me to leave, I wanted to stay in the hallway for a quick getaway.

Bryan sat cross legged on his bed with his laptop on his thighs, papers and books strewn around his bed. He had his glasses on and his hair stuck up in the back. He didn't look up at first, typing away on the keyboard with a pen between his teeth. I stayed where I was, waiting for him to realize it wasn't Troy at his door. When he finally did glance up from his laptop he did a double take. The clacking of the keys stopped as he stared at me.

"I can come back if you're busy," I spoke first, eyeing the mess of papers on the bed.

"No, that's okay." He closed his computer and scanned the bedroom, looking at the mug and water bottles on his night stand. The pile of clothes on the floor. I didn't care about the mess. "I would have cleaned up if I knew you were coming home."

Home.

"I didn't want to risk you telling me not to come," I admitted, still not moving an inch.

"I wouldn't have."

A silence fell over us, uncomfortable and uncertain. I decided to take the first jump off the cliff. I stepped into our bedroom and closed the door behind me. Bryan and I needed privacy, especially after the conversation I had with Troy.

"I had a whole thing worked out in my head on the way over, what I wanted to say but now I don't know where to start." I looked down at my shoes.

Bryan took a deep breath. "Then maybe I can go first?"

"Okay."

"I've missed you," he whispered. "I wanted to call you the moment you drove off but I wanted to give you space. Clearly you needed some alone time to figure out if you still wanted to do this and I didn't want to push you further away. I don't want you to take my silence as complacency."

"I kind of assumed you were the one deciding if you wanted to stay together or not."

Bryan's face fell. "Because me crying and begging you not to walk away during our argument gave off the impression that I don't want you anymore?"

"Of course not. I needed time to process. Truth is, I'm still angry but I don't like the radio silence between us. I've had a hard time sleeping without you."

"I don't know what to say to that," Bryan admitted, running his fingers through his messy hair. "I'm sorry about everything. I'm sorry I yelled at you. I feel like such an asshole."

"I yelled back."

"Yeah but you had a reason to. You were right. I should have told you that Serenity and I had history weeks ago, but I had just gotten you back and I was afraid of fucking things up between us. Which I did anyway, so I guess that's all moot. You had just found out everything with Hannah and I was scared you would think I'm not worth it."

"You are worth it."

"Cheating on Hannah and keeping my past with Serenity a secret are red flags that I'm embarrassed of. I didn't want you to think less of me, or look at me differently."

"I don't. I'm sorry I blew up," I apologized. "I understand why you didn't want to tell me, even if it did hurt." I picked at the cuticle of my thumbnail. "It's hard for me to admit this but I'm jealous."

"Whitney." Bryan got off the bed and stood in front of me, reaching out to take my hands in his. "I wish you could see yourself through my eyes because you have no competition. I love every single inch of you, including your soul. You are everything to me. Everything. Whatever you need me to do to help you trust me again, say the word. If you want that list, I'll write it right now. Whatever you need, I'll do it."

"I don't want a list, Byn." I slid my hands from his and pulled him into my arms. He held me against his body, warmth flooding my core. "No more surprises."

"I promise."

"I'm not mad at you for having a past. I have one too, but I think I take for granted that none of my exes live in town. None of them even know what state I live in. But you grew up here. We're in our twenties. I knew you had a life before me. It rocked me that Serenity was such a big part of it."

"I know," Bryan muttered against my hair, pressing a soft kiss to my crown. "I'm sorry. I didn't handle any of this very well."

"Neither did I."

"The last few days I've been agonizing over that fight. I hated it. My parents used to fight like that and I swore I'd never act that way."

I lifted my head from his chest to meet his eyes. "We're going to argue and disagree. Couples fight sometimes."

Bryan looked down at the floor. "The fighting between my parents got worse as I got older. They'd scream at each other in the kitchen after Rose and I went to bed. Break dishes and shove each other into the walls. Sometimes they didn't even wait until we were out of the room. It was ugly and toxic and abusive. After that fight with you, I was terrified that I'm turning into him."

I cupped his cheek. "You would never take it that far. You'd never lay a hand on me."

"No, of course not." He kissed my hand.

"Hey, we're okay." I smiled up at him. "We both said things in anger, but I love you and I want things how they were before this stupid fight. I don't want Serenity to fuck up another aspect of my life."

"I can't say I'm sorry enough."

"You don't have to." I leaned up and pressed my lips against his. "I forgive you. Do you forgive me?"

"I was never mad enough for you to need forgiveness."

Bryan's eyes burned into mine before he grabbed my face and pulled me back in for another kiss. His tongue ran against my bottom lip and I parted my lips against his, deepening the kiss. His hands traveled down my back and grabbed my ass, lifting me up with an ease that still shook me. Bryan held me against his chest as he turned and laid me down on the bed, the papers crumpling beneath us as he climbed on top of me.

Before I could voice my concern of messing up whatever he worked on, his lips collided with mine again. I ran my fingers through his hair, grabbing the back of his head to pull him closer. I needed him closer.

His hand slid under my sweatshirt, grazing across my stomach as it danced up my chest. His thumb brushed against my nipple through my bra. I gasped against his mouth as his hand traveled to my back. I arched as he undid the clasp of my bra, watching him carefully lift my sweater and shirt over my head. His eyes came back to mine and he dropped my bra on the carpet. With a blink of an eye he was on top of me once more, pressing his weight against my body.

"I love you," he said into my neck, leaving a trail of soft kisses down my skin. "I love you so damn much."

"Show me," I whispered. His eyes darted up to meet mine, desire burning behind them. "Show me how much."

Bryan unbuttoned my pants and slowly slid them down my legs. Within moments, I lay bare before him. He slid off the bed and grabbed my thighs, yanking me towards the edge. Every molecule of my being rose to high alert as he knelt down and kissed my inner thigh. Those gorgeous green eyes traveled up my naked body until they locked into mine.

"You are everything I've ever dreamed of." He kissed a little further in. "And you aren't leaving this bed until you believe it."

Anticipation bubbled throughout my body as my core turned to molten lava. I braced myself, but Bryan preferred to take his sweet time. He pressed another kiss, watching me groan with impatience.

"This is my favorite part," he whispered. "Watching you come undone."

Finally, he gave in to me with a long, slow sweep of his tongue. I shuddered at the impact, clenching my thighs around him. He pushed my leg up onto his shoulder, giving himself more room as he draped his arm across my stomach to hold me in place. He gently caressed my skin as his tongue got to work, sweet and slow. I reached down and laced my fingers in his, squeezing his hand. He took the hint and slipped his tongue inside, using his free thumb to rub lazy circles around my most sensitive spot.

I bit my bottom lip in an attempt to silence myself but a moan vibrated in my chest as he replaced his thumb with his lips and began to suck.

I wrapped my fingers in his hair and pulled him closer, grinding my hips against him. He hummed against me, picking up the pace. Keeping his mouth in place, he slipped a finger inside me. I arched my back, closing my eyes and focusing on his touch, on his movements.

But intrusive thoughts kept creeping in. The sounds of concrete blasting over me from the Renati's attacks. Their screams of pain from Rayn's fire. Erebus hooked up to all those wires and tubes.

"Hey." Bryan lifted his head to look at me. "Relax, baby, stop getting stuck in your head."

"I'm sorry, I'm just–"

"I promise you'll feel better after an orgasm. Lay back and let me take care of you."

I nodded and lay my head back on the bed, closing my eyes as he eased back into his rhythm. My mind went blank and I focused on his touch. The way he caressed my skin with his fingertips, memorizing every curve and dip of my body.

Desire pooled in my core, heating my soul. A whimper escaped my lips and excitement sparked in Bryan. He readjusted himself, putting my other leg up over his shoulder, giving himself two free hands. He spread me open and slid two fingers back inside, responding to every move and noise I made. My breathing picked up and my hips bucked against him as the pleasure built inside of me. My thigh muscles tightened around him and I put my hand over my mouth to swallow any noises. I had made a conscious effort to not let my voice echo through the house when Bryan was between my legs, as difficult as it often was.

This wasn't the all consuming, earth shattering finish I normally received from my lover. This had been sweet and slow, a gentle reminder that we could still be vulnerable and fragile with one another. A show of his love and devotion no matter what the future held for us. I could almost feel his smirk as I came crashing down.

"What about you?" I panted, reaching out for him.

He shook his head, grabbing my hand before I could touch him. "No, this was for you."

"Are you sure?"

"Trust me, I get nothing but pleasure from making you come." Bryan lay down next to me on the bed and pulled me against his chest. I nuzzled in, finally feeling at home.

Gradually, my pulse slowed down and my breathing returned to normal. Bryan grabbed a blanket and pulled it over me.

"So, what are all these papers?" I asked.

"There's this class I have to take to get into the credential program and the professor is making everyone do this stupid research paper before the semester even starts. It's a requirement to stay enrolled."

"And we just ruined them?"

Bryan kissed my forehead. "It's not a big deal, I'm almost done anyway."

I nodded and traced the wrinkles in his shirt. While the tension from the night's events brewed under my skin, I melted into Bryan. The release he'd given me did relax my muscles as I let out a deep breath. The future may be uncertain, but at least Bryan and I were okay again.

"You okay?"

I nodded.

"Baby, talk to me."

"Troy's mad at me," I whispered. "I wasn't going to say anything because in the moment it didn't bother me, but I know your friends are important to you."

"Did he say something to you?" Bryan's muscles tensed as he went to sit up, but I put my hand on his stomach and eased him back onto the bed.

"He's worried about you. All he sees is me hurting you and I don't blame him for assuming the worst. It's not like you can tell him the truth about any of this."

"Regardless, he shouldn't have said anything to you."

"Don't make a deal of it. I don't want him to hate me."

Bryan kissed my forehead. "He doesn't hate you. I told him why you were mad at me. Troy doesn't need to know about witchcraft to know you'd be upset about Serenity."

I sniffed. "When we broke up, Ashley barely spoke to me for a month."

"I'm sorry. They're protective. Troy is spoiled because he's been with Emma for so long. And I've never worked with any of Ashley's exes so I can't honestly say I would behave any differently. But I won't sit by and let them be dicks, I promise."

"Troy wasn't a dick. He just let me know he wasn't happy we were fighting."

Bryan tightened his arms around me. "Well, that's all behind us now, yeah?"

I nodded, letting the night's events run through my mind like a flip book. I sat up abruptly as the reality of my actions washed over me. I grabbed a handful of blankets and held it over my chest. "I fucked up."

"What?" Bryan asked, pushing himself up on his elbows.

"We went to the old hospital tonight. We got Lauren's bracelet and kicked the Renati in the shins on our way out but—"

"Wait, is everyone okay? Is Rose—"

"Rose is fine. We're all fine, but Serenity was there and someone asked how we knew about the hideout and...I fucked up."

"What did you do?" Bryan's emotions froze under his skin.

"I repeated what you said to her in the parking lot. Sometimes all you need is someone to listen. She knew..." I paused. "She knows you tricked her."

Bryan cursed under his breath. "Why did you do that?"

"I was mad," I confessed. "Mad at Serenity. Mad at everyone. I wasn't thinking. I put a target on your back. Fuck." I grabbed the roots of my hair, hating to admit the words in my head out loud, but I felt the need to be open and vulnerable. A tear slid down my cheek. "I wanted her to know you picked me."

Bryan's gaze held mine for a long moment before he spoke. "There has never been a competition between you and Serenity for my affection."

I wiped away another tear. "I spiraled. I'm so sorry."

Bryan ran a comforting hand up my spine and wiped the next tear away with his thumb. "I chose a side. *I* made that choice. Serenity already knew that. She would have figured it out that I leaked the information eventually. She's too smart to not realize it was me. It'll be fine."

"Do you actually believe that?"

He let out a deep breath. "Part of me does. The part that hopes the person I knew is still in there somewhere. Hey," he cupped my cheek. "I love you."

"I love you too." I cleared my throat and swallowed the rest of my tears. "Speaking of the person you knew...there's something I've been wondering about."

"What's that?" Bryan traced my jaw with his fingertips.

"What is the whole yogurt on the shirt thing?"

"Wow, you remember every little detail."

I shrugged. "I'm not going to lie, I fixated on everything you said to her. You still care about her and that's hard for me to swallow."

Bryan sighed and pulled me against him. I rested my head on his chest, focusing on his heartbeat. "Emma and Serenity are a year younger than Troy, Ash and I. My first day of sophomore year, they were freshmen. We were in the cafeteria at lunch and someone knocked Serenity's tray against her chest. She had an open cup of yogurt and it went everywhere. All over her shirt. She started crying and ran into the bathroom and I felt so bad for her. I went after her and offered her my shirt."

"Wow," I whispered, overwhelmed with his kindness for a complete stranger.

"I got detention for breaking the dress code but it was worth it. Troy met Emma that day. Not that they wouldn't have met anyway but I like to think I helped bring them together."

"Did you go to class shirtless?"

"Yeah." He laughed under his breath. "I got sent to the office the minute I walked into class. Em and Serenity ate lunch with us from then on. They are the ones who took Troy and I to the party where I met Ash and well, here we are."

"Where you sang Misery Business on her table?" I smirked.

His eyes widened. "Of course she told you about that."

"You are such a good guy," I breathed, wrapping my head around his history with the Drake sisters. "You really are the nicest guy I've ever met."

"Yeah, well, it hasn't always been beneficial," Bryan's voice trailed off. "Maybe if I hadn't gone after Serenity, maybe things would be different now."

"I don't think so." I leaned up and kissed his cheek. "I think everything happens for a reason."

Chapter Thirty-Three

POWERLESS

Whitney

"Are you sure you want to spend your last day at the cottage?" I asked Bryan that weekend as I lounged on our bed.

"Yes," he answered without skipping a beat as he pulled his jeans up over his hips. "I'm going back to FBU tonight. I'm spending every free second I have with you."

A smile swept across my face, watching his shirt lift up to expose the skin above his jeans as he put on a hoodie. "I want that too."

"It's more than that." Bryan reached out and took my hand in his. "This fight going on between you guys and the Renati...it affects more than your inner circle. It affects the whole town. Everyone here will get taken down in the crossfire, like that village where the hunters started. I want to help."

"You've done a pretty good job so far," I said, lacing his fingers with mine. "I don't want you coming on any missions."

"I'd probably be in the way," he agreed, rubbing the back of my hand with his thumb. "But I want to help plan out the next move. I know this town. I want to keep Rifton from burning to the ground."

I nodded. "You're right. I shouldn't have pushed you away."

"None of that matters now." He pulled me gently towards the door. "Let's get this portal thing figured out."

An hour later, our entire crew stood in the living room of the cottage. I couldn't help but admire the mixed group we had formed over the last few months. I never imagined when we moved to Rifton that this would be the end result. My eyes lingered on my brother.

Dmitri looked so young surrounded by older men. The roundness of his face gave away the years he trailed behind the others. Nic may have been the shortest of the men, but his sharp facial features showed his years. Even Bryan seemed older standing amongst the men. Aden and Warren both towered over everyone, though Aden stood with broader shoulders and a wider chest. Dmitri looked like a child beside the rest of them.

Even more reason I wanted to keep him out of the fighting.

"I don't understand why we are bringing home every stray we find. At least the hunter serves a purpose." I realized Nic referred to Bryan.

Rose shot back at him. "A stray? My brother is the only reason we got the ledger *and* Lauren's bracelet back."

"Why are you so concerned about me being here?" Bryan asked Nic. "I don't have to prove anything to you."

"You aren't equipped like we are. You wouldn't last a minute out there." Nic's tone remained firm as he crossed his arms.

"Then teach me. I already know how to shoot." Bryan turned to Aden.

Aden scoffed. "I have been trained to hunt and survive since the day I learned to walk. You do not become a hunter overnight."

"I'm a quick learner. And besides, the hunting part is not what I'm interested in. Surviving on the other hand–"

"Your first mistake is assuming they are not one in the same," Aden replied sternly. "Not everyone is made for this life."

"Why have you already dismissed him? Bryan is intelligent and resourceful, he's already helped us," I spoke up in defense.

"From what I've heard, it sounds like you could use all the assistance you can get. You won't find anyone out there more dedicated to their safety than I am." Bryan gestured towards me and the other girls.

"You are powerless," Nic matter of factly stated. "End of discussion."

"I may not have powers, but I am not powerless!" Bryan shouted across the room. "The only thing you have over me is the ability to manipulate kinetic energy into heat and I'm not the least bit intimidated by it."

"Listen," Lauren eased. "I know you guys are Magisters, but we are the last complete generation of Elementals. We are the holders of the Shepherd's lost talismans, aren't we?"

"Yes," Harmony hissed.

"Then shut up and listen to us," I finished Lauren's sentiment. "We want Bryan here."

Nic rolled his eyes. "It doesn't matter. Now that you have Lauren's talisman back, the Renati will be planning retaliation. They'll be ready to strike and they know we are coming for the Shadow Realm portal next. We have to stay one step ahead. So–"

"No," Harmony cut him off with an ice cold glare. "They don't want our advice. They don't want to listen. They can let us know when they've figured it out."

"Honey, will you join me in the garden?" Amilia turned to Harmony with a sigh. "There's something I wish to discuss with you."

"Sure, Mia," Harmony replied warmly. She took Amilia's arm as the two of them left the room.

"You aren't going with them?" Rose asked, turning to Nic and Warren.

"No," Nic answered, sitting down on the couch.

Warren let out a sigh and turned to us. "What do you girls have in mind for the portal?"

"The potion was easy enough, since the bulk of the magic is in our blood." Rose scooted to the edge of her seat. "I traded out borrult for sorrow root. Sorrow root symbolizes an ending, closing of a chapter, if you will. Since borrult only blooms with the dawn, it made sense."

Warren's eyes widened in amazement. "You are brilliant, Rose."

"Now we just have to get the Renati taken care of," I said.

Brooke pursed her lips. "I don't see us fighting off Renati while we focus on a spell powerful enough to close it. The meadow portal had no distractions, but getting out of the old hospital was so hectic. I barely remember half of it."

"You need a decoy," Dmitri replied. "The Magisters and I could–"

I cut him off. "I'm not using you as bait, Dmitri."

"I'll die before I let someone lay a finger on him," Nic stated. "But he's right. The rest of us will keep them off your backs while you close the portal."

"You'll be outnumbered, even with Aden's help. You'll wear yourselves down before we even get set up," Brooke pointed out.

Warren shook his head. "We'll be fine."

"I thought we burned the ledger so the Renati couldn't track Elemental supporters and we could, I don't know, get some damn support?" Lauren murmured sarcastically.

Warren shrugged. "It is, but most of them left Rifton. They will come back, but in the meantime we are working with a skeleton crew. I have faith in us."

"The Hallow," I said, watching Nic's reaction carefully.

He side-eyed me. "How do you know about the Hallow?"

"Question is, why haven't you told us about it?"

"I suppose it hasn't come up organically." Nic tilted his head.

"This is me bringing it up."

Warren's gaze wandered over to Lauren. "So, that's where that went."

Lauren raised her brow in surprise. "What do you mean?"

"It's not nice to take things that don't belong to you, Lauren," Warren warned.

"Yeah, and keeping secrets doesn't make friends," I argued.

Warren turned to me and hardened his eyes. "We are your Magisters first, friends second."

Nic took a step forward. "Whit, we will get to the Hallow, I promise you. But we can't leave Rifton while that portal is open if we want a town to come home to."

"How were these witches able to leave town without being tracked?" Rose questioned. "That's the purpose of the ledger, isn't it?"

Warren and Nic looked at one another, as if silently wondering if they should tell us.

"They destroyed their own pages. Severed the connection between their blood and the ledger." Nic moved his hands as he spoke. "That's how Audri was able to hide out for so long."

I nodded, finally understanding the bigger picture. "That's where you went to get the spell? The Hallow?"

"No, but I hope you understand anonymity is part of the deal," Warren said.

Bryan crossed his arms. "There isn't any Elemental support left in Rifton?"

Nic turned to Bryan, annoyed. "Mia has been in touch with some old friends, but not many of them have the balls to go up against the Renati." He turned to me. "Return of the Elementals or not."

"Closing the portal will gain their trust." I put the pieces together. "Once we prove that we can protect them against the Renati, they'll be more willing to stand behind us."

Nic smirked at me. "I agree."

"The big question is, do we strike now or wait?" Rose asked, running her fingers through her hair.

"Strike now," Lauren answered.

At the same time Brooke said, "Wait."

"We do the opposite of whatever the Renati is expecting from us," Rayn stated.

"Which is?" Nic asked curiously.

"Serenity knows Bryan is the one who told us about the old hospital, so that was a one and done deal," I told the room. "Unless we can figure out how to be a fly on the walls, we are running off guess work."

"Brooke, can you astral project yet?" Warren asked, turning to look at her.

Brooke shook her head. "I don't think so?"

"Fucking Finn, never there when we needed him," Warren grumbled. "He could astral project, send his subconscious out from his physical body."

"That's a cool party trick," Rose remarked.

"It wasn't easy though. He always passed out afterwards," Nic replied. "We don't have the luxury of time to unlock new powers. We need something now."

I reached into my pocket and gently ran my thumb along the blue lace agate, realizing we weren't the only ones keeping an eye on the Renati's movements. Hopefully, this last resort would be the ticket. I opened my mouth to announce my idea to the group but decided against it, letting out a sigh instead. To everyone else, I appeared frustrated with the lack of progress and I wanted to keep it that way. I thought of Abe and continued to rub the stone. After we finished at the cottage, I'd rush to our usual meeting place.

"I have to get to work." Lauren pushed off the wall and grabbed her bag. "I don't know what we are going to do, but we can't waste time debating it. We need to act."

Nic ran his hands over his face. "I agree, but if we act too hastily, it won't end well."

Rose groaned and stood up, stretching out her back. "Brooke and I need to head out anyway. They only wanted her gone for an hour."

"Yeah, I'm closing tonight. I need to jump in the shower," Rayn said.

All that time talking in circles and we were in the same spot we were when the day began. Everyone trickled out of the room until only Nic, Bryan, Aden and I remained.

Bryan stood still, his eyes on Nic.

"Got something to say?" Nic asked, holding out his arms.

Bryan narrowed his gaze. "I don't like the way you look at her."

"At who?"

"Whitney."

Nic scoffed. "Oh, don't be so thick headed to think someone is infringing on your territory. I like my girls a little bit older."

"You look at her like you love her."

"I do love her," Nic snapped. "I'd kill for her. I'd die for her like my own blood, like someone would do for their sister or their child. She's one of the only friends I have in this fucking world, so you're damn right I love her."

Bryan fell silent, turning his head away from Nic. When Bryan didn't speak, Nic continued.

"Those girls are going to face challenges in this war that you can't fathom. I don't give a shit about you. You're powerless and therefore you're worthless to us. The least you can do is knock off your petty jealousy and get out of our way."

"Dominic." I made my presence known, my gaze burning holes into him.

Nic's eyes met mine, unapologetic and fearless. "You know it's true." He turned to leave the room.

"Apologize."

"Whitney, please don't." Bryan's voice was small. I could tell he wanted me to let Nic walk away but I grew tired of the mask Nic wore whenever someone else was around him. Sick of him being two different people.

"I will not." Nic crossed his arms.

"You will because I'm asking."

"As the holder of a talisman?"

"As your friend." I stepped towards him. "As someone who loves you just as much. If you cared about me in the least, you'd be nicer to the love of my life. You will treat him with respect if you want to keep mine."

Nic's gaze lingered on me before the mask fell away. I finally saw my friend standing before me.

"I didn't have to be that harsh," Nic muttered. "I apologize for my approach."

"Dominic," I said sternly through my teeth.

"I apologize," Nic repeated. Bryan still wouldn't look him in the eye. "I know how it feels...to see the woman you love depend on another man. I'm sorry I put that on you." Nic sighed and closed his eyes, letting his shoulder fall. "I'm stressed out."

Bryan finally met Nic's gaze. "We're all uneasy."

Nic gave me one last look, waiting to see my silent approval before he took his leave.

I followed Bryan out of the front door, speed walking to keep up with his long legs. He didn't glance over his shoulder as I huffed after him. It wasn't until he got into the driver's side of his Jeep and closed the door that he acknowledged me.

"Hey, are you mad at me?" I asked, climbing into the passenger's seat.

"No," he answered quietly. "I'm…I'm sorry."

"Bryan, Nic can be such an asshole. *I'm* sorry." I reached out for his hand. "I don't know what his problem is, it's probably not even you. He's not always like this."

"Why do you hold him in such high regard if that's how he acts?"

I paused, wondering why I felt so defensive of Nic. "Sometimes I feel like I'm the only one who sees what's under the mask he shows everyone else. We're going through the same things. Nic is someone I can talk to and he knows how I feel."

Bryan took an uneasy breath before he spoke. "I don't know how I feel about that."

"What?" I asked, confused. "He's supposed to be my mentor."

"And I'm supposed to be your boyfriend."

"It's not like that between Nic and I."

"I know it's selfish not wanting you to be close to another man." Bryan met my eyes with intensity. "But there's a connection there and I…I don't know how to feel about it."

"Bryan, I don't want anyone else," I soothed him, touching his face. "Nic has never once made a move and I'd never let him. I promise you."

"Whit, I've never had a relationship like this before."

"With a witch?" I asked, trying to lighten the mood with a half-laugh.

Bryan chuckled under his breath and reached for my hand.

"You've had plenty of other girlfriends," I said.

The word plenty put an odd look on his face as he chewed on his bottom lip. "No, I haven't. I've never moved anyone in before. I've never felt this intensely for anyone. I thought I knew what love was, but then I met you and it's like I'm feeling it all for the first time." Bryan's voice turned to a whisper. "I know how it feels to lose you, and I'm terrified to go through that again."

I stared at him, absorbing every word he spoke. Hurt echoed in his eyes, but love accompanied it; so much love that it warmed every corner of my being.

"I feel the same way about you." I touched his face again, feeling his stubble against my fingertips.

"I want to be the person you bring your problems to. You can talk to me, too, Whit."

"I do talk to you. I love you." I held his gaze.

He smiled softly. "I love you too. I know I seem like a jealous jerk, I'm sorry."

"Don't be. I'm going to talk to Dominic, okay? He'll ease up on you, I promise. I'd do anything for you," I smiled at him, running my fingers through his hair. "But first, I have a lead I think might help us. Can we go up to the Eagle Loop Trail?"

"Sure," Bryan said, pulling away from the curb.

Bryan waited for me at the trailhead while I trekked through the winter forest. With each step I took, the stone in my pocket's vibration quickened against my leg. I found Abe resting his back against a tree, waiting for me.

"Is Dmitri okay?" Abe asked, pushing himself off the tree.

"Yeah, everyone's fine," I answered, not realizing that he probably panicked since I called him outside of our usual supply drop. "I have something to ask. Have you still been watching the Renati?"

"As best as I can without getting caught, yes. Mostly the old D-" his voice cut out. "The burnt building. I haven't been stupid enough to get too close."

"That's perfect, actually. We have to close that portal before things get out of hand. When have you seen the least amount of people there?"

"Um," Abe pondered for a moment. "Usually early morning, right before the sun rises is when I've seen only a few keeping watch. The times I've seen the most people there is earlier in the night. Once it gets around 5:30 in the morning I think they figure if you were showing up, you would have by then."

I nodded, making a mental note of everything he said. "Good, good. That's useful."

"You aren't going to take Dmitri with you, right?"

I broke eye contact with Abe. "He doesn't listen to me when I tell him no, so I don't have much control over if he goes or not."

Abe stepped forward with wide, panicked eyes. "He has to listen to you. He can't be there, Whitney. That protection spell I did was only temporary. They'll kill him without blinking just to hurt you."

"He went with us when we attacked the old hospital and the other Elementals kept him safe. They wouldn't let anything happen to him."

"He can't be there," Abe repeated. "You have to be smarter about this, you can't risk him like–"

"And what are *you* doing to keep Dmitri safe?" I cut him off. "You hide in the woods saying you're staying away for his own protection but if he's in danger either way, you should be there to help keep him safe. I used to think the same way about my boyfriend, I used to think that if I kept him far away from everything he'd be safe. But a Shadow still attacked him, and thankfully I was there to get him out alive. We can't protect them if we leave them alone."

Abe shook his head, avoiding eye contact. "I can't."

"Then you're a coward," I hissed at him, pulling the blue lace agate from my pocket and dropping it on the ground. "You must not care about him as much as you claim."

"I *love* him," Abe shot back, staring down at the stone lying at his feet.

"I don't believe you. All you ever do is hide in the shadows. I respect the protection spell you did for him, Abe, but sometimes you have to face your demons. If you actually loved my brother, you'd get off your ass and do something. You'd fight with us."

"Whitney," Abe's voice caught in his throat. "I can't. I'm trying to keep my parents safe too."

I scoffed. "That didn't stop them from killing Lauren's mom and putting her dad in a coma."

He looked away, a tear falling down his cheek. "I can't."

"That's too bad." I turned on my heel and left Abe alone in the woods.

CHAPTER THIRTY-FOUR

MENTAL FORTITUDE

WHITNEY

Lauren and Ashley were already behind the counter when I walked through the front door of the Corner Cup the next day. That familiar and comforting bell chimed above my head, welcoming me in. My friends were completely unaware I had walked past, even though I'd wished them a good afternoon. I went into the back to put away my things and grab my apron. Even as I walked behind the bar, tying the strings behind my back, they still didn't look my way.

They both leaned against the counter; Lauren cleaned up with a damp cloth as Ashley filled the large espresso machine with more coffee beans. Lauren moved slowly down the counter towards the machine, inching into Ashley's space. Ash seemed nervous, her hands clumsy as she moved the bag away from the machine too fast and spilled coffee beans all over the floor.

"Fuck," Ashley cursed under her breath, squatting down. She began scooping the beans into a pile, sighing in frustration.

Lauren knelt down on the floor next to her, offering words of comfort. "It's okay, these things happen. It wasn't even that much."

Lauren scooped up a handful of beans and slid them back to the main pile at the same time Ashley reached out. Their fingers grazed as they slowly looked up into one another's eyes. A small smile curled the edges of Ashley's lips but Lauren's gaze was more intense, smoldering almost, pouring her entire being into Ashley's eyes.

I hated to interrupt but a customer stood at the register. "Good afternoon, what can I get started for you?" I asked the woman.

They both jumped, and Lauren pulled her hand away from Ash's in a snap.

"Oh, Whit, hi. I didn't know you were here." Ashley cleared her throat and stood up. "I'll go get the broom."

"No worries." I put the customer's order into the computer and began making her tea.

Lauren stood as well, wiping her hands on her jeans. "Hey, you okay? I heard about the fight between Nic and Bryan."

I nodded. "I'm taking care of it." I peeked over my shoulder to make sure Ashley was still in the supply room. "You and Ash are precious."

Lauren cleared her throat. "We're just friends."

"Sure, totally," I smirked. "Very friendly indeed."

"You have to be fucking kidding me." Lauren's chest puffed out and she pressed her palms down on the counter as the bell to the front door chimed through the dining area. I glanced in its direction to see the last person on earth I expected to walk through those doors.

"We have to stop meeting like this," I mocked as Serenity Drake slithered towards the register. Her makeup had been applied extra thick to hide the remnants of a black eye delivered by yours truly.

Serenity shrugged. "It's a public place. Most people like coffee."

"Good thing there's another shop down the block." Lauren seemed ready to jump over the counter and beat the shit out of Serenity in the middle of the dining room. I was ready to join her.

Ashley's voice spoke up over my shoulder. "Serenity, you can come in here and order coffee but stop harassing my employees. I'm dead serious, girl, I'll have you banned if you become a problem."

Serenity's dark eyes scanned the chalkboard menu above our heads as she chewed on her bottom lip. "Do you still have peppermint?"

"Yes," I answered monotone.

"Peppermint sounds good. A large."

"A peppermint what?" Lauren asked but I held up my hand.

"Make something with peppermint so she can leave."

Lauren bared her teeth before she turned toward the bar and whipped something up. Ashley had most of the coffee beans swept off the floor and went to dump the dustpan into the trash can. I glared at Serenity as she stood off to the side. It was degrading that she could come into my place of work and taunt me, forcing Lauren and I to serve her knowing that we had physically fought days before. Serenity knew she couldn't beat us in a magical brawl, so this was her way of getting under our skin.

"Thanks for coming in, have a blessed day." Lauren set the coffee down on the counter in a to-go cup and glared at Serenity.

Serenity moseyed over, taking her sweet time picking up the cup and took a slow sip before she set it back down. "It's not pepperminty enough."

"Oh for the love of–" Ashley groaned and stood in between Lauren and I. "Serenity, that's it. I don't want you here anymore. I mean it."

Serenity shrugged and picked her drink back up. Her eyes slid to me as she smirked. "Say hi to Byn for me." She took another sip from her coffee as she strolled out of the Corner Cup.

My blood boiled under my skin. I ran my hands down my arms to keep myself busy, to force my mind to focus on anything besides leaping over the counter and drowning her on the sidewalk. The rage that coursed through my veins suffocated me. Hatred filled every corner of my being, my lungs filled with screams I couldn't release. My fingers trembled, itching to wrap around her throat and squeeze. I needed to break something. I wanted to break every last coffee cup on the wall.

"Whit." Ashley's warm hand rested on my shoulder, reining me back in. "Breathe."

"Did you know she and Bryan hooked up?" I whispered to Ashley.

She paused, licking her bottom lip. "That was a long time ago, Whitney. Don't let her get under your skin. You're letting her win that way, when you let someone have that much power over you."

I knew she was right. I knew how unhealthy my spiteful emotions were and that I only poisoned myself but Ashley didn't know the whole story. She looked at me and saw a jealous girl who couldn't stand the thought that Serenity had slept with her boyfriend years before she met him.

Ashley didn't know that Serenity kidnapped my sister and tried to murder us. She didn't see Rose fly against a brick wall and fall unconscious by Serenity's hand. She didn't see the large scar on my arm from Serenity's knife or the rage in her eyes as we tried to kill one another. Bryan's history with Serenity was the only forgivable aspect of this whole thing, yet it made me look like an idiot.

I nodded, swallowing every ounce of negativity I felt, burying it deep down in my core until it didn't feel so consuming. "I'm fine."

Ashley gave an empathetic half-smile before she headed back to the supply room.

Lauren stood at my side, resting her body against mine. "It'll be over soon. It won't be like this forever."

"I keep telling myself that too," I answered, staring at the front door. A chill ran up my spine as a woman came in. My blood pressure rose until I saw her face. Not Serenity.

"We're going to pull this off," Lauren reassured both of us. "Serenity will get what's coming to her."

I nodded, knowing exactly what my next move needed to be.

After I clocked out for the day, I followed Lauren to the cottage. I head straight to Nic's room, ignoring everyone's greetings as I passed them. I knocked on the door and waited a few moments before I heard his voice on the other side.

"I have to break Serenity's mental walls," I announced, opening the door and shutting it firmly behind me. "I want to end her, once and for all."

"Oh, hi. My day was okay, thanks for asking. Can't complain too much on my end, I suppose. You seem tense. Rough day at work, dear?" Nic leaned back in his chair, crossing his ankle over his knee.

I groaned and sat on the edge of his bed. "Yeah, shitty day."

Nic waved me off. "So, go complain to your boyfriend."

"Nicky..."

"What are you doing here?"

"Making sure you and I are okay."

Nic sighed. "You and I are fine. We have limited time to kick the Renati while Erebus is vulnerable and your boyfriend thinks amongst all the weight on my shoulders, I'd try to sleep with you? I hope you know if I wanted to, I already would have."

My face heated as I replied, "You're a good guy, Nic, but you're not *the* guy. In Bryan's defense, he's not the only one who has made comments like that."

"I don't care," he stated matter-of-fact. "All I care about is killing Henry Drake. All I care about is keeping you alive and seeing the light leave Erebus' eyes."

"Vengeance is a dangerous game, Nic."

"I don't care. It's all I have left." He paused. "What happened at work?"

"Serenity Drake is taunting me."

"That's about all she can do."

"I need to practice charming. I can't beat her until I can get into her head."

"So practice. What do you need me for?" Nic asked, tilting his head.

I sighed and rubbed my face. "I don't know…I need to practice on someone who isn't Dmitri. Someone who can actually block me out."

Nic tapped his knee with his thumb. "You want me to find a witch for you to charm?"

I nodded. "That would be helpful, yes."

"That's all you needed to say," Nic replied, getting up from his seat. "I happen to know someone who is a master at mental blockades. Serenity Drake will be easy pickings if you can get through this one."

"Who?" I asked, following Nic out of the room as he headed down the hall and into the kitchen.

He gestured to Amilia, who stood at the sink, washing her hands. "Whitney needs to practice charming on someone who actually knows how to block." Nic raised a brow at Mia.

She turned to face us as she dried her hands on a towel. Uncertainty gleaming in her eyes. "Is that so?"

"You want me to charm Mia?" I gave Nic a sideways glance.

He shrugged, casually walking out of the room. "You wanted a challenge. This is the best I can come up with on a moment's notice. Have fun, you two."

Amilia held her hand out to the small breakfast table in the far corner. She waited until I pulled out a seat and sat down next to me, the chair creaked against the hardwood as I scooted in.

"Before we begin, why are you so determined to learn how to charm?" Amilia asked, folding her hands on the table. "Dominic and Warren knew I wouldn't approve of this, or else they would not have taught you behind my back, which I'm assuming is what happened?"

I took a step towards Amilia. "We need to have weapons in our arsenal if we are going to stand a chance of winning this thing, Mia."

"Even if those tools go against the Elemental Code?"

"Yes," I answered with confidence. "I promise never to use it for ill will, or to harm anyone. But you have to admit, it does give us an edge over the Renati, since they can't charm us back."

Amilia sighed and rubbed her forehead as she turned in her seat to face me. "I'm not happy about this, but I agree to help you practice. I won't teach you how."

"I already know how." I rested my spine against the chair back to give myself some sort of physical balance as I let my mind relax.

Amilia sat sturdy and solid like a force to be reckoned with. Her face remained unreadable, her mouth a thin line as she neither smiled nor frowned. Her blinks were slow and at ease as she took in steady breaths. Her composure was admirable, completely voiding herself of anything that could make her look weak.

I did my best to collect myself in the same manner, but my nerves still swam around in my stomach. I let all excess thoughts fall to the wayside, steadying my trembling fingers as I slowly sent my powers out, searching for a weak spot.

Only there wasn't one.

I tilted my head down, narrowing my gaze into Amilia's eyes, focusing with every last shred of power I had. Amilia locked her mind tight as a fortress without a single entrance point. I pushed deeper, knowing there had to be something. Anything that would have the slightest bit of give as I nudged against it. My power slid forward, finding resistance but still making headway. I pushed harder, and not even a moment later my powers slammed against a brick wall.

"You pupils dilated," Amilia replied, her voice void of emotion. "You gave yourself away."

"You didn't feel me pushing on the weak spot?" I asked.

Amilia shook her head. "No, but your face told me you found one. You carry your emotions on your sleeve, Whitney. Charming is about subtly. Try again." She waved her hand for me to continue.

I scanned Amilia's face; the dark circles under her eyes and the definition of her cheekbones. Had she lost weight? "Are you okay, Mia?"

"Yes." She nodded. "I'm tired, dear, we've all had a lot going on. Try again."

I strained my powers, shoving them at Amilia's mental block. She pushed me out every single time. I kept my composure, leaving my face blank and my fingers still until Amilia placed her hand on mine.

"You're bleeding," she replied, reaching for a kitchen towel. I didn't feel the wetness trickling down from my nose until she pointed it out.

I cupped my hand under my chin to keep the blood from staining my shirt as Amilia handed me the towel. I let out a defeated sigh and looked up at her. "How did you get so good at blocking?"

Amilia laughed. "I'm fifty-one Whitney. When you're my age, you'll be even stronger." She patted my shoulder in support.

Fifty-one. I hadn't given much thought about what my life might be like when I was Amilia's age. Or if I'd even make it to my thirties at this point. I had faith that the girls and I would succeed, but the looming question that weighed me down...What if we didn't?

My mother never made it to her fifties. I doubt when she woke up that morning she knew it would be her last day. I doubt she had any warning or slightest indication that everything would come to a halt. I didn't expect any different. I didn't expect the ending to come with a flashing neon sign. None of it mattered anyway unless the girls and I could close the portal to the Shadow Realm.

"Whitney? Did you want to try again?" Amilia asked, watching the wheels in my head turn.

"Yes," I answered, readjusting myself in the chair to get comfortable. I kept the cloth held to my nose and relaxed. "I don't have anywhere else to be."

CHAPTER THIRTY-FIVE

DEBTS AND FAVORS

RAYN

I scanned over the list of tables at the hostess station of Giani's, making sure I hadn't skipped over anything. Even though I stood in the restaurant and functioned normally, my mind was elsewhere. Mentally, I prepared to finally close the portal to the Shadow Realm that night, to return to the remnants of Dragonfly Mystic. It had been a long time coming, and while I was definitely irritated at how long it took to get to this point, I acknowledged that things could be much worse.

Erebus probably still lay in his hospital bed. The Shadows were out and about but they hadn't started attacking people like I assumed they would have. Something had to be keeping them at bay. I didn't understand why the Shadows toyed and taunted us but never made a legitimate attempt to kill us. It had all been too easy, as if they were lying in wait, preparing for something bigger.

I just hoped the Renati didn't know the Elementals were doing the same thing.

A chill crept up my spine. The familiar sensation that something watched me from the darkness. I peered out the large panes of glass in the front of the restaurant but I only saw the blurry outlines of the streetlamps. Even though the Shadows didn't always make themselves known, I knew what it felt like to have their eyes on me. I busied myself with the list of reservations, picking up the pen to draw small circles on the top of the page. Anything to keep my mind occupied.

As much as I tried to bury the memories from my time at Dragonfly Mystic, I still remembered the smell of incense and essential oils blending together in the air. The feel of the counter where it dipped in the middle from years of wear and tear. The sound of the creaking ladder leading up to the library on the second floor. The way Tom's fingers would always find part of my body as he walked past, a discrete display of affection. I was in a hurry to close the portal, same as the others, but I could hold off on going back to the scene of the crime. Thinking about Dragonfly Mystic brought all the haunting memories of Halloween flooding over me.

I closed my eyes as the phantom feather touch of Tom's fingertips turned into a grip around my neck, constricting my air flow. I winced, wanting out of my body, out of my skin. This was a place my brain only went to when I allowed it, and I rarely allowed it.

"Ray?" a familiar voice asked from the other side of the podium.

I opened my eyes. "Hey, B."

Brooke stood in the entryway of Giani's with her parents, her brown eyes wide with concern. She stepped closer and lowered her voice. "You okay?"

"Oh, yeah. Yes, I'm great. Welcome! Table for three?" I flashed my best customer service smile and grabbed three menus from the stack behind me.

"Mom, Dad, this is my friend Rayn," Brooke reintroduced us even though we'd already met.

"I remember," Brooke's father replied, unimpressed. "You helped her sneak out and brought her home past curfew."

"Dad!" Brooke hissed. "That is *not* what happened."

"I didn't know you were still friends with those girls." Brooke's mother looked me up and down with a worried glare.

I wasn't sure how to reply to that, especially since I was clocked into work. I smiled instead and led the way to an empty table across the dining room. "Alex will be your server this evening," I said, pretending I didn't hear Brooke's parents. "Enjoy your meal."

"Rayn," Brooke whispered in an attempt to get my attention but I slipped back to the hostess station without a word.

This was not the time or the place, especially in front of Brooke's parents. After escorting a couple with a reservation to their table, I checked my phone to see a text from Brooke.

I'm sorry.

I messaged back. **It's okay, really. Let it go, B.**

Brooke did not let it go. I heard Brooke and her parents arguing about it as I walked past to ask my manager a question.

"What has gotten into you?" Brooke's mother asked in a hushed tone. "You never used to talk back to us like this. Is this because of these new friends you've made? They don't appear to be good influences on you."

"Mom, that isn't what's happening."

"What are we supposed to think? You lied about taking your medication and you know how off balanced you get. I don't...*we* don't want you to revert."

Brooke briefly glanced up at me, as if she knew I overheard it all. I widened my eyes, trying to mentally call out to Brooke to not piss off her parents the night we planned to close the Shadow Realm portal.

Brooke looked away from me and down at her hands. "I'm sorry. I'm stressed out. Senior year hasn't been easy."

"College will be even harder, Brooke, you have to get a handle on your emotions," her father said. "You can't have another breakdown when you're away from home...claiming you're seeing things."

"You're right."

I swallowed my anger and counted down the minutes until I could take a break in the back. My shift would be over in a few hours. I needed to stay focused and Brooke needed to stay out of trouble. I hadn't realized how much I took for granted that Brooke would be able to put our mission first like the rest of our generation. Her parents knew nothing about the magic in Rifton, and what they did know, they thought was a mental disorder. Brooke was still months away from eighteen and we needed to play smarter.

Luckily, Brooke's family finished their meal while I was on break and when I came back, their table sat empty. I sighed in relief and spent the rest of my shift centering myself for the task ahead. One thing swirled around in my mind, louder than anything else.

I needed to make sure Dmitri would be safe. This was different than attacking the old hospital. Dmitri had been on the sidelines. This time, he'd be in the center of the action and it didn't sit well in my stomach. I trusted the Magisters to keep an eye on him, but they wouldn't be the only ones there. I wanted to ensure that everyone who wasn't actively focused on closing the portal knew that keeping Dmitri from harm's way was the top priority.

After closing, I caught a ride with Whitney back to the cottage. Instead of heading inside, I went around the side gate to the back yard. I knew Aden would be alone in the garden shed rather than in the house with everyone else. He may have been helping us out, but that didn't mean he felt like one of us. As apprehensive as everyone was about having a witch hunter around, I was sure Aden did not feel any more comfortable being surrounded by witches.

Gently, I knocked on the door, alerting him to my presence. To my surprise, the spell that Amilia swore she'd keep on the lock was not there. I pushed the door open and found Aden sitting on a box, cleaning his gun. I took a step back at the sight of the firearm in Aden's hand. He glanced up to see the fear in my eyes and quickly set it down on a plastic tub.

"Sorry, I'm preparing for tonight," Aden apologized.

I stepped into the shed and closed the door behind me. "Are you ready?"

"I should be asking you that question. I'm not doing anything I haven't already done."

I paused. "You're fighting *with* witches, that's new."

"The killing isn't."

I winced at how easily the words slipped from his tongue. I wondered if they ever tasted like acid. If Aden ever felt regret about the things he'd done, or the witches he'd killed. Sure he'd admitted that at the end he disagreed with the methods. But he didn't like the *way* the witches were killed, not that they were murdered in the first place. That bothered me to my core. I wanted to ask, but I feared that if I pushed too hard, he would leave again. Aden probably wouldn't go back to his pack, but that didn't mean he had to live in garden sheds. He didn't have to stay with us if he didn't want to.

None of it made sense to me. Usually I looked past things I didn't understand and accepted people at face value, but Aden was a puzzle I wanted to solve. How could a man who showed little to no regret for hunting people down with a crossbow draw the line at killing me? What made me so different from the countless other witches who came before me? How long had he been hunting people in the forest? Aden wasn't much older than me. I had never asked, but he didn't feel as old as the Magisters.

"How old are you?" I asked, feeling like this was a safer question than whether or not he prayed for forgiveness at night.

"Twenty-seven." Aden leaned back. Eight years older than me. "Why?"

"I just realized I never asked. I'm nineteen."

"I know," Aden answered, catching me off guard.

I furrowed my brow. "You do?"

"Your sister told me."

"Um, when did this happen?"

Aden's eyes remained unreadable. "The night my pack came to your house. She told me you were nineteen and that I needed to leave."

Of course she did. "I didn't know she did that."

"Your family is supposed to protect you."

I tilted my head. "Do I need protection from you?"

"Is there something on your mind?" Aden asked, watching me closely. "The real reason you're here?"

Aden saw through me like a freshly-cleaned window. "I want to talk to you about something."

Aden furrowed his brow. "Is everything all right?"

"I'm nervous," I admitted, sitting down on the box next to him. "It's a big deal that we do this right. The Renati aren't going to let us close this portal without a fight."

"Do you think you and the other witches are prepared?" Aden asked.

"As prepared as we can be. We have the spell, we have the others to distract the Renati. I don't know how to be more prepared."

"Your state of mind is everything in situations like this. I have seen hunters with all the preparation in the world still be taken down because they were not focused. You have to stay focused, and right now you seem scattered."

"How so?"

"You're fidgeting. Your eyes are wandering."

Was I? I hadn't noticed. I laced my fingers together and rested my hands in my lap. Turning to face Aden, I took a deep breath. "I'm trying to calm down."

"What do you typically do to center yourself?"

"Meditate," I answered.

"So, let's meditate."

"Together?"

"Why not?" Aden shrugged.

I expected a jolt of nerves to shoot through my body but I felt a calming presence wrap around me like my favorite hoodie. Aden closed his eyes and shifted his weight, getting comfortable. The plastic bin he sat on shifted, and I hoped the contents were sturdy enough to hold him. I stared at his face, at the relaxed curves of his eyes, the sharp lines of his chin. The stubble that had taken over his jaw since he'd been at the cottage. His long hair pulled up out of his face, loose strands whispering across his forehead.

"You're not meditating," Aden whispered, his eyes still closed.

I smiled. I had no idea how he knew but somehow I wasn't surprised at all. I closed my eyes and tried to imagine myself somewhere relaxing. At home by the warm fire or nestled under a pile of thick blankets. Nothing stood out to me. Nothing felt as safe or calming as sitting there with Aden.

Slowly, the tension in my shoulders eased. I unclenched my jaw and breathed out the stress held deep in my muscles. I felt weightless, my boots resting flat on the floor. Another deep breath, breathing out the uncertainty of what our futures held and the trauma of my past. When I breathed in, I took in the scent of pine and clean soap. Aden must have just showered.

"I have a favor to ask," my voice filled the silence.

"So ask."

I let out a deep breath. "I'm worried about my brother. He's so determined to throw himself in the middle of all this." I bit my bottom lip. "Can you please watch out for him tonight? I know the others will be watching out for him too, but I'd feel better knowing everyone is putting his safety first while the girls and I are closing the portal."

"I will."

"Really?"

"Why did you ask if you didn't think I'd do it?"

"I'm just...I figured you would but I'm surprised you agreed without any convincing."

"You don't have to convince me to help you. Ever." Aden's eyes held something I had never seen echoed back to me in a man before. The intention to keep his word.

My chest constricted around my racing heart. A warmth spread through my body like wildfire. Not even my powers filled my soul with this much heat. Usually I barely noticed the fluctuation in my body temperature, but this was a fever I'd never experienced before.

Without a second thought, I filled the space between us and placed a kiss on Aden's cheek. His facial hair scratched against my lips.

"Thank you," I whispered. "For looking out for Dmitri, for saving me...For coming back."

His head slowly turned towards me, pouring himself into my gaze. "There is nowhere else I'd rather be."

Chapter Thirty-Six

SACRIFICES

Whitney

The energy around the charred remnants of Dragonfly Mystic shifted as we approached. The air hung heavy and thick, coating the inside of my lungs and making it difficult to take a deep breath. Weathered yellow caution tape blocked off the area even though most of the debris had been cleared out months ago. The city acted swiftly to make sure the evidence of our battle was taken care of. The City Council could haul away the burnt lumber and hang up signs to keep out the public, but they couldn't hide the energy of the portal.

This portal wasn't like the one in the meadow. This portal was visible to a witch, waves of energy rose up into the air like a heatwave. We could see it. We could feel it. I paused at the edge of the parking lot, waiting for a Shadow to crawl from the depths of the Shadow Realm, claws and teeth at the ready. But everything remained silent and still. A false sense of security.

"Ready?" Rose asked, coming up next to me.

"As I'll ever be," I answered, taking the first step.

Ray, Brooke, and Lauren followed closely behind us. Luckily, the darkness rising up from the Shadow Realm wasn't the only energy buzzing through the air. The vibrancy that connected our powers rippled, building each of us up. Individually, none of us would have stepped near the portal's circumference, but together we might be able to pull this off.

Rose pulled out the potion she'd made and removed the top, pouring the golden liquid over the edge of the portal. Without hesitation, she retrieved a small dagger from her bag and sliced her palm, quickly handing the dagger to Brooke who followed suit. The girls all cut the same part of their hand, careful not to go too deep. Rayn winced and gritted her teeth as she handed the dagger to me. I cut quickly so I didn't have the chance to second guess myself or think about the pain. I wiped the dagger off on my jeans and slipped it into the pocket of the small bag we brought with our supplies. Sure, it was unsanitary for us to all cut open wounds on ourselves with an unclean knife, but we were short on time and Brooke would be able to heal us afterwards.

We held out our hands, letting our blood drip onto the ground. Close enough to the portal for the blood to touch it but far enough away we didn't risk falling in or being caught off guard by a Shadow coming through from the other side. I squeezed my hand, forcing more blood from the open wound to drip into the swirling magic. I let the stinging pain course through my veins, focusing on it to keep myself anchored on our task.

Rayn reached her hand out. I took hers in mine and Lauren's in the other. The five of us created a semi-circle around the portal. Our blood mixed together as it did the night Tom and Serenity tried to murder us where we now stood. The night we unwillingly resurrected Erebus.

I closed my eyes as I centered myself, feeling the power of my generation ripple under my skin. Each of their energies felt slightly different. I could tune into each one and tell who the vibration belonged to. We stood as one, holding tight to one another, putting all of our focus into closing this portal once and for all.

A slight flicker in the energy sparked, sending chills through my body. I felt the magic around the portal shift, as if we had weakened it somehow. The buzz of the energy dimmed. I dove deeper into my own power, expending everything I had until a voice over my shoulder shattered my concentration.

"Well, well," a chuckle cut through the silence. A voice I had grown to hate with every fiber of my being.

My eyes snapped open.

"Drake," I muttered, watching him carefully as he slowly circled around us. My power bubbled inside of me, ready to strike, until I realized he wasn't alone.

I didn't recognize some of their faces, but I knew the darkness in their eyes. The hatred they had for us. Finally, the members of the Renati showed their faces. I guess with Erebus back they felt more confident than when they hid in the shadows like cowards.

Before I had a chance to react, an energy wave hit me like a ton of bricks, knocking me onto my ass. I scolded myself under my breath as Rayn stepped in front of me. A ring of fire erupted around us, inches from the Renati, causing them to leap backwards to keep from getting burned. Rayn's fire kept the Renati from getting close, but it didn't stop their spells.

And our backup remained nowhere in sight.

"Aden!" Rayn shouted into the abyss.

No one answered.

I jumped to my feet, dodging another energy wave that blew Rayn and I's hair into our faces. There was no way we were going to be able to simultaneously fight off the Renati's attacks and close the portal.

"Get back in here!" Lauren winced, holding her trembling hands over the portal in an attempt to hold onto the active spell.

Rayn kept the ring of fire around us as I joined my generation at the edge of the portal, throwing my energy back into the mix, strengthening the spell. We wouldn't be able to finish without Rayn who had to do other people's jobs of protecting us.

"The almighty Elementals, all alone," a slender woman next to Serenity chuckled. "Let this be a reminder that you are nothing compared to Erebus and his faithful."

"Oh, fuck off," I snapped over my shoulder, holding the spell steady.

Ice cut through the air, slashing the slender woman across the face. She fell to the ground, clutching her wound as she cried out in pain. Henry Drake jumped back as a fireball landed at his feet. Nic stepped out from behind the charred brick and threw another fireball that Drake barely ducked under.

"Finish the fucking spell," Nic ordered, releasing another hate-filled attack at Drake.

Henry Drake laughed at Nic and stepped closer to him. "Round two, Grant?"

Nic yelled out in frustration as his next attack missed Drake once again. I had to peel my eyes off him as he lunged towards Drake, tackling him to the ground. Drake screamed out as Nic burned him with his hands. Nic clung to Drake as the flames seared through his jacket. Serenity released an energy wave, knocking Nic off of her father. I choked on the smell of burning flesh.

"We got caught up. Half of the damn Renati is out tonight," Harmony informed us as she turned her attention to Serenity and hardened her second ice layer. Harmony pulled her arm back and sucker punched Serenity across the face.

Aden released a bolt from his crossbow and took out the slender woman who had been cackling with Serenity. A quick, clean kill. I kept my hand over the spell but my attention was split, scanning the hectic mess for Dmitri.

"Whitney!" Rayn's voice brought me back to the spell, back to why we were there in the first place. Why the Magisters were fighting so hard to keep the Renati off our backs. Finally, I spotted my brother glued to Warren's side, safe and sound.

I let my surroundings go silent as my mind slipped into a meditative state. My powers washed over me, pouring from my body as the tingle of my generation's powers mixed with mine, standing together as one entity.

A wispy paw reached out from the swirling magic and clung to the edge. Smokey talons dug into the pavement as a Shadow pulled itself from the other side. Brooke startled, jumping back as the Shadow emerged in front of her.

"It's not fully formed yet!" Rose yelled.

Brooke kicked at the Shadow, sending it back over the edge in a cloud of smoke. Seeing the Shadows coming through rattled my soul and I pushed everything I had into the spell. Every drop of magic that coursed through my body poured out of my being. My knees trembled and I was sure my body would give out when the energy from the Shadow Realm portal fell silent.

It finally closed.

A trickle of blood dripped from my nose, the metallic taste coated my tongue as my head spun from using too much magic.

My eyes flew open at a familiar gasp of pain behind me.

Serenity tightened her grip on Dmitri, holding a knife to his throat.

Nic scrambled away from Drake as Serenity spoke. "Take another step and he's dead."

Nic halted, his face draining of color. Henry Drake tried to get up but fell back to the ground, whimpering at the large chunks of charred flesh covering his body. Harmony was on her knees, panting as she lifted her head to glare at Serenity. If looks could kill, Serenity would have fallen to her death. Warren held out his hands as if his gentle actions would cause Serenity to show mercy. Even Aden lowered his crossbow. We all stood at the mercy of Serenity fucking Drake.

"Right where I want him." Serenity smiled, tightening her grip on Dmitri's neck. His eyes widened in fear but he clenched his jaw trying to hide it.

I took in a deep, steadying breath as I held Serenity's eye gaze. "Let my brother go."

"You think I don't know what you're doing?" Serenity scoffed as she pushed me from her mind.

I hardened my gaze, letting the hatred fuel me. I ordered once more, with feeling. "Let my brother go."

Her mental barricade shoved against me. Fuck. I spent too much energy on the spell to close the portal. There wasn't anything left to save my brother.

"Let him go." Nic's eyes focused on Serenity.

She refused to look at him, making her mind a steel trap. "All that power and you still can't keep your family safe."

Hatred flooded my core as Serenity and I glared at one another. I didn't know how this whole thing would go, but I knew it would end with one of us killing the other. "There isn't a damn thing–"

A blur tackled Serenity to the ground, freeing Dmitri from her grasp. The second Serenity hit the asphalt, Nic and Harmony scrambled to Dmitri, dragging him to his feet. Nic stepped in front of my brother, flames roaring from his fingertips.

Abe Roberts fell onto his back from a blow Serenity landed in the middle of his chest. Serenity growled through her teeth as she hurled a chunk of debris at Abe, debilitating him. Dmitri rushed to his side but Harmony grabbed hold of his torso, clinging to him.

"No, Mit!" she shouted.

I mustered the little energy I had left and threw a thin icicle at Serenity, stabbing her in the calf. She screamed a deep rage as she thrusted all her energy at Abe. A vine sprouted from the ground and wrapped around Serenity's ankle but with a hard yank of her foot, she broke the root with ease. Rose tried again but the vine lay limp on the concrete and she fell to her knees, hyperventilating.

Lauren had blood dripping from her ear and Rayn could not even muster a flame in her hand. Brooke put out her hand as her power fizzled through my body. She stumbled to her knees. *This* was the exhaustion Nic and Warren had described, spending so much energy that simple actions were near impossible. The girls and I didn't have any power left to help Abe and the Magisters stood in silence, letting him risk his life like he didn't mean the world to Dmitri.

The Magisters saw Abe Roberts as collateral damage.

Talons tapping on the concrete echoed through the burnt remnants of Dragonfly Mystic as Big Boy crawled up over the rubble. The winged Shadow snarled, showing its fangs as it lurked closer to Abe and Serenity.

"Get out of here!" Abe shouted at us. "Go! Please!"

"The portal is closed, we need to go." Nic kicked Henry Drake in the ribs before he extinguished his flames and grabbed my hand.

"I can't leave him here to die." I turned back to Abe in time to see him hit the concrete with Serenity on top.

Nic yanked on me. "Don't make me carry you out of here."

I ripped my hand from his grasp as he scrambled for me again and made to bolt across the ruins to help Abe. But Nic grabbed me, tightening his grip. I turned to face him, grabbing his shirt. "Please, don't let him die."

"We need to go."

Tears sprung from the corner of my eyes as I begged. "Please don't do this. He matters. Help me save him." I grabbed his face, forcing him to look me in the eyes. "Please, Nicky."

That final plea attached to his nickname softened his brow. Nic stared back at me for a moment before he threw his hand out over my shoulder, thrusting an energy wave towards Serenity and Abe. They both went flying across the concrete, but the energy wave didn't seem to bother Big Boy at all.

Nic mustered a fireball and hit the winged Shadow in the face. It stumbled backwards long enough for Dmitri to break out of Harmony's hold and run to Abe. Serenity pushed herself back onto her knees but Warren sent her flying once more in a gust of wind. Dmitri grabbed Abe and pulled him to his feet. Wrapping his arm around Abe's waist, they limped away from the Renati. Abe tripped a few steps in and pulled Mit down with him. Before I could move a muscle, Aden rushed past me and picked Abe up. Aden threw Abe over his shoulder and grabbed Dmitri's arm, pulling them both along with him like a couple of rag dolls.

Nic grabbed me again and lifted me from the ground, following our group away from Dragonfly Mystic.

"Dad!" Serenity sobbed, pain caught in her throat.

The Shadow's growls erupted behind us as Big Boy jumped to his feet and charged us. We rushed back to where we had parked the cars down the street. Nic threw fireballs over his shoulder, but his aim was sporadic and the winged Shadow dodged the attacks with ease. Other large Shadows that had previously come through the portal joined in the hunt, sprinting after us as we made our escape.

Nic dragged me along behind Aden, who still carried Dmitri and Abe. The Magisters did their best to help the girls and I flee before the Shadows got too close. I chose to ignore their snarls and the sound of their talons against the asphalt.

When we reached the car, I fumbled with the door and climbed inside. Aden came up behind me, shoving Dmitri and Abe into the backseat with me.

"You okay?" Nic asked.

After I nodded, he left the car and ran to the other girls, loading them into the back of Lauren's car. Aden slammed the door shut and followed closely behind Nic. I grabbed Dmitri and gave him a quick scan, but my head spun and I couldn't focus on one thing. Black spots took over my vision and my entire body went limp.

"Whitney?" I heard my brother's frantic voice.

"I'm fine," I answered, hopefully out loud.

Harmony climbed into the driver's seat and Warren got into the passenger's as they started the engine.

Dmitri wrapped an arm around me and pulled me into his chest. I leaned into him, squeezing my eyes shut. Everything spun, even with my eyes closed. My stomach did flips and I clenched my teeth.

"Hey," Abe's voice spoke and a warm hand rested on my arm. "Deep breaths. Deep, long breaths. It'll pass. I've gone through this before and it won't last long. You did it, Whit. You closed the portal."

I put my other hand on the back of Abe's and clasped it in mine. I wanted to speak but I was afraid of what would follow if I opened my mouth.

The car jerked as Harmony pulled away from the curb, speeding back to the safety of the cottage. I groaned as she took a corner too fast. I knew their main priority was getting us back to the cottage where the Renati were unable to touch us. We had to get to safety before we could even take assessment of what happened. So I fell back and let the Magisters take charge of the situation. I felt too worn down to fight with them anyway.

"I can't believe you threw yourself at Serenity. You could have gotten yourself killed," Dmitri said, but not to me.

Abe sighed, holding my hand tightly in his. "You two were right. I couldn't hide out there forever."

CHAPTER THIRTY-SEVEN

INVOLUNTARY COMMITMENT

WHITNEY

"What an absolute cluster fuck." Rose collapsed on the nearest couch as we walked into the cottage together. "Everytime we face those bastards, we never truly win."

"Never truly win?" Harmony asked, crossing her arms. "We closed the portal! We retrieved Lauren's talisman! We have done nothing but win against the Renati, ungrateful child."

"Then why do I feel like I've been beaten to death?" Rose groaned, covering her eyes with her open hand.

Amilia stood in the dining room, where various potions, salves, and healing herbs lay spread out across the table. She held her green-stained hands over her mouth and stepped towards Dmitri and Abe. "Abe Roberts? You're alive?"

Abe nodded. "I, um, I hope it's okay that I'm here."

"Of course it is." Dmitri spoke for Amilia.

Mia's gaze fell down to Abe's side where his sweatshirt was soaked in blood. "You're hurt?"

Abe nodded with a wince.

"Why didn't you say anything?" Dmitri demanded as Amilila escorted Abe to the table.

Amilia and Dmitri tended to the cut along Abe's ribcage and my balance slowly returned to my body. Rage coursed through me, boiling my blood. I couldn't stand still, storming around the living room searching for something to unleash on. My hands found Nic's chest and I shoved him as hard as I could. He stumbled back, caught off guard by my attack.

"The fuck?" he yelled.

"What happened to dying before you'd let them hurt my brother?" I shouted.

"Whit, we all did everything we could to keep Dmitri safe." Warren stepped in.

"If Abe hadn't come back and saved him, Serenity would have killed him and his blood would have been on your hands!"

"None of us would've let that happen," Nic reassured me.

"Bullshit." I hissed. "You all stood there and watched. I had to *beg* you to do anything. Fucking beg you, Dominic."

Harmony turned to me with crossed arms. "We were all ready to attack her at once, Whitney. You can't feel our powers but all of us were ready to take her out. Did you want Dmitri to get hit in the crossfire?" Harmony glared at me.

"No, but–"

"Have some fucking faith in me," Nic snapped.

Amilia put her hand on Dmitri's shoulder. "Why don't you take Abe into the guest bath and help him get cleaned up?"

Dmitri nodded and led Abe down the hallway.

"Dmitri is alive and the portal is closed," Lauren announced, finally noticing the dried blood around her ears. "When do we leave for the Hallow?"

"You don't," Harmony replied sternly.

I turned back to face her. "Wait, what?"

"You five will not go to the Hallow," Harmony repeated. "We, the Magisters, will go as your representatives and gather what we need."

"The hell you will!" Rayn shouted, raising her voice at Harmony.

"And you agreed to this?" I asked Nic who remained suspiciously quiet.

Before Nic could answer, Harmony spoke again. "You girls don't listen. You will get yourselves killed before you ever reach the Hallow. Besides, we know how to get there, and you do not. We have made the executive decision to not share that information with you. When we, as your Magisters, feel you are ready, we will bring you to the Hallow. I will not allow you to embarrass the name of the Elementals in front of those we desperately need to impress. You aren't experienced in building these kinds of connections and we already have a history with these people."

I stood speechless; my mind unable to form a complete sentence as I processed the stone wall placed in front of us. Nic and Warren were abnormally quiet, meaning they actually agreed to this ridiculous plan.

"We have the talismans, not you," Rayn stated, betrayal in her voice.

"You know, back in the reign of the Elementals, being a Magister meant something. We were respected and heard. The younger generations knew their place. You would benefit from remembering that time," Harmony spat again. "This whole thing is dead in the water if anything happened to a single one of you. We have to keep the five of you alive and this is how we decided to do so."

"Nicky." I turned to him again but he refused to make eye contact. "Coward."

"Honey, I think we're being too harsh," Nic finally spoke.

"Don't you *dare* call me that," Harmony snapped. "And don't you dare second guess the decision we already made because your favorite student stomps her feet."

"Harmony is right." Amilia replied from the dining room. "You five girls will stay here with me and continue your training while the Magisters visit the Hallow. They already have a personal connection with their leadership and it will be a quick, painless trip as long as everyone plays their parts."

"When have the girls ever sat with their hands in their laps waiting for instruction?" Nic asked, finally taking a stand. "If we don't involve them in this, they will go on their own and then they *will* get killed." He turned to Amilia. "And it will be your fault."

Amilia stepped back in shock. "I have kept these girls alive before you strolled back into town, Dominic, do not speak to me with such disrespect."

"May I speak to you in private?" Nic asked, stepping closer to Amilia.

"I already know what you are going to say. The answer is still no, Dominic."

"Fine, we'll have an audience then. Mom, I don't understand why you hide things from them." Nic relaxed his shoulders, attempting not to come off as an attack.

"What do you mean?"

"Please, don't. They know you aren't telling them the truth. I already rummaged through the books you hid and showed Whitney everything. There's no reason to keep them in the dark, you never did that with us."

Amilia widened her eyes and gasped. "I'm doing what I can to protect them. You have no idea what they've already been through."

"I do, though. I know about the possession and the Shadows. I understand all that. What I don't understand is treating them like infants."

Harmony came to Amilia's defense. "They aren't mature enough to handle this like we are."

"But this isn't about us, we aren't the ones the talismans went to. They don't belong to us, they belong to the girls. Without proper training and information, they're walking blind into the lion's den."

"I've let them read every book on that shelf, Dominic."

"Don't pull that shit with me, Mom. I know those aren't all of your books."

"Nic, don't be an asshole!" Harmony intervened again. "Mia raised us, she knows what she's doing."

"But she's not raising the girls like us, we weren't lied to."

Amilia jabbed her finger into Nic's chest. "I treated you like equals when I should have been treating you like children, which you were by the way. It remains my biggest regret in this life."

"But Mom, it's different now. We are older and we have lived and learned. I hate to say it this way, but it's not up to you anymore. It's up to us, we are the Magisters. They are the new generation and we need to be teaching them everything we know."

"Well, I suppose my opinion is irrelevant then."

"No, not at all. It's like...you know, when grandparents try to raise their grandkids instead of trusting they raised their own kids to be capable enough to do it themselves."

"I did not raise capable adults."

Nic's shoulders fell. "What do you mean?"

"I let you all run wild and practice whenever you liked on whatever interested you, and look at what good it did? You knew everything and we lost three of you. I lost my own child."

"And if I hadn't showed up that night on Halloween, three of the girls would be dead because you left them in the dark."

"Well thank the generations you finally decided to pull your head out of your ass and come home to save us, Dominic." Amilia threw her kitchen towel at Nic's feet before she stormed out of the room.

"Do you ever know when to shut up?" Harmony asked, shoving past Nic to follow Amilia. She turned over her shoulder and said to Warren, "Do not let things escalate."

Warren let out a sigh, rubbing his face with an open palm. He looked at Nic with dark circles under his tired eyes. "Mia and Honey are not completely wrong."

"Neither am I," Nic argued back.

Warren shrugged. "You've always done whatever you want, Nicky, I won't waste energy arguing with you." He left the room, defeated.

"We already know the entrance to the Hallow is Falcon Ridge." Lauren turned to Nic. "At least tell us where to go from there."

Nic looked at each of the girls before his gaze settled on me. "Please, Whitney, promise me you will not go to the Hallow without me."

"Why do we need you?"

Nic chortled, shaking his head. "Just don't, please. The forest isn't safe."

"Okay," I lied. "I promise."

"Thank you." He ran trembling fingers through his dark hair.

I turned to the girls and Aden as Nic left the room. I shook my head, knowing they would understand what I meant without having to speak a word.

"We need to go somewhere more private." Brooke whispered, motioning towards the kitchen.

"The cottage is the only place protected. Where else do we have to go?" Rose asked, stepping in towards our group as the girls and I huddled together.

Aden lingered towards the back, giving us space. He had stayed quiet during the altercations, knowing it wasn't his place to chime in or offer an opinion. The leather of his jacket creaked as he crossed his arms.

"Rayn and I put a spell on our bedroom. No one can hear us talking from there." Lauren whispered, leading the way down the hall. Aden followed silently behind us after Rayn gave him a nod. None of us spoke until the door firmly shut and we were sure the spell was still active.

"Brilliant thinking, to charm your bedroom." Brooke sat down on the edge of Rayn's bed.

"Amilia and the Magisters are too nosey. I don't trust them not to eavesdrop," Rayn replied, sitting down next to her. "So I think we are all in agreement that we will not be playing along with that bullshit plan."

"Absolutely not." Rose shook her head. "We have to bring the Elemental support back to Rifton."

"And fast before the Renati can recuperate from what happened tonight." I agreed. "Henry Drake may be down for the count now but he won't stay there."

"We haven't done anything to make the Magisters think we aren't capable. It's like they want the credit for taking down the Renati or something." Lauren crossed her arms and leaned against the wall. "We're the ones with the talismans, they chose us. Do we really think whoever lives at the Hallow would leave their homes to come back here for half of a generation?"

"I know they have history with them, but you'd think if they wanted to show capability they would take us with them." Rayn motioned around the room to all of us. "You know, the complete generation with the talismans?"

I chewed on my bottom lip. "I don't know what they're thinking, but there has to be a reason Nic doesn't want us to go alone."

"Because it's dangerous and they don't think we can handle ourselves." Brooke met my gaze. "The Magisters are pretty vocal about how inferior we are."

I shook my head. "Nic doesn't think we're inferior."

Rayn let out a sigh. "Whit, Warren and Harmony don't seem to care what Nic thinks." She looked around the room at each of us. "We should be the ones going to the Hallow. If they don't want to accompany us, that's fine but they shouldn't stop us from going."

Lauren pushed off the wall. "We need to leave, like, now."

"We should leave after my mom's wedding this weekend." Rose nodded. "She's getting married in Falcon Bay and none of the Magisters nor Amilia will be there. No one can stop us. That gives us a few days to prepare."

"Perfect," I said, turning to Aden. "Will you come with us?"

Aden shifted his weight. "Won't these witches be a bit apprehensive when you show up with a hunter?"

"Maybe at first. Once we reach the Hallow, you can stay back and the girls and I will go in first to explain the situation." Rayn glanced up at him with soft eyes.

Aden agreed, putting far too much trust in us that we'd be able to convince an entire compound of witches that he had no intention of harming them. "My allegiance is to you. I will go where you go."

"Okay," Lauren sighed as nerves rattled around in my stomach. "We leave for the Hallow in three days."

Life did not stop because we had a rough night. The world kept spinning and the Corner Cup still needed to operate. It was the only reason half of our group had any money, and Lauren and I were both scheduled to open.

"Not to be a total dick, but you two look like death," Robby commented at 4:30 the next morning when we approached the front door together.

"How charming." Lauren faked a smile as I unlocked the door.

"I'm sorry, that slipped out." Robby let us go ahead of him. "If we aren't too busy maybe you should take turns napping in the break room."

"Sure," I answered, knowing that wouldn't be an option.

The day turned out to be busy as everyone had moved past the holidays and were now fully engaged in desperately attempting to cling to their resolutions. We quickly ran low on sugar free syrups. I stared at the empty barstool at the bagel counter, thinking about Bryan being in Falcon Bay all week. At this point in the morning, he should have shown up for his first class of the day. I pictured him with tea in a to-go cup as he sat towards the front of class. He probably would have been wearing his glasses and his favorite green hoodie with his backpack on the floor at his feet. I found it comforting that he was out in the world living his most normal life and far away from the mess that Rifton had become. If Bryan had been in Rifton, I had no doubt Serenity would have gone after him last night after we nearly killed her father.

It was also around the time that Rayn and Rose should be starting the history class at the Community College they'd signed up for together, which is why seeing them rush through the front door confused me.

"Lo!" I called back to Lauren in the storage room. She came up to the register as Rose and Rayn hurried towards us.

"Guys, we have a major fucking problem," Rose said in a hushed tone, tears welling in her eyes. "They committed Brooke."

"Who did?" Lauren asked.

"Her parents. They've admitted her into the mental ward of the hospital."

I took a step back, unsure I had heard her correctly. "Why would they do something like that?"

Rose wiped a tear from her cheek. "B texted me right before her parents took her phone away. 'They're doing it again'. I knew immediately what she meant."

I let the words sink in. "We have to get her out."

"We should charm everyone and walk out with her," Lauren suggested.

"How are we going to maintain eye contact with every member of the hospital staff at once?" Rayn asked, her hands shaking.

"We just have to distract them long enough to get her out." My hands trembled as I clung to the edge of the counter. "We are leaving for the Hallow day after tomorrow, we have to get her out tonight."

Rose nodded. "I'm so pissed."

"Me too," I agreed. "But once we are in the forest, none of this will matter. We won't be coming back to Rifton for who knows how long. Brooke's parents can be as mad as they want but they won't care about Brooke sneaking out of the house when Rifton is burning to the ground."

"The hospital should have less staff and security after hours," Rose said. "My mom is always complaining about how short staffed they are at night. That's the time to go."

We only had one shot at this. If we weren't able to get Brooke out of the mental ward tonight, our entire plan of leaving for the Hallow was dead in the water.

The sun sank behind the mountain, casting a darkness across Rifton. Since visiting hours at the hospital had ended, we couldn't waltz into the front door and casually stroll to Brooke's room.

Lauren walked through the automated doors, cradling her left arm, wincing in pain. She hissed and squeezed her eyes shut as she approached the front desk.

"Can I help you?" the receptionist asked, her eyes trailing down to Lauren's arm.

"I fell in the yard and I think I broke my elbow. That stupid tree root," Lauren replied, gently rubbing the supposedly broken area.

"Okay, let's get you checked in," the receptionist clacked her long fingernails on the keyboard and asked Lauren some basic questions before she got up from her desk and went into a small room behind the reception area.

Rayn, Rose, and I seized our opportunity and rushed past the waiting room. Lauren winked at us as we skirted past her and headed down the main hallway deeper into the hospital.

"The mental ward is up this way, on the third floor," Rose whispered as we turned a corner down another deserted hall. "I remember seeing it on the directory near the elevators."

Before we reached the elevators, a nurse holding a clipboard turned the corner, almost running into us. He didn't seem to expect anyone to be roaming the halls.

"What are you doing here?" he asked, looking at each of us and waiting for an answer.

I locked eyes with him and let my magic slowly slither its way into his mind. He had no guard up, letting me in easily.

"We aren't here. You're exhausted and must be seeing things," I said in a soothing tone.

His eyes glazed over and he gently nodded. "Yeah, I'm tired."

He shuffled past us, dragging his feet on the floor as he went about his business. I gently reeled my powers back in and pushed the up arrow on the elevator buttons.

"Impressive," Rayn replied as the doors dinged and slid open.

We walked into the elevator and pressed the button for floor three.

"It's easier to charm the powerless," I said to my sister. "The Renati, on the other hand? They've had years of training to put up mental blocks. I don't know if we'll ever break those."

Rose tapped her heel nervously. "We will."

The elevator lifted us up with a jerk, dinging twice before the doors opened once more. A large sign on the wall in front of us provided a list of the third floor offices. An arrow pointed to the right, directing us towards the mental health ward.

"Okay, I'll distract whoever is at the front desk and then you guys get Brooke." Rayn cracked her knuckles.

A nurse at the front station sat on her phone. Rayn approached the counter and chatted her up in the politest customer service voice she could muster. "Excuse me? I'm so turned around here. I'm looking for the closest coffee kiosk. My sister just had a baby and those nurses over there are *not* very helpful at all. They told me I could find coffee on the third floor but it seems I've been sent on a goose chase."

"There is a vending machine at the other end towards the therapy rooms but that's all that we have up here," the nurse replied.

"Could you please show me? I don't want to waste any more time than I already have. I need to get back to my little nephew."

Listening to Rayn's story, I realized she'd never be able to have an experience like this. Bragging about becoming an aunt from her sister. I found it hard to ignore the excitement in her voice as she fabricated her story. Maybe she'd always wanted it but never had the heart to tell me that my choices of remaining childless hurt her in any way.

Before I could think too much on the subject, the nurse led Rayn out of the mental health ward. Rose and I hid behind a corner that led to a janitor's closet as they passed by. Rayn gave us an indiscreet thumbs up as she led the nurse away from her station.

"Let's go," Rose whispered as we tiptoed into mental health. She headed straight to the door at the side of the nurse station, the one clearly leading to the patients. A card scanner on the wall stared back at us, but we didn't need to worry about that. Rose waved her hand over the handle and it clicked open instantly.

"Now the tricky part," I whispered to Rose as we snuck down the hall, keeping our heads on a swivel to look for staff. "We have no idea what room she's in."

Rose shook her head. "I only know she's here because of that text."

I chewed on my bottom lip, trying to formulate some kind of plan when we ran into another nurse wearing scrubs with cartoon dogs all over them.

"Can I help you?" she asked, setting her charts down on a nearby counter.

"Yes," Rose spoke up quickly. "Yes, you can, um..." I felt Rose's powers simmer under the surface as she locked eyes with the nurse, spinning her a tale of how she needed someone to talk to. Rose grabbed my hand and pushed me past them. Rose kept her charm locked in tight as I ventured down the hall. I waved my hand over the next door, unlocking it.

"B," I whispered, opening up a door to an empty room. I moved onto the next. "Brooke."

"Whit?" her small voice answered back.

I slipped into the room and gently closed the door behind me. Brooke sat curled up on the bed with her knees hugged to her chest. She wore a hospital gown and socks. Her short black hair was pulled back into a messy ponytail and her bloodshot eyes were ringed with smeared makeup.

"Where are your clothes?"

"I-I don't know." Brooke answered. Her gaze looked distant.

"They drugged you."

She nodded.

"Okay," I affirmed, not a moment to lose. I went to the cabinets but each of them were locked. "Brooke, do you have any idea where your things are?"

She shook her head, squeezing her eyes shut. I let out a frustrated sigh and grabbed under her arms, helping her off the bed.

"Where are we going?"

"I'm getting you the fuck out of here. Can you walk?"

"I, uh, I think so?" Brooke slid off the bed and stumbled forward.

I caught her in my arms. "Shit, okay. Everything is okay. I'll carry you out of here if I have to."

I helped Brooke across the room, her feet dragging as she shuffled across the floor. I poked my head out the door to make sure the coast was clear. Not a soul in sight.

I put my arm around Brooke's waist to steady her and we made our way down the hall where Rose and Rayn waited for us.

Rose rushed to Brooke's side as we came into sight. "B, are you okay?" Brooke silently nodded as Rose wrapped her arm around Brooke. "Let's get her out of here before someone else sees us. I don't want to have to charm anyone else."

"Rosie?" a familiar voice asked behind us. Rose froze in place, her eyes widening. She turned slowly, coming face to face with her mother. Nancy's eyes were wide with confusion, glancing at Brooke in a hospital gown hiding behind me. "What are you girls doing here?"

"Y-you work in pediatrics, what...what are you doing up here?" Rose stumbled over her words.

"I think the more pressing issue is what the hell are you girls doing? Why is Brooke in a gown?" Nancy scanned us all but her eyes settled on me, a mix of disappointment and rage in her gaze.

A tear fell down Rose's cheek as she made solid eye contact with Nancy, lowering her head slightly in concentration.

"Mom," Rose's voice shook. "You didn't see us. We aren't here."

Rayn and I looked at one another in shock.

"Of course I see you. What are you talking about?" Nancy took a step forward.

"Mom." Rose's tone sharpened and she clenched her jaw. "You didn't see us. We aren't here."

Nancy's eyes glazed over and Rose took control. Nancy nodded slightly and walked past us down the hall. Rose waited until Nancy turned the corner before she grabbed Brooke again and headed to the elevator.

"Rose–" I began but she cut me off.

"Let's get Brooke out of here. I don't want to talk about it."

Chapter Thirty-Eight

OLD GRUDGES

Whitney

"Here, drink this." Rose handed Brooke a small potion vial in the backseat of my car. "I figured they would medicate you, so hopefully this counteracts whatever they gave you."

Brooke took the vial and drank without a word. However Rose figured out how to even make that kind of potion left me amazed at her abilities. Brooke remained quiet for another few moments before she spoke again. "Thank you for coming to get me."

I looked up in the rearview mirror as I came to a stop at the next red light. I turned in my seat to look at her. "It wasn't even a question."

"We'd never leave you in there, B." Rayn took Brooke's hand in hers.

Lauren turned in the front seat as well to face the other girls. "Why on earth would your parents lock you up like that?"

Brooke let out a deep sigh and squeezed her eyes shut. "It was my own fault...I got too comfortable and practiced at home. But usually when my bedroom door is closed, they leave me alone. I wanted to practice healing myself. I've never been hurt like you guys have and I know I can heal you, but what happens if the Renati gets to me? I cut myself to practice mending the wound and, well, let's just say my mother has the worst timing."

The car behind us honked, bringing my attention back to the road. The traffic light had turned green. I continued down the road, listening to the girls talk as I gripped the steering wheel with white knuckles. Rage coursed through me thinking about what Brooke's parents had done. I finally spoke. "That isn't your fault, Brooke."

"It is though," she answered. "I should have never done that at my house."

Rose huffed. "So your mom walked in and thought you were cutting yourself?"

"She lost her shit. It was the final breaking point. All she saw was me hurting myself, not taking my medication and sneaking around behind their backs," Brooke explained.

Lauren shifted in her seat. "I can see how that would look on the outside."

I pulled into the driveway of the cottage, relieved we made it there without any issues. The girls got out of the car and headed up the driveway.

"I am in so much trouble with them, guys, they are going to absolutely lose it when they find out I'm gone." Brooke wrapped her arm around Rose's waist as they walked towards the front door together.

"I know, but in a few days we are heading to my mom's wedding and then none of it will matter," Rose answered.

Brooke scoffed. "They'll have cops all over town. My parents know Nancy's wedding is this weekend, they'll assume I'm with you and come to Falcon Bay."

"If your parents showing up is a possibility, we will prepare for it. We just have to get through tonight and tomorrow," Rayn reassured her. "Your parents are never going to lock you up again, Brooke."

"Charm them," Lauren answered simply.

"We can't charm everyone whenever it's convenient, it's not moral," Brooke answered. "Especially my parents."

"It may be against the Code, but you have to admit it's a useful skill. We charmed plenty of nurses to get you out of there in the first place," Lauren answered. "Rose charmed her own mom to get you out of there."

"Anyway," Rose spoke before Lauren finished her sentence. "Your bag for the Hallow is in Ray and Lauren's room so at least we can get you in some real clothes. I don't know what to do about your phone."

"I don't need my phone. Everyone I want to talk to is right here." Brooke nodded as we walked into the cottage together.

Bryan sat in front of the fireplace chatting with Dmitri and Abe in hushed tones. They dropped whatever they discussed the moment we walked in, both of them trying to play it cool but Bryan's heart thud loudly in his chest. His nerves swam through his veins and echoed back to me in his furrowed brow. Even without our empathic connection, I'd know he worried by the way he tapped his fingers against his thigh. Dmitri didn't look up as he fiddled with his thumbs. Brooke scurried past them to the bedrooms with Rayn close behind her.

Dmitri finally looked up as they passed by. "Why is B wearing a hospital gown?"

"Don't ask." Rose put up her hand. "I thought you were staying in Falcon Bay until Saturday," Rose said to Bryan, wrapping her brother in a hug.

He rested his chin on the top of her head. "I changed my mind."

"You okay?" I asked, looking back and forth between the three guys.

Dmitri nodded, holding Abe's hand firmly in his. Seeing Abe sitting next to Dmitri at the cottage was surreal. I couldn't tell if my speech truly helped things at all, but I'm glad we finally got him out of that hunting cabin.

"We're worried, that's all. There's a lot happening." Bryan admitted with a weary smile as the rest of the cottage's occupants came into the living room from the kitchen.

Rayn quietly emerged from the hallway with Brooke dressed in jeans and a hoodie.

"Oh, good, you're all here." Amilia sat down in her favorite chair by the bookcases and folded her hands in her lap. "I wanted to take a moment to speak with you all before the Magisters leave to attend business at the Hallow."

Lauren rolled her eyes as her shoulder thudded against the wall. She crossed her arms in annoyance and slouched into the corner. Everyone else took seats and waited for Amilia's speech but I stayed put. I didn't want to sit. I didn't want to listen to more bullshit about how the girls and I were too immature to handle our own fight. I had grown tired of hearing about all the things members of our crew thought I was incapable of.

Bryan stood beside me, wrapping his arm around my waist and snuggled into my side. His hand slipped under my hoodie, his thumb gently grazed the skin above my jeans. The action calmed me and sent a spark of heat through my body all at once.

"I know these have been trying times, and I appreciate the way you have all stuck together, taking the time to work with one another and bond as a family. I know I haven't always made the right decisions and I know you have all disagreed with my choices at one time or another, but I don't have a handbook for any of this either. You can imagine my surprise when Abbie's powers finally surfaced, and there were thick ivy vines covering the ceiling of her bedroom. I thought she was playing and went into her room to check on her but there it was, the evidence of elemental magic back from the dead.

I was in disbelief for days, wondering if I had dreamed the entire thing when she brought home a friend from school who had accidentally started a fire on the playground. Then one by one, they found their way to us, to my coven. We were delighted, as if we had been chosen to care for such special children. As if we were the ones who had been given the sacred gift. But I learned quickly when Abbie died that gifts can be taken as easily as they are given. Audri had the same fear and excitement in her voice the day she called and told me she had two little Elementals who needed a home and she would make sure they had a mother. Stories of the generations were told to us as children in place of fairy tales. Great fables of honor and righteousness, but the reality is not so pristine as the stories would have us believe."

Amilia paused to wipe a stray tear from her eye and continued on with her speech.

"But now we have a chance at redemption. A chance for justice to those who we have lost along the way, and the opportunity to fight for a better future for the ones who have yet to come. I'm honored to be a part of this journey, and I care for every single one of you deeply."

"We love you, Mia." Harmony smiled, putting her arm around Dmitri's shoulders and gave him a gentle squeeze.

Amilia smiled back, taking in a steadying breath. "We must all remember what is at stake, and that we will all play different, yet important, roles."

Her speech should have filled me with fuzzy feelings. There should have been a warmth in my core. But I knew the underlying message to Amilia's words: know your place. I doubt she would have felt the need for this performance if the girls and I had done as we were told.

It was almost amusing; Amilia and the Magisters didn't know about Brooke being committed or us bending the rules of the Elemental Code to break her out. They didn't know about our plans to run off to the Hallow and bring back our supporters ourselves. But I smiled at her anyway, genuinely meaning the adoration I felt for her yet knowing I couldn't trust her with everything.

Harmony looked back and forth between Warren and Nic. "The three of us have some preparations to make. I found some things I believe will be beneficial for the girls to study while we're gone."

"I don't think that–" Nic didn't get the chance to finish his sentence.

A sonic boom exploded in the cottage, shattering every window in the house. Glass flew across the rooms mixed with splinters and shards of wood paneling. Something slammed against me, knocking me to the ground as I crashed. The weight was familiar, something I'd felt on top of me a thousand times.

Bryan wrapped his arm around my head, shielding me from the wreckage. I squeezed my eyes shut on impulse, stifling a scream as shouts and panicked cries erupted throughout the living room. I jerked my shoulders, trying to get Bryan off of me as reality sunk into my bones.

The cottage was under attack.

"Get off!" I shouted at Bryan and gave him one final shove before he shifted his weight off me.

I jumped to my feet, hoping to take a moment to assess the damage when an energy wave crashed into the center of my chest, sending me tumbling over an end table.

"Byn!" Rose's voice shouted from across the room as I fell.

I scrambled to my feet and Rose rushed to her brother's side, jumping in front of him and throwing up a shield. Soft waves of energy glistened in the light from the magic flying through the room.

The Renati were everywhere. They were fighting with Harmony in the dining room. Dmitri and Abe released energy waves towards the kitchen as witches came in through the back. Chaos ran wild throughout the cottage. I couldn't take a moment to assess the damage or count heads to see where our people were.

Underneath the window that exploded first, Warren lay limp on his side. Blood pooled underneath him as the light glistened off his torso. I took a step towards him, realizing the light glistened off long shards of glass impaled into his body. The window couldn't have possibly shattered that way on its own. The manipulated shards must have been intentional, an attack from the Renati before Warren could shield. His unblinking eyes stared back at me as a thick shard of glass protruded from his neck, blood trickling down his adam's apple.

Oh, shit.

I began to move towards Warren's body when a Renati witch appeared in my face. Next thing I knew, my back slammed against the floor with the witch on top of me. Her long, sharp nails dug into my skin, causing me to scrunch my shoulders and recoil in pain. My vision blurred with tears as I tried to push her off with my knee.

Catching me off guard had given her the full advantage to pin me to the ground, using her powers to hold me down with a strength I couldn't fight against. I grit my teeth, glaring into her hateful eyes. My hands slid up from her shoulders and wrapped around her thin neck.

She punched me across the face. The pain stung deep in my cheek, and I realized I had forgotten all about my second ice skin amongst all the chaos. I hardened my exterior instantly.

She punched me again, and cried out as her knuckles cut against my ice-covered body. Thick frost bled from my fingertips, cracking as it spread from my grip up her neck. Her body chilled, slowly turning to solid ice. She screamed in obvious pain, fear reflecting back at me in her dilated pupils. Her mouth gaped open in a permanent cry for help as she froze and fell off me, shattering onto the hardwood.

Holy shit I had no idea I could do that.

The frost remained on my fingertips as I jumped up onto my knees, my head darting to either side for whoever would dare come at me next. I finally found Rayn, flames burning brightly from her fingers as she stood with Nic, stopping any Renati from coming in through the living room windows.

"Nicky, Warren is—" I stumbled back as an energy wave hit my chest.

My head shot up to meet the gaze of dark, spiteful eyes.

"How many times are we going to do this?" I asked Serenity, who appeared surprisingly calm amongst all the chaos.

"As many times as it takes." Serenity thrust another energy wave at me but I deflected it with a shield. "Your old party tricks won't work for much longer."

I levitated a fallen lamp off the floor and hurtled it towards Serenity, knocking her back a few steps. She snarled at me and held up her hands. I braced for impact but nothing came. The fighting stopped as the Renati ceased fire. I spun around, watching all of them freeze in place. Flames still burned from Rayn's fingers as she panted, looking around with confusion. Nic moved across the room to Warren and fell to his knees next to him.

"No. No, no, no," Nic repeated with trembling hands. "Brooke!"

Brooke took a step to rush in their direction, but froze in place as a chill crept through the cottage. Footsteps echoed across the room. Everyone turned towards the hole that had been blown through the front door.

I knew who had entered Amilia's home before I turned to look.

Erebus no longer had cords and monitors attached to his feeble body. He stood tall and proud, his slender figure covered in a simple black jacket and pants. His pale hands swung casually at his sides as he strolled into the house with all eyes on him. The Renati members turned to pay him respect with a bow of their heads.

None of us dared to move. The last few times I had faced Erebus, he had been weak and barely breathing. But this man had a rage in his eyes that could knock me over with a single glance, and that rage locked onto me, seeping into my gaze.

A fireball flew across the room and my sister's powers tingled under my skin. Erebus didn't look towards the flames, his eyes remained on me. He held up his hand and extinguished the fireball with a splash of water. Droplets from his deflection dripped to the ground as he smirked at me.

Erebus had used *my* powers, but that had to be impossible.

Erebus was not an Elemental.

Stepping away from him, I cast out a wave of ice. The sharp icicles hurtled towards him but before they could pierce him, flames erupted from his fingertips and melted my ice into a puddle at his feet.

I met my sister's gaze from across the room as Erebus had used water and fire to counter our attacks. Confusion tore through me. How was that possible?

"We meet again," Erebus spoke to me, his glare pouring hatred into my core. No one had ever looked at me like that before. Like their sole purpose in life was to rip my throat out with their bare hands. "It's been so long, Thomas."

I furrowed my brow in confusion and took another step away from him. My voice sounded foreign as I spoke. It trembled and shook as much as my limbs. My voice betrayed me, laying the terror I felt out for full display. "I-I'm not Thomas."

Erebus scoffed. "Your face may have changed but your heart has not."

Another wave of sharp ice hurtled towards Erebus but not from my hand. Harmony flung herself forward, throwing her attack at him from one side at the same time Nic and Rayn combined their fire into a massive fireball that crashed down at Erebus from his other side. Both elements were deflected by a shield I didn't see him erect.

His hand moved to wrap around my throat.

"Whitney!" Bryan's voice rang out, muffled from the other side of the shield.

Magic attacks and bolts from Aden's crossbow bounced off the magical barrier around me as Erebus squeezed against my airway. I gasped for air and wrapped my hands around his wrist. He lifted me off the ground, the toes of my sneakers scraping against the floor. I tightened my grip on his arm in an attempt to pull myself up and bring some relief to my lungs but he only squeezed harder as panic rang through my body.

My powers trickled from my fingertips in desperation. As my second ice skin took over my body, Erebus pulled his fire powers out and quickly melted the barrier. His hand burnt the skin around my throat and the last bit of air I had in my lungs erupted in a scream. Tears sprung from my eyes as my skin throbbed under his touch.

My vision began to speckle with black spots as I attempted one last time to defend myself. This was it. This is how it would end for me. Here at the vengeful grip of a man who had sat in darkness for centuries waiting for this exact moment. My powers surged from my body, rattling the shield around us. I didn't have to shatter it, just weaken it enough for the rest of my crew to get through.

Through my blurred vision, I saw enough of Erebus' face to see the smirk curl across his lips and a black feathered dart stick into the side of his neck.

With a hiss, Erebus dropped me to the floor. He ripped the dart from his neck and turned towards Aden, throwing his hands out but nothing came. His powers were blocked, but those darts were only temporary.

The battle erupted in the cottage once more as the remaining Renati members threw everything they had at us in an attempt to protect Erebus until his powers returned. Pieces of debris flew through the air as both sides unleashed our hatred of one another. Brooke blurred across the room to where Nic remained at Warren's side.

I shuffled across the floor to get out of Erebus' range of motion. My vision finally returned as hands grabbed my shoulder and pulled me up onto my feet. If I didn't know the touch and feel the panic swirling behind them, I would have attacked. I grabbed a hold of Bryan as we backed against the wall.

"You need to get out of here," I rasped, pushing him down the hallway. "You and Mit need to go."

"I'm not leaving you." He grabbed me and pulled me down as the ceiling above us exploded from an energy wave.

I didn't have time to look up and see where it came from before I moved towards the hall, dragging him with me. "Stay here." I pushed his shoulders against the wall as if it would secure him in place and keep him safe. "Don't get hit."

I jumped back onto my feet and tried to assess the situation but everyone else moved a mile a minute, throwing magic around the room that destroyed the cottage with every blow. I scanned the room, frantically searching for my little brother.

Dmitri stood against Abe's back, the two of them pressed against one another as they defended their respective direction. Dmitri threw a shield up across the room as Brooke knelt down at Warren's side, her magic swirled around in my stomach. Nic jumped to his feet and ruthlessly lit a Renati member on fire before shoving them through a broken window with an energy wave.

They all looked exhausted. Soon our energy would be spent, leaving us weakened. We had to get the Renati out of here before that happened.

I found Serenity fighting with Rose. Vines had broken through the floorboard but were halted by Serenity's shield. The moment I'd been training for. I mustered every last ounce of magic I had and threw an energy wave at Serenity so hard it shattered right through her shield.

The room went silent. The screams of everyone around me vanished. The sound of spells bouncing off the walls dissipated as I locked eyes with Serenity, scratching down her mental walls.

"Leave." I ordered through my teeth.

Serenity began to scoff when something in her gaze shifted. She shook her head, pushing me out but I forced back in. Blood trickled down from my nose as her mental wall shattered.

"Leave and take your followers with you." I demanded again as Serenity's eyes glazed over. Her lips parted as her jaw fell open. Her head became heavy, slowly tilting to the side. Her breathing mellowed and her hands swayed at her sides.

"I..." she started to say. "I can't–"

"Leave."

She turned on her heel, moving as if someone above her controlled puppet strings, slowly shuffling her feet towards the door. The two remaining Renati members stood still with wide eyes and open mouths, letting their guards down enough for Rayn and Lauren to get into their heads and order them to follow Serenity.

The three of them walked out of the hole blown in the wall where the front door once stood.

The only member of the Renai left in the living room was Erebus, and Aden's dart had finally worn off.

Black smoke swirled around Erebus as he conjured something deep in his soul. A form of magic that I'd never seen before. I took a step back, preparing a shield but something in the back of my mind told me whatever Erebus brewed would break right through my defenses. The darkness wisped around his fingertips before he shouted and thrust everything he had at me.

I threw up a shield last minute as the dark magic came hurtling towards me, impressions of skulls appeared in the smoke as it shot across the room. I braced for impact but before the magic could even touch my shield, a blur darted in front of me, arms thrown out wide as the dark magic consumed all the light in the room.

A gasp escaped Amilia's lips before she fell lifeless to the ground.

Harmony's scream filled the cottage, piercing my ears.

No possible way I stood before Amilia's body. She had survived so much before this, she couldn't have been taken out so easily... I stared down at her lying at my feet, waiting for her to twitch. Waiting to see her chest slightly rise and fall with a breath, but nothing happened.

Erebus' hand wrapped around my throat again and my gaze met his. His once-glowing red eyes were now a warm shade of brown, almost human. He squeezed gently to assert dominance and I let him, still in shock from watching the last link I had to my mother die in front of me.

"I could kill you right now, but I want you to suffer," Erebus said in a soft voice, his thumb grazing down my jaw line. "I want you to feel every agonizing moment as I kill everyone you love until the only thing left is this hollow shell you call a body."

Erebus let go of my throat with a shove and I stumbled backwards. My head grew heavy and the room spun. I reached out for something, anything to steady myself. But there was nothing there. I collapsed on the floor as everything went black.

CHAPTER THIRTY-NINE

THE AFTERMATH

WHITNEY

It was raining. Water droplets poured over my shoulders, running down my back. Strands of hair stuck to my face. I squeezed my eyes shut, letting the water bring me back from the brink of insanity. I inhaled deeply, longing for the scent of wet earth and crisp air but the rain didn't smell right. When I finally opened my eyes to sleek white walls, I realized I was in the shower. How did I get here? I glanced down to arms wrapped around my waist, holding me upright against a warm body. Gently, I ran my fingertips along the freckles and little blonde hairs covering his skin.

Bryan.

"You passed out," he whispered in my ear. The stubble of his facial hair scratched against my skin in a familiar comfort. "This is all I could think to do."

I knew this bathroom. We were still at the cottage. The attack. Harmony screaming over Amilia. Had I imagined all of it? *Please*, my mind begged. *Tell me it was a horrible dream...*

"Mia," I whispered.

"I'm so sorry."

Not a dream then.

"Who else?" The words lodged themselves in my throat even after I spoke, afraid of hearing the answer.

"Brooke tried to help Warren, but..." He paused, rubbing my arm. "He was gone before she got to him."

I put my weight on my feet, straightening my back to hold myself up but Bryan still held on tight. We were both fully dressed, sopping wet clothes stuck to our skin as the warm water fell over us.

"The girls are okay," Bryan reassured me. "Dmitri is okay."

Dmitri.

Panic coursed through my veins as my throat constricted making it difficult to breathe. I turned to face Bryan, the water from the shower still running over us both.

"Byn, you have to promise me something."

"Okay." He nodded softly.

"If anything happens to me–"

"No," he cut me off. "No, we aren't doing this."

"Yes we are. Listen to me," I pushed, holding his face in my hands. He stared back at me in silence. "If anything happens to me and Ray, you have to take care of Dmitri."

He didn't speak. Bryan closed his eyes and took a deep breath before his gaze finally met mine again. He nodded.

"I need you to say it aloud. I need to hear you say it."

"Okay."

"Say it."

His breath caught in his throat. This was a very real possibility. "I will take care of Dmitri."

"I know it's a lot to ask, and he's almost eighteen, but that doesn't mean he'll be able to afford to be independent and–"

"Whitney." Bryan cut me off, placing his hand on the side of my face. "I will always take care of him, no matter what happens."

"Thank you."

I couldn't face what I needed to do next without knowing someone looked out for my brother. I had planned to leave Dmitri with Bryan and Amilia when the girls and I went to the Hallow but...but I should have known by now that I would always need a backup plan. The thought of leaving either Mit or Bryan behind ate me alive but at least this way they would have each other. Bryan would have someone to take care of to distract him from Rose and I disappearing and Dmitri would have someone stable to lean on. With Bryan, Dmitri would always have a roof over his head and food on the table.

I reached behind me and turned the water off, both of our clothes soaking wet.

"I forgot to grab towels," Bryan muttered, peeling his wet shirt off his chest.

"I don't care." I stepped out of the tub, creating a puddle on the tile floor below me. I squeezed the water from my hair and opened the bathroom door.

"She okay?" Nic asked, looking at Bryan and I as we walked into the living room, our clothes dripping water behind us.

"I'm fine." I snapped, scanning the room. Amilia and Warren's bodies were gone but the blood remained. Fucking blood everywhere. "Are my girls okay?"

"Physically, yes," Nic answered softly. His eyes were bloodshot and swollen. I ignored the signs that he'd been crying and swallowed my desire to crumble onto the floor and implode. I cleared my throat and trudged through the broken wood and glass shards of the living room into the kitchen.

Rose and Rayn stood in front of the sink.

"You're okay." Rayn threw her arms around me and pulled me in close. "And soaking wet...After you collapsed everything was so fucking hectic." She squeezed me as her tears soaked into my drenched shoulder.

Engulfed in the warmth of my sister's embrace, my hard exterior cracked. A tear fell down my cheek. She pulled back to take a look at me and wiped the tear away with the back of her fingers. "It all happened so fast."

I nodded, afraid that if I spoke the tears would never stop. Rose put a trembling hand on my shoulder.

"Brooke tried to revive Warren until she nearly passed out," Rose replied. "Mia too. She did what the spellbook said about mending tears in the soul, but..."

"She can't bring people back," I whispered.

We'd always wondered how far Brooke's spirit powers expanded, but this answered one of those questions. Rose rubbed my arm before she passed by me into the living room.

Rayn wiped a tear from her own cheek. "It's like the car wreck all over again. Shattered glass."

Amilia throwing herself in front of me and then crumbling to the floor replayed in my mind. I didn't even know for sure if Erebus' spell would have penetrated my shield. It was stupid of her to throw herself in harm's way like that when I might have been able to protect myself. She didn't have to die. She didn't have to die protecting me. We didn't have to lose Mom or Warren either. Senseless losses.

My chest constricted as tears stung my eyes. I fought them but my heart grew too heavy as the reality of the night's events sunk in.

I took Rayn's hand in mine and walked back into the living room. Rose sat next to Brooke, gently stroking her dark hair. Nic had crumbled to the floor with his face in his hands. Bryan grabbed a broom and began sweeping up the debris that covered the living room floor. The back door opened and fear shot through my blood. I startled as Harmony, Dmitri, Abe, and Lauren came into view. I threw myself at my brother, wrapping my arms around him so tightly I felt the air constrict in his lungs. He held me back, nuzzling his face into my shoulder.

"We can't right now," Dmitri said, pulling back to hold me at arm's length. "We can't break down right now. We have to re-secure the perimeter. We have to get this place cleaned up and make sure we're safe. We can't take for granted that they'll retreat for the night."

"You're right." I nodded, hardening myself. I glanced around at everyone, most of the eyes in the room were on me.

"Hell of a charm you pulled back there." Nic lifted his head to look at me.

"It's the moment you trained me for. What was that magic? The black smoke?" I asked Nic, rubbing my arms for warmth but the cold seeped into my bones. For the first time in my life, I actually shivered.

Nic shuddered. "I honestly have no idea. I've never seen it before."

"It's a killing curse." Harmony answered, her voice cracked as she spoke. "Magic brought over from the Shadow Realm."

"Wait, I thought witches didn't exist in the Shadow Realm?" Rayn asked, confused.

"Only monsters," Harmony whispered. "But there is raw energy that can be manipulated if you know how. When Erebus first rose to power, he thinned the veil between the realms, using the energy of the Shadow Realm to alter reality and spellwork here in our world. The Shepherd's may have banished him but they didn't completely seal the veil."

Nic crossed his arms. "Where did all that come from?"

"Mia told me all about it years ago," Harmony answered. "After you left."

"I have a book about the Shadow Realm and it didn't say any of that." Rose left Brooke's side.

"What book?" Harmony asked.

Rose stood next to me, linking her arm in mine. "I found it at Dragonfly Mystic before it burned. Written by Margaret Daniels."

"Oh." Nic lifted his brows. "Maggie has been busy."

"You know her?" I asked, turning to Nic.

Nic nodded. "She's from here. Used to be part of Mia and Audri's coven. Did the book say anything about the veil?"

Rose shook her head. "It wasn't very helpful. Harmony?"

Harmony wiped a tear from my face. "I don't know how to heal the veil."

This is bigger than we thought, Rayn's voice replied in my head.

They might know more at the Hallow. I tried to reassure her but neither of us felt comforted.

"How did they even get in here?" Lauren asked, rubbing her arms. "The cottage was supposed to be safe. What the fuck happened?"

"Amilia put up the protection spells herself." Harmony motioned around the living room. "No average witch should have been able to break them, not even the entire fucking Renati should have been able to break them."

"Erebus isn't an average witch," I whispered.

He had blown right through our defenses like a wet piece of paper.

"What are we going to do about Mom? We need to call Warren's dad." Nic got onto his feet and turned to Harmony, who wiped away more tears. Harmony shrugged and Nic let out an irritated sigh. "We can't exactly tell the police that the Renati waltzed in here and murdered them."

"And why not?" Lauren asked, crossing her arms. "Why shouldn't we turn them in?"

"Because the Chief of Police is Renati," Nic answered through his teeth.

"I will take care of that, okay?" Harmony ran her fingers through her hair. "It's late. Get this house cleaned up and put back together. I'll call 911 in the morning and come up with something."

"Honey–" Nic began.

Harmony cut him off, her eyes thick with tears. "You think she and I never had this conversation, Dominic? I'm the executor of Mia's estate. I know how to handle things." A sob escaped Harmony's throat as her icy gaze hardened on Nic. "This is un-fucking-be-lievable."

Nic furrowed his brow, but didn't respond.

"They both died. They're both gone. Warren and Mia are dead," Harmony sobbed, her chest bobbed as she hyperventilated. She grabbed the front of her shirt as tears streamed down her cheeks. "This...this cannot be happening."

"Harmony." Nic reached out for her but she shoved him away.

She struck him with a closed fist, pounding against his chest. "They left me! They left me here with *you*!"

"I'm sorry..." Nic's voice caught as he grabbed her hands, attempting to retain her.

I couldn't move. I froze in place watching Harmony strike out at him. One final blow landed on Nic's chest before he wrapped her in his arms and pulled her close.

She struggled at first but collapsed into him a moment later. Harmony cried out in a pain that chilled my blood. She grabbed fistfulls of Nic's shirt and screamed.

"I know, Honey. I know," Nic whispered into her hair, tears streaming down his face.

I turned away from them, unable to keep my own emotions trapped in my chest. Rayn approached them, putting a hand on Harmony's shoulder.

"Let's go outside, Honey," Rayn whispered. "Let's get some air."

Harmony slipped out of Nic's arms and walked with Rayn to the back porch.

Aden spoke up, clearing his throat. "We're vulnerable here, sitting ducks. It's time to abandon the cottage and move onto safer ground."

Abe rubbed his eyes with the balls of his hands and released a breath. With a wave of his hand, the splintered wood on the floor floated up into the air and fused back together. Within moments the window seal was reconstructed, the glass a solid sheet like it had never been touched. Bryan stopped sweeping, watching Abe's magic with wide eyes.

This all had to be a dream. I would wake up at any moment. I'd wake up in my bed with Bryan's arm draped over my waist, his body heat radiating into my back. My alarm would be blaring, waking me up for an early morning shift at the Corner Cup. I'd tell Lauren about the weirdest dream I had the night before as we wiped down the counters together.

"I need to talk to you." Nic grabbed my elbow and dragged me down the hall towards the bedrooms, pulling me back into reality.

"What?" I yanked my arm from his grip and followed behind him.

"Listen to me," he whispered, closing his bedroom down behind us. "This is going to postpone things. Harmony and I need to stay here, we can't go to the Hallow."

"Nicky–"

"I'm not stupid. I know you were going on your own," he continued. "It's not an easy place to reach and it's dangerous in the woods, take the hunter with you. I'm sure you were already planning to but just in case." Nic grabbed the roots of his dark hair. "You want to follow the trail that leads around Falcon Ridge towards the waterfall. When the sign for the waterfall comes up, go left into the woods. There won't be a trail or any signs to follow so this is where you're going to have to rely on Aden's tracking skills. I'll draw you a map from what I remember."

Nic paced across the room towards the dresser. "The Hallow is protected by a magical barrier and it's not easily penetrated, but there will be weak spots you can get through if you push hard enough. The forest is different behind the magical barrier, it's close to the center of the Allurement. You remember what those are right?"

I nodded. "The centers of magic that attract witches."

Nic let out a deep sigh. "The earth isn't the same, okay? The plants, the animals...they're stronger and bigger because the oxygen levels are higher. The magical barrier keeps out pollutants and isn't visible to powerless eyes." He made a half circle with his hands, as if showing me the shield's shape. "Rayn will have to watch her magic, things catch fire easier within the barrier. When you get to the Hallow, show them the talismans immediately. They'll attack on sight if they think you're infiltrating. Show them the talismans and tell them I sent you. Ask for Roberta, she's the one in charge. Tell her Mia is dead and you need the missing pages from the Shepherd's book. Do you understand?"

I stood with my mouth hanging open, staring at him, trying to process the info dump. "How–"

"The Hallow is where I ran off to before I went south to California. I stayed there for a year with Roberta, she'll get you what we need. Tell her Audri was your mom. Tell her I'm the one who sent you. You have to leave as soon as possible. Shit is hitting the fan here." Nic put his hands on my shoulders.

I nodded, letting it all sink in as my heart fell into my stomach. I knew we were leaving for the Hallow, but now that someone else knew too, it finally felt real. The gravity of our reality hung heavy on my shoulders. "Left at the waterfall."

"Pack well. It snows in the mountains." Nic smiled though his eyes were lined with tears. "Don't worry about water, you can refill everyone's bottles with your powers. Rose can help compensate for food, so don't pack more than you need. If you're weighed down, it'll make it harder to run. Enchant your bags to fit more."

He turned around and opened the bottom drawer of his dresser. He pulled out a thick leather bound book, nearly identical to our spellbook. "If Harmony knew I was giving you this, she'd kill me."

"What is it?" I blinked at the book.

"Your spellbook belonged to the Martyrs, the generation that Erebus killed. This book belonged to the Shepherds." He handed it over.

"Harmony said all those books had been lost years ago." My heart pounded in my throat.

Nic looked down at the weathered cover. "Many were, but not the two that matter most."

"And this has been sitting in your dresser all this time?"

Nic shook his head. "No, we were packing it to take to the Hallow with us. Since we're no longer going, you'll need to take it with you. Roberta is hanging onto some very important pages that are missing from this book, she won't give them to you unless you have this. Roberta has been away from Rifton longer than I have, she may need some convincing at how bad things have gotten here."

"Roberta knew my mom?"

"She was a coven member with Mia and your mom. Being Audri's kid will work in your favor."

"Okay," I whispered, pulling him into a hug. "Okay. We're leaving after Nancy's wedding."

Nic wrapped his arms around my back and held me close. His heart beat loudly against my chest. He whispered into my shoulder. "Good. You're stronger than you think, okay? Don't doubt and don't second guess yourself. You can do this, and we'll be here when you get back."

"My brother–" A sob caught in my throat.

"Dmitri will be fine, I will take care of him, I promise." Nic huffed. "Bryan too. I've got them. I'll see you soon, and please, do not get yourselves killed."

"Nic?" I breathed into his shoulders. "Is Erebus an Elemental?"

Nic took a shaky breath; his back rose and fell under my hands. "I don't know. Everyone always said that Erebus killed the last of the Elementals before us, but...he has our powers."

"We're missing a big piece of the puzzle."

Nic held me at arm's length and forced a smile. "That's why you need to go to the Hallow. Get the missing pages from the Shepherd's book. I'll do what I can here."

"What are the missing pages for?"

Nic's eyes wandered down to the aquamarine around my neck. "To unlock the magic trapped inside that pretty necklace of yours. It's our only way to win this thing."

ABOUT AUTHOR

Meg Lynn has been writing for most of her life. She wrote her first short story in third grade and has been creating fantasy worlds ever since. Meg is a Northern California girl married to her high school sweetheart, they have three beautiful children and three cuddly cats. She received a bachelor's degree in Social Science from CSU Sacramento and loves coffee, books, and witchcraft. When Meg isn't writing, editing, or marketing you can find her binge-watching TV, playing BioWare games, or shuffling a tarot deck.

www.meglynnbooks.com

@meglynnwrites

ACKNOWLEDGMENTS

Dave, no one has heard about these books more than you. You have been there through every trial and achievement of this journey and I'm so grateful to have such a supportive partner in you. Thank you for believing in me and helping make my dreams of being a published author come true.

Mom, thank you for always supporting my dreams. Thank you for listening to all my ideas and reading all the different versions of my books.

Kerry, thank you for always reminding me that my voice matters, on and off the page.

Sarah, you are the hype woman of my dreams. I'm so glad this series brought us together. Thank you for being such a supportive fan of my books and for being the sweetest friend to me.

Sydney, the best editor I could ask for. Thank you for putting so much care and attention into my book babies.

My beta readers, thank you for your honest opinions and for taking the time to read my story while it was full of plot holes and typos.

My friends, the ones who have been listening to me talk about publishing these books for years and ordered the first round of signed copies. Thank you for everything.

And as always, thank you to Starbucks and Taylor Swift for giving me the drive and motivation to continue this journey.

www.ingramcontent.com/pod-product-compliance
Lightning Source LLC
Chambersburg PA
CBHW031842310726
48972CB00005B/1374